Curse of the Spanish Gold

MOUNTAIN MEN BOOK 2

TERRY GROSZ

WOLFPACK PUBLISHING

Print Edition

© Copyright 2018 Terry Grosz

Wolfpack Publishing
6032 Wheat Penny Avenue
Las Vegas, NV 89122

ISBN: 978-1-62918-499-9

Library of Congress Control Number: 2018951316

Curse of the Spanish Gold

TERRY GROSZ

Contents

Prologue

SEVERAL YEARS HAD PASSED since the violent battle in 1836 between trappers Jacob and Martin, and their Snake Indian wives, and a Gros Ventre raiding party in the Wind River Mountains of present-day Wyoming. Leo and Jeremiah, fellow trappers and adopted sons of the embattled Jacob and Martin, had watched in anguish from a safe distance as the trappers' wives (whose men had been ambushed and killed earlier in the day) tried to hold off the same raiding party. The younger men knew they were so heavily outnumbered that to interfere in the battle at that moment would mean instant death.

Riding to the burning cabins after the raiding party had left, Leo and Jeremiah were beside themselves with joy when they saw the small sons of trappers Jacob and Martin, who had been killed earlier, emerging safely from their hiding place in the outhouse. They had been hidden there by their mothers, who had calculated that no attackers would look there. After burying their adopted parents' burned and mutilated bodies, they gathered up the now parentless Jacob and Martin (each named after his father) and rode to their own nearby cabins. They found their wives scared but undiscovered by the raiding party and hurriedly made plans to leave the dangerous area the following morning. When daylight came, the little group gathered together the last of their belongings, loaded their pack animals, and left this formerly happy land. The recent numerous Gros Ventre Indian incursions into their trapping area had made life there untenable.

As they fled southwest, Leo and Jeremiah were surprised to cross the tracks of the same retreating and heavily decimated Gros Ventre war party that had killed the children's parents. The war party had originally headed north toward present-day Montana, only to have its route blocked by the Gros Ventre's mortal enemies, the resident Snake Indians. Those Snake Indians were now swarming across the land looking for the remainder of the raiding party.

Come nightfall, a vengeful Leo and Jeremiah

tracked down the remaining members of the Gros Ventre raiding party and extracted the full and bloody final measure of frontier justice as the raiders slept. They saved the cruelest punishment for the raiding party's war chief. He died screaming as emboldened wolves, crazy with the smell of blood from the many nearby dead warriors, tore his body to pieces where he had been left tied to a tree and mutilated.

Continuing south, the little party finally arrived in the area soon to be known as Fort Bridger, Wyoming. This area was well watered by numerous streams and had mountain grasses that came belly-high on their livestock. The land was also littered with herds of bison as far as the eye could see, interspersed with fleet bands of pronghorn and large concentrations of the lords of the plains, the graceful elk. To the south of this pristine area lay mountain ranges covered with evergreen timber and holding abundant populations of black and grizzly bears along with Rocky Mountain bighorn sheep. After carefully looking around, the men decided that this would be the site of their new home — a place far from the murderous Blackfoot Nation Indian bands, where one could raise a family in relative peace.

Continuing to trap furbearers and hunt buffalo for their skins after building their new home, the men began a slow change from mountain men to hunters, trappers, and small-scale tillers of the soil. These new pursuits more than supplied their families' needs and made their desire for the more violent frontier lifestyle a thing of the past.

During the following years, Leo and Jeremiah, as masters of frontier survival, began the deadly serious job of training young Jacob and Martin as they had promised their parents over their freshly dug graves. This promise was kept to a degree that only the two murdered trappers and their wives could truly have appreciated. Leo and Jeremiah knew their adoptive fathers would want the very best of frontier survival training and skills imparted to their sons because they had lived and died by those same standards. The West was a harsh yet beautiful land to the practiced eye but deadly violent to those who looked and could not see. The only way to survive was to become woods-wise, understanding of animal and Native American behavior, weather-smart, skilled in the trade of "kill or be killed," and cautious yet alert to the rustling winds of change.

By 1843, life in their little valley had become even more interesting and comfortable for the two frontier families. Longtime trappers Jim Bridger and Louis Vasquez settled in the area and built a crude log trading post nearby named Fort Bridger. Its purpose was to serve as a trading post for the area's growing number of residents and those now starting to head west in wagon trains on the nearby Oregon Trail. These groups migrating westward were in many instances led by mountain men, who were wise in the geography and ethnology of these new horizons. Bridger and Vasquez soon found the trickle of Argonauts turning into a flood of westbound hopefuls. Soon the fort was a thriving center of trade for the remaining mountain men married to the land and to their Indian wives, the military, the Mormons, and others headed for a new life in the far western lands of promise.

Still lurking unknown to Leo and Jeremiah lay the Curse of the Spanish Gold. The older Martin and Jacob had acquired golden ingots in a trade with a Ute chief at a rendezvous many years earlier. The ingots had been taken by the Ute chief and his warriors from a Spanish mining camp after they had killed the entire party of miners and the priests who accompanied them. Before his death in that battle, a Catholic priest had cursed the yellow metal ingots that drove men to an unholy madness that exists to this very day.

After that battle, the Ute chief laid claim to the hoard of 126 golden ingots, and the Curse of the Spanish Gold began. Over the next year, that chief lost two of his sons to savage grizzly bear attacks, and another son was severely injured in a fall from a horse. When the trappers Jacob and Martin gave the Ute chief a magnificent grizzly-claw necklace, the chief, not to be outdone, gave them the cursed golden ingots in return. With the ingots once more passed the Curse of the Spanish Gold!

Several years later, Leo and Jeremiah picked up the ingots that had been scattered about after the deadly battle at the trapper's cabin in 1836 and kept the gold for the orphaned children. The Gros Ventre had left the gold behind because they placed no value on the yellow metal. The Curse of the Spanish Gold once again passed with the possession of the ingots. All the men in the raiding party that had killed the trappers and their wives had handled the golden ingots, and several days later they died horrible deaths at the hands of Leo and Jeremiah. Years later, Leo and Jeremiah were in turn killed by a Lakota raiding party in an early-morning raid. When their adopted sons, Jacob and Martin, returned to the battle site, they buried their adopted parents and dug up the hidden Spanish gold from beneath the burned-out cabin. With that, the Curse of the Spanish Gold passed on to the boys.

Chapter One

THE ODYSSEY BEGINS

LEO, JEREMIAH, AND THE TWO BOYS, who were fast becoming men of the frontier, left their home; a cabin nestled in a thick grove of cottonwoods, early one morning and headed for Fort Bridger. Today would be the start of an adventure that the boys were looking forward to, although they were also a little apprehensive about what the following days might bring.

Leo and Jeremiah had spent years working with the boys, teaching and honing their frontier skills to the point where there was little difference among the four in those abilities other than experience. Leo and Jeremiah had been pleased with the boys' progress through the rigors of frontier survival training as they grew older, stronger, and wiser. Both young men, like their fathers before them, had adapted well and quite easily to the frontier teachings—so much so that soon they had gained an understanding of life on the frontier that was far beyond their years. They were crack shots with their rifles and pistols and skilled in knife use, including those skills necessary to defend oneself in a fight to the death. They were their adoptive fathers' equals in tracking and trapping. They easily spoke various dialects of the Lakota, Crow, and Snake languages and were equally at ease with the talk of the plains, namely, speaking in sign. Reading the weather and animal signs and learning the ways of Native Americans came easily to the boys. So did the making and use of the ancient Native weapon: bows and arrows. At age seventeen, both young men stood slightly over six feet in height, weighed about 200 pounds, and were strap-steel tough from many hours of hard labor on their folks' farms and small ranches.

Their adoptive Lakota mothers, White Feather and Prairie Flower, had taught the boys the domestic ways of the frontier, including making clothing, caring for hides and furs, becoming familiar with the many medicinal properties of native plants, and making even a mountain lion or bobcat loin taste good in a Dutch oven. They had also taught the boys how to treat wounds and sew up any torn flesh that was damaged so extensively that it couldn't be left alone to heal by itself without fear of infection. The women also taught them to respect Mother Earth, honor the gods, and understand the way of the ancients.

The young men couldn't wait to begin their new adventures. Little did they realize the many trails they would travel and the dangers they would experience before they laid their heads down on Mother Earth for the last time.

Reining up in front of the fort's open outer gates in the summer of 1852, the boys were amazed at what lay before them. They had never been to the fort before. Fort Bridger was a collection of rough-hewn cottonwood logs forming a palisade within which was a small number of crudely made hay sheds, cabins, and storage rooms in addition to the trading post. To the south were about thirty Indian tepees occupied by white fur trappers and their Native American wives. Herds of horses and oxen belonging to Bridger roamed at will in the fort's adjacent grassy fields. On this day, the tranquil scene was accompanied by the ringing of blacksmiths' hammers clanging off iron rims being reset on the spokes of a traveler's wagon wheel, the din of children playing around two different wagon trains circled outside the fort, and the barking of numerous dogs. The pungent smell of lye soap from the laundresses doing the weekly wash commingled with the fragrant aroma of baking bread. A sound foreign to the young men's ears was the groaning of a hand-pumped organ and voices singing to the heavens in hopeful tones.

Dismounting, the four frontiersmen made their way through the gates into the center of the fort. Off to one side sat what was called the trading post, a building made just as crudely as the fort's palisades. Hitching their horses, they went inside, where the young men met with many more new sights and smells: curing hides, gun oil, freshly baked bread and pies, made by the ladies in the wagon trains and exhibited for sale on a nearby counter, and both stale and fresh tobacco. At the far end of the wooden counter were salted and brined fish in open barrels and smoked slabs of bacon stacked up in greasy heaps. Beneath all these odors was the underlying pungent smell of stale sweat from unwashed bodies.

They heard laughter from a group of men nearby—voices that were liberally spiced with strong whiskey, from the raucous sounds. Before them were furs by the bale being traded and others packed for travel. The fresh-meat smell of elk and buffalo hindquarters hanging from the rafters, still dripping blood onto the dirty wooden floor, hung heavily in the air. It was all topped off by the thickness of the confined, oppressive, stagnant summer heat.

Hanging back, the two young men followed the leads of their adopted dads. Planning on drawing on their credit with the trading post from previous fur and hide sales, Leo and Jeremiah motioned Jim Bridger over. As he approached, the boys observed a powerfully built man who moved with the grace of a deer. After much back-slapping and a long pull by each man from a gallon jug of whiskey concealed beneath the counter, the three men got down to the business at hand.

"These here young'uns are getting ready to go out on a hunt to make meat for our families," Leo informed Bridger. Bridger looked seriously at the two boys and then, with no sign of emotion, brought his eyes back to Leo and Jeremiah. "They will need to be supplied for at least a ten-day trip out onto the plains, and that is why we are here. I will need to use a portion of our credit to procure some powder, caps for their Hawkens, two nipple picks, a couple extra skinning and gutting knives, a steel, two sharpening stones, and two pounds of your long-leaf Virginia chew. They will also need a six-quart Dutch, a boilin' pot, an ax, and a couple of fire steels," said Leo as Jeremiah nodded in agreement. "Then they will need a large sack of your salt yonder and two pounds of pepper. While you're at it, Jim, throw into that mix a jug of your bear lard, a jug of honey for biscuits, ten pounds of flour, and a two-pound sack of sugar cones. And they will need five pounds of your dried pintos there and a large bag of coffee beans," continued Leo as his experienced eyes roamed across the selection of goods on the shelves behind the counter.

"That we'un can fix right up," said a grinning Jim Bridger, who was quick in taking in the order, and a sharp man when it came to bargaining. Turning, he beckoned for one of his clerks to give him a hand pulling together the goods just ordered. Soon the wooden counter began to fill with stacks of the items Leo had requested. As each requested tool was laid out on the counter, Jeremiah carefully examined it for any flaws from shoddy manufacturing. He also checked the beans and flour for any signs of weevils. Pleased with each item as it arrived, he replaced them on the counter and grinned at Bridger through his massive beard.

"That will about do it," said Bridger as he looked up at his two grizzly-bear-sized friends, men he knew from long-past rigorous days of trapping wet and cold on the beaver streams. "I will remove the cost of these goods from what I owe the two of you in credit from previous fur deals. That is, unless you have a problem with that."

"That'll be fine with us," replied Leo with a

smile, knowing they had made a good trade and gotten the supplies needed to make the boys' upcoming trip safe and successful. "At least they're covered in the food and 'chew' department," thought Leo.

"Well, if that be a deal, I can't let the two of you out of sight without sharing a bit more of my snakebite medicine afore you go," Bridger replied with a smile, as if he needed to justify the snort of whiskey the three friends were soon to share.

The boys, knowing their places, stood silently, delighted by the friendship the three mountain men openly shared. The trading, drinking, and palavering over, the four walked back out into the bright sunlight carrying armloads of their trade items. Greeting their eyes were friendly Indians, trappers, travelers, children, and numerous dogs along with a few domesticated pigs looking for food scraps. The boys grinned at the activity playing out before their eyes, a far cry from the quiet and solitude they had grown up with in the wilds. Yet they were already missing the comfort of home and wishing they were once again back within its less busy and noisy confines.

With their newly acquired supplies loaded on two pack animals, the four turned their backs on the noisy fort and headed out into the comforting and well-loved quiet of the high intermountain prairie toward their homes.

Chapter Two

ON THEIR OWN

ARRIVING HOME just in time for supper, Jacob and Martin gulped their meals, hardly tasting anything. The boys hurried to eat so they could finish organizing for the first hunting trip of their lives on their own. Dreams of coming home with pack animals loaded with meat and hides danced in their heads, as happens with young men about to embark on a vision quest. Hardly sleeping a wink that night, the young men were up long before the crack of dawn the next day and soon had their horses and mules fully loaded for their grand adventure. This trip promised a lot of hard work and the element of danger. But it would also usher them through the passage from boyhood to manhood.

Their mothers put a large breakfast of elk stew

thick with gravy along with Dutch-oven biscuits and coffee on the table, and the two boys fell to like there was no tomorrow. They knew that the buffalo had moved many miles to the east to avoid the humans in their valley. If they were to find the great herds, they would have to ride long and hard that first day. Supper, if any, would be late at night, and jerky would have to sustain them throughout the day's hard ride. However, that was not a bother because they were young, well equipped, and currently loading up on a great breakfast. What more could the young men want?

That answer was not long in coming. Leo and Jeremiah emerged from their cabins carrying two old but perfectly functioning Hawken rifles in their hands. Without a word, the men took the boys' newer rifles and fastened them onto the first animal in their pack string for easy and fast retrieval in case of an emergency. Then the boys were handed the two older Hawkens as their primary rifles. Both boys just looked at each other in amazement. The Hawkens had belonged to the boys' biological fathers...They had been retrieved from the dead Indians after Leo and Jeremiah had exacted the supreme measure of justice from the murderous band who had killed their parents years earlier. For years the Hawkens had hung on the wall in the back of the cabin as if awaiting an important event. That event had arrived, and now the rifles were in the hands of their rightful owners.

Fingering the Hawkens and admiring the still precise tools they were, both boys found their eyes misting up. They were holding their dads' rifles and had been given the honor of continuing their use. Looking into the eyes of their adoptive fathers, they saw that they held tears as well. A coming of age was taking place that morning, and both boys had been given the ultimate gift to herald such an event. They could feel the energy such a symbol represented and seemed to grow even taller and more mature as a result. Yes, such rifles would fit into their lives and continue the tradition their fathers had started.

Looking back as they dropped over a hill, both men waved at the four figures silently standing by their cabins watching them go. All waved back, and the young men's adventures now began in earnest. To bring home great amounts of buffalo or elk, they had to find the creatures and be successful in their stalking and shooting. Then the real work would begin as they removed the hides and prepared the meat. To avoid spoilage, they had to kill and work fast—and do so without attracting the attention of the hostile Lakota in the area who would be out hunting as well.

∽∾

JACOB AND MARTIN CRAWLED through the dense brush surrounding a small grove of cottonwoods to get closer to the herd of buffalo calmly feeding upwind some forty yards away. Crawling up to the base of a small cottonwood, Jacob slowly rose up into its branches so he could steady the big Hawken as he prepared to shoot. Pushing through those branches and leaves, Jacob and Martin, who was rising on the opposite side of the same tree, found themselves instantly engulfed by swarms of angry bald-faced hornets from a large nest hanging on a limb they had bumped! Screaming and yelling in abject pain as the swarm repeatedly stung the two intruders, the boys fled the scene, lucky to hold on to their rifles. The offended hornets followed them for another hundred yards, administering what they thought was the appropriate justice for disturbing their peaceful nest. As if that were not enough, the buffalo, seeing two human beings fleeing across the prairie in plain view and waving their arms like banshees, lit out for quieter parts, leaving only the dust of their passage and fresh droppings on the ground as a reminder of their earlier presence.

That evening, both boys sat close to a small, densely smoking fire in an attempt to keep the hordes of mosquitoes from their exposed, throbbing flesh. They both had swollen ears and lips and welts on their hands, noses, and cheeks. Their eyes were almost swollen shut. As if that were not enough of a mess, the boys applied their precious bear cooking lard to the affected places, hoping to reduce the pain, as their mothers had taught them. Then they settled into their sleeping furs amid the constant whining hum of a million mosquitoes. But the mosquitoes were almost drowned out by the growling of their empty stomachs as the big guts ate the little ones, since supper had stampeded off earlier.

They might have thought matters couldn't get any worse until Martin woke up to something licking the bear grease off his face. Roughly shoving the unknown creature away in fright, he jumped to his feet and yelled. Jacob leaped to his feet with his pistol and knife in hand, ready for the action that was sure to follow, based on the volume of Martin's hollering.

"Agggguhhh!" yelled Jacob as a large, very surprised, and pissed-off striped skunk righted himself after being tossed roughly aside. Stamping his front feet, he let go with both barrels into the jumping and hopping men from a distance of no more than six feet. Instantly both men fell to the ground, blinded, as the spray flew right into their open eyes and mouths. As they knelt on the ground, frantically rubbing their eyes, the skunk let go with another barrage — this time at a distance of no more than three feet. With that blast, both men rolled away and jumped up to blindly run away from their smelly adversary. Jacob ran full- bore into a cottonwood tree, knocking himself out in the dark. Martin fared little better, blindly running the opposite way and dropping suddenly into a seven-foot-deep ravine holding a small creek—and hitting his already swollen lips on a protruding root on the way down.

The next morning found two sad-looking and disgruntled hunters, and a campsite in disarray. The young men looked like death warmed over and smelled even worse! To make matters worse, the mosquitoes, undeterred by their bad looks and evil smell, bored in unmercifully. After moving their camp to a more breezy location to be rid of the smell and mosquitoes, the youths spent the next two days healing up without any thoughts of making meat.

Setting their triggers, Jacob and Martin each selected a fat buffalo cow and squeezed off their shots. Both cows instantly jumped up under the impact of the heavy .54 caliber slugs, dropping to the ground and groaning out matching death rattles. Even before they ploughed into the dirt, two more cows were staggering after having been quickly hit with slugs from the boys' reserve Hawkens. The men hurriedly reloaded as the herd began to shuffle off, and before the animals got far away, four more cows soon lay kicking their last on the ground. The herd, smelling the blood and finally realizing that this was a place of danger, moved off in the buffaloes' typical ground-eating shuffle, with tails held high.

The boys stood up from their places of conceal-ment with grins of success. Before them lay eight fat buffalo cows, representing a hell of a lot of good meat and one heck of a lot of work. Jacob went back for the horses and pack animals as Martin began the long, messy process of gutting and removing the meat and valuable hides. Hard work aside, the boys felt nothing but elation. This was their first hunt on their own, and, setting aside a small problem with the hornets and that damn skunk, they were now successful hunters in their own right. To make matters even better, they had done it with their dads' rifles. Whether they knew it or not, their rite of passage had now truly begun.

Finally getting back to their campsite, the boys tiredly collapsed at their new campfire, sit-ting there as fresh buffalo meat began cooking on sharpened green willow sticks. After gorg-ing themselves on about five pounds of freshly cooked meat, they began building small cotton-wood-limb meat racks with low-heat smoking fires underneath. They cut the meat from the huge hams, shoulders, and loins into strips and laid it over the racks for smoking and drying. They knew it was something to kill so many big animals, but the most important part was to see that the meat was correctly processed. By daylight, over half the meat was in the process of being smoked and dried. After a short break for breakfast of more skewered fresh meat, they continued into the evening, processing the rest of the meat so it could be dried and smoked. Dried and smoked, the weight of their hunt would be far lighter to transport home and would avoid spoilage from being flyblown.

Soon the boys slipped into a deep sleep brought on by the day's exertion and slept soundly until first light. As Martin cooked some buffalo back straps and a pot of beans, Jacob tended the smoking fires and turned the meat so it would continue to dry. Sitting across from each other, they began to laugh at one another. The swelling from the hornets was almost gone, but Martin still had a split lip from falling into the ravine and hitting the root stub. Jacob still had a large cut on his forehead from running into the cottonwood tree in the dark. And that awful skunk smell still permeated their entire camp and their buckskins. As the boys broke a sweat processing the meat, they began to smell even more strongly of that holy-hell skunk smell once again.

"I think we could call this look and smell one

of success," uttered Martin through his swollen and split lips with a slight, mischievous grin.

Jacob just leaned back and roared a hearty laugh, saying, "I am sure glad our moms and dads cannot see us now."

Fact of the matter was, their parents couldn't see anything.

Chapter Three

LEAVES WITH THE WIND

RISING FROM HIS SLEEPING FURS at the crack of dawn upon hearing the horses and mules shuffling nervously around in their corral, Jeremiah grabbed his Hawken and walked to the front inside wall of his cabin. He peered carefully through the nearest shooting port. Seeing nothing in the early light but nervously milling livestock and suspecting a nearby grizzly, he opened the door. *Zippppp—thunk* went an arrow into the cabin wall, inches from his head.

Quickly drawing back the hammer on his Hawken and yelling, "Indians," to warn his brother in the adjacent cabin, Jeremiah desperately looked for his assailant in the half light.

Zipppp—thump went the next unseen arrow into the side of Jeremiah's neck with such force that it shot clean through the muscle and tissue and slammed quivering into the wood facing of the opened front door behind him. As the arrow passed through the neck, it ripped into an internal carotid artery. Dropping his rifle and clutching his neck, Jeremiah staggered out into the front yard in agony as blood gushed uncontrollably through his fingers. *Zipppp—thump, zipppp—thump* went two more arrows into his chest and stomach as he staggered forward, then fell face first into the dirt. No longer could he see the welcome first light in the sky to the east, only a darkness closing in from the sides of his eyes along with a quietness now descending over the roaring sounds in his brain.

Boom went Leo's Hawken, and the bullet found the Indian who had shot the first arrow into Jeremiah's neck. Ironically, Leo's shot hit the Indian in the same spot where the arrow had struck Jeremiah. The man died in moments as his blood gushed out from a torn artery over the dusty ground next to the corrals.

"Aye-aye-yahaaa," yelled a second Indian as he jumped on top of the inert Jeremiah and, swinging his knife wildly, scalped him in one swoop.

Boom went Leo's reserve Hawken, and the Indian had scalped his last enemy as the heavy bullet smashed through his chest, tearing out a chunk of his spine as it exited his body.

Two more Indians made a run for Jeremiah's open front door, only to be cut down in their tracks at the stoop by a fast- shooting Prairie Flower with her double-barreled fowling piece. Four more Indians materialized from behind the horse corral in the swirling dust cloud kicked up by the panicked horses, only to have one killed outright by a pistol shot from Leo as they ran across the front yard. The other three reached the front door of Jeremiah's cabin only to have one killed by a point-blank pistol blast from Prairie Flower. The other two made it into the cabin, and the screams of Prairie Flower told Leo they had begun hacking her to pieces.

Slamming shut his front door, Leo grabbed the fowling piece held by wooden pegs over the front door and, sighting through a shooting port, cut in two another Indian running across his field of view. White Flower was hurriedly reloading his two Hawkens.

Wham, the front door was ripped off its leather hinges by the combined weight of three Indians hitting it simultaneously! In a second, Leo was on top of the Indians on the floor where they had fallen, using his pistol and slashing knife with a fierceness born from desperation.

Boom went his pistol, and at such close range the ball passed through the Indian on top and into the second one lying underneath, killing both instantly. The remaining Indian staggered to his feet only to have Leo's knife plunged to the hilt into his chest.

By now screaming Indians were streaming through the cabin's front door. Leo killed two more with his knife and one with his tomahawk while White Feather dispatched another with a close- in shot from a freshly loaded Hawken. However, the odds were too great, and both died moments later in the melee after killing two more Indians with their knives.

By now the cabin was filled with the dust kicked up by the nervous horses in the nearby corral, white clouds of black-powder smoke from close-quarter shootings, and a dozen yelling, victorious Indians.

Soon the cabins' contents were turned upside down as the Indians looked for anything of value. Rifles, pistols, axes, cooking pots, furs, barrels of powder, lead ingots, and the like became the proud booty of the victorious raiders led by Lakota subchief One-Eye-Only. Having survived the onslaught, he was now concerned. Sixteen of his raiding party of twenty-eight lay dead or dying in and around the trappers' cabins. The two trappers and their wives had put up a tougher resistance to the surprise attack than he had expected. To lose so many warriors would disgrace him as a war-party leader in the eyes of his tribe. However, his thoughts soon turned to a small degree of happiness when he saw that they had acquired four of the famous Hawken rifles, two fowling pieces, six pistols, several bundles of high-quality furs, many buffalo skins, four brass pots, and sixteen horses and mules with all of their tack.

With this trove of treasure plus all they had taken during their previous raids in the valley, One-Eye-Only began to think he might still return to his tribe with honor.

As the winds from the eastern plains blew as they always did in the afternoon, One-Eye-Only led his tired and decimated band toward the protective cover of the southern mountains. From there they would travel back to their tribal encampment on the eastern prairies and spread among the members of the tribe the goods taken on these raids. The wealth in equipment, horses, weapons, and furs that his raiding party had taken from six other hapless settlers and their families was considerable. And that was before they had attacked Leo, Jeremiah, and their wives. In fact, every horse and mule they had taken was loaded with possessions once owned by those settlers. In addition, they were in possession of twenty-three scalps from the hated whites. The scalps of the Indian women killed in the raids were left where they had fallen because they were deemed not worth a warrior's time. As they trekked away, they left the two cabins and storage sheds once belonging to Leo and Jeremiah burning. With that smoke spiraling upward in dense clouds, the legacy of this family of former mountain men and their Indian wives became part of the fabled history of the frontier.

As a matter of course, two of the trappers' own, yet unharmed, would carry forth and serve their memories well as they moved throughout the West now and in later years. However, the curse of the Spanish gold ingots remained buried beneath their burned cabins. That curse had struck once again, and if and when the golden ingots were dug up, it would be transferred, unbeknownst to them, to the boys.

Chapter Four

HOMECOMING AND THE RECKONING

COMING BACK from the prairie country to the southeast, Jacob and Martin were hot, tired, smelly, and happy. They were returning home victorious from their first quest as lone hunters for the family and had survived what the forces of nature had thrown against them. They had grown from the experience and expected now to be treated as men in their families. They also expected looks of respect from their dads and some great home cooking from their moms. Yes, they thought, this would be a great homecoming, one long to be remembered...

Pulling up over the last rise before their parents' cabins, both boys were shocked to see that their homes were not on the horizon! Stopping in surprise, they looked again for the familiar silhouettes, only to find nothing. Spurring their tired and heavily loaded mounts, they trotted on to their home sites. Blackened ruin greeted their eyes, along with the four bloated and mutilated bodies of their parents! They jumped off their horses and ran to the inert bodies, only to discover that their parents were now with the Cloud People.

Fighting back tears of anguish and rage, the two began examining the ruins and piecing together the events that had led to the deaths of their parents. Before long, they had discovered the Indians' hiding places before the battle. From the arrow shafts left behind, Jacob and Martin discerned that the raiding party had come from one of the many bands of Lakota in the area. They figured out the raiders' escape route into the southern mountains and memorized what they needed to know from the tracks of the horses and mules the Indians had taken with them. They calculated how many Indians had been involved in the attack, based on their footprints. And from the dried, dark pools of blood scattered around the battlefield, they deduced approximately how many Indians had been killed in the battle.

After burying their loved ones in a single grave (Leo and Jeremiah's wives had no biological children. Just the adopted boys of Jacob and Martin). Then they checked the ash piles to see if anything of value remained. They found nothing out of the ordinary. Then Jacob remembered the ingots of Spanish gold that their biological fathers had left them. Knowing the ingots had been buried in the northeast corner of Leo's cabin, the boys took their knives and began digging. Soon a large cast-iron pot emerged, and in it were the yellow bars their parents had considered of great value. They discovered that all 126 ingots remained intact, and that the pot had been buried deeply enough that the gold had not melted in the heat of the cabin fire.

Filling their saddlebags and those of all the pack mules with the precious yellow metal, they remounted their horses. Instead of a homecoming surrounded by love, they had entered a dark world of death, ashes, and a lost childhood. They sat there on their horses and vowed vengeance on the killers, driven by a cold determination that came from the genes of their biological fathers and the intense training of their now dead adoptive parents.

That vengeance turned to fury as they tracked the Indians to where they had left their dead high up on burial scaffolds in a grove of cottonwoods. The young men pulled down all the scaffolds and scalped and mutilated the bodies. The remains were left for the meat eaters so that, according to Indian culture and tradition, the dead would wander forever outside the Happy Hunting Grounds, looking for their missing body parts.

Then, with heavy hearts filled with a murderous hatred for those still alive who were responsible for the destruction of their lives and their family, they turned their horses away from the old home site. Now they reached out into the frontier that was to be their new home. Little did they realize that the Curse of the Spanish Gold had also found a new home.

Chapter Five

THE RETURN TO FORT BRIDGER IS FOLLOWED BY A DEADLY SURPRISE

REINING UP IN FRONT of Fort Bridger, the boys sat for a moment with their heavily loaded pack string and thought back to the happier time of their first visit. Then, without further delay, they spurred their horses into the inner compound. Hailing Jim Bridger from among a group of fur buyers with a wave, the boys dismounted and stood quietly waiting for him.

After greetings and a firm handshake all around, Martin said, "A raiding party of Lakota killed our parents and burned their cabins a few days back."

Surprised and stunned over the news and the loss of his friends, Jim took a step back and just shook his head, saying, "That can't be. Them two was as tough as a she-grizzly with cubs. There was no way in hell they could be taken face to face. What in damn nation happened?"

"As near as we could tell, they was ambushed, probably at first light. There were about thirty of them devils, but they paid heavily for attacking our moms and dads if the number of burial scaffolds we found says anything," Jacob said coldly.

"And those Indians we found in their burial scaffolds will never enter the Happy Hunting Grounds now that we are done with them," Martin uttered just as coldly.

Bridger, still stunned by the news, looked long and hard at the young men and then said, "What are your plans? Do we need to get up a group of trackers and run them murderous savages to ground so this doesn't happen again?"

"No," Martin quietly replied, with Jacob nodding in agreement. "We will kill our own snakes in due time. But right now we have fresh and dried meat to sell. With that and any remaining credit our folks had with you, we need to resupply."

"Then we will begin tracking those responsible for killing our parents and kill every one of them," Martin said quietly and in a deadly flat tone.

"We sure can use the meat, that's for certain," replied Bridger, looking over the heavily laden pack string. "Them folks in the wagon trains are always fresh-meat hungry, it seems. Move your pack string over to that shed, and I'll have my men unload it. Then we can move into the store and see to it that you have what you need to pursue them killin' sons'a bitches." His lips tightened and his eyes narrowed. After a moment's thought, he said, "You sure you young'uns don't need some help? It sounds like there is still a passel of them killers on the loose, and they sure as hell will be watching their backsides for anyone cold- trackin' 'em."

"I thank you, Jim, but we will take care of them just as sure as if Leo and Jeremiah were still alive and needing to settle up the score. They be dead men, sure as shootin'," said Jacob with a look in his eye that was very clear in its meaning.

Jim recognized that look, having borne the same one himself many times over the years when he was in a killing mood. He nodded and said, "Let's go to the post. I'm sure I have something there all three of us could use about now, and then we can settle up on your folks' credit and what you brought in today." Jim and the two young men walked over to the trading post. Inside, the three of them went to the counter, and Jim brought out his books.

"Looks like your folks had $101.23 and a half cent on the books," mumbled Bridger as he struggled ciphering over the figures in the book (Jim Bridger was basically illiterate).

About then three of Jim's employees entered the store and told him the fresh meat, hides, and dried meat would bring about $60 on the market.

"If that be the case, you boys have $161.23 and a half cent's worth of credit coming. You can have anything in this here store you see. But if I was you, I'd get several kegs of powder, four horse pistols, some pig lead, and bullet molds for the pistols and Hawkens. Them rifles eat a lot of lead. Then I'd add a couple Green River knives, several tins of caps for those smoke sticks of yours, some horse and mule shoes with nails, and a couple of square axes." Jim offered these suggestions based on his frontier experiences and knowledge of what faced the boys in the days ahead. He also offered his advice to the boys because he know that was what Leo and Jeremiah would expect from a close friend under the circumstances.

"That be good for a starter," Martin agreed. "But we'll need some staples as well because we may not be back for a spell."

With that, out came the jug from under the counter. After each took a long pull, they wiped their mouths on their sleeves, and the ordering began. Jacob and Martin ordered a host of supplies designed to hold them for a long time on the trail. They also ordered several bags of grain because they intended to push their mounts hard in order to overcome the lead the killers now had on them. They realized grain-fed horses could go faster and farther than those subsisting only on tough mountain grasses.

When finished, they discovered they had a problem. The cost of the supplies they had ordered far exceeded their credit. They put their heads together, and after a short, quiet discussion, Jacob left the trading post. He returned to the counter carrying two gold ingots, which he laid down on the counter top, saying, "That ought'a just about cover what we owe you for the rest of them goods."

Bridger nearly fell out of his moccasins, as did the three employees looking on when the glitter of the ingots greeted their eyes. Even in the soft light of the trading post's interior, the ingots seemed to blaze with a devilish shine.

"Holy cow! Where in God's good name did those come from?" Jim exclaimed as he lifted and fingered the heavy ingots. "I would say from the markings on the bars, they be Spanish gold," he proclaimed in amazement before the boys could respond to his first question.

"According to family history, our real dads got them in trade from the Northern Utes many years ago at a rendezvous," Jacob explained in a matter-of-fact tone.

"We figured since we still owed you some money for the goods we needed, it was time to use the gold. 'Sides, it makes our load a shade lighter," Martin added.

"I would have offered you two credit for those goods if necessary. That's the least I could do for the kin of two very dear friends," Jim said.

"No, that wouldn't do. We have the means to square with you, and that is what our family would have wanted," said Jacob with a finality that told Jim the deal had been struck.

None of them foresaw the impact those glittering gold bars would have on those observing the transaction. As well as the impact on the boys down the trail as the curse continued to work its fatal and magical ways...

Chapter Six

THE BOYS BECOME MEN

JACOB AND MARTIN REMEMBERED that when they had come home from the plains to the southeast, they had not crossed any tracks from a large number of horses and mules such as the number that now made up the killers' stock train. Keeping that in mind, the boys retraced their earlier route. Knowing the main bands of Lakota were on the plains for the most part, making meat, they figured the killers in the war party would soon leave the mountains to the south, hide their tracks, and then head east toward their villages on the prairies. The boys also figured they could cut several days' lead from the killers and maybe intercept them, crossing their old trail before they got among their tribal members, if they took an angled route to try to find their trail. On the second day of skirting the base of the mountain ranges to the south of Fort Bridger, they cut across the tracks of a large pack string of loaded horses and mules. Their plan had paid off, and now they were setting out on the trail of tracks that from all indications were less than a day old.

After tying their horses and mules close to their sleeping area, the boys built a small fire and slowly cooked some fresh venison from a deer that Jacob had killed earlier with his bow and arrow to avoid alerting their quarry. As near as the boys could figure, they were about four hours behind the killers of their parents. The trick of bringing grain for their horses and mules to keep them fresh but fast had borne fruit of the deadliest kind, if those being pursued had only known.

Slipping into their sleeping furs, the boys began thinking through what they would do once they ran the killers to ground. Even though the war party far outnumbered the two of them, Leo and Jeremiah's frontier survival teachings had been well learned. Both boys possessed the deadly killing instincts of their biological dads, and to them, this venture was nothing more than the extermination of a nest of nasty varmints that needed to be destroyed. Those vengeful thoughts continued until they slipped into a fitful sleep.

Jacob woke from his restless sleep with a start

but without any discernible movement other than opening his eyelids. Something was wrong, and he quickly became aware that someone was in their camp. Reaching slowly across his bedding in the dark, he put his hand over his sleeping brother's mouth as he closed his other hand over the comforting butt of his close-at-hand pistol. Martin, ever woods-wise, awoke with no start or other movement. He too was instantly ready to face the danger his brother's hand had told him was near. By training, both boys slowly laid their pistols across their chests on the sleeping furs and quietly cocked the hammers against the sound-dampening fur. Nothing moved or made a sound as Jacob frantically used his senses to try to locate the intruders.

All of a sudden, there they were! Two darkened forms rose up from the ground at the very feet of the two boys' sleeping furs until they were standing over them. Pow — pow went Jacob's and Martin's pistols in bright flashes, almost at the same moment. The muzzle flashes blinded the two boys' night vision as they quickly rolled off to either side from under their sleeping furs. Quickly discarding their fired pistols, they grabbed and cocked their second ones, pulled from their sashes in one practiced motion. The quick move to one side from their beds after firing a weapon was a lesson the boys had learned from their adoptive fathers, who in turn had learned it as young adopted men from the boys' biological fathers.

Boom—boom went two rifle flashes from the dark as the unseen assailants sent hot lead slugs and flame from their rifle muzzles into the sleeping furs, which just seconds before had been occupied. In fact, the shooters were so close that shooting into the furs set them afire.

Lunging toward where he figured his shooter was standing, based on the rifle's flash, Jacob fired his pistol point-blank in that direction. The flash from his pistol illuminated a man standing just feet away, hurriedly reloading his rifle. In an instant Jacob was on him, repeatedly plunging his knife deeply into the man's vitals. Warm blood spewed over his hand and arm as his blade found the man's heart, and the pungent stink of urine from the dying man soon also scented the cool night air. Throwing the dying man to the ground, Jacob turned and desperately tried to find his brother in the dark now that the illumination from the small blaze in his sleeping furs had gone out. Quickly moving to the sounds of a nearby struggle, he grabbed his Hawken from his bedside and discovered a pile of men moving violently on the ground by his feet. Grabbing the man on top of the pile and throwing him off to one side, he screamed out his brother's name.

"Here," shouted Martin as he jumped up from under the bloody body of another man he had just gutted with his knife.

Whirling, Jacob took aim from the hip at the shape of the man he had tossed off the heap, who was now trying to untangle himself from some bushes. Boom went the Hawken, and the sound was quickly followed by a groan as the heavy lead slug found its mark. Jumping onto the moving shape, Jacob soon discovered that the man had been gut-shot and was no longer a danger.

Grabbing the man's rifle so it could not be used against them, Jacob hurriedly tossed some dry pine needles on the coals of their fire, and soon a flaring light softly flooded the bloody scene. Martin was covered with blood, but the worried Jacob soon discovered that it was only the blood of the man whom he had disemboweled.

At the end of Jacob's and Martin's sleeping furs lay the two men killed by the boys' pistols, their bodies still twitching occasionally. Off to one side of Martin's bed lay another man, still quivering from the great loss of blood that occurs when one is knifed deeply in the blood-vessel-rich guts. The man Jacob had knifed after missing him with his second pistol shot was obviously now trapping in the Happy Hunting grounds.

Now that things had quieted down, Jacob and Martin began examining the five men they had just killed or mortally wounded. They were surprised to discover that three of them were the men who had watched them pay Jim Bridger with the gold ingots! Martin reached over and grabbed the dying man whom Jacob had shot with his Hawken. The man screamed in pain at being so roughly handled but was alive enough under questioning to tell the boys that the five of them had followed them and planned to kill them for the rest of their gold.

Jacob cleanly cut his throat to the spine after that information was revealed, putting him out of his misery.

Neither of the boys, who were fast becoming men, slept much during the rest of the night, especially after a grizzly bear, smelling the blood, came into camp and dragged away one of the dead men. Within moments, he commenced loudly tearing apart the body and eating it just a few yards away.

The next morning found the boys slowed by the addition of the five men's horses and pack mules. Those animals were so jaded that they made travel difficult, but still they pushed on after their family's killers.

From their place of observation the next evening, they could see several small lights from campfires blinking out on the prairie in a grove of cottonwoods. Tying their animals in a distant plum thicket, the boys prepared for the battle to come. Again, they gave no thought to the odds against them, just the killing that was soon to follow.

Rigging elk-leather slings, each boy placed two of the recently killed trappers' primed and ready-to-fire rifles over their shoulders. Then, with a Hawken in each hand, they started their sneak down into the Indian camp. After an hour of deliberate stalking and slow sneaking, they were in position to overlook the Indians' camp from a distance of a few yards. There were eleven sleeping Indians and one nodding off and on as he guarded the large stolen mule and horse herd. The one on guard soon died quickly and quietly at the hands of Jacob and his sharp knife. After another half hour of careful sneaking, the boys were within feet of the eleven sleeping men. Carefully laying down their extra rifles after cocking them against the quiet of their buckskin shirts, the boys looked at one another. The odds were great, but it would take a lot to overcome what they felt in their hearts, and they could almost believe that the odds were in their favor. The Indians' two campfires burned brightly, clearly illuminating those sleeping on the ground. That would make the killing a lot easier.

The brothers were excellent shooters, especially when dedicated to the moment in pulling the trigger. Jacob whistled loudly, and when the sleeping Indians jumped to their feet in confused alarm, the first two up took rifle slugs in their guts. Then all hell broke loose! As the Indians struggled to wake up, grab their weapons, and defend themselves all at once in the face of danger, one man after another was smashed with a heavy rifle slug from their assailants until eight of them lay on Mother Earth for the last time. The remaining three tried to fight off their assailants with their rifles, but two died from the enraged Jacob's and Martin's pistol shots at close range. When the remaining Indian tried to fire his flintlock, it misfired. Standing there defenseless, he began singing his death song, only to have it cut short by a pistol shot from two feet away from a wild-eyed Martin.

The boys scalped and mutilated all the dead Indians so they could never enter the Happy Hunting Grounds. The two boys, if hardened hearts were any kind of measure, were fast becoming men of the frontier. They left the Indians' bodies where they had fallen for the scavengers and other Indians to discover. Come daylight, Jacob and Martin were pushing a large and fully loaded horse and mule pack string back to where they had left their own animals.

"Jim, come here. You won't believe your eyes," said a skinner in Jim Bridger's employ.

Jim ran up to the Fort Bridger lookout and stared in disbelief at the sight below: a pack string numbering sixty-nine horses and mules! Leading the herd was Jacob with his own pack string and a bell mule. Bringing up the rear was a very dusty Martin, covered in dried blood.

"Holy catfish," said Jim as he scrambled down from the fort's walls and ran out to greet the two young men. He thought, *Them boys sure do have a passel of their dads in them!*

"Where in thunder did you lads get such a string of horse and mule flesh?" he asked, out of breath in the emotion and excitement of the moment.

"Well, two horses and six mules be our'n. Those sixteen horses and mules on the outside of the herd belonged to our folks. The rest belonged to those killin', thievin' Indians and five of your men from the fort," replied Jacob as Martin rode up beside his brother.

"So that's where those varmints went," Bridger uttered disgustedly. "One day they was here, and the next, after you two left, they was gone along with two of my best horses and a belly-load of stolen supplies. You say them varmints be dead?"

"Sure did," replied Jacob with a wry grin.

"Couldn't have happened to a nicer bunch of polecats. They was nothing but trouble when they was here with their drinking, whoring around, and all," continued Jim. He disgustedly spat a long stream of tobacco juice onto the dusty ground at his feet.

"You can pick out what is your'n, Jim, and what animals is left that we don't want for our pack string, we will try and sell to the people in the wagon trains or to you," Jacob said tiredly.

"If you don't have any particular druthers, I could use some of those mules, that be for sure," replied Jim. "And the horses go without sayin'."

"Take your pick, Jim, and if you don't mind, we will take some supplies and our two gold bars back in trade," replied Jacob.

"That be a deal," Jim replied with relief. "Ever since them gold bars been here, they have been cursed. It seems everyone has to see them, and I can't get a lick of work out of my men for all the talkin' they seem to do on the subject. They spend all their time trying to figure out where you might be and how many more you have. It is almost as if I were cursed by ownin' them."

For the next several days, Jacob and Martin rested at the fort as Bridger's guest. They sold all the Indians' scalps for hard cash to a passing contingent of Mormon solders. The extra mules and horses that Martin, Jacob, and Bridger didn't need disappeared into the ranks of the settlers in the wagon trains to replenish their exhausted stocks of animals. The boys had recovered their adoptive dads' Hawkens and pistols from the Indians, along with the rifles from the five men from the fort hell-bent on stealing their gold. In addition, they had taken all the other rifles from the dead Indians. Jacob and Martin figured they would use those flintlock rifles in trade with the Indians along the trail for whatever they needed. Before everything was said and done, the boys had all the supplies they needed and all their pack string could carry. They also had over $2,900 in cash from the scalp and livestock sales. They left the other items retrieved from the Indians' pack string, loaded with goods stolen from the valley's settlers, at the fort for Jim to return to anyone still left alive who could claim them. If no owners showed up, they instructed that those items be given to any settlers in the wagon trains in need of such supplies.

Jacob and Martin were now men who still had many adventures ahead of them, along with numerous turns and surprises in their trails of life as they made their way in the West. And westward they would go, as would the Curse of the Spanish Gold...

Chapter Seven

A SURPRISING STEP BACK INTO THE PAST

FOR THE NEXT SEVERAL YEARS, Jacob and Martin wandered southern Wyoming and northern Colorado like falling leaves in a November storm. They seemingly had no real purpose as they trapped and hunted off the land. Selling meat, buffalo hides, and the furs from their trapping, the two managed to make a good living. But something was missing in their lives if their random wanderings accounted for anything.

As they sat on logs by their campfire one evening in 1855, watching several slabs of elk meat cooking on willow sticks, Jacob said, "Brother, what say you we go south to Fort Vasquez on the Platte River? If'n we did, we could see what that neck of the woods has to offer. We can still hunt for a living, then sell our meat and hides at the fort and probably do better than we are doing here at Fort Bridger. 'Specially since this area seems to be dying out as the wagon trains are passing it by for shorter routes to places west. Plus, it is an area we haven't seen.'"

Fort Vasquez was near the present-day town of Platteville, Colorado. Martin sat for a few moments, gazing into their fire, and then looked up and said, "That has to be better than what we are doing now. I hear tell at Fort Bridger that Fort Vasquez is really growing, and they have a need for just about everything. I still have a hankering to go further west and see that there Pacific Ocean someday afore the worms get at me. Brother, I am game, since that is at least heading somewhat in the right direction for where I want to go and have a look-see."

The next morning found the two men with their pack string drifting south out of the old fur trappers' rendezvous site at Encampment in Wyoming toward what is now called North Park in north-central Colorado, near the present-day town of Walden.

"We still have some daylight," Jacob said after many hours of travel, looking back over his shoulder at his brother. "What say you we keep moving south toward those nearest mountains and hole up for a spell?" He pointed to a line of timber at the end of the sagebrush flats they were traveling through.

"Sounds good to me. Besides, these animals need a few days of heavy feed and rest, or they will become worn out and footsore. There seems to be plenty of buffalo and elk sign in the area, so I agree. Let's find a spot out of the wind in the timber and do some hunting and resting up before we push on south to Fort Vasquez," Martin agreed.

Without a word in return, Jacob pointed the pack string to the south and headed for the first timber in the area, which today is near Rand, Colorado. He kept the pack string heading for the nearest edge of timber as he kept a careful lookout for any hostile Indians. Moving into the comforting quiet of the timber, Jacob headed for an open spot near a small stream that looked like a good spot to set up camp. As he approached the chosen site, he was surprised to see an abandoned small log cabin already occupying the clearing.

"Must have been from some earlier mountain man fur trappers," he mused as he lightly swung down from his saddle.

Martin had already dismounted and was stiffly walking around with sore knees as he went looking for the best area in which to set up their camp.

"No matter how you cut it, that old cabin is in the best spot," Martin finally said. "Whoever built this place sure made it hell for stout. Aside from some trash inside and a broken front door, it is livable, and the roof still appears sound. Why don't we camp here for the night? It sure don't seem its original owners will be back anytime soon," he said with a twinkle in his eyes and an easy laugh.

"Sounds good to this tired old carcass. Let's get to unloading before this incoming afternoon storm hits and get our gear under cover," responded Jacob as he eyed the darkening oncoming cloud cover from a thunderstorm.

Then the two woods-wise men suddenly noticed many things out of place. Surrounding the cabin in the limbs of the trees and stuck in the ground were old lances and numerous feathered items almost reminiscent of an old Indian burial ground.

"Jacob, see what I see?" asked a now cautious Martin, aware that it was not "the way" to set up camp in an Indian burial ground, if this was in fact one.

"Sure do, but this doesn't appear to be a burial ground. I don't see any old burial platforms anywhere. Do you?" he responded, looking into the surrounding trees.

"No, and if I was a betting man, I would say this area has some other kind of special significance. But what it represents I have no idea," quietly replied the still watchful and cautious Martin.

Carefully looking over the area once more with practiced eyes, the brothers decided it would be all right to camp there, but all the Indian items left behind and their unknown significance still spooked them a little.

"This is the land of the Northern Arapaho," Jacob mused, "but I'll be damned if I can cipher the meaning of what is scattered all around this cabin."

Finally convincing themselves that they were not trampling on a sacred site of the Arapaho, the men set about their business but kept their rifles close at hand. Within an hour, the horses and mules had been unloaded, hobbled, and let out to feed under the men's watchful eyes. Soon Jacob had a fire going in the old cabin's fireplace and a pair of Dutch ovens alongside, one holding biscuits and the other filled with thick slices of sizzling bacon.

Soon the old cabin smelled better than it had for many years. Bringing the livestock in for the night, Jacob observed that Martin had repaired the old corral near the cabin, and into that went their stock for safekeeping. The front door had also been repaired with several fresh straps of leather from their packs, and it now hung as it should. Breaking out a large candle, Jacob lit its wick with an ember from the fireplace and set it on an old table in the center of the cabin. Soon the cabin was bathed in soft light from the fire and the candle, and the cooking food began to smell heavenly to the hungry men. Sitting on the still intact sleeping platforms in the cabin, they shoveled great chunks of biscuits sopped in honey along with slabs of sizzling bacon into their mouths until it was all gone.

Sitting with his tired back against the wall, Martin bit off a big chunk of good Virginia chewing tobacco from a soft deerskin pouch, closed his eyes, and let the juices work their magic inside his mouth. After a time, he opened his eyes and let his gaze roam over the inner structure of the cabin, looking for any leaks as the heavy rains began quietly beating on the sod roof.

Then he saw it! Carved in the ridgepole of the cabin were the words, *This here cabin is the property of Jacob and Martin.*

Jacob saw his brother's reaction and, thinking danger was near, slowly reached for his Hawken as he looked around for the problem.

Martin, never taking his eyes off the carving in the log beam, slowly rose and stepped over for a closer look. Jacob didn't say a word but just watched his brother for the explanation he knew was sure to come.

"Jacob, remember Leo and Jeremiah telling us stories about our dads and how when they were younger they trapped in this here neck of the woods?"

"Sure do. What the hell is going on with you, Martin?" asked a still puzzled Jacob.

"Remember the story about how they killed a large white buffalo and the Arapaho Indians in the area considered it sacred? And remember they made warm cloaks from the white buffalo hide and one day were surprised by a mad bunch of Arapaho and feared death at any instant?"

"Yeah, yeah, but what does that have to do with you acting all out of sorts?" demanded Jacob, getting more frustrated by his brother's actions by the moment.

"I think I have figured out why all the sacred Indian feathers and such are outside our cabin. For some reason, this cabin is sacred to the Arapaho, and I think this here carving holds the key," slowly uttered Martin. He gestured for Jacob to come have a look.

Jacob, with a look of puzzlement on his face, got up from the old sleeping platform on which he had been sitting and walked over to where Martin now stood. Looking where Martin was pointing, Jacob froze in his tracks. Their adoptive parents had taught both boys how to read and write, and what he saw sent shivers clear down to his moccasins.

Running his fingers over the carved words, Jacob could hardly believe his eyes as he began to feel a connection with his dad and uncle from a time long past.

The boys' eyes met in disbelief. Thoughts of their adoptive parents' teachings about their fathers began to whirl around their heads just as the bald-faced hornets had done on their first hunting trip. Soon they were running their fingers over the carvings as if the words could speak and tell them about their respective dads. The feelings they now shared were of love, closeness, history, sorrow, and things that never were, all wrapped up in one. Jacob and Martin found their eyes filling with moisture as the cabin now seemed to grow even "hotter" from the cooking fire in the fireplace.

Sitting back down, they just looked at each other for the longest time.

"Do you think those words in the main beam were carved by our dads?" asked Martin.

"How many other Jacobs and Martins have you met in our travels?" asked Jacob.

The boys slept rather fitfully that evening, and the first thing they did in the morning was go back to the main beam and make sure the carving was still there.

Notwithstanding the questions they now carried in their breasts, they shot and killed a buffalo that day for fresh meat. Hauling in the shoulders, hams, and blackstrap, they commenced processing the meat into jerky for the trip ahead over the Rocky Mountains to where Jim Bridger had told them Fort Vasquez was located. They weren't sure what kind of hunting they would find on the trail.

While Jacob tended to the jerky and checked the livestock to make sure the animals' shoes were still in good condition, Martin remained in the cabin melting lead and pouring a small mountain of bullets for their rifles and pistols.

"Martin, I need you out here right now, and bring your rifle!" called Jacob, obviously riled and concerned.

Stepping through the cabin door with his rifle at the ready, Martin was surprised to see about thirty mounted Arapaho warriors quietly sitting on their horses in front of the cabin, glaring down at the two of them. The party had arrived as silently as ghosts from times past. For the longest time no one moved, and with odds of fifteen to one, the brothers knew they were dead if the warriors proved hostile.

Then an old Indian rode forward a few feet and said, in perfect English, "I am Bison Path, chief of the Northern Arapaho. Are those the magic buffalo guns that never miss?" He pointed to Jacob' and Martin's Hawkens.

As Jacob tried to understand what he meant by the question, his racing mind finally understood. Leo and Jeremiah had taught the boys that their dads were such good shots with their Hawkens that they hardly every missed.

Gambling, Jacob thought he would give his idea a try. He said, "Yes, these are the guns that never miss, and this is the very one that killed the great white buffalo many moons ago." He patted the stock of his Hawken. Boy, did that stir them up, he thought, watching the ripple of movement as the warriors nervously fidgeted on their horses.

Martin, not understanding Jacob's drift, just held his ground, ready for whatever came his way and hoping it wouldn't be an arrow, lance, or speeding rifle ball.

Jacob continued, "We two are the sons of the mountain men who came here many moons ago, killed the great white buffalo, and treated the Arapaho as brothers."

Another ripple of apparent understanding went through the mounted warriors.

By now Martin had his brother's drift and, without making any menacing moves, pointed out a rock many yards away, raised his Hawken, and fired. The flat-sounding whock of the heavy lead slug hitting the rock squarely was audible to all. Without further ado, Martin set his empty Hawken against the front of the cabin and, reaching through the open door, took out his reserve Hawken just in case. However, the point had been proven to the warriors gathered at the sacred place for the mountain men who had killed the white buffalo. The bullet had hit the rock at a distance their flintlocks could not even approach.

A murmur of excited talk moved through the Indians, and Chief Bison Path got off his horse and walked over to Jacob. Grabbing his right forearm in friendship, the old man smiled and then warmly embraced Jacob. Then it was Martin's turn for the same treatment. Soon all the Indians were talking excitedly at once over their discovery at what they called "Big Medicine's" cabin.

Bison Path raised his arm for silence and when he had the stage asked, "Would the two 'spider people' like to go on a buffalo hunt tomorrow?"

Jacob and Martin understood the Arapaho name for white men. Knowing they still needed more meat for their trip to Fort Vasquez, Jacob said, "We would be happy to help our brothers kill some buffalo."

Those words made Bison Path happy, and he said his hunters would meet the sons of Big Medicine at their cabin the next day at daylight. He quickly mounted his horse, and after a friendly wave of his arm, the warriors rode off into the timber behind the cabin.

Jacob and Martin stood there in amazement, watching the Arapahos ride off. Instead of being killed they had been invited to go on a friendly buffalo hunt with their newfound friends. They also now understood the significance of the Indian decorations around the cabin.

"It sure was a good thing our dads killed that sacred white buffalo and were good to the Arapaho, or we would be dead and cooling critters about now," Martin said with relief.

"We best get ready for the hunt, and Lord help us tomorrow if we miss," Jacob replied seriously.

Chapter Eight

THE HUNT AND MUCH MORE

THE NEXT MORNING at daylight found Jacob, Martin, and about thirty Arapaho warriors heading north into the sagebrush flats and rolling hills of present-day North Park, Colorado, looking for buffalo. It didn't take long to find several herds, but they spent a few hours scouting them all for the one with the best nearby cover from which the hunters could approach unseen. After a herd had been selected, Jacob and Martin left the Indians behind because they had only the shorter-range flintlocks. Jacob and Martin then crawled up a rise careful not to be silhouetted, and looked over the top. There below them lay about a hundred buffalo, resting or feeding, unaware of the danger nearby. Getting into shooting position, each man shot a cow and then, crawling back out of sight, hurriedly reloaded. Two more shots, and two more cows struggled on the ground, life ebbing. Because the herd could not see the danger, only small puffs of white smoke, the animals continued peacefully resting or feeding. Soon eight more cows lay on the ground, and now the smell of their blood was beginning to alarm the herd. A large cow began to nervously move away, and Jacob used his reserve Hawken to kill her before she could stampede the herd. With the confused animals now in a stand, the killing continued as six more buffalo hit the ground. As another cow began to nervously move off, Martin killed her with his reserve Hawken, and the killing continued until another eight buffalo were on the ground. By now the Hawkens were too hot to hold, so Jacob and Martin let the rest of the herd walk away. They had twenty-eight animals down and figured that was plenty for all. The two men stood up in plain view and beckoned to the Indians sitting patiently out of the herd's sight in a nearby draw. The buffalo, now seeing the danger, rumbled off into the sagebrush with their tails typically held high as Jacob and Martin smiled at their success. They had not missed a single shot!

The rest of the day was spent butchering the animals. Soon the horses, travois, and pack mules were loaded with all the meat and hides they could carry. What remained of the kill was left to the ever-present skulking wolves, coyotes, and meat-scavenging birds.

That evening Jacob and Martin were the guests of the Northern Arapaho Tribe, and much gorging on fresh buffalo liver, hump ribs, and small intestines took place. In addition, much speech-making went on about the return of the white buffalo killers and their rifles that never missed but killed with one shot. Finally Jacob and Martin excused themselves because they still had their share of the meat to care for. They headed back to their cabin in happy, stuffed silence.

For the next several days the two men did nothing but cook, eat, and process their meat into mounds of jerky. On the third day after the hunt, they heard a lot of horses coming their way. Not sure of the riders' intent, they grabbed their rifles, stood, and waited. Soon warriors led by Bison Path swung into their clearing towing numerous pack animals loaded with dressed furs.

"We have come to trade with the ones whose rifles never missed," stated Bison Path.

After a hurried conversation with Martin, Jacob went back into the cabin to their stash of supplies. He returned carrying six flintlock rifles. Upon seeing such bounty the Indians began talking excitedly among themselves. The talking got even more animated when Jacob went back inside and returned with another six rifles. When he made a third trip and came out carrying six more, there was pandemonium over the display of such riches. Since these Indians had been nothing but their friends, Jacob and Martin had decided to honor them with the most important trade item for a frontier Indian These rifles were the ones taken from the five men from Fort Bridger who had tried to kill them and the Lakota responsible for the deaths of their adoptive parents, so it was no skin off their noses to trade them. They had been carrying the guns around for several years, and it was the right moment to get rid of them before they rusted into uselessness. Plus, they would need the pack animals that had been carrying the rifles to carry the furs soon to be received in trade from the Arapaho. Jacob went back to their storage pile and came out one more time with bags of flints, powder, bullet molds, and some pigs of lead to go with the rifles. The excited conversation had long since died away, and amazed silence reigned. The Indians could not believe the life-giving bounty lying before them.

Stepping forward, Martin began the trading. A mad scramble ensued among the Arapaho. Many wanted to trade for the rifles, and as it turned out, there were just enough to go around to those possessing only bows and arrows. Soon Jacob and Martin were in possession of a small mountain of furs from bobcat, wolf, coyote, lynx, beaver, and river otter. There were also many beautifully tanned buffalo hides that would bring top dollar on any market. As the trading ended, the feeding and gorging on fresh buffalo meat that was customary among white and Indian friends began. Jacob and Martin unlimbered the cooking sticks and pots full of beans and rice, and soon everyone could hardly move as another evening of feasting and storytelling faded into night.

There was yet another surprise in store for the trappers. The Indians knew they wished to go to Fort Vasquez, which was across the mountains and out on the plains. Bison Path stepped forward to tell Jacob and Martin that his tribe would furnish four guides to help them over the passes and into the head of the canyon leading to Fort Vasquez. Jacob and Martin accepted, smiling at another good turn of events.

On their last morning at their fathers' cabin in the early summer of 1855, the men checked their equipment, loaded a small mountain of furs onto their pack animals, and prepared to leave. They visited the cool quiet of the cabin one last time and ran their fingers over the carved words in the ridgepole as they tried to connect with what was left of their pasts. Both vowed never to forget what little they knew of their early heritage. Then they put the immediate past behind them and mounted up. With one backward glance, they rode off into the next stage of their lives— lives that would soon see more adventure along with an event that would change both of them forever.

Two days later Jacob and Martin bade farewell to their Arapaho guides as they sat on their horses on the top of present-day Berthoud Pass (a route that had been discovered by Jim Bridger) looking into Clear Creek Canyon far below (Originally Clear Creek had been named Canon Ball Creek by French explorers and later Vasquez Fork by Louis Vasquez). The Indians told them to follow the stream down and they would find Fort Vasquez one sleep on the plains to the south and east of the mouth of the canyon. They also informed them that they would find many tribal members living along the rivers, led by Southern Arapaho Chief Left Hand, who was also friendly to the spider people.

Slowly working their way down the steep, densely timbered canyons with their heavily laden pack strings, Jacob and Martin marveled at the numbers of mule deer, elk, moose, and big-horn sheep they ran across. They thought it was truly a hunter's paradise for anyone who wished to be in the business of feeding the meat-hungry mouths at Fort Vasquez along with any military contingent that might be in the vicinity. They thought they would return to this bountiful area, plying their trade as hide and meat suppliers to the good people of Fort Vasquez. Things were looking up for the two men without any roots who carried such violent memories from their pasts.

Chapter Nine

FORT VASQUEZ BOUND

THE FIRST EVENING after leaving their Northern Arapaho Indian guides, Jacob and Martin feasted on the back straps from a freshly killed bighorn sheep. As the meat sizzled deliciously in its heavy fat around their fire, the tired men failed to see the small ribbons of liquid silver melting from the rocks around their fire pit and trickling out from under the hot coals... The oversight would be remedied days later, but in another, much more valuable form.

The next evening found them at the mouth of Clear Creek Canyon, facing the open plains. Suddenly they heard a loud crashing noise in the creek bottom below, and both men went for their Hawkens in case danger presented itself. However, it was only dinner in the form of a cow elk, which soon lay on the hillside cooling as they finished gutting the extremely large and fat animal.

Realizing that if they went any farther that evening they could very easily miss the fort in the darkness, they skinned out the front and hind-quarters of the elk and removed the back straps. The rest was left for the scavengers and was soon claimed by a pack of seven wolves who, from all the noise they made consuming the remains, were more than happy to find a free dinner.

Early the next morning, with the elk quarters hanging from the heavily loaded pack animals, Jacob and Martin set out for their first look at Fort Vasquez. After a day's ride to the south, they stumbled upon the fort. What a disappointment! It was nothing but a few crude mud-and-log huts; tepees; and numerous framed tents posing as saloons, eateries, stores, and a butcher shop dotting an area around a small fort surrounded by low mud walls.

The fort and its surrounding area, however, were bigger than Fort Bridger. And so was the noise level: guns fired into the air, music coming from the tents marked as saloons, and clanging of the ever-present blacksmiths' hammers as the men passed along a dusty row of tepees and huts outside the mud enclosure. Before they had gone far, a butcher with a blood-splattered apron, seeing the elk quarters hanging from the pack saddles, ran out into the dusty street and hailed them with a wave from a grease-covered beefy arm.

"You boys want to be let free of carrying that there elk meat?" he asked hopefully.

Not having thought of that, the two just looked at each other for a moment. Then Jacob said, "Sure, how much you offering?"

"I will give you a dollar for each hindquarter and fifty cents each for the shoulders," the butcher said quickly.

"You got yourself a deal," said Jacob as he swung the pack string toward the front of the man's tent, which had a board hanging from its main support pole marked, "BUTCHER SHOP."

Moments later the meat had been hauled into the man's tent and laid on several rough-cut boards across the tops of some wooden barrels that served as a crude counter.

"There you be," the butcher said as he counted out three dollars into Martin's hand with a happy grin.

"You boys be new hereabouts, I suspect, not having seen you before," said the friendly butcher after introducing himself as Harold. "How'd the two of you like to make some more money?"

"We just got here and thought we would take a look-see around," said Jacob.

"She isn't much but soon will be, I suspect,"

Harold said. "Especially if people keep flooding into her like they have been lately. In fact, the only thing keeping this area from becoming a land boom are those damned thieving and killing Sioux, Northern Cheyenne, and Comanche Indians farther to the east on the plains. They be a real problem, and if you're not careful, they'll lift your hair quicker than a weasel kin spit."

Jacob and Martin just smiled. Having come from Indian parents, and having been victims of more than one raiding party themselves, they understood some of the bad feelings and prejudices many people harbored about their kind.

"In fact, the Sioux and Northern Cheyenne are so bad out on the plains south and east of here, it is hard to get good buffalo meat because if you go out to hunt, it just might be your last," Harold explained. "That is why we are eating elk, mountain sheep, and goats instead of good buffalo meat." Jacob and Martin understood him to mean pronghorns when he said "goats," as that was the common name for such animals. "Say, you boys never answered my question about wanting a good job. How about it? Want to be my hunters and provide the butcher shop with elk and sheep so I can sell it to the good people around here? I will pay you top dollar and buy everything you can supply." He sputtered the offer quickly, as if not wanting to lose a good opportunity.

"Sounds like you have a deal," said Jacob as

Martin also nodded in agreement. "We have a temporary camp not far from here and will operate out of there until the game becomes scarce. Then we can move farther up into the canyon and hunt from there as well."

"That'll be good," said the butcher. "But you boys need to be careful up there too. Them killin' Northern Arapaho may not want you trespassin' and killing off their game."

Jacob and Martin just grinned at each other. Their relationship with Bison Path gave them little concern for their safety, and he had given them safe passage throughout his territory to hunt and trap as they pleased.

Jacob and Martin spent that evening at Fort Vasquez, taking in the sights, such as they were. They also spent some time trading the small mountain of furs they had received from the Northern Arapahoe. This allowed them not only to stock up on supplies but also to start an account at the store based on the credit that remained. They also witnessed two killings in a tent saloon and one out on the street and quickly decided frontier civilization was not for them. Bedding down by a corral outside the fort, the two men had a good night's sleep as their pack string and riding horses got a good graining from the liveryman.

Next morning at daylight they headed back

up Clear Creek Canyon until they found a good campsite near the present-day town of Idaho Springs. Finding a cold stream entering Clear Creek from the west, they set up shop on a small flat. Cutting some nearby trees, they soon had a partial log cabin built into a nearby hillside, effectively making a log-and-dugout home site. Over the next two days they built their roof and made several log sheds for the pack animals along with a stout corral. Then, while Jacob made permanent meat-hanging racks, Martin dragged dry logs next to the cabin site so they would have firewood for the coming winter.

Having completed their home, the men set about hunting. Soon the meat poles hung heavy with elk and bighorn sheep carcasses. Then down to Fort Vasquez they went with a fully loaded pack string of fresh meat for their butcher friend. They were surprised to find that the butcher shop had doubled in size. In a second tent another man, an Old Country German who spoke only broken English, had established a sausage- making operation in conjunction with the friendly butcher's fresh-meat business. When Jacob and Martin reined up in front of the butcher-shop tents with the heavily loaded pack string, Harold was beside himself with glee. He had wondered what had happened to his hunters, fearing the worst from the Northern Arapahos. But the meat bonanza in front of him soon made him forget his fears for the hunters' safety and sent him into a happy, toe-tapping tizzy.

"I'm glad to see you two fellas. I had given you up for lost. Now that you're here, though, you can see why I'm so relieved. I also set up a sausage-making business, and without you two delivering meat, I would have lost my shirt. In fact, an army quartermaster came by last week and said they would buy five hundred pounds of hard sausage every two weeks if I could supply it," he happily informed them.

Jacob and Martin smiled. They hadn't figured on such a big job coming their way, but now that it had, they knew they could live in the area as long as they wanted and support themselves as hunters. Plus, it sure as fire beats the cold feet and legs that come from trapping beaver, especially come winter, thought Martin with a knowing, been-there grin.

Harold settled up with Jacob and Martin to the tune of $25 and immediately began deboning the meat for resale to the townsfolk and making it into sausage. Jacob and Martin headed for a large tent marked with a sign reading, "Jake's Emporium." They had noticed the place emitting some of the best smells they had ever breathed when they had ridden by earlier. After eating two freshly baked apple pies, they sluggishly climbed into their saddles and headed happily for their home site back up the canyon.

Chapter Ten

A DISCOVERY CHANGES THE DAY

QUIETLY SNEAKING UP behind a canyon rim in early fall 1855, Jacob and Martin cautiously peered over the edge. Not thirty yards below was what held their attention: six large bighorn sheep rams lying on a small, sunny bench off to one side, overlooking the canyon below. They were in such a position that if danger presented itself, all they had to do was jump up and sail over the rim into the canyon below in order to be safely away. However, they had not planned on being stalked from above by such hunters as Jacob and Martin. Within moments the crash of two heavy rifles being fired echoed off the canyon walls, followed by the report of the two reserve Hawkens firing just split seconds later. The two smaller bighorns, upon hearing the noise, jumped up and sprang off the bench, hurtling out of sight into the canyon in a cloud of dust. The four larger rams lay as they had slept on the bench, never again to roam their high mountain ridges.

Martin began gutting the rams so they would not spoil as Jacob went back up the mountainside to bring their horses and pack animals down from where they had been hidden. When Jacob returned, he helped Martin finish gutting the animals and cut off their massive heads. Since the horned heads brought no money at Fort Vasquez and just added extra weight to the pack animals, they always discarded them alongside the gut piles. When finished, both men looked as if they had just emerged from a slaughterhouse; they were covered with blood from having to awkwardly clean such large animals on the steep side of a hill at the cliff's edge.

Moving carefully down the steep hillside, leading their heavily loaded horses and pack animals, they finally arrived at a little creek near the present-day town of Black Hawk, Colorado. There they let the hardworking horses and mules blow and water in the creek until they'd had their fill. As the animals fed on the lush grasses in the creek bottom, the men took deep drinks from the cold running water and then commenced washing off the dried blood caked on their knives, arms, moccasins, and pant legs.

As Jacob vigorously washed the blood off his arms, a glint in the gravel of the streambed caught his eye. Stopping for a moment and then reaching into the water to pick up the glittering item, he was surprised to find himself holding a large gold nugget weighing several ounces!

"Martin," he said, "can you beat this? I just found myself a gold nugget!" He held it up for his brother to see.

Martin examined the nugget in his brother's hands and then without a word, reached down and picked up a nugget from the streambed at his feet that was at least twice the size of the one Jacob was holding!

"Can you believe this? Here is another one!" he said, surprised and starting to get excited. Like most mountain men, the brothers had never bothered to pursue the mineral wealth of the land over which they roamed because in the wilderness such things had little or no value. However, gold was a cat of another color!

Before they realized what they were doing, the men had picked up over a pound of the bright yellow nuggets at the edge of the riffle where they were standing. Over the next hour they continued picking up the yellow metal off the gravel bars by the handful. Soon a small mound of the precious metal lay glittering on a flat rock beside the stream.

Pausing to consider, Jacob said, "We need to keep this quiet, my brother, or this country will be flooded with gold seekers, and there will go our peace and quiet, not to mention our hunting grounds."

Quietly thinking over his brother's warning, Martin slowly nodded in agreement as he placed another two handfuls of the shiny nuggets on the flat rock, which was becoming crowded with the precious metal. The gold bug had bitten, and hard, as the brothers continued gathering the shiny nuggets from the streambed, working both up- and downstream from the spot where they had first seen gold. In a short period of time, they collected over thirty pounds of nuggets, and there was still more as far as they could see, gleaming on the gravel bars up and down the fast- flowing stream!

Realizing it was getting late in the day and they needed to get back to their camp with the meat so it could be cleaned, skinned, and cooled out, the two men mounted their horses and left the fabulously rich find. Now they had other things on their minds, namely, some beans, bacon, and biscuits. But they didn't leave without first stuffing all their saddlebags full of the precious metal!

After caring for the bighorn sheep meat so it would glaze over in the cool night air, the men fed their horses and then went inside the cabin for their evening meal. As the beans bubbled away in a pot over the coals, Martin fried several pounds of bacon in two three-legged frying pans standing over more hot coals and made a batch of Dutch-oven biscuits. Jacob gathered up the heavy saddlebags of gold nuggets and brought them into the cabin for safekeeping.

Amid the good smells of their meal, the men dumped their find onto a hide stretched across a makeshift table. There was so much gold that many nuggets fell off the table and onto the dirt floor in a glittering array.

"Do you know what we have here, brother?" asked Martin, grinning.

"Sure do," replied a grim-faced Jacob. "We have the ruination of our life as we know it in this neck of the woods if word of this gets out."

"That's true, but if we do it right we can make sure we have plenty for any kind of life we care to live. And that includes buying some land to settle down on before anyone realizes what is here," replied Martin with a knowing grin. "I suggest we haul the meat we have on the hanging poles down to Harold tomorrow so he can make his sausage and the like. Then we should beat it back to our creek and get some more nuggets before anyone else discovers our find. After all, that creek isn't far from the mouth of the canyon and all those people in the fort."

"As usual, brother, you make good sense," said Jacob. "At first light we'll haul the meat down to Harold, and once that is done we need to go to the emporium and purchase some tanned elk skins to make into large sacks in which to haul our gold without raising any suspicions. After all, we need the room in those saddlebags to haul jerky and our possibles," said Jacob as he began to really get the gold bug.

The next morning the men hid their gold, burying it in two green sheep hides above their cabin and covering the spot with a large rock that took both of them to move. Later that afternoon they delivered the sheep meat to a very happy Harold. Then, trying to act casually, they went to Jake's Emporium like ordinary shoppers. They purchased several kegs of powder, more primers for their rifles and pistols, another shovel, flour, cornmeal, jugs of honey, and four tanned elk hides. That evening, as usual so as not to arouse any suspicion, they slept at the corrals just outside the fort and, as before, were gone at first light.

From about noon on, the two men mined the surface gold in their little creek, finding enough loose gold to fill their eight saddlebags once more! When they arrived back at their cabin in the evening, Martin tended to the horses as Jacob went inside with the four tanned elk hides and began cutting and sewing together long tube-like leather pouches that could be filled with gold nuggets and easily carried on pack saddles. That evening after supper they filled several of the tubes with gold nuggets, sewed the tubes shut, and hid them in a hollow tree above their cabin.

The next day the two men found a herd of elk and killed four. They spent the remainder of the day quartering the elk and bringing the meat back to their cabin to hang on the meat poles so it would cool and glaze. Dawn the following morning found them on their gold-nugget-littered creek, filling their saddlebags once again. This time they started on Clear Creek at the mouth of their little stream and worked upstream. They figured if they picked that end of the smaller stream clean of gold, anyone who came prospecting up Clear Creek might pass it by. That way they might be able to postpone a major gold rush in the canyon. Once again they quickly filled all their saddlebags with the precious yellow metal. On the way home they crossed paths with a small herd of bighorn sheep and managed to kill three rams. Arriving late back at their cabin, they unloaded the meat, cleaned it up, and hung it on the remaining meat poles. Then, after a meal of cold beans and sizzling hot fried bacon, the two worked late into the night cutting and sewing together elk-skin bags, enough to hold their gold nuggets from that day's prospecting and the previous days' finds still buried in the green sheep hides under the boulder above their cabin.

As they sat there in the candlelight, Jacob figured they had a small problem. They now had at least 400 pounds of gold nuggets stashed away on the hillside and in their cabin. In addition, they had at least 125 pounds of gold in the Spanish ingots their parents had saved for them, although they didn't intend to do anything with that gold at the moment. They figured their current pack string would be doing well just to haul all their goods and equipment, so they didn't really have any way to transport another four hundred pounds of newfound wealth.

"The next time we are in Fort Vasquez, we need to see if we can buy at least two more good riding horses and a couple of hell-for-stout mules," said Jacob, trying to calculate their new 'gold discovery' needs.

"I agree, and if we're able to purchase extra stock, it shouldn't arouse any undue suspicion because we're hauling in so much meat for Harold," Martin answered with a grin.

The next morning the men buried their latest hoard of gold nuggets under a burned-out log and then urinated on the freshly turned soil to discourage any curious digging animals. They loaded their entire pack string with meat and headed into town. On the way Jacob killed a fat cow elk, and they loaded its hindquarters and back straps onto the already groaning and loudly complaining mules as well.

If nothing else, we'll look more like the hunters we are, arriving with this huge load of meat, thought Jacob with a devious smile that barely showed through his massive beard.

That afternoon the two brothers unloaded their pack string in front of Harold's Butcher Shop as the happy merchant did a jig in front of his meaty riches. The army was coming by at the end of the week for the first installment of sausage and hard salami, and with the meat he now had, he could fill the order. In addition, a farmer who had just given up farming and ranching on the eastern plains had brought all his cattle and pigs into town to sell before the hostile Indians stole them. Harold and his employees were in the process of butchering those meat producing stock animals, which would go into his meat market as well.

After procuring powder, lead, beans, bacon, dried apples, and two freshly made pies, the brothers headed for the corrals outside the fort. After polishing off their pies, they approached the owner of the corrals, who was also the busiest local blacksmith in town. Two of their mules needed new shoes, and after arranging for that service, Jacob asked the blacksmith if they could purchase more horses and mules for their meat-hauling pack string. As it turned out, the same farmer who had brought his pigs and cattle to town had also brought his draft horses and plow mules to sell. As luck would have it, he had just sold those animals that morning to the black-smith.

"Well, you boys came at a good time. I am of a mind to sell everything to anyone with enough hard cash to pay for 'em," he said as he care-fully looked over the heavily bearded, muscular mountain man standing before him.

"Care if we take a gander at them?" asked Jacob.

The liveryman continued to look doubtingly at Jacob and Martin as if they had a good case of the "graybacks," or lice.

"Where the hell a couple meat-hunting drifters like the two of you gonna find enough hard cash to pay for such animals?" he asked suspiciously.

"We have some money left over from our ear-lier meat and fur sales at Fort Bridger and some from the butcher in town," replied Martin, a bit pissed at being treated like the drifters who hung around the fort looking for handouts.

Sensing that he had angered a couple of poten-tial customers, the liveryman backed off a bit and began to act like the astute businessman he was.

"Well, them is very valuable animals. Which ones might you be interested in?" he asked.

"If they are good and sound, we might like at least four mules that are hell-for-stout and a couple extra riding horses in case we cripple one of ours going up and down those rocky canyons. Them two draft animals might just be what we need for hauling heavy meat loads out from the mountains as well," Jacob said in a flat tone designed not to arouse any interest in the real need for the unusually large purchase by two men who were not farmers.

"Well you can take a look at them, but I will need $1,600 in trade for the lot you just described or $1,000 in hard cash," the liveryman said, still looking intensely at the two brothers and prospective customers. "That is what I would ask from the army when they come by at the end of the week, if they be interested and could get it, they being so hard on their horses and all."

For the next half hour Jacob and Martin looked the animals over and were pleased with their condition, teeth, and ages. There were four strong mules broken to pull a plow or wagon, three good-looking riding horses, and the two heavy-boned draft horses. Going on intuition and knowing the army would purchase the riding stock posthaste once the supply officers were aware of their existence, Jacob and Martin made a quick decision. They arranged to purchase the animals and their tack on the spot, leaving $50 as earnest money from their recent sale of meat to Harold, with a promise to pay the balance once they returned in a week.

At dawn the next morning they departed, Jacob leading their original pack string and Martin the horses and mules purchased from the liveryman. Although they made a conspicuous sight, everyone knew they were major meat suppliers for Harold, so no one suspected the real need for the extra horseflesh. On the way home Jacob and Martin killed two fat elk, and by the time they arrived at their cabin, it was dark. Martin cared for the animals while Jacob began dinner with a pot of cold beans as a starter, an entire elk back strap staked over the coals, and a Dutch oven full of biscuits.

At dawn the next morning, after a breakfast of the other elk back strap and biscuits, the men took the two new mules and hunted their way down to their golden creek. Working above where they had left off the time before, they continued picking up the rich surface gold until they had once again filled their eight saddlebags to bursting with the precious nuggets. They hunted their way back to their cabin in the afternoon, killing a large bull elk and a full-curl bighorn ram on the way.

That evening, as supper was cooking, Jacob used up the last of the tanned elk hides purchased at Jake's Emporium to make storage pouches for the nuggets. Upon finishing the pouches, he filled them with their latest discovery. When he had sewn the open tops together, they had compact leather tubes full of gold ready for hiding or easy hauling on their pack animals.

Sitting back and looking at their latest lumpy bundles of gold pouches, Jacob said, "Martin, near as I can figure, we have at least five hundred pounds of gold nuggets! We are rich men." (This amount of gold would have been worth about $128,000 in the money of the day, with raw gold bringing $16 per ounce.)

Martin smiled, remembering the day when they had innocently watered the horses and washed off in their little stream of riches. He quietly thought that if the Indian raiding party hadn't attacked their adopted parents' at their cabins all those years earlier, they would still have been in the Fort Bridger area and never would have stumbled over this source of great material wealth.

"I don't know how much further our little stream will run gold, but I suggest we keep working it because it's just a matter of time until people coming from Fort Vasquez or new arrivals from back East heading for the gold fields in California fan out and discover our secret," said Jacob.

"I agree. Let's ride this horse just as far as we can, and when the hills explode with gold seekers, we need to take what is ours and get the hell out of the area," said Martin, looking introspective as he realized the changes a gold rush and thousands of clamoring people would bring to their quiet backwoods lives.

Dawn the next morning found the men on their horses climbing high onto the ridge overlooking their creek and the now golden changing aspens in the canyons and hills below. They spooked a moose out of a drainage heavy with springs and willows just below the ridge top, and it took both of them shooting their heavy Hawkens to bring down the beast before it ran deeper into the canyon, which would have made it a chore to haul out. It took them the better part of the morning to get the animal cut up and loaded onto the two stout mules. Both animals had been used extensively before the men had acquired them, as was apparent in their gentle nature—especially when asked to take on such a task as carrying heavy, bloody, and strong-smelling animals on their backs in rugged mountain country that was almost straight up and down.

Heading down into the steep drainage with their heavy loads, the men took their time in order not to injure the pack animals. When they reached their gold laden creek they continued working upstream from where they had finished the last time as their animals took time to load up on the lush grasses that grew along the banks. As had been the case before, nuggets littered every gravel bar and eddy, and in no time they had once again filled their saddlebags with the precious metal. Mentally marking the spot where they finished, the brothers headed up over the ridge and set a course for home. When they arriving at their cabin, they slid into their familiar mode of work. Martin grazed the livestock on the nearby hillside, curried the animals' coats, and watered them in the small creek running next to the cabin before putting them into the corral for the night. Once finished, he brought in an armload of wood for their fire and sat down at the table with Jacob, who had taken care of the moose meat so it would cool and glaze. With those chores done, they prepared supper, filling the cabin with delicious smells.

"Tomorrow we need to go right to our stream and mine it first thing. Then we need to hunt that hogback above the creek by our cabin," said Jacob as he swallowed a piping-hot biscuit slathered with dark honey.

"I agree," said Martin. "I've been hearing elk bugling up there for the last few days, and that might be a good place to load up with more venison."

For a long time it was quiet as the two men ate, and then Jacob said with a grin, "With what we brought down the mountain today, we have at least seven hundred pounds of gold nuggets—and that doesn't count the gold we have in our Spanish ingots!" Martin smiled and said, "I still want to see what the old-time mountain men used to call the Big Water, or the Pacific Ocean. Then we can buy that big ranch we always wanted, settle down, quit Indian fighting, and have a passel of kids. I figure our gold will just about do the trick and then some."

Jacob shook his head at his brother's single-mindedness when it came to seeing the Pacific Ocean. But in the back of his mind, he wanted the same things—someday...

The two men set out before daylight the next day, but this time they took their two larger and two smaller mules. That way, if they found the elk, they could bring back a load of meat, then head to Fort Vasquez the next day to sell it and settle up with the liveryman for their livestock purchase. When they reached the spot on the creek where they had finished gold hunting the last time, the two brothers tied off their stock on long ropes so the animals could feed and headed upstream on foot. For a long time their work was just as before. In every riffle and on the back sides of eddies, they picked up handfuls of loose gold nuggets. Coming to a large cut in the cliff face through which the stream passed, Jacob paused in order to figure a way through the rough terrain without getting wet. Then he saw it! Where the creek cut through the rock formation lay an exposed vein of gold at least a foot wide and a foot and a half high.

"Well, I'll be damned," said Jacob, "will you look at that!"

Martin scrambled around his brother and stopped short, looking at the riches in the rock formation.

"What the blazes do we do now?" he asked.

"Damned if I know, but we can't leave it here," said Jacob, dumbfounded.

They stood looking at the mother lode in amazement. Neither of them knew a thing about hard-rock mining, so they bypassed the rich vein and continued to look for the loose gold in the stream above the cut. However, they discovered none above the vein. Apparently the vein was the source of the loose gold they had found downstream.

Taking what they had discovered that day, they mounted up and, with the puzzle about what to do about the rich vein swimming around in their heads, hunted their way back to the cabin. They killed a large, fat grizzly bear that they found digging out a yellow-bellied marmot from under a rock. The great bear never heard the shot or saw the man above him pulling the trigger. Jacob and Martin knew they now had almost a full winter's supply of excellent cooking oil once they had rendered the fat from the great bear.

Loading the fat bear tried the patience of the larger mules, who refused to take on the quarters because of the strange smell. The two smaller mules, who had previously been loaded with bear meat, took on the load, but not without rolling their eyes to make sure everything was all right. As they worked down the ridge above their cabin, each man managed to take an additional large bull elk in the rut, and by the time the best parts of those animals had been strapped onto their pack animals, they had more than a load.

Elk back strap, beans, biscuits, and honey made up their dinner that evening, drowned with large tin cups of steaming-hot thick black trapper's coffee. Once again the men hid their latest finds of gold, this time in an unused cast-iron boiling pot in the woodpile under some limb wood. They were rich men, and if they could find a way to get at the gold in the vein, they would be rich beyond belief. However, therein remained a puzzle the men would have to work out before someone else beat them to the find of a lifetime. They didn't dare purchase a pick or a breaking hammer in the settlement because of the risk of catching everyone's eye and curiosity.

Little did they realize the key to that puzzle was fast approaching, and from a point on the compass that would be truly amazing.

Chapter Eleven

A BLACK MAN COMES, AND TROUBLE FOLLOWS

STEPPING OUTSIDE the cabin at daylight to attend to a call of nature, Jacob saw what appeared to be a black bear feasting on a hindquarter of the moose they had shot two days earlier as it hung swinging from the meat pole. Racing back into the cabin, he yelled to Martin as he ran back out with his Hawken.

As he drew down on what he had thought was a black bear, Jacob was surprised to see over his rifle barrel the face of a half- naked black man of immense height and proportions! Grabbing Martin as he ran by Jacob to get a shot, he held down the barrel of his brother's rifle so Martin wouldn't also mistake the man for a bear. Standing there in amazement, the brothers gawked at the amazing sight.

Finally Jacob yelled, "Hey, that there moose hindquarter belongs to us!"

Surprised by the appearance of the two men, the man tiredly held up his hands in resignation and stood still with a baleful look on his face. As they got their first real look at him, the brothers continued to stare in astonishment. The man stood at least six and a half feet high and in better days had probably weighed at least three hundred pounds. His arms and legs spoke of nothing but power.

Keeping his Hawken at the ready, Jacob said, "Come here, you. We won't hurt you."

For a moment the man didn't move or take his eyes off the armed brothers. Then he frantically looked around for an avenue of escape. Seeing none, he finally came out from behind the moose quarter and slowly walked over to them.

Damn, thought Jacob as the black man loomed over him, he is even bigger than he first appeared to be! "Who the hell are you, and where did you come from?" he asked.

"My name is Cain, and I'm a runaway slave. I escaped ten days ago from my master, Ben Lord, at Fort Vasquez and have been on the run in these mountains ever since."

Jacob and Martin just looked at each other in amazement. First, they had only ever seen three black men in their lives before, all at Fort Bridger;

all three had been servants traveling west with families on the wagon trains. Second, the man spoke better English than the two of them. Third, he was an immense human being but appeared to be as docile as a baby bird.

Jacob shocked his brother with his next words. "If you can wait a spell, my brother and me will fix you some vittles and hot coffee. That is, if you would like that instead of that there raw moose hindquarter, which we mean to sell if you don't eat it to the bone."

"I would be obliged," said Cain, "as I haven't eaten since I escaped until this morning."

The men stood for a moment looking at each other until Jacob smiled and said, "Come on, Martin, let's see if we can fix this man some eats before he commences to eating our moose once again."

Cain sat outside the cabin on a log because there wasn't enough room for him inside while the brothers turned to making breakfast. Just in case Cain suddenly became a dangerous wild man, the brothers carried their pistols at the ready in their sashes.

Breakfast consisted of two Dutch ovens full of biscuits, a frying pan full of partially cooked bacon (Jacob figured it best to leave a lot of fat on the meat so the black man could replenish his own fat reserves), eight moose steaks in two other frying pans, and two pots of scalding black coffee before Cain appeared to be filling up. Not much was said as the three men ate, but they spent a lot of time looking at each other. The brothers felt awe and respect for the starving gentle giant trying to square up his stomach with the little guts. Cain stared at the two mountain men as if this moment might disappear into thin mountain air as a figment of his starving imagination, and the grub along with it.

Finishing, Cain said, "I can't pay you for your hospitality, but I can work off the grub doing whatever you need around the cabin. Then I have to skedaddle before my master runs me to ground and beats the living tar out of me once again for escaping."

Jacob and Martin just sat there. They had been raised in the rough-and-tumble wilderness and were tough, hard-hewn men. Yet here was a man who had led a life of slavery and abuse and appeared as gentle as all get-out. Already, in the short time they had been together, Cain had begun to win their hearts.

"Cain," said Jacob, "is your owner really out there somewhere looking for you?"

Cain said immediately, "Yes, he is, and if he catches me he will beat me within an inch of my life. I just had enough of the beatings, starving, and poor treatment while he always lived high on the hog, so I up and ran away. I am still his property, and he won't give up until I'm back in his clutches because he paid $1,000 way back in Virginia for me. I am dead or of no use to anyone anymore, as far as I am concerned." Cain dejectedly looked down at his ragged pants and bare, bleeding feet.

"No man has a right to own another!" said Martin through clenched teeth.

"That's right!" Jacob agreed strongly, upset over what he was hearing.

"As long as you're with us, no one will make a slave out of you ever again," added Martin, very determined and not really realizing the ramifications of his words.

"The two of you don't fully understand. I am Ben Lord's property under law. He paid for me fair and square, and now he can do with me whatever he wants under the law," Cain said quietly and without any emotion.

"Where does this Lord fellow live again?" asked Jacob.

"He lives in a back room in Jake's Emporium at Fort Vasquez. He is a wealthy land speculator and buys and sells town lots around Fort Vasquez and on a site along Cherry Creek," answered Cain.

"Cain, we have to run our meat to Fort Vasquez to sell before it spoils. That will take us a long day, and then we will be back. Why don't you stay here at our cabin and wait until the two of us can figure a way out of this mess for you?" asked Jacob.

"I would like that, but I had better keep on running. If I don't, I might get you both in trouble with the law and Mr. Lord as well. Besides, I'm a slave, and that's my lot in life — to serve him or others like him," Cain said resignedly.

Those words inflamed Jacob and Martin. Having been raised in the west as free men, not obliged to anyone except themselves, they didn't think any human being should believe it was his lot in life to be a slave.

"You will wait here for us, and upon our return we'll figure a way out of this mess," Martin said sternly as Jacob nodded in agreement.

Cain helped the brothers load the meat onto the pack animals, and they asked him to feed and water the remaining livestock while awaiting their return. Jacob went to their stash of coins from the sale of the Lakota horses and mules at Fort Bridger and took out the $950 they owed the liveryman; then the brothers left for the fort with their pack strings heavily loaded with fresh meat. Behind them stood a forlorn-looking figure, hoping against hope that Martin and Jacob's words would somehow ring true.

Arriving in Fort Vasquez, the brothers unloaded the meat at the butcher shop. Harold was especially happy to get the moose meat because of a high local demand for the excellent-tasting venison. When they picking up supplies at Jake's Emporium, Jacob and Martin overheard talk about an escaped slave and learned that a party of men was out hunting him. Pretending to be uninterested in the news about the manhunt, they went about their business. After getting their supplies loaded, they hotfooted it down to the livery stable and paid off the liveryman. With no further delay, they headed back up Clear Creek Canyon toward their cabin.

Arriving home about one the following morning, they were surprised to see dim candlelight shining from a window in their cabin. There was a fire blazing in the fire pit in the front yard and a large stand of horses not belonging to them tethered nearby. Tying up their pack string out of sight of the tethered horses so they wouldn't alert those inside, Jacob and Martin began their stalk to get closer. Quietly walking up to the front door, the brothers hesitated and then jerked it violently open. Storming inside, they found the cabin crowded with eight men, all trying to sleep. Their surprise was complete, and Jacob and Martin covered them with their rifles as they leaped to their feet. Sitting in one corner of the crowded cabin was Cain. He was tied up and had been badly beaten about the face, back, and shoulders.

"Hold your fire! I am Ben Lord, and I can explain," said a short, fat, balding man.

"Best get to explaining before I start shooting," Jacob uttered through clenched teeth, "since this here is our cabin, and you varmints don't belong!"

"We have been trailing this here slave who belongs to me for the last several days. His trail led to this here cabin, and when we opened the door, we found him hiding inside. I am doing nothing but claiming my property, and once we got some sleep, we was going to take him back to Fort Vasquez," said Ben Lord. He seemed perplexed by the turn of events as he stared at the business end of Jacob's and Martin's unwavering rifles.

Still holding Lord in his sights, Jacob said, "How much you want for the slave?"

"I don't want to sell him," said Lord with a less-than-calm, surprised voice.

"How much did you pay for him?" Jacob demanded.

"He cost me $1,000 in hard coin way back in Virginia a couple years back," responded Lord, still confused by the line of questioning.

"I will give you $1,200 for the man in hard coin and gold if you will sell him to me," Jacob responded, still very angry.

Martin continued to back his brother's play, but the offer to buy Cain caught him as much off guard as Ben Lord. Neither of us believes in slavery, so why buy a slave now? he wondered, looking hard at Jacob as if that would bring an answer.

"I think $1,200 would be a fair price. But the only way I will take it is in silver or gold," wheezed Lord, still nervous at the rifle barrels pointing at his guts and very surprised by the offer.

Carefully walking over to Cain, Jacob cut him loose. Walking back to the doorway of the cabin, Jacob handed Cain his rifle and said, "Watch them. If they move, send them over the Great Divide."

Cain took Jacob's rifle, and the look in his eyes showed that Jacob's words would be well heeded if he had his druthers.

Turning to Martin, Jacob said, "I will be back shortly," and he went out the door into the early-morning darkness.

Twenty minutes later Jacob returned with a saddlebag in hand. Walking over to the table, he dumped the last of their gold and silver coins out on the table. He counted them out as everyone under the muzzles of the rifles looked on in amazement at the hoard of wealth of a kind rarely seen on the frontier.

"There be $800 here," Jacob said. Then, with a quick movement, he threw two of their Spanish gold ingots onto the table, saying, "That will square the deal, agreed?"

Lord reached over with fingers still greasy from supper and fingered the golden ingots.

"Where'd you boys get these?" he asked with obvious greed in his voice.

"Do we have a deal or not?" asked Jacob, ignoring Lord's question.

"Sure do," said Lord as he scooped the coins and gold ingots into his hat, "but you never answered my question on where those Spanish ingots came from."

"Traded some horses for them off a Ute Indian some years back," lied Jacob, hoping to throw Lord off the golden and seemingly still cursed trail.

The look on Lord's and the others' faces showed disbelief, but under the circumstances, they held their tongues.

Martin roared to life, saying, "Now you all get the hell out of our cabin. You are stinking it up!"

The eight men started to grab their sleeping rolls and rifles but were cut short by a gruff command from Jacob. "Leave them rifles, pistols, and knives here, boys," he said with finality in the tone of his voice.

The men hesitated, and Martin said, "Obey my

brother or you will all die here in this cabin, and then we will burn it to the ground to get rid of your stinking carcasses. Then no one will ever be the wiser about what happened to you miserable wretches."

The tone of his voice told the men that to disobey would mean death. Their weapons were slowly lowered back to the floor of the cabin or stacked against its walls.

"You can pick up your rifles, pistols, and knives here at the cabin in two days. They will be left inside for safekeeping, and you can claim them then," said Jacob.

It would soon be first light, and the men left only to bed down by the corral for the remainder of the darkness. Jacob, Martin, and Cain did not let their guards down. At daylight they stood in the front yard and watched the eight manhunters thread their way back down Clear Creek Canyon until they were out of sight as they headed back to the fort. Little did Lord and his party realize that the Curse of the Spanish Gold now partially rested in their saddlebags and would be exacted to the fullest measure on a soon-to-come date...

"That about cuts it," said Jacob. "We need to move on now because I feel they will be back in force and try to have their way with us for the rest of the Spanish gold if we are not careful."

Martin nodded in solemn agreement and said,

"You are right. If we stay there will be some killing, and that we don't need. Besides, it seems every time we bring out those Spanish gold ingots, trouble is not far behind us. That would have gone double if we had used some of our nuggets to seal the trade."

Cain, quiet until then, said, "Thank you both for my freedom. But I fear if Ben can get me back, you will have spent your money and gold in vain."

"That ain't going to happen," uttered Jacob, "without a whole lot of killing, and it won't be us gettin' killed if that be the case!"

Before leaving the cabin, Jacob and Martin outfitted Cain as best they could. He now carried his own Hawken, two pistols, and a sharp gutting knife from their stores. Since they did not have any buckskin shirts big enough for him, he had to be satisfied for the moment with a buffalo-robe cape worn loosely over his massive shoulders. He rode Dander, one of the hell-for-stout mules, and helped in leading the two draft horses, who were loaded with very heavy packs containing numerous lumpy elk- skin pouches.

By noon that fall day, as the three men looked back into Clear Creek Canyon from the top of what is today Berthoud Pass, they saw no sign of pursuit. Jacob had altered the rifles and pistols of the men who had taken Cain before leaving them in the cabin so that if anyone tried to fire them, they would misfire. By the time the alterations could be discovered and rectified, Jacob hoped the three of them would be out of reach in the high country and back with their friends the Northern Arapaho.

Just smart business altering their rifles if they catch us not looking, he thought with a grin as he kicked his horse in its flanks.

The three men made a grand picture as they rode down the back side of Berthoud Pass in all its fall glory, wending their way through the heavy stands of lodgepole pine into the lush mountain valleys and into the territory of Bison Path, chief of the Northern Arapaho, with their long pack strings. Jacob recognized a small stream rushing down the canyon and followed it downward, leading their heavily loaded pack strings out of the heavy timber in and around the less dense stands of spruce and aspen until they reached an open, high mountain valley floor. Cutting across the headwaters of the Colorado River, they headed up and over what is today called Willow Creek Pass. Along the way Jacob noticed the vast amount of beaver ponds and dams in the watered areas. We need to trap these waters in the future, he thought with a grin of anticipation over the advent of the fall trapping season, soon to be upon them.

Unknown to Cain, Jacob was leading the way to a little cabin near a small spring in a grove of trees that the Indians had decorated with sacred items of respect...There they would winter, trap beaver along the Michigan River, and make meat from the many buffalo in the sagebrush flats north of their cabin. The days ahead were looking good...

As for the vein of pure gold that they left behind, it would be discovered in 1859 and lead to a local gold rush near the present-day town of Black Hawk, Colorado.

Chapter Twelve

FALL ARRIVES WITH ALL ITS FURY BEFORE THE WINDS OF WINTER HOWL

BEFORE THE MEN made it to the old cabin, they were intercepted by a small band of Northern Arapaho who had been out hunting. After exchanging greetings, Jacob let the Indians know they were heading for the old cabin for a winter stay. This excited the Indians, but not as much as seeing a black man for the first time in their lives—and a huge one at that!

Leaving the band of Indians and leading their pack strings to the cabin, the men dismounted and removed the loads and saddles from the animals. They hobbled the animals and let them out into the nearby meadow to feed and water while the three men set about enlarging the horse corral and strengthening the support posts in order to hold their increased numbers of livestock. During this process of digging holes and setting additional posts, the brothers were amazed again and again by Cain's great strength. He easily lifted logs that would have taken both of the brothers to lift. When the corral was finished, they moved all their gear into the cabin, and Jacob set about building another sleeping platform for Cain that was befitting of his height and great size.

For the next week the men busied themselves hauling in winter firewood, hunting buffalo with the Indians, making clothing for Cain, and drying great amounts of meat for the time when the snow would be too deep to hunt or move about easily. Figuring that Cain was not only built like a horse but ate like one, Jacob saw to it that their jerky and smoked-meat stores were very substantial. The three men also built a large aerial cache house next to their cabin to store their overflow provisions. During this time the brothers let Cain in on their secret relating to the hoard of gold nuggets and Spanish ingots.

Cain was amazed as he let some of the nuggets slip through his large hands and fingers, then let them drop back into the elkskin sacks.

"As you can well imagine, we need to hide our fortune," said Jacob.

"There's a small rocky outcropping behind our cabin in which we could store it if you think it would be secure there," said Martin.

"I've been thinking the same thing," said Jacob.

"It's mostly out of sight and out of the weather, so our leather bags won't rot. Plus, we can bury the whole mess under some loose rocks and dirt out of sight of prying eyes," continued Martin.

"Then it's done," said Jacob. "Tomorrow we will bury the gold in a dry cache and cover it well enough that it won't be discovered by anyone nosing around when we aren't here."

The next day found the three men digging out dirt and wood-rat debris from under a rocky overhang and hiding the gold in a typical trapper's cache of log walls, floor, roof, and dried leaves. Several hundred pounds of loose rock and dirt over the cache's roof logs completed the task in such a way that no one would be any wiser about the golden hoard hidden therein.

During the process of getting ready for winter, the Indians came calling many times. They were still amazed by Cain's color because they had never seen a black man before, and they were also astonished by his great size and strength. They held many contests of speed and strength, and Cain emerged as the winner most of the time. When an Indian bested him, which didn't happen often, it was cause for great celebration in the Indian camp.

Cain, because of his uniqueness, was also able to bed many of the Arapaho ladies—at their requests.

Leaving the cabin one fall morning at daylight, the three men went into what is today the Michigan River drainage to trap beaver, which were now in their prime. After setting out twenty traps, they commenced hunting the willows and killed a large cow moose for camp meat. Returning to their recently set trapline, they found about half the traps full of prime, blanket-sized beaver. Even though a beaver pelt was worth only a dollar because silk had replaced the demand for beaver hats, the men still trapped them for old times' sake. Resetting those traps, they loaded the beaver on their pack string along with the moose meat and headed back to their cabin before an oncoming winter rainstorm drenched them.

Rounding the trees below the cabin, the men filed into the corral area and dismounted to unload the moose meat and beaver carcasses. They hobbled the animals and let them out to feed and water in the nearby meadow. Turning toward the cabin carrying armloads of beaver to be skinned and hooped, along with the moose quarters, they were suddenly confronted by six white men holding leveled rifles as they quickly emerged from their hiding places inside the cabin and fanned out in front of the door.

"Drop what you are holding and turn around," yelled a red faced, excited Ben Lord.

For a long moment the three men just stood in amazement at the sudden change in their fortunes. Then they did as instructed, turning and facing away from the six men holding rifles. There were three loud thuds from rifle butts, and the lights went out for the brothers and Cain.

When the three men awoke, they found themselves tied to adjacent separate trees. Unable to move or fight back, Jacob and Martin could only watch as Ben beat Cain within an inch of his life with a bullwhip. That whipping opened up great gashes in Cain's heavily muscled flesh. Jacob and Martin quietly tried to loosen the ropes that bound their hands as the beating went on, but the armed men accompanying Lord had tied them too well.

After Ben had beaten Cain almost senseless, he started in on Jacob with his bullwhip, asking where the rest of the golden ingots were hidden.

Jacob coldly answered, "That was all there were."

A smash in the face from the leaded butt of the bullwhip brought tears of pain to Jacob's eyes and a burning rage to reach out and squeeze Ben's neck until he quit wiggling.

As blood ran down Jacob's face, Lord stuck his furious face in Jacob's and said, "Tell me where the gold is, or I will beat you within an inch of your life same as I did the nigger!"

Rage surfaced in Jacob, and he spat into Ben's leering face. That was the last thing he remembered as Ben beat him about the head and shoulders with the leaded butt of the whip until he was senseless. When he came to twenty minutes later, Jacob swore to his maker that Lord would die a horrible death if he ever got free from his ropes. That rage became even more intense when Lord turned on Martin, beating him unconscious as he tried to get the secret of the location of the Spanish gold ingots from him as well.

Leaving the three badly beaten men tied to the trees, the six invaders had a good laugh, then went into the cabin to get out of the lightly falling cold rain to eat and sleep. The three captives, soon soaked by the cold winter rains and stiff and sore, could only imagine what was to befall them come daylight.

About two in the morning Jacob felt a knife cut his ropes, and he fell stiffly and awkwardly to the ground. Painfully rolling over, he stared up into the worried face of his friend Bison Path. Then he heard Martin and Cain fall with soft thuds as well. In a few moments the men were able to work the stiffness out of their arms and legs until they could stand.

Bison Path helped them stumble away from the cabin and out of earshot while a number of his braves surrounded the darkened cabin and watched it for any sign of discovery. After walking several hundred yards into the dark timber behind the cabin, the men found themselves by a small fire and were able to warm up, partially dry out, and collect their senses.

"What do you want us to do to the bad spider people, my friend?" asked a worried but obviously revenge-minded Bison Path.

"We are going to kill every one of them!" stated the fast-reviving Jacob, who was now so full of rage and hatred that his whole body was violently shaking...and it wasn't from the cold.

Looking at his brother and Cain, Jacob could see the rage in their eyes by the dancing light from the fire.

"When we're ready, we'll return to the cabin. If my Indian brothers will give us some knives, we will go into the cabin and kill every man there," Jacob said coldly.

"And if we are unsuccessful and some bad men try to escape, I would hope our Indian brothers will kill them as they exit the cabin," Martin added.

The look in Bison Path's eyes told them that no man from Lord's party would leave the forest alive that day.

Jacob grabbed Bison Path's arm in friendship and agreement as he was handed a long-bladed knife. Two braves standing nearby handed knives to Cain and Martin at Bison Path's request. With that, the three men and a dozen braves quietly returned to the darkened cabin, which was being guarded by another band of heavily armed Northern Arapaho.

Jacob slowly opened the front door as the returning thunder of the winter's rains on the sod roof muffled any sound. He moved to his right and was followed by Martin, who moved to the left in the darkness inside. Cain silently moved into the middle of the cabin, blocking the door to stop anyone lucky enough to survive the brothers' attack. If the beating Cain had taken from Lord meant anything, that survivor trying to escape from the brothers' wrath would die from a broken neck or back at his hands.

Boom—boom! roared two rifles, going off simultaneously as two men awoke when Jacob stepped on them by mistake in the early-morning darkness. The first ball tore along Jacob's left side, ripping away hardened muscle and cracking two ribs. The man firing that rifle, illuminated by the fireball at the end of the barrel, died immediately from a knife thrust deeply into an eye socket. The second shot tore harmlessly into the timbers of the cabin above the door. With that, total terror reined within the darkened cabin as the invaders awoke to their worst nightmare. *Boom—boom— boom* went three more rifles in quick succession.

One ball hit Cain in the point of his left shoulder, tearing out a two-inch chunk of muscle. Cain, in turn, hit the closest man so hard in the neck with his knife blade that he severed the shooter's spine, dropping him instantly. Martin, unnoticed by everyone, swung his knife with such force that he beheaded his target, a small man just rising in alarm from his sleeping furs on the floor.

"I surrender, I surrender!" screamed Lord as he struggled to his feet and then tried to escape. Cain broke Lord's neck with a loud snap audible over the melee still going on in the darkened cabin as he tried to escape by running out the front door.

Boom went another rifle in Martin's face, leaving him with a powder burn along his neck and shoulder. That shooter died as Martin's knife plunged repeatedly into his chest until the man sank to the floor, a lifeless, bloody rag.

Whack went the sound of a tomahawk hitting the steel of Jacob's knife in the darkened cabin. Losing his knife with the strike, Jacob lunged forward and, grabbing the man by the head, bit off the assailant's ear as he gouged out the man's eyes with his fingers. A terrible scream erupted as the man sank to the floor under the savage onslaught, only to have his neck quickly snapped by a furious Cain before Jacob could finish the job.

The morning light was just starting to illuminate the room as the men paused in their killing fury, recognizing each other in the moment. The cabin smelled strongly of blood, black powder, and the urine and feces expelled by the dead men.

"Are you all right, Martin?" yelled Jacob.

"I have a powder burn, but I think I'm all right. How about you?" said Martin.

"I hurt like hell on my left side where I was shot. Cracked ribs for sure, since I heard them break when the ball hit," Jacob said flatly as he started coming down from his violent adrenalin driven emotional high.

"Cain, you all right?" Martin asked worriedly.

"I'm fine. I took a ball in the shoulder, but it's only a flesh wound, I think," Cain said quietly as he explored the damaged and bleeding area tenderly with his fingers.

Several worried heads peered into the open doorway as the Indians approached to see what had happened during the furious exchange. They soon parted, and in walked Bison Path with concern written all over his face. Upon seeing his friends all standing, he smiled a huge smile of relief.

The three men set to helping each other patch up their wounds. Jacob was hurt the worst with his broken ribs, but he had a whole winter in which to recover. All they could do was clean out his wound and tie it up tightly with a piece of tanned elk skin. By then several Indian women had arrived on the scene and patched up Cain and Martin with their herbal remedies. In the meantime, the warriors hauled the dead out of the cabin. They were dragged by ropes tied to the Indians' horses across the meadow and piled up in a small gully. Because the Indians considered them to be evil, the dead men were deemed not worthy of scalping. Within days all that was left were meat scraps on the bones for the ravens, crows, and magpies to enjoy after the prairie wolves, coyotes, and bears not yet in hibernation had eaten their fill.

For their help and rescue, Bison Path and his people were given the six assailants' horses, pack animals, rifles, and supplies. However, Jacob kept the two Spanish ingots he had used to purchase Cain, which he recovered from Lord's saddlebags before giving up all the men's tack to the Arapahos. It seemed that Lord and his men had felt the ultimate sting and curse of the Spanish gold...

Ͽᴖᴗᴗ

THE REST OF THE WINTER of 1855 went quietly as the men trapped beaver and other fur-bearers until freeze-up. When the snows came, they retreated to their cabin to fix equipment and horse tack for the next spring. During times of good weather, when the snows were not too deep, they hauled more firewood, trapped pine marten and lynx, and visited their friends at the Arapahos' camp. During those sessions the men traded their excess supplies for the well-dressed furs taken by the Indians during their fall and winter trapping excursions. Soon their little cabin was literally filled to the rafters with piles of furs. During the winter the men healed from the fight with Lord and his henchmen. However, in the close confines of the small cabin and the deepening snows, they waited with keen anticipation for the spring thaw and what the new trapping season had to offer.

Jacob and Martin frequently made the time to study the ridgepole with their fingers, feeling their fathers' carved names as if to draw out the last ounce of family history. That history seemed to speak more and more often of mortality...

Chapter Thirteen

SPRING AND A TRIP NORTH

WHEN THE SPRING of 1856 came, the men looked forward to a good year and put the previous winter's events behind them. They began trapping for beaver on the Michigan and Illinois Rivers once again, and soon a small mountain of pelts adorned the back of their already crowded cabin. In addition, they continued hunting buffalo on the sagebrush plains to the north, and before long a pile of tanned buffalo hides filled one of their lean-tos.

One late-March morning, as the skies spoke of more snow to come, the men moved in single file along the Michigan River, checking their traps. Jacob was in the lead, followed by Martin and then Cain, who was leading the pack animals.

Crash—wham! A huge bull moose, apparently

asleep in the dense undergrowth and startled by the quiet approach of Jacob's horse, jumped up and immediately charged. The speed, surprise, and energy of an enraged 1,500-pound animal striking the side of the horse from less than ten feet away knocked Jacob and the horse to the ground. Pinned under his horse, Jacob heard his leg and two of those on his mount snap like rifle shots. As the horse screamed in pain, Jacob passed out, still under the weight of the frantically thrashing, terrified animal.

Awakened moments later by extreme pain, Jacob became aware of the moose's slobber-covered nose resting wetly on his face. Martin and Cain were yelling, and Jacob smelled the comforting odor of freshly fired black powder from rifles fired seconds earlier into the still enraged bull.

"Jacob," Martin yelled, "are you all right?"

"'Course I'm all right. I always lay under a horse and bull moose for the hell of it," Jacob called back. "That damn moose broke my leg, which hurts like hell, and I now have a horse with broken legs still squirming on my bad leg. Do something."

"He's all right," Cain said in relief. "If he can bellow at us like that after being hit full-on by a bull moose, he'll survive." Grabbing Jacob's still thrashing horse, Cain lifted its head and slit its throat clean to the spine, killing it within moments as it bled out. Then, grabbing the dead moose by its head, Martin and Cain rolled the body off the still quivering horse and Jacob. They then lifted the front end of the dead horse high enough for Jacob to painfully drag his body and broken leg out from under it. That effort and the pain of his broken, twisted leg hanging up on some crushed willows beneath him caused Jacob to pass out again.

Awakening, Jacob found that his leg had been splinted and that he was lying on a makeshift travois that also carried several beaver carcasses and the back straps and one hindquarter from the moose that had almost killed him. The remaining hindquarter was carried by their pack horse along with several more dead beaver. An unexpected drop as the travois passed over a small creek bank caused Jacob to pass out yet again from the pain in his leg, and he made it back to the cabin without any further felt suffering.

The next time he awoke, it was to the smell of fresh moose steak frying in bear grease and the pleasant feeling of the sleeping furs in his bed. Propping himself up on his elbows, he saw Cain struggling to hoist the moose quarters onto the meat pole in the front yard. On the other side of his bunk, by the fireplace, Martin was occupied with cooking dinner. The heavenly smell of sourdough Dutch-oven biscuits reached Jacob's nostrils, and if his leg hadn't hurt so badly, he would have been pleased.

"Awake, are you?" asked Martin, still worried as he strode over to his brother's side.

"Yes," answered Jacob as he ran his hand over the now tightly wrapped break in his leg.

"It's a good thing we have extra horses since you lost yours to that damned moose," Martin said with a wry smile.

"Leave it to you to worry about a damn horse over your brother," Jacob shot back. But he smiled his thanks for the others' help in surviving what would have been a fatal backcountry encounter if he had been alone.

The light in the cabin dimmed as Cain's huge frame filled the doorway.

"Who's going to take over his chores until he heals up?" asked Cain with a large grin on his weathered face, as if he didn't already know.

"That does it!" exclaimed Jacob, albeit with a grin of his own. "After all I have done for you two miserable wretches, that's all the concern I get as I lay here almost in death."

The men had a hearty laugh over Jacob's bad luck, and the three were no closer now than if they had all been biological brothers. In the end, Jacob enjoyed that fresh moose-steak dinner more than he had enjoyed any other moose meals in the past.

Several more deep snows confined the men near their cabin and the Indians to their camp until the end of April. By then Jacob was able to get around with a homemade crutch as he and the others prepared for the summer.

"The beaver are about gone in all the river bottoms, and the buffalo have moved farther north as a result of the Indians' presence and our hunting pressure," Cain mumbled through a gigantic mouthful of steaming-hot elk stew and biscuits.

Jacob and Martin nodded in agreement as they filled their mouths with the gravy-laced, thick, delicious stew as well.

"I say we move on farther to the north and try our luck," Cain continued.

Martin looked over at Jacob, the nominal leader of the group, to see what he thought.

Swallowing a mouthful of the elk stew, Jacob helped himself to another cup of strong black coffee and sat thoughtfully for a few moments as he looked into the dying embers of the fire as if that was where the answer lay.

"I've been thinking the same thing. It'll do us no good to stay here and continue to trap in an area now lacking critters. Our trapping success with marten, fox, and wolves is down as well, and it does us no good to have to ride five miles one way in order to get into the buffalo so we can make meat. What say we move north and west over toward the Sweet Water River and do some serious buffalo hunting for hides. We can take them over to Jim Bridger at the fort, if he is still in business, and replenish our supplies there. From there we can continue moving north and east up through South Pass and into the Popo Agie to continue trapping and hunting buffalo if that suits our fancy."

"That ain't getting me any closer to that big pond out west and a place where we can settle down and raise a passel of kids," Martin said slowly, reminding his brother of his lifelong Pacific Ocean dream.

"What about you, Cain? What are your druthers to that way of thinking?" asked Jacob.

"Well, as the two of you already know, you are my only family. I sure would favor eventually going farther west and away from the likes of Ben Lord. But whatever you two decide to do, count me as a throw-in," he replied quietly.

"I hear tell from our Arapaho brothers that many wagons with white tops are coming down through South Pass and going to a place they call California. What say we move in that direction as we continue hunting and trapping. Then, if we find that our kind of business and lifestyle is gone, we can hitch up with some of those wagons and all go to California. That way Martin can see that big pond he is always talking about. Not to mention, Cain will be rid of slavery issues, and all of us can settle down and start families," Jacob proposed thoughtfully, trying to read his brothers' faces for their reactions to his newest proposal.

"That sounds better to me than the earlier plan," Martin exclaimed with a smile.

"Then north it is," said Cain with a tinge of excitement in his voice for the first time in many months.

"Then it's agreed," said Jacob, letting a bit of excitement creep into his voice as well. "We'll leave this valley and head north, and if that does not pan out, west it is."

That evening the men went to the rocky ledge behind the cabin that held their secret stash and retrieved their leather pouches, still holding the gold nuggets along with the Spanish gold. Several of the bags had been nibbled on by dusky-footed woodrats, but Martin had them patched up in no time. Back at the cabin, the men loaded the gold onto newly constructed pack frames for the two draft horses to see if they were capable of carrying the heavy cargo by themselves. They made a few adjustments to the frames in the form of underpadding, then unloaded everything after finding the draft horses stout enough for the loads they were to carry.

The Dutch-oven apple pie that Cain made with

soaked dried apple slices went down very well that evening. It might have gone down even better if the brothers had known what magic was in store for them at Fort Bridger...

Chapter Fourteen

A FORTUITOUS MEETING

WHEN LATE SPRING CAME, and the grass was sufficiently high for horses to live on, the men loaded up and headed their large pack string northwest. Before departing, Jacob and Martin each visited the carvings made by their fathers on the main ridgepole of their cabin in order to make their final farewells. As they rode out, the caravan was quiet for many miles. Jacob and Martin were silent because they were leaving a little piece of their lives forever. Cain, realizing the historical importance of the moment, remained at a distance out of respect for what it represented to the brothers.

When dark came on the first day, they were camped along the North Platte River near present-day Saratoga, Wyoming. Martin hobbled the horses and mules, then turned them out so they could feed on the lush grasses along the river-bank. Jacob set to making a fire and cooking the evening meal while Cain built a large lean-to and set up the rest of their camp for the night. Dutch-oven biscuits and beans soaked from the day before cooked merrily over the fire, as did several slabs of back strap from a freshly killed buffalo calf taken on the day's journey. Soon Jacob signaled that the chow was ready, and the men fell to their meal with the gusto born of hard living on the frontier. Finishing up the last of the beans and biscuits, Cain laid his huge frame against a nearby downed cottonwood log, placed a huge chew of tobacco in his cheek, and closed his eyes in contentment. Martin brought the livestock closer to camp to avoid the loss of such a valuable resource to bands of wandering Indians as Jacob walked to the nearby river to find some sand to scrub out their dishes and cooking pots.

Jacob carefully stepped off the high bank of the river and down onto the rocks at its edge, feeling some pain and weakness in his still healing leg from the moose collision. Bending over at the water's edge, he took several handfuls of sand and scrubbed the plates and bean pot, then rinsed them off in the river's cold waters. Gathering up the plates and bean pot, Jacob turned and found himself looking directly into the eyes of an Indian lying under the edge of the riverbank not eight feet away!

"Hey-hey-hey!" he yelled in surprise as he dropped the plates and bean pot on his feet. Still startled by the close encounter and hopping in pain from the impact of the cast-iron bean pot on his moccasined toes, he stepped back into the river, slipped on the wet, mossy rocks, and fell full length into the cold water. Cain and Martin were up in an instant, and, grabbing their rifles, both men ran to the river's edge to aid Jacob in whatever danger he had stumbled upon.

Lunging up out of the cold water, blowing hard, Jacob stared at the Indian, still lying motionless under the riverbank, as he bellowed out, "What in tarnation!"

Cain and Martin stood on the edge of the bank with their rifles at the ready, looking on in surprise at Jacob standing in the river, soaking wet and behaving like a damn fool, and seeing nothing else.

"Under the bank at your feet," Jacob yelled as he pointed his finger in their direction.

Cain and Martin stood on the bank, puzzled by what Jacob was trying to tell them because they couldn't see anything under the bank overhang.

"Indian, you damn fools. He is lying right there under the riverbank at your feet!" yelled Jacob.

Cain stepped off the bank and, upon seeing the

Indian lying there motionless, reached under the overhang, grabbed him by the throat, and jerked him up in front of his massive frame. The Indian went limp and passed out in the big man's hands. Not understanding what was happening, Cain tossed the body up onto the bank by Martin's feet like a sack of barley.

Jacob staggered out from the water and up onto the bank next to his brother to examine their find. The men found themselves looking down at an Indian boy, probably Lakota based on his garb, with an Arapaho arrow sticking out from the thickness of his upper thigh. He couldn't have been more than fifteen years old, and had likely been injured for some time. His gaunt features spoke of many days without food, and the arrow wound was badly infested with maggots. It quickly became apparent that he had been in a fight with the Arapaho and somehow had escaped unnoticed. Feverish, he had probably scrawled to the river looking for water.

Jacob picked up the scattered dishes and bean pot while Martin and Cain took the Indian boy to their camp to see what they could do for him. Stripping off the still unconscious boy's leggings, the three men carefully examined the wound. It was a high thigh wound, and the arrow was still sticking out from where its head had penetrated the leg muscle to the edge of the bone. Live maggots dripped from the festering wound as Jacob reached down, took the arrow's shaft into his hand, and looked up at his brothers' faces, figuring that since the boy was still unconscious, it was the time for direct action. Reading their eyes, Jacob shoved hard on the arrow's shaft until it broke free from the thigh bone and ripped through the remainder of the muscle, passing out the other side. Pus, maggots, and discolored blood literally poured from the exit wound. After heating some water to cleanse the wound, Jacob and Martin were surprised to find Cain quietly kneeling at the boy's side. With his powerful hands, he gently massaged the wound until he had pressed out all the maggots, sour blood, and pus. Opening the wound channel with his knife, carefully so as not to further destroy any more muscle tissue than he had to, Cain poured in some of their whiskey until it flowed freely, mixed with bright blood, out the exit hole. The boy moaned in pain but remained unconscious while Cain ministered to him. Cain washed the wound vigorously with warm water and wiped it dry. He trimmed away the putrid flesh with his knife, poured some gunpowder into the entry hole, and set it ablaze with the end of a burning stick from their campfire. The flame flared up briefly when it came into contact with the gunpowder and then died out as the smell of burning, rotted flesh hung heavy in the damp evening air. Then he wrapped the leg, making sure the exit hole could drain freely. Finally he gently raised the still unconscious boy and placed him on some of his own sleeping furs under the lean-to. Martin and Jacob were amazed at the tenderness they had just observed. How a man so large could act so gently yet kill so quickly and violently was almost beyond their comprehension.

The next morning the men woke to find the boy sitting up on Cain's sleeping furs with a worried look on his face. Jacob could just imagine what was going through his mind now that he had been captured by two heavily bearded "white-eyes" and one huge man who was all black. A large helping of hot bacon and biscuits slathered with honey, which the boy greedily devoured, seemed to convince him that he would not be eaten by the strangers anytime soon. That good feeling continued when Cain gently cleaned the wound and, satisfied with its progress in just one night, rebound it with another soft, tanned rabbit skin tied firmly with an elk-leather thong.

Jacob and Martin had learned some Lakota in their youth. Using a mix of Lakota and sign, the universal talk of the plains, the three men tried to explain to the boy that they meant him no harm and were trying to heal him. After that the tired, weak youth seemed to relax, but his eyes never left the men as they went about their camp chores.

"Jacob," said Cain, "the boy needs to rest some afore we drag him along on the trail."

Jacob looked over at Martin, then turned and said, "We ain't in that big a hurry, so I reckon we can wait around for a few days to see how he mends. In fact, maybe by then some of his kin will come looking for him and can take him home."

The men spent the next four days along the river, waiting for the boy to heal well enough to travel. In the meantime, they learned that the boy's name was Walks-in-the-Sun. They also learned that his band of Lakota had been surprised by a larger band of Arapaho while buffalo hunting; during the running battle Walks-in-the-Sun was wounded, fell off his horse into the tall grasses, and was left for dead on the battlefield. When he felt it to be safe to move, he stumbled to the river and hid in its brush, hoping he wouldn't be discovered and killed by the Arapaho. After the Arapaho war party moved on, the boy attempted to walk downstream to where his people had last camped, but he found that they had fled the country. Weakening and unable to walk any farther, he had hidden by the Platte River until discovered by the trappers.

On the fifth day the men gathered up their belongings and headed northwest across the

Muddy River and into the area known as the Great Divide Basin, a massive sea of nothing but sagebrush and prairie grasses. The lands were full of game, and the men made use of the easy availability of good meat, especially buffalo. Behind their pack string rode Walks-in-the-Sun, comfortably laid out on a travois. With plenty of food and rest, his leg healed quickly, and soon he could hobble around camp with the aid of a cane made from a tree root. His improvement created a new concern for the men: What should they to do with the lad once he was able to move more freely? For the moment, they continued traveling northwest, hunting along the way. Jacob and Martin noticed that Cain rarely left the boy's side, and a deep, abiding friendship began to develop between the former slave and the injured youth.

Soon the little party arrived on the bank of the Big Sandy River where it makes an abrupt turn almost due north. For the last three days they had been surrounded by thousands of elk and buffalo, and today was no different. Except for some Indian sign, they appeared to be almost alone among the great expanses of sagebrush and herds of wildlife. Looking over the area from a rise in the rolling hills, Jacob sat on his horse and surveyed the land below. Before him some hundred yards away lay a small creek entering the Big Sandy, fed by clear water coming from a nearby hillside spring. This would be enough water for all our needs and our livestock if we were to live nearby, he thought. He also noticed a small wooded area close to the spring where anyone camping would be out of the wind and sheltered from winter storms. Seeing Jacob sitting there quietly scanning the countryside, Martin and Cain rode up beside him and looked over the area as well without a word spoken.

Finally Martin asked, "Are you thinking what I am?"

"I'm thinking this would be a good place to set down some roots for winter. The area is alive with game, and the Indian sign is few and far between. There's plenty of fresh water and firewood close at hand, and it's well pastured. The Big Sandy is nearby, with lots of beaver sign, and we would be out of the weather and off the beaten path," Jacob answered quietly.

"The time is right for us to begin setting up our winter camp. We have plenty of time to gather our winter's supply of meat, build a cabin with corrals, and stockpile firewood before the snows fly. Plus, the area would be great for our livestock even in the worst of weather because of the cover it affords from the winds," Martin said, smiling.

"What do you think, Cain?" asked Jacob.

"If we were to build a cabin in that small area to the left among the cottonwoods, it would be in a great position to defend against attack. Not to mention, it's close to a good source of water and feed for our livestock," Cain replied thoughtfully, pleased that he was being asked for his opinion.

"Then let's make our winter camp in that grove of cottonwoods and get on with the chores of making meat for the winter and building ourselves a cabin," said Jacob.

With that, the three men and Walks-in-the-Sun, now riding his own horse cut from the pack string, spurred their horses down into the wooded valley to make their winter camp.

Chapter Fifteen

ONE BIG SURPRISE FOLLOWED BY ANOTHER

THE LOUD AND NERVOUS braying of Dander, Cain's riding mule, caused the men to look up from their labors in building the walls of their cabin in the cottonwood grove. Not sixty yards away sat thirty mounted and fiercely painted Lakota Indians, quietly surrounding the trappers' herd of grazing horses and mules. To the men's amazement, the band had sneaked that close to the hardworking trappers without being detected. Grabbing their close-at-hand rifles, the three men quickly faced the threat. Then out from the cottonwood grove to the left and right of their cabin thundered another thirty or so mounted Lakota, who were also fiercely painted for war! Totally surrounded, the men realized that to try to fight their way clear and retreat to the cover of the partially raised cabin walls was to court immediate death from a hail of arrows and bullets. Howling and yelling, the obviously agitated and excited Indians were a hair-trigger pull away from descending upon the hapless trappers, but they were restrained by a powerfully built man who was obviously some sort of a chief. From his position in front, sitting on his horse calmly studying the situation, he stared long and hard at the cornered trappers. Then, abruptly holding his right hand up for silence, the chief began questioning the trappers in sign as to why they had invaded the sacred hunting grounds of the Lakota and were now building a cabin on their lands without permission.

Stepping forward, Jacob replied in sign, "We are here in friendship and did not know these lands were sacred to the Lakota."

The chief answered in sign, "Lay down your rifles, or all of you will be killed."

Realizing that to lay down their rifles would take away any chance they had to live, Jacob took a gamble, knowing the Indians respected courage. He told the chief in Lakota, "We feel because of all the fierce warriors in front of us, that to lay down our rifles is not a wise or good thing to do."

The chief appeared startled at being answered in the Lakota tongue instead of sign and sat for a long moment, staring hard at Jacob.

Off to the south, the trappers now saw what appeared to be a dust cloud from a larger band of Lakota on the move and coming their way. Jacob realized that they were now really in trouble! The warriors would fight even more fiercely than before with their women and other tribal members looking on.

Then, to everyone's amazement, Walks-in-the Sun strode purposefully out of the grove of cottonwoods where he had been taking care of a call of nature and walked between the group of Indians confronting the trappers and the newfound friends who had nursed him back to health. Crossing his arms in a defiant manner, Walks-in-the-Sun stood looking at the startled Indians. For a long moment no one moved, and Jacob thought that, unarmed as he was, the brave young man was probably about to die for his brave but foolish act.

Then, raising his right hand, Walks-in-the Sun said in Lakota, "Father, I have returned from the land of the Cloud People. I was wounded in the fight with the Arapaho but escaped and hid by a river. These three trappers found me and treated my wounds. Today I am all but well because of these men and now am very happy to see you and the rest of my people."

The three trappers stood there thunderstruck. Just moments before they had been preparing to die quickly in battle, but now their act of caring for the wounded Indian lad was quite possibly bearing fruit of a bountiful kind. Then they heard several loud screams and saw two Indian women running through the mounted warriors. They threw their arms around Walks-in-the-Sun, and talking, crying, and hugging, all three fell to the ground in a happy pile. In the meantime, not a warrior moved or took his eyes off the three armed trappers. To their way of thinking, the trespassers were not out of the woods until their chief said so.

Rising up from the ground, an adult Indian woman ran to the side of the chief and, through tears of happiness, grabbed his leg and spoke rapidly in Lakota. "Our son has returned from the dead! He says he was saved by these men, and now he has returned to us. Please do not harm them, for they have given us back our only son and our daughter's brother," said the joyful woman.

Jacob and Martin, understanding most of what she had said, stood waiting to see what would happen next. Cain, taking his cue from the brothers, remained alert because, to his way of thinking, they were still in hot water if the stern look on the chief's face meant anything.

"White man, is it true what my wife says? Did you save Walks-in-the-Sun after he had been wounded?" the chief asked Jacob.

"It is true what she says. We did find your son and treated his wounds. After he healed we did not know what to do with him, so we took him in as one of our own to care for," replied Jacob, not removing his eyes from the chief's hard stare.

Walks-in-the-Sun walked over to the chief, reached up, and clasped his father's forearm in happiness and respect. Tears came quickly to the chief's eyes and left just as rapidly before anyone else noticed.

"I am glad you are back, my son. It has been many dark days since you were wounded and left for dead. Now you are back, standing in honor, and have brought three friends. If they are your friends, then they are mine as well," said the chief, with a smile now cracking through his sun-weathered face.

Turning, the chief raised his right arm and said to his group of warriors, "The white men and the one who is dark as the night without any moon are friends and forever to be treated as such."

The warriors remained stoic in their looks, but Jacob could tell the chief's words had been heard. With a wave of his arm, the chief hailed the warriors still holding the trappers' livestock hostage, and they rode closer to join the group around the chief. Once again, for the benefit of those men, the chief repeated the story of his son's return and his words of friendship for the trappers.

Turning, Jacob said, "Cain, we are to be treated

as friends. Walks-in-the-Sun is the chief's son, and he has just saved our lives."

Cain got a huge grin on his face and only then relaxed his tight hold on his Hawken, as did the others.

The chief dismounted and without saying a word walked over to Jacob. He clasped Jacob's forearm in a sign of friendship and then did the same to Martin. Walking over to Cain, he grabbed his hand and turned his arm slightly to more closely examine the color of the man's dark skin. Satisfied it was the real thing and not just war paint, he also firmly grasped Cain's massive arm and, stepping back, clearly marveled at the other man's huge size.

Turning to his warriors and the rest of the tribe, the chief said they would all camp next to the spring for the evening and honor the gods with a feast for bringing his son back from the dead.

Turning to the warriors at his side, the chief said, "Go and kill some buffalo, for we are going to feast tonight in honor of these three men who saved my son."

Jacob, sensing an opportunity, raised his hand for attention, then said to the chief, "May we go as well to help kill some buffalo? We have rifles that shoot very far and can kill buffalo before your warriors can with their bows and arrows."

"If the white men and their black friend who

saved my son wish to come, then we would be honored," said the chief with a lot more lightness in his voice than when he had first arrived.

That evening, as the Indian camp prepared a feast with the ten buffalo killed by Jacob, Martin, and Cain with their long-shooting rifles, the three men gathered some gifts from their trading stock. These gifts were to be presented to the Indian chief and several subchiefs for allowing the three of them to live in the cottonwood grove for the rest of the summer and winter and for letting them trap beaver in the Big Sandy.

Loaded down with the gifts, the three men rode into the Lakota encampment. Stopping at the chief's tepee, they dismounted and were instantly swarmed by dozens of children wanting to touch the saviors of the chief's son and closely examine the hugeness of the black man called Cain. Soon they were joined by the chief, whom they now knew as Many-Horses-Walking; his wife, Singing Wind; their daughter, Falling Star, and Walks-in-the-Sun. Inside the chief's tepee. It was then that the trappers presented their gifts. To the surprise of Jacob and Martin, Cain had a Green River skinning knife, which he presented to Falling Star, Walks-in-the-Sun's sister.

Later that evening Jacob had to tell and retell the story of how he had found Walks-in-the-Sun, and Cain had to explain how he had saved the young man with his knowledge of treating wounds. The party went long into the morning as everyone ate until they were stuffed and then ate some more. During the feast Jacob and Martin had Singing Wind and Falling Star at their beck and call. It seemed as if the two women couldn't show enough appreciation for Jacob and Martin's care of their son and brother. Cain was another matter. Everything he even seemed to want was given to him instantly. It was apparent to Jacob and Martin that the Indians considered Cain something very special. His close friendship with Walks-in-the Sun also seemed to make a huge difference in how he was treated, and Falling Star seemed to take to Cain especially. There were many looks between the two of them at almost every opportunity.

After leaving the feast, the three men could hardly wiggle because they were so full as they nestled down in their sleeping furs. They had to get some sleep because the next day they had to put up the main beams, log subroofing, sage-brush, and dirt on their cabin's roof. That was a chore that would take a lot of hard work.

Rising early the next morning, Jacob tended to breakfast, Martin to the horses and mules, and Cain to the gathering of firewood and water. After breakfast they began work on their roof and made rapid progress well into the afternoon.

Just as they finished, a group of Lakota arrived, led by Many-Horses-Walking, who invited the three tired men on another buffalo hunt.

Thirteen buffalo later, the women and small boys came from the Indian camp by the spring, and the serious butchering and hauling back of the meat began.

At that night's feast the men were requested to tell their stories time and time again of how they had saved the chief's son—especially the part where Jacob had fallen into the Platte River. There was much laughter and celebration, and once again Jacob and Martin marveled at the treatment Cain received at the hands of the Indians in general and Falling Star in particular.

The next day found the three men hard at work once again around their cabin. Jacob, like his father, had a knack for building things. He made and hung the front door, cut shooting ports into the cabin walls, built sleeping platforms for the three of them, and finished making the table and chairs. Then he began work on their stone fireplace. Martin and Cain dug post holes and built a stout corral for their herd of mules and horses. By the end of the day, they were dead tired and famished. Having only jerky on hand made them rather grouchy at having to eat that meager kind of fare until they saw Falling Star and Singing Wind approaching their cabin leading a pack horse. They walked out to meet them and were warmly greeted. Then the women set to work around the cooking fire. Soon the delicious smell of roasting buffalo meat, com cakes, and a stew-like dish filled the air. The men sat around on the new chairs Jacob had built for them in front of their new home, smoked their pipes, and waited for the evening meal to come. Soon the food was ready, and as the men filled their plates, they noticed that Falling Star filled Cain's plate—and with the choicest of morsels! Again the men were favored with outstanding treatment as thanks for their rescue and care of Walks-in-the-Sun. Later that evening they gave some tobacco to Singing Wind to take back to the chief in thanks for the meal, and Cain escorted the women back to their camp.

Over the next two weeks the three men dragged in mounds of winter wood, finished the stone fireplace, and cut hay by hand and spread it to cure for winter. They also killed buffalo, made meat, and visited with their Lakota friends. That meant attending several more feasts and performing shooting, races, and other feats of strength and skill.

One morning Many-Horses-Walking rode over to the busy trappers' camp and informed them that his band of Lakota was moving on to greener pastures to the north. Their herd of over three hundred horses had eaten all the feed for some distance around their camp. He asked if the trappers wished to come with the band, saying they would be welcome additions to his tribe as the friends they were.

Jacob thanked the chief for his offer and the friendship they had shared over the past weeks but answered, "We will remain here because the beaver trapping and buffalo hunting is good. Plus, we have fewer livestock, and we can survive on the remaining grasses along the river and in the meadow at hand."

"I understand," said the chief. "Your new home is here, and the hunting is good. Just remember, you will always be friends and are welcome to stay here as long as you wish without fear from my people. We will be leaving at first light, so I say thank you for returning my son from the land of the Cloud People, and may the sun always smile on your trails." With that and a wave of his arm, he rode back to his camp.

That evening around their dinner fire, the talk among the trappers was subdued. Cain hardly said a word the whole time. Sitting outside in front of the cabin in the cool of the evening after dinner, the three men sat and smoked their pipes in silence.

That silence was finally broken as Cain tapped the ash from his pipe, rose, and turned to face

Jacob and Martin. "I would like to go with Many-Horses-Walking and his people tomorrow when they leave for the north," he said!

Jacob and Martin sat there, stunned.

"But we just got our cabin built and are almost ready for fall and winter trapping," Jacob responded, still surprised and not knowing what else to say.

"I know, but I feel my life will be best spent with the Lakota. Their lifestyle is like mine. They harbor no ill will against anyone different from their own kind, unlike many of the whites, and I just feel I would be happier with them. Nothing against the two of you. You have been like brothers to me and saved my life. But I feel that when you move on to other places with more white people, the hurt will return because of the way people with small minds act toward someone my color. No, I feel that in the long run I would be happier living among my new Lakota friends. I have made up my mind. I will take what supplies you can share and go with the Lakota when they leave tomorrow. Plus as you may have noticed, 1 have taken a shine to Falling Star, and she to me. Hopefully her father will let me marry that woman, and we will have lots of children. And if any are boys, 1 will name them Jacob and Martin after my brothers."

Jacob and Martin still could find no words.

Finally Martin got his voice and asked, "Are you sure? The three of us can have a very good life once we move west with the gold. You are right; we are like brothers, and to separate now will be a huge loss."

"Yes, I am sure. I have been thinking about this ever since I met Falling Star. She is the one for me, and with that in mind, I wish to be the one for her," Cain quietly replied.

"Then it's done," Jacob said with a forced smile, rising from his wooden bench.

"Go forth, my brother, and know we support you and will always have a place for you and yours in our homes once we get to California," said Martin with as happy a tone as he could muster under the circumstances.

There was much back-slapping and well-wishing all around. "What about your share of the gold?" asked Martin.

"Where I am going I have no need of such things," said Cain. "The two of you keep my share. Maybe someday I will come to California and take the two of you up on your offer of golden wealth."

"Damn," said Jacob, "we have got to get going if you are leaving at first light. We need to get you outfitted for your new life."

For the next two hours the men busied themselves collecting Cain's supplies for his new life on the plains with the Lakota. Kegs of powder, pigs of lead, skinning knives, sharpening stones, beaver traps, an extra rifle, rifle parts, bullet molds, spices, and horse tack were all added to the growing pile of necessities. Then the men went to the corrals and separated two pack horses and two riding horses. Cain's hell-for-stout riding mule, Dander, was left behind because the men figured a mule would only slow down the Lakota as they traveled or hunted; hence the switch to horses.

Having completed those chores, the men sat outside their cabin, lit up their pipes once again, and, with a hefty cup of whiskey each, sat in the dark amid the constant hum of the ever-present mosquitoes and quietly contemplated their futures. Before light Jacob was up and cooking breakfast, and Martin and Cain were saddling the horses and loading the pack animals. They could hear the stirring from the Indian camp some distance away.

After breakfast the men sat outside in the cool morning and, without much talk, waited for the inevitable. Soon the smell of prairie dust wafted their way as the Indian camp was pulled and the band started on the trek to the north. Passing in front of the trappers' cabin with the rest of the band, Walks-in-the-Sun broke out of the pack and rode over to his friends. Dismounting in one fluid motion born from many years in the saddle, he walked over to Jacob and Martin without even a trace of a limp. He gave each man a hug, then turned and remounted without any words being spoken to Jacob and Martin.

"It is time, my brother," Walks-in-the-Sun said to Cain.

Cain rose and gave a bear hug each to Jacob and Martin. Then, without a further word, he mounted his horse and, with a wave of his massive arm, rode with his pack string in tow into the band of Indians still streaming by. Soon the caravan had passed, leaving only the dust hanging in the air and the fading sounds of talking, laughter, and barking dogs. Slowly those sounds and smells died away as the rays of the fall sun began to heat up the morning air.

"We still have a passel of work that needs doing, and best we get to it," said Jacob, still sorrowing over their loss of a brother.

"I wonder if our trails will ever cross again?" said Martin to himself and the prairie winds.

The rest of the day was spent building another lean-to to protect the small mountain of curing hay for their horses and mules. The ache of their loss was not far from each man's breast. In fact, several times during the day the brothers found themselves looking to the north as if expecting Cain to reappear on the horizon, coming back their way.

Chapter Sixteen

FORT BRIDGER AND THE START OF A NEW LIFE

FOR THE REST OF THE FALL of 1856 and into the spring of 1857, the men hunted buffalo for their skins and trapped beaver and river otter for their pelts in the backwaters of the Big Sandy. Buffalo hunting was good, and soon they had so many hides that it was about all their horses and mules could carry or pull on travois along with all their other gear. Added to that were four bales of prime beaver and otter pelts from the Big Sandy and several marshy areas near their cabin. It was obvious that for the most part the beaver would be trapped out by the end of spring, and they would have to move on if they were to survive in the fur and hide business.

One late-spring afternoon, after they had fleshed out and hooped their recent catch of beaver, Martin sat back in his chair and looked over at his approaching brother. "Say, brother, this ain't getting me any closer to that big saltwater pond out west in California I always wanted to see."

Jacob, rounding the side of the cabin with another armload of wood for their evening fire, said with a grin, "Then I suppose we best do something about that itch of yours that needs scratching." Laying his armload of wood next to the fire, he turned and said, "What say we head for Fort Bridger just as soon as the horse feed greens up? Once there, we can sell our hides and furs, then hitch a ride west with one of them wagon trains going to California."

Martin looked up from sharpening his fleshing knife on a whetstone and grinned, saying, "That sounds okay with me 'cause neither of us ain't gettin' any younger by the day, you know."

Jacob grinned. His brother had always had the wanderlust in the family, and it was time to satisfy that curiosity. He was right in that they were not getting any younger, and the fur trade, except in buffalo skins, was sliding downhill. In addition, some of the Indians in the area were getting downright nasty and killing the white men flooding onto their hunting grounds. Yes, Jacob thought, Martin might just have something in this going-west thing of his.

"Besides," continued Martin, "maybe we need to go to California to the gold rush and make our fortune like all those other people we heard about last time we was at Fort Vasquez."

Jacob grinned at his brother's humor about the gold, since the two of them were already sitting on a fortune of the precious metal. That plus the Spanish ingots they still had from their parents all but assured they would never have to work again once they got to civilization.

The next morning the brothers had decided for sure it was time to move on. Rounding a turn on the north side of the Big Sandy, they happened on three wagons that had probably been part of a larger wagon train. They had apparently left the protection of that larger group and wandered south looking for a piece of land on which to settle. The still smoking remains of their wagons bore mute testimony to the poor wisdom of that decision. Riding among the smoking ruins, the brothers saw nothing but death and destruction. Everyone had been killed, the wagons looted and burned, and the livestock run off. The arrow shafts left behind showed that it had been Lakota who had discovered the small group of wagons and decided to settle the score in part for the wholesale invasion of their lands by whites in ever growing numbers.

After dinner that evening, with the memory

of having buried all the bodies in a mass grave, the brothers sat quietly smoking as they watched their way of life in their corner of their world slowly dying out.

"The grass is almost high enough in places to travel, feedwise, so I say we pull our traps tomorrow and head for Fort Bridger," Jacob said slowly.

Martin said, "I'll have the animals saddled and loaded at dawn if you care to clean out the cabin and fix us a breakfast that will hold us until dark. I think it only wise to get the hell out of here in case someone has changed their minds about us being protected by the word of Many-Horses-Walking, especially if another chief is now in charge."

"I hope Cain is still all right," Jacob replied thoughtfully as he aimlessly pushed some un-burned sticks back into the fire with the toe of his moccasin.

By daylight the brothers had packed up and set a course for Fort Bridger, but not before each man had chiseled his name into the main beam to let the next visitors know that this was the cabin of Jacob and Martin. Neither man looked back as they rode over the many small, rolling ridges leading away from their cabin as they headed southwest across the Green and Muddy Rivers toward the home of their old friend, Jim Bridger.

❧❧

SWINGING OVER the last rolling hill into Fort Bridger, the brothers stopped and quietly studied the sights before them. The fort had seen better days, and the air surrounding it was full of dust from a nearby herd of horses and mules nervously milling about. A short distance from the herd were fourteen gleaming white wagons drawn up in a defensive circle a few yards from the main gate They heard barking dogs and could faintly smell the evening dinners being prepared. Looking over at each other, the brothers grinned and headed their heavily loaded pack and travois string toward the fort's welcoming open gate.

"Welcome back, you two," said Jim Bridger, now more grizzled and stoop-shouldered, as the men came through the gate.

"Glad to be back, you old varmint," said Martin as he jumped down from his saddle, not showing any stiffness from his long hours in the saddle.

Jacob lifted more stiffly from his saddle but dropped to the ground easily. Then he stood beside his horse holding on to the saddle horn until the life came back into his sore knees and still painful leg from the earlier moose wreck back in what is today Colorado.

"You old he-grizzly, I see you still have your hair and a grin to match," Jacob said with a smile as he forgot his pains. He walked over to the old man and gave him a bear hug out of deep respect.

"Where be you two from now, and where you heading next?" Jim asked with a twinkle in his eyes, knowing the two boys had one hell of a wanderlust ever since their families had been laid waste by the Indians.

"We be here for a spell to trade, resupply, and then head for that big salty pond called the Pacific Ocean to the west, if Martin has his say," Jacob replied with a grin.

"Yeah," added Martin. "That is, if we can hitch a ride with a wagon train a-goin' in that direction for the protection the extra shooters would offer and the company it bears."

"Well, if that be your choice, ye be in luck. See that wagon train out yonder by the grove of cottonwoods? They be a-splittin' up. They lost their wagon master to a horse wreck and it now seems many of the folks have had enough of the dust, distance, Indians, bad grub, alkali water, and never-endin' routine of slow travelin' every day to a land beyond their lookin'," replied Bridger.

Both boys looked in the direction Bridger pointed and saw a small wagon train comprising only fourteen wagons. They were drawn up into a tight, well-formed circle, and the wagons for the most part looked none the worse for the wear. They were dusty from the many miles of traveling but appeared at first glance to be soundly built and well maintained. Maybe that was because of the man mountain who appeared to be a blacksmith, who was currently tending to one of the rear wheels on a wagon. Jacob observed the man's industry, which gave him the feeling of a well-managed wagon train. To have such a person along was certainly a boon, he thought as he continued looking over the group appraisingly. Turning, he said with a smile, "That be well and good, but for now we have business with you and yours, Jim. We have a load of good furs and hides we need to be rid of and figured you'd be just the man to fix that itch."

"If that be the case, let's get crackin'," replied Bridger, never the man to turn down a good deal, especially in the fur and hide business.

With that, the men and pack strings made their way into the central portion of the fort as Bridger led the way.

"Casey, Jonathan," Bridger yelled at two men lounging by a set of corrals, "pull the furs from this here pack string, grade them fairly because they be friends of mine, and give me a tally. The three of us will be in the store taking the miles of dust off our tongues and firing up our bellies with some old trapper's top-knot remover."

Inside the cool of the trading post, Jacob and Martin glanced at each other, realizing that not much had changed since the time they had been there with their fathers just before their first buffalo hunt. The moment also brought back sad memories of what they had discovered upon their return to their homesites.

Jim, sensing their sadness, interrupted their thoughts. "Here, this ought to cut the dust and cure what ails the two of you." With that, he pulled the familiar earthen jug from under the counter and handed it to Martin for a pull.

Taking a long swig of the intense liquid, Martin almost choked. Coughing back the urge to spit out the fire sliding down his throat, he grinned in embarrassment at Jacob as he handed him the jug. Jacob, realizing it had been some time since the two of them had tasted really strong whiskey, took a gingerly sip, and he too almost coughed up the contents.

"What the devil you got in this here jug?" he whispered through clenched teeth, with still watering eyes and a seared throat.

"Ain't that stuff a beaut? It's uncut whiskey I got from the wagon train that is calling it quits. It came clear from Kain-tucky, and I was lucky to buy all five barrels they had to offer. Seems it is as high a proof as one can make and is made for cutting with branch water before one sells it. However, I have developed a hankering for the strong brew, and man, it sure cuts the dust or whatever else ails a body!" Bridger replied with a grin. "Care for another swig?"

Both men, although almost gagging on the intense liquid, kind of liked the smooth aftertaste, so they took another long pull. By now their guts were reeling from the brew, and they figured two swallows were enough! Especially if they were to dicker over the price of their furs and trade goods on the shelves in Jim's store in good thinking order.

Jacob and Martin were surprised at the large amount their mountain of furs and hides was worth. Looking over at a grinning Jim Bridger, anxious to trade now that he realized the base he had to operate from, Jacob brought him up short.

"Jim, instead of settling up just now, I think we best hold off a spell. If Martin and I are to go west, we will need a wagon to haul our goods. That means we will need something to trade for a wagon if one is available from that group going back East. Bottom line, if we trade some of our credit for your supplies to anyone willing to sell their wagon, that will give us a wagon and the seller the necessary supplies to make it back to civilization," said Jacob. "What do you think, Martin?"

"That be damn good thinkin' to my way of figurin'," Martin slowly replied, looking intently at Jacob. "That way we won't have to go into our gold stash to buy the wagon and create a ruckus based on the greed the sight of that metal brings to most everyone."

"You boys still carryin' around all them damn cursed golden ingots?" asked Jim.

"Not only that, Jim, but numerous pouches of gold nuggets we discovered in a creek many miles back by Fort Vasquez," Martin replied, knowing Jim would keep their secret.

"That be good figurin'," replied Jim. "Ain't no use creatin' a ruckus unless one has to, and that usually ends in a blood-lettin' when the sight of that metal is involved."

"Then we will go meet them folks and see who wants to go and who wants to stay," Martin said. "We will approach those wantin' to go back and see if we can buy one of their wagons in exchange for goods from Jim's store or the last of our coin. If anyone is willin' to double up with their neighbors who also want to return, then we will have a deal,"

Martin looked at his brother, who nodded in agreement. "Sounds like you boys have a plan as strong as a beaver dam," Jim replied with a smile that registered even on his weathered face. "Your folks, God rest their souls, would be a damn sight proud of how you two turned out."

With those words, another long pull on the jug was in order. The three men shook on the trade credit issue, and then Jacob and Martin strode out into the bright sunlight of the fort's stockade. Leaving their livestock and gold in Jim's care, they headed over to the wagon train he had identified as the one caving in at the seams with those who wanted no more of what the West had to offer. As they approached, they noticed a number of men gathered around a central campfire with many downcast faces and not much talk.

Walking into the ring of circled wagons, Jacob said, "Hello, the campfire. Care if my brother and I join you?"

The men looked around in surprise at the two approaching massive and heavily bearded strangers, then rose in unison, as was the custom of the day when greeting strangers. There were handshakes all around as the men made room for Jacob and Martin to sit among them on some logs pulled up next to the fire. Soon cups of hot coffee were thrust into the two brothers' hands, and much small talk was made about the weather as Jacob and Martin waited for the right opening.

Jacob spoke first after the moment of politeness had passed. "Folks, I am Jacob, and this is my kid brother, Martin. Our parents and our stepparents were killed some time back by Indians, so the two of us up to now have made our way as fur trappers and buffalo hunters. Life has been good to us, and we have seen and experienced many beautiful and some not-so-wonderful things in our travels. In our minds, however, it is now time to move farther west. My brother and I wish to see this place called California, the Pacific Ocean, and any other sights that neck of the woods has to offer. Then we would like to settle down on a ranch in the Sierra Nevada Mountains and raise a passel of kids. We just came in from our latest trapping sashay in the lands to the south and met with Jim Bridger. We told him of our desire to go west in a wagon train, and he mentioned you folks were thinking of breaking up, with some going on and some returning home. If that be the case, my brother and I have something to offer you good folks wanting to proceed. We can carry our own share. We are experienced frontiersmen and excellent shots, and, having come from families of fur trappers, we know 'the way' of many tribes of Indians we might run across. We would like to join the group that is going westward. With our knowledge of the land in that direction, for a ways, anyway, and that of some of the tribes of Indians, we feel we can add to the group and its chances for success."

Jacob paused and waited for a response. For a long time none of the men from the group spoke. They just looked at each other with enormous surprise. The explanation for such looks of surprise on the men's faces was soon forthcoming as they interrupted Jacob's words in a FAR different manner than he had meant.

Then one man rose and, looking intently at Jacob

and Martin, said, "I am Chris Grosz. I am traveling with my wife, Lisa, our daughter, Laurel, and
son, Gabriel. We set out from Kentucky because
our farmland had given out, and it appeared the
open lands to the west were our salvation. Now
we are at a crossroads. This here wagon train is
intent on splitting up and reducing the chances of
folks like myself to realize our dreams. My wife
is a crack shot, as am I, and we wish to continue
on to California. I am a blacksmith by trade and a
gunsmith by avocation. As such, I can add those
skills to a wagon train if we are to go on."

With that, the man sat back down on his log.
Jacob looked long and hard at the man who had
just spoken. He was a huge man, probably six
feet tall, weighed at least three hundred pounds,
and had arms as thick as most men's thighs! He
also had a look in his eyes that was as kind as any
he had seen. But Jacob also recognized in those
eyes a fire that told him here was a real man who
could be depended upon come hell or high water.

An older man rose from the logs around the
campfire, and looked at all the other men and
then at Jacob and Martin. Finally he said, "My
name is Daniel, and these men at my side are my
sons, Zeke and Jeremiah. We are from Salt Lick,
Kentucky, and are here today because our farms
have also played out. I am here with my wife,
Betsy. Zeke is here with his wife, Margaret, and

Jeremiah is here with his wife, Constance, and their sons, Bill and Lemuel, and daughter, Sarah. We come with three wagons, are well stocked in livestock, and are outfitted with provisions. If we had our druthers, we are all for pushing on to California and seeing what life there will bring."

He sat back down. Jacob thought from the looks in his eyes and those of his sons, here were three tough families, born in adversity and ready for what the frontier further west had to offer.

Then all of a sudden Jacob realized that the men who had spoken so far were looking at him as they would a wagon master, as if they expected him to lead them west because of his frontier experience. His heart almost skipped a beat. Neither he nor Martin knew the way to California, the best feed grounds along the way for the stock, or where to find good water and firewood. Most importantly, neither he nor his brother knew the nature or even names of many of the Indian tribes along the way, especially those further to the west.

Holy cow! he thought. This was not what he'd had in mind when he and Martin had approached the men around the campfire to see if they could join those choosing to carry on the westward journey.

Before Jacob could fully mull over his dilemma, a stocky man rose and said, "My name is Otis

Barnes, and me and my kin are from Tennessee. My lands were being overrun by Southern rabble seeking to support slavery. I am not for enslaving any human being. My wife, Alberta, and I wish to continue to California with our daughter, Nancy. Count us in if there is to be a train going west. I bring good livestock as well as a wife who is the best cook going, and I can shoot with any man." With that, the quiet man, as Jacob came to judge him, sat back down.

Another, older man rose and quietly faced Jacob and Martin. "My name is Martin Jones, and I am a full-blooded Delaware Indian. I am the neighbor of Daniel's clan from Salt Lick, Kentucky, and like his lands, mine have played out. My kin came from Ohio but were driven off their lands by crooked land speculators, and because of that, we moved to Salt Lick, where a man could be free. I bring three sons, their wives and children, and a Celestial woman I won in a shoot-off. We too wish to continue to the lands farther west. My family is very woodswise. We are great hunters and fear no man. My only problem is that three of our mules have gone bad lame, and I have not been able to replace them so that we can continue on as a family. There are good mules here at the fort, but the price is more than we can afford. So we are stuck in limbo unless we abandon one of our wagons and double up in those remaining."

By now Jacob was becoming concerned. His eyes met Martin's, and he saw that his brother now also sensed what was happening — a situation where they might find themselves leading a wagon train filled with families west over lands they themselves had never seen nor visited.

A slightly built man with spectacles, puffing on an old pipe, rose from his seat by the campfire, saying, "My name is Howard Larson, and I am a doctor. I am with my wife, Mary Ann, and daughters, Donna and Linda. I am not a very good shooter, but my livestock are sound, and our supplies are adequate for the trip. I would be obliged if we could continue with the others going west."

As Howard sat down, Jacob's head was swimming with the misunderstanding he and his brother were facing. But before he could say anything, another man rose and said, "I am Marvin Clary, and I am a cousin to Otis Barnes. I too was having problems with proslavery groups burning my crops since I wouldn't allow slaves to work my lands. Facing that kind of violence, and before I ended up shooting those hind ends, I decided to get out while I could. I am with my wife, Lorraine, am accomplished with a rifle or pistol, have good stock, and wish to continue west to California with the others if that comes to pass."

Jacob started to set the issue straight with the

folks around the campfire when one of the tallest and strongest-looking men he had ever seen rose from his seat by the fire, saying, "I am Richard Grosz, brother to Chris, the blacksmith. I too am a farmer and rancher from Salt Lick, Kentucky. I got into a shootout with two brothers who had pushed the limits of their drunk and stolen several of my cattle. Not wanting to rightfully return my stock, they went for their shooting irons when accused, and now they lie under the ground. However, they had a clan of seven brothers and three uncles who were on their way to avenge their deaths, and that was too much for my brother and me to handle in a fair fight. I want to raise my family in safety, so here we are on the way west to start a new life. I too am a crack shot with a rifle and pistol, fear no man in a fair fight, and bring good livestock and sup-plies to the wagon train. My wife, Carrie, and my older daughters, Amanda and Katelyn, are excel-lent shooters and afraid of no man as well. We wish to go to California and start our lives anew and would welcome the chance to go along with that wagon train if there is to be one."

Before Jacob or Martin could explain, another man rose from his seat around the fire.

"You boys have need for a good wagon?" he asked.

Jacob replied, "Yes, sir. We was hoping to

purchase one from someone not continuing on to California who would have no need for it."

"That be me, I reckon. I not only lost my wife to an accident, but both of my children took sick with consumption, and now they are lying along the trail in unmarked graves. I plan on going back with another couple who lost their kids as well and sharing a wagon. But you can't have my livestock. We will be taking them with us on the return trip in case any of my friend's stock turn up lame or stole by them damn thieving Indians," the man replied softly.

"What will you take for your wagon?" asked Jacob, postponing the wagon-boss issue for the moment.

"I will take $40 in coin or trade if ye be interested," the man mumbled in obvious resignation.

"You have a deal," said Jacob, catching approval on Martin's face as he spoke even though the wagon and its condition were sight unseen.

Then silence reigned around the campfire as the rest of the men stared at the fire in acceptance of the fact they would soon be returning home and never going to see the West.

"By damnit, we are going on too!" another large man said loudly, rising from his seat. "My name is Mark Webb. I am a farmer, and my land played out as well in Virginia. Too many years of planting tobacco, I would guess."

Mark was a well-built man as Rich Grosz but not as tall. However, he appeared just as determined if the fire in his eyes and stern look on his face meant anything. He continued, "My wife, Kathy, who is with child, my young son, and I wish to be considered if there is a wagon train going west to California. I am still well provisioned, and my stock is in good condition. Plus, we have kin in Sacramento as well as in the gold fields on the Feather River. By gum, we mean to start a new life somewhere out there for our family, hellfire be damned! And like my new friend Rich Grosz there, I fear no man, be he red or white."

Jacob had to smile even though he found himself in a pickle. Here was a man almost the size of Rich Grosz, and if the intense look on his face said anything, he would stick alongside his friends come hell or high water — and woe betide his enemies as long as he held a rifle, powder, and shot.

Jacob, still bothered by the notion that the folks wanting to go to California were thinking of him as a genuine wagon master and wanting to clear up the issue, suddenly felt his brother's reassuring hand on his shoulder.

"The two of us need to talk this over for a spell and will get back to you by suppertime," Martin announced with his characteristic happy-go-lucky grin.

"We usually have a community supper around the central fire come sundown," Otis Barnes said with a smile. "Come have supper with us and meet the rest of our families." With that, the group broke up, and the men from the wagon train went off to tell their families about the possibility of new "wagon masters." Walking away from the group, Jacob said to Martin, "What the damnation are you thinking? We don't know the trail once it gets beyond Fort Hall, and you know it!"

"As always, brother, you are right. But those people wish to continue their travels. That's the way we wanted to go all along, and those who spoke up comprise fourteen wagons counting what we put together. That is a safer way to travel than on our own, and we know the best trail blazer in the country in Jim Bridger. He has been to California and back several times. He can help us and maybe make some maps to show us the way. Hell, it can't be that bad! All we have to do is follow the trails left by others who went before us," Martin countered with a grin.

Looking at his brother, Jacob could see nothing but enthusiasm and determination in his eyes. And Martin did have a point. All they had to do was follow the earlier trails to get to California...

Jacob began to feel better after several hours with Jim Bridger, several deep pulls on the contents of Jim's fiery jug and time spent exploring Bridger's towering knowledge of the exact lay of the land all the way to California. Having been there personally several times over the years. Jim drew several maps showing the major landmarks along the way once they got to and beyond Fort Hall. He followed those geography lessons with instructions in where to find good water and where to be extra alert to avoid livestock-stealing Indians. There were many trails to follow west and several passes through the mountains, but Jim laid out several options for the boys, one of which led to Oregon and the other to California. Then it was time to tap the earthen jug full of good Kentucky whiskey again so the boys could boost their confidence with a little liquid frontier courage...

Some time later Jacob and Martin met with the man willing to sell his wagon. They settled up with him using the last of the coins they had inherited from their fathers when they were young men just getting started themselves in the fur trade many years before. Looking carefully over the wagon that they had just purchased, Jacob and Martin were pleased. It had been built hell-for-stout by a builder in St. Louis, Missouri, who obviously knew his trade. He had used the finest oak and hickory throughout, and straight-grained woods at that. The recent owner had maintained the wagon well, and it had two spare wheels and an extra singletree lashed under the wagon in case the current one broke. The brothers planned to use their two draft horses as wheelers to pull the wagon, aided by two other stout horses from their pack string as headers. Since they would be traveling light because they planned on buying most of what they needed in California with their stocks of gold, a heavy team was not really needed. They would need the wagon only to carry their sacks of gold, food, bedding, extra firearms, sacks of livestock feed, and associated gear. Other than that, they would carry little compared to the others in the wagon train. Jim would equip them with the proper harnesses and other tack from the pile of gear discarded at the fort by earlier travelers as they tried to lighten their loads in order to continue their travels along the Oregon Trail.

Leaving their new wagon, Jacob and Martin headed over to the central cooking fire to meet the rest of those who were soon to become their charges. Soon they were undergoing what seemed to be endless introductions of wives and children from the thirteen wagons wishing to push on to California. One young woman caught Jacob's eye immediately, and he could not take his eyes or thoughts away from her once he had seen her. She was tall for a woman her age, had long, brown hair that hung below her shoulders, was slender as a willow, and walked and talked with a grace long beyond her years. Her name was Amanda, and she was Rich Grosz's older daughter. He had never seen such beauty in a woman and found it hard to breathe or take his eyes off her while she was, by chance or design, serving him supper that evening. Martin was smitten by a young woman in the contingent as well. During the many introductions, he was introduced to the Celestial woman belonging to the Delaware Indian and patriarch Martin Jones. Neither Jacob nor Martin had ever seen an Asian person before, much less one who was so beautiful. She was very tiny, but her coal-black, dark flashing eyes and long, beautiful black hair spoke of her origins among an ancient race in a land far away. Later in the evening Martin discovered that her name was Nguyen Ahn Sang, but the Delaware families called her Kim. Martin could hardly believe what was happening to him. Here was a women he could easily fall in love with in a heartbeat under the right circumstances.

Suffice it to say, Jacob and Martin were finding this wagon-master job better than either of them had expected...

Chapter Seventeen

MAKING READY

RETURNING TO THEIR SLEEPING area in the fort, Jacob and Martin walked in silence as they thought of what lay ahead of them as wagon masters for a bunch of hopeful people, and what they were feeling after having just met two charming women.

❧❧

"YOU BOYS GOING TO SLEEP ALL DAY?" asked Jim Bridger.

Exhausted by the previous day's events, neither man waved at Jim from their sleeping furs to signify that they were awake.

"Best the two of you roll out because we have a passel of things to go over afore sunset if the talk from the wagon train about you two leading them west is for certain," Jim continued with a smile.

Rolling out of their furs, the men washed up as best as they could. For some reason, they found themselves trying to trim their unruly hair and beards for once so they would look more like men than mad grizzly bears.

After a hearty breakfast of moose steak, fried mush, honey, and some of the thick black liquid Jim called coffee, Jacob and Martin quietly sat down at the table with Jim.

"I intend to butt in on the affairs of you two boys because your dads would have expected that much of me. And, if the same circumstances ever came up, me of them. Now, do you men have at least two wagons in which to carry forth?" he asked.

Jacob and Martin looked at each other for a moment in surprise. Jacob said, "No, Jim. We just purchased the one wagon from a man who was not going on and willing to sell, figuring that was all we would need for the trip."

"Thought so," Jim replied in a fatherly tone. "The two of you are setting out on an endeavor that may well kill you and all those innocent folks you are leading. Did you ever think of that?" There was a trace of real seriousness in his voice that the boys had never heard before.

"No, sir," Jacob and Martin replied in unison, a bit taken aback. Jim's seriousness was kind of like the way their dads had spoken to them when

the boys had screwed up or failed to pay attention to their early training.

"Well, you will need a second wagon. The two
of you are taking innocent folks into the great
beyond, and you had better be prepared. That
means one wagon for what you will need and an
extra one full of supplies in case someone on your
wagon train runs short or wrecks their wagon,
including the two of you. Then comes the issue
of what kind of livestock you are going to use to
pull the wagons," Jim growled, enjoying his new
paternal role.

Jacob, embarrassed at having overlooked the
obvious need for a second wagon, lamely ar-
gued, "We have a set of draft horses, two other
hell-for-stout horses, and four large mules for
the wagons and other heavy work in our current
pack string."

"Not good enough. The grasses on the trail are
not the best for horses pulling heavy loads and
just bearable for mules. Many won't make it, or
you may destroy them before the day is done
if they have to depend on those kinds of range
grasses to survive. Besides, so many have gone
before you that most of the good grass will be
grazed down to a nubbin," Jim replied.

Damn, thought Jacob as he looked over at
Martin for support. Good ole Martin, ever the
quiet one, was having none of it. He was leaving

his older brother to do the thinking, or heavy lifting, and to get the ass-chewin' for being wrong.

Seeing no help coming from that quarter, Jacob said, "Well, if that is not good enough, what do you suggest, Jim?"

"Oxen," he replied. "They can eat a bale of weeds and still last a full day on the trail pullin' a heavy load, unlike horses or mules. To my way of thinkin', them last two types of critters belong in pack strings, not pullin' heavy-loaded wagons on an overgrazed trail. Besides, oxen are less prone to stampedin' or catchin' everything that comes along, plus most Indians with any sense will not run off with your slow-movin' oxen unless they are starvin' and need something to eat," he continued.

"Where the hell we supposed to get eight oxen?" Jacob blurted out in exasperation at having been so shortsighted.

"Right here at the fort. For the last year or so I have traded one good, well-rested ox for two jaded ones when the wagon trains came rolling in. As it now stands, I have over one hundred rolling fat head of oxen in the pasture just behind the fort," Jim replied with a twinkle in his eye at having finally gotten the boys' attention.

"Then if they are for sale, my brother and I will trade in most of our pack string and some of our credit from our trappin's for what we need,"

Jacob replied after a quick look over at his weasel of a brother for confirmation.

"I don't think so," replied Bridger. "You boys need to keep your other stock for the trip as well. Never can tell when you will need them to hook up to the wagons and help the oxen pull a steep hill or move a wagon out of the mud or quicksand during a river crossing. No, I suggest you keep your pack string for riding or trade when they are needed. Now, who is going to drive those two wagons of yours?"

From the looks on both boys' faces, he could tell that was another thing neither had thought of. Jacob sheepishly replied, "Well, we can drive our own teams."

"That really makes a lot of sense," Bridger replied with the fatherly sharpness in his voice again. "Who is going to do the scouting for a place to camp at night, kill some meat for supper, or be on the lookout for hostiles?" His stem look concealed his joy at being able to help the sons of his dead trapper friends from times past, especially when it came to the really serious part of growing up.

Jacob and Martin looked at each other again, in agony. This wagon-master job is sure turning out to be a pain in the ass, Martin thought. Jacob worried about just how little he and his brother knew about the business they had now gotten themselves into.

184 | TERRY GROSZ

Jim continued, "Now, as to supplies for the two of you. I would suggest three barrels of flour, one barrel of sugar, one barrel of cornmeal, four twenty-five-pound sacks of coffee beans, and a new coffee grinder. You will also need oxen, horse, and mule shoes with associated nails for your livestock and those of your wagon train in case they haven't thought of it. Then, if's it were me, I would add four twenty-five-pound kegs of powder, six jugs of honey, a hundred pounds of beans, one hundred pounds of bacon, and a hundred pounds of rice." Writing down what Jim was advising on a small board, Jacob scribbled furiously. Then after a short pause, Jim continued as if talking to himself, "Then I would add four sacks of salt, two sacks of pepper, some extra cast iron in case you break what you already have, and several extra wheels, both front and back. Also, I would add some extra leather strapping in case you bust some harnesses along the way and have to mend them. Seeing you may have to detour a bit, I would suggest some extra axes, saws, and shovels so you can get out of what you got yourself into. Lastly, I would suggest several kegs of whiskey, some buckets, a water barrel per wagon, and a passel of trade items for the Indians you will run into along the way. And, oh, several buckets of good axle grease as well as some bear grease fir your cooking' would be helpful."

Jim paused as if gathering breath and then thought better of going on. He had already over-whelmed the boys with what they had forgotten and felt it best to hold his tongue and fill them in later on what they still needed as it became nec-essary. It was during that moment that the boys realized that even though their credit from the trapping was substantial, they would not have enough for all Jim proposed as well as items to be added later.

"Jim," said Jacob, "I think my brother and I now realize the seriousness of what you are say-ing. You are right, and the both of us appreciate you standing in place of our fathers. We will be short in our credit from our trappin's, but we have other means for paying you in full, as our parents would have wished."

Jim just looked at the two young men, proud as punch as if they were his own, as their parents would have been as well had they lived.

Jacob continued, "We have needs for livestock replacement, topping off of supplies for the oth-ers wishing to continue west, and two men to drive our wagons. Most of our concerns for our travelers my brother and I can fix. However, do you have any idea who we can get who is honest and hardworking to drive our wagons while my brother and I scout and ride herd?"

"Jus' so happens I have a couple of good men

in mind who would fit that bill," Bridger replied with a grin. "To the south of here about three miles are two brothers, Dave and Jerry Hall. They trapped with me up on the Yellowstone in '30 and '32. Both are damn good men, getting long in the tooth but honest and God-fearing. I would be right proud to serve with either or both of them if asked. And I would bet both would lunge at the chance to go west and see what is over the mountains and on the other side, 'specially from the safety of a wagon seat."

Excited over the prospect of having a couple more men for the wagon train who had Jim's blessing, Jacob said, "Jim, will you point me and my brother in the right direction so we can meet these men and decide for ourselves?"

"That be easy," Jim said. "Follow me."

Walking out from the fort, Jim stopped and pointed to a belt of trees jutting out in the grassy plains several miles below his fort. "They be nestled in a small cabin at the foot of that finger of trees," he advised. "It be easy to find, and I am sure the Hall brothers would appreciate the company, especially if you boys were to bring a jug."

"That will suit us just fine," said Jacob. "My brother and I will ride out that way and be back in time for dinner at the central fire at the wagon train. Then we can share the good news of having two more men to help carry the load, provide security, and point the way if they pan out and wish to join us in our travels."

"I'll go and get our horses saddled and ready to ride," said Martin, and with a nod from Jacob he was off to the corrals.

"Now all I need to do is find another good wagon, and aside from provisioning, we should be ready to roll," Jacob mused aloud.

"Look no further," said Jim with a grin. "I have two wagons out back of the fort that I bought some time back from several families who had been partially wiped out by cholera just outside St. Louis. Then both the menfolk were crippled up by accidents, and what was left of their numbers turned back, but not before selling me their wagons. One is in pretty good shape. The other is somewhat the worse for wear. But you can buy the good one and part out the other one so you have some spares for the good wagon in case they are needed."

"You have a deal. My brother and I will look them over when we get back from visiting the Hall brothers," said Jacob as Martin approached with their saddle horses.

"Hello, the cabin," shouted Jacob an hour later.

As they approached, the brothers could see a neatly built cabin with a small corral off to one side but easily defensible in case someone tried to rustle the stock. A tall, slender man emerged from the cabin carrying a rifle and squinting into the daylight. Upon seeing the two riders coming toward him, he waved a friendly greeting. Soon another man stepped from the cabin, also with rifle in hand, and stood behind his brother to see what developed.

Stopping in front of the two men, Jacob said, "This here is my brother, Martin, and I am called Jacob. Jim Bridger sent us to look you fellows up."

"What fer?" asked the taller one with a smile of recognition at the mention of Jim's name.

"We are fixing' to put together a wagon train to go to California and need two drivers for our wagons. Jim said you two might be willin' to take on that chore and go to California to see what is over there. If the two of you are eager to do so, my brother and I are willing to offer you payment upon arrival and 'found' throughout the trip," replied Jacob.

"Light down and sit a spell," said the taller one as he leaned his rifle against the front of the cabin. His quiet brother did the same. Then both men strode over to Jacob and Martin and warmly shook their hands.

"From the looks of your garb, the two of you be mountain men sure," stated the shorter of the two men, who had introduced himself as Jerry.

"You be right as rain," said Martin. "We both came to this valley after our real parents were killed off in the Wind Rivers by the Gros Ventre many years ago. Our stepparents were killed in this here valley some years back as well by a band of Lakota."

"Them that was responsible have bones that are now scattered to the four winds," Jacob added. "Since then we was trapping and meat hunting in the land of the Arapaho far to the south. Realizing we are not getting any younger, the two of us decided to go west and see what those new lands have to offer. Coming to the fort, we hooked up with our old friend Jim Bridger and found a wagon train going west that could use our help. We need two good wagon drivers who might know the country about to be traveled, so here we are."

"Well, Jim be right. The two of us have been wanting to go west and see what is over yonder. But we felt we was gettin' too old and never would get that chance. Sit down and let us jawbone over just what you two are trying to do and when," said Dave.

The four men spent the next two hours getting to know each other. As Jim had suggested, the sight and contents of a jug of good liquor aided the flow of the conversation considerably.

Jacob and Martin found that they liked the two

reserved brothers more and more as they talked. It appeared that Dave and Jerry were intrigued by the prospect of going west with a gang of folks who could more than defend themselves. Soon the stories flew, and Jacob and Martin lost track of the time until the jug was empty and the brothers realized the sun was setting.

"Gentlemen, we need to get cracking and get back to our wagon train and let them know of the changing events since we saw them last," said Jacob.

"What be you men's thoughts? Any hankering to throw in with us on the trip to the west?" Martin asked hopefully.

Jerry and Dave looked at each other, and then Dave said, "When would you folks be gettin' under way?"

"Just as soon as we replace some livestock, patch up our wagons, and get provisioned," replied Jacob.

"Be three, maybe four days at the most. Have to keep our eyes on the mountain snows closing down the passes in the Sierra Mountains and make sure we get there before that happens," said Martin.

"Count us in," said Jerry as Dave nodded in agreement.

"Oh, by the way, me and Jerry have been as far as the Humboldt afore most of our party got kilt off and me and my brother got run back to where we came from by the Paiutes," Dave said casually.

Jacob and Martin looked at each other and then grinned huge grins beneath their massive beards.

"That be great! The two of us have never been past Fort Hall. If you two have been to the Humboldt, that will be a great help to us as we guide the wagons west," Martin exclaimed.

"Well, that won't be no problem," said Dave.

"After that we will just follow the tracks left by the many others afore us," said Jerry with a smile and a bit of unsteadiness from too much of Jim's hard liquor.

"Won't be the first time any of us have gone into the great beyond partially blind," said Jacob with a look of relief.

The four men shook on the deal and agreed to meet three days hence for a planned departure on the fourth day of the week.

That evening Jacob and Martin could hardly contain themselves over the information they had for the folks of their wagon train. On the way back from their visit to the Halls, the brothers could hardly get over their good fortune. They now had two more experienced mountain men to provide security and help lead the way to the Humboldt River and Sink. They had drivers for their two wagons, and the four men had gotten along very well. Jacob and Martin had decided to have all their folks load up on supplies at the fort and replenish their existing livestock with oxen from Jim's reserve herds. They would pay Jim with credit from their furs and some of the gold nuggets from their cache. They had listened to Jim and now understood that taking a group of people west meant undertaking a lot of responsibility. They would see to it that before they left the fort, their wagon train would be well supplied with provisions and outfitted with fresh livestock.

That evening after supper around the central fire, the women and children melted back into their wagons and chores while the men going west gathered around the campfire for the latest news. When everyone was accounted for, Jacob rose and addressed the group.

"Men, my brother and I will lead you to California! We have never been there ourselves, but with Jim Bridger's directions, help from Dave and Jerry Hall, who are two old mountain men, and a well-marked wagon trail to follow, we feel it will not be hard to reach California."

For a long moment the men wishing to proceed west smiled. Then they jumped up and began slapping each other on the backs as they excitedly talked about the adventures and new lives that lay ahead.

Jacob continued, "First of all, starting tomorrow all of you with horses pulling your wagons will meet with Jim Bridger. There you will acquire four oxen with one extra for each of your wagons in case you lose one to an accident, becoming foot sore, or the fever."

There was a nervous murmur from the men. Sensing their concern and speaking for all of them, Rich Grosz rose and said, "That will be impossible for most of us. For the most part, we have used the last of our monies just to get this far. None of us have the resources to change our animals from horses and mules to oxen at this stage of the trip." The other men mumbled their concerned agreement.

"That will not be a problem. Jim Bridger has a concern that horses cannot safely pull our wagons over the next thousand miles eating what grasses they can find in the western desert facing us. Oxen can eat just about anything and can pull heavier loads, so oxen it will be. As to your concerns, me and my brother will pay for the additions to your stock trains. We will also keep our old stock because we will need them to assist along the way and to pull our plows and ride once we get to California."

The men sat silent, thunderstruck by Jacob's generous words.

"Now for the next thing. My brother and I will

inventory your wagons to see what you have and what you might need. All of us will carry several barrels of flour, cornmeal, bacon slabs, axle grease, oxen, horse, and mule shoes, extra rope, additional leather to repair harnesses and reins, extra wheels, and the like. Those lacking what we feel you will need will meet with Jim Bridger and provision up to the standards we set. Those supplies needed to top off your loads will again be paid for by me and my brother. Once we leave this area, things we will need for every-day living and traveling might be a bit sparse to acquire along the trail. I know Fort Hall is over the horizon, but that is at the end of the supply route. They might not have much of anything in the way of supplies. So we need to make sure that once we leave this place, we can make it to California on what provisions we are carrying," Jacob stated flatly.

By now the women from the wagon train had gathered behind their men, after hearing their concerned murmuring. Jacob could see Amanda smiling at him through the crowd and almost forgot what he still had to say. Overcoming his distraction, Jacob continued, "As I said earlier, we will be adding two more men to our group. They are the Hall brothers, longtime mountain men living nearby who also want to see the west afore they pass over the Great Divide. They have been as far west as the Humboldt River and Sink, which is on our way. They will be driving our two wagons and will provide even more security with their Hawken rifles, not to mention their partial knowledge of the way west."

Rising and standing beside his brother, Martin said, "We will be leaving in four days. I would suggest the women get their washing done for the following week on the trail and their baking and bean soaking as well. For you men, I suggest all of you have Chris Grosz examine and repair any of your firearms. And you, Chris, any spare gun parts you are lacking, I suggest you see Jim Bridger and get what you can from his stores. Whatever you come up with, tell Jim Bridger we will square that with him afore we leave. If any of you need some heavy lifting done and are unable to do so, get ahold of Rich, Mark, Otis, or Marv Clary. We are also fortunate to have a doctor on this trip. Howard, I would suggest you go and see Jim as well and provision up with whatever salves or medicines you may need for the trip from whatever he has in the fort's stores. We will pick up those expenses as well. Once on the trail, my brother will ride point, and I will ride alongside and at the rear of the wagons in case we have any problems. As you did before you got here, we will walk many times along the way to reduce the weight and rest our stock. Those folks who are driving their teams and are concerned with the livestock changeover will find the oxen much easier to control. They move more slowly and do not frighten near as easy as horses and mules. I expect the men to be armed at all times and either walking alongside the wagons, driving their wagons, or riding their livestock close at hand.

"The young boys in the group who are able will be responsible for our horse and mule herds and must be alert at all times. Several armed men will be chosen each day to ride with the herders because we will have a very tempting herd of animals in the eyes of the Indians." With that he stepped back, aware that Kim was looking at him intently, causing him to blush and, like his brother, almost forget his words.

"We will leave at daylight every day unless emergencies befall us. I am hoping to make between ten and fifteen miles per day. If we are successful in that endeavor, we should be able to stop around four in the afternoon, build our fires, and cook our suppers. If anyone has any concerns, they are to let either me or my brother know as soon as possible. We are also to treat our livestock well. Without them we will not make California before the snows close the passes. In case of Indians, we will circle the wagons, and me, my brother, or the Halls will go forth to parley to see what they want. Under no circumstances will anyone fire on an Indian unless his life or the lives of his loved ones or his neighbors are in danger," Jacob said, surprising himself with the tone of command he was taking on.

Jim Bridger, standing at the edge of the crowd of folks who were not moving on but who stood there listening, smiled. Yes, he thought, their folks would have been right proud of these two young men.

༺•༺

THE NEXT MORNING, while the folks in the wagon train were getting fitted up with their new oxen, Martin and Jacob, having a final personal chore before them, left the group in Jim's trusted hands. Riding out to the old homestead and then to their parents' graves, the two boys slowly dismounted. Putting a few wilted flowers they had picked along the way on the now almost indiscernible gravesites, they said their final good-byes. Then, without another word, they mounted their horses for a final time at their old homestead and rode silently back to the fort.

༺•༺

DAY TWO of the preparations found the fort a living mass of energized people. Jacob and Martin were busy inspecting the conditions of the wagons and the supplies they carried. If any needs were discovered, the wagon owners were dispatched to the fort to address those concerns. Soon Jim Bridger's storerooms in the fort were looking a bit barren in some places, and still the frantic pace continued.

Taking time out of their day, Jacob and Martin collected the stores they would personally need for the trip, adding a dozen sacks of oats and grain, gun wadding, extra primers, blankets, several tanned buffalo robes, whetstones, axle tools, and the like. Then they met Bridger behind the fort and selected the wagon he recommended. The three of them soon took apart the old remaining wagon, keeping several wheels for replacement for their new one. Jim then led them to a small corral by the edge of the fort. Standing there were ten of the best-looking oxen Jacob and Martin had seen. They were huge and in very good condition.

"There you be, lads, the pick of the litter," Jim proudly proclaimed.

Jacob and Martin could not have been happier with Jim's surprise.

"I am having my men build the tack necessary for those oxen along with some extra sorts for the trip ahead," Jim continued with a proud smile.

The boys were overwhelmed at the man's far thinking generosity.

"Jim, we can't thank you enough," said Martin as Jacob nodded in agreement.

"No need, boys. That is the very least I can do for the kin of some of my best friends afore them damn savages killed them. This is nothing more than they would have wanted of me, and so be it," he said quietly. "Besides, some years back a mountain man and close friend named Harlan Waugh left me a pile of credit with one of our rendezvous traders. That was afore he and his son went after several other bad seeds who had kilt his kin. He never returned from that chore. But afore he left, he told me to use the credit he had left me to open up a trading post when my bones got so brittle that I could no longer tolerate the cold trapping waters, and my back could no longer bend enough to trap beaver. In return for his generosity, I am passing along some of his kindness to you two boys, sons of mountain men."

"What about the low stock of your remaining supplies?" Jacob asked.

"Our folks have about cleaned you out," added Martin.

"Not to worry. I have my annual supply train coming sometime next week or the week after, and with that, I will be set for what winter has to offer. You boys did me a favor cleaning me out of my old stocks, so don't worry none about ole Jim," he said with a grin.

&

DAY THREE found the air around the wagons smelling of lye soap and the delicious aroma of baking bread. Dave and Jerry Hall showed up, trailing a pack string loaded with their belongings. Soon their belongings was stowed in one of the boys' new wagons. Dave and Jerry were introduced all around to the folks in the wagon train during the evening meal. In the process, Jacob and Martin had a chance to talk to the two young women they found so intriguing. They also discovered that Martin Jones and Rich Grosz watched Jacob and Martin like hungry hawks would a mouse when they were around their girls. It was clear that the two fathers were interested in the well-being of their young ladies and very suspicious of the two mountain men or any male suitors, wagon masters or not.

That evening come suppertime, the entire wagon train turned out for a celebration heralding the next day's adventure on the trail west. For that evening's supper there were fresh trout caught in the streams on the valley floor fried in bear grease, deer and pronghorn steaks smothered in wild onions sizzling in cast-iron frying pans, homemade bread and biscuits, thick, rich gravy, rice pudding cooked in a cast-iron pot, apple pies, and hot coffee to round out the fare. Out came a fiddle handled by Marvin Clary and a banjo strummed by Otis Barnes, and soon the night air fairly hummed with activity as many of the folks began dancing. The dust rose high from all the flying feet and swirling long dresses as the dancers lathered up the celebration. Finally it became necessary to bring pans of water to wet down the earthen dance floor to settle the dust created by the many happy, flying feet and whirling dresses.

Jacob, Martin, and the Hall brothers sat at the edge of the group watching and smiling at the mass of folks oblivious to the perils that lay ahead on the worst part of the trail yet to come. They all would be facing about four more months' worth of tough traveling if everything went well. And that didn't include hostile Indians, alkali dust, hordes of mosquitoes, endless hot sun, bad water, disease, accidents, lack of firewood, weather, and everything else that might trouble a body.

Jacob spotted Kim working her way toward Martin. She said something to Martin that made him blush — then up on his feet he went with Kim into the swirling mass of dancers.

Martin looks like a bear cub playing with his feet, thought Jacob as he laughed at his brother's clumsy attempts at dancing.

Then it was his turn to look funny as well. Amanda, with her dad's approval, worked her way through the crowd and, standing in front of Jacob, held out her hands, beckoning for him to stand. Jacob found himself just as clumsy as his brother when it came to dancing. He felt like a millipede, he had so many feet, all going in the wrong direction.

When he stepped on Amanda's feet for the tenth time, she stopped, laughed easily, and said, "I will teach you how to dance on this trip if you and my dad will let me."

Jacob mumbled something he couldn't remember the next day and was glad to sit down. After all, he was the wagon master. But my, how his heart was beating! In fact, it hadn't beaten that fast during any of the close escapades he had had during the earlier years of his life.

Chapter Eighteen

THE WAY WEST AND A SURPRISE OF UNUSUAL DIMENSIONS

DAWN THE NEXT MORNING found the air around Fort Bridger full of dust and filled with the noise of cracking whips, barking dogs, yelling men, creaking wagons, and a meadowlark calling softly off in the distance. In the middle of all that chaos moved Jacob and Martin, keeping things organized and moving. As the sun rose and quiet returned to the valley, they found fifteen wagons in a line and ready to go. Off to one side stood a smaller group of folks watching with downcast faces and heavy hearts. They were the ones who for various reason were returning home, beaten by the hardships of the westward journey.

"Wagons, ho," yelled Jacob as he turned his horse toward the northwest and Fort Hall.

Standing nearby, watching that moving mass

of humanity, stood Jim Bridger, who had been a towering mountain man in his time. The sight of the caravan heading out and the departure of his two friends from long past, who he suspected would never return, made him feel as if time was leaving him behind. The fur trade that he loved was almost gone, as were many of its participants. The great herds of buffalo were disappearing, or at least had been run off by the noise and smell of humans, as were the bighorn sheep and lordly elk. The tribes of Indians were getting harder and harder to live with in light of the mass of humanity invading their lands, and meetings between the settlers and the native peoples were now often turning deadly. The number of wagon trains coming to his fort annually was diminishing because those travelers had discovered shorter routes, and his body was telling him it was time to slow down, rest, and reflect on the storied past.

As the last wagon rumbled out of sight over a distant hill, Jim sadly headed for the comfort of the earthen jug under the counter in his store. Sitting on top of the counter over his jug of "old top-knot remover" was a foot high mound of gold nuggets that Jacob and Martin had left to pay off their debts to a man to whom they were forever indebted. Jim didn't put his earthen jug down until later that afternoon. It seemed as if it took a lot longer that particular day to salve his old war wounds.

Off at the edge of the timber a short distance from the fort, a lone wolf howled. His howl was not returned, and its message was soon borne away in the whispers of the west winds like many other events now long past...

Jim Bridger died years later and was almost blind at the time of his death. However, he always wished he could return to his beloved mountains one last time, even though he could not now see them. He is buried in the State of Kansas...

THE FIRST DAY the wagon train only made about ten miles as the group worked out the tangles inherent in the operation. That evening several fires were made as different groups prepared their supper and rested from the day's travails. The wagons were in a tight circle, and after the oxen and other livestock had been watered and allowed to graze, they were brought into the circle for protection from roaming bands of Indians and other predators. Jacob, Martin, and the Hall brothers made their campfire separate from the others as they cooked their meal in tired silence. Martin was one mess of dust from head to foot, having followed the dusty train as he rode from side to side, watching his charges. The Hall brothers were sore from riding on hard wagon seats all day, as was evident when they ate their dinners that evening standing up. Last but not least, Jacob's knees were telling him that riding a horse all day was not as much fun as it had been during his younger days.

The next ten days were more of the same, only the caravan was now making about fifteen miles per day as everyone began settling into a pattern of travel and routine—as much as they could on the ever-changing trail.

One evening when Jacob and his crew were cooking their supper of biscuits, beans, and bacon, Daniel, the older man from Salt Lick, Kentucky, came over and quietly sat down with the men. He had brought a pie his wife, Betsy, had made in a Dutch oven. That quickly brought smiles to the four men's faces when the heavenly smell reached their noses.

"How about from now on the four of you join my clan for supper? I have more and I would bet far better cooks than you four, and it would make for a merrier group if you were to join us," said Daniel. When saying those words, he looked long, hard, and strangely carefully at Jacob's face.

Rich Grosz's camp was right next to Daniel's, and Daniel's and Martin Jones's clans always ate together. That meant Jacob would be closer to Amanda and Martin to Kim, who was traveling with the Jones family.

The four men looked at each other, and Jacob, feeling a consensus, said, "We would be glad to join your camp, but only if we can help out with the grub."

"Suit yourself," said Daniel. "After all, you folks bought many of our provisions anyway."

"Then it is done, and we would welcome any cooking better than the Hall brothers' sad attempt at feeding the four of us," Jacob said with a teasing smile. That statement got a burned biscuit bounced off his head by Jerry Hall, their camp cook for the evening.

With that invitation Daniel left, and Jacob and Martin made their rounds around camp and outside it for some distance, looking for any signs of trouble. A lone wolf's howl was their only reward for vigilance, and it gave Jacob and Martin pause.

Life was good on the trail, and soon it would take an even more spectacular turn in the lives of Jacob and Martin.

At the end of the next day, after the wagons had been circled and the stock fed and watered, Jacob, Martin, and the Halls went over to join Daniel and his sons, Zeke and Jeremiah, by their cooking fire. A large pot of beans, bacon, and wild onions merrily boiled away, filling the cool night air with delicious smells along with the heavenly perfume of biscuits and a pie baking in two Dutch ovens at the fire's edge. Having finished their chores, Martin Jones and his three sons ambled over to Daniel's cooking fire as well. In the meantime, the men's wives scurried around to get supper ready. As the men made small talk about the day's journey, the welcome clanking of metal plates, utensils, and coffee cups being taken from the grub box could be heard. Soon great mounds of beans and biscuits were heaped on the plates, and the cups were filled with a black liquid so hot it was hard to hold the metal cups with bare hands. The men ate as if they meant it, and their wives and children ate quietly with them. When supper was finished, the men broke out their pipes as the women cleaned up. Talk centered around the arrival in Fort Hall in several days and the constant close presence of game. Several of the men wanted to hunt the next day for some fresh meat, and Jacob concurred.

"Tomorrow before we stop for the evening, why don't several of you break away from the train and kill the camp a deer or pronghorn," suggested Jacob. "However, don't ever lose sight of the wagon train, no matter what. That is your only protection, so take heed. We are in Lakota Indian country, and they don't cotton to white men killing their game. In fact, just before my brother and I came to Fort Bridger, we buried some folks from three wagons that had strayed into Lakota territory looking for homesteads and figured dead wrong."

The men nodded in agreement with Jacob's stern warning, full well knowing the frontier could be a deadly place. Even though they had Howard Larson along, an arrow or rifle ball in the wrong place could be hard for a doctor on the trail to fix.

As they sat around the fire enjoying their meal and a smoke afterward, Jacob noticed that Daniel kept looking at him as if he were seeing something extraordinary. He also realized, even though it was less noticeable, that Martin Jones was staring intently at Martin. By now he and Martin were getting a little uncomfortable under the older men's stares. Then they discovered that Zeke and Jeremiah were studying them closely as well.

"Where you boys from again?" asked Daniel, out of the blue.

"We was born in the Wind River Mountains north of here. Our moms were from the Snake Tribe of the same area, and our dads were mountain men," said Jacob, still feeling uneasy at the intense, piercing looks he and his brother were getting.

"Did either of you really get to meet your dads?" asked Daniel.

"No, not really," said Martin. "They was killed by the Gros Ventre when we was just little guys."

Now Martin Jones and his sons were looking openly at Jacob and Martin as if something were seriously wrong.

"Why all the questions?" asked Jacob, who was becoming a little irritated by their traveling companions' bad staring manners and personal questions.

"What were the names of your dads?" asked Martin Jones, ignoring Jacob's question as his sons kept looking intently at the two men.

"What the hell is going on?" asked Martin, who was also becoming perturbed. Out West a man's name and background were private territory that strangers should not try to enter and explore. It was neither polite nor wise to do so.

"No offense, gentlemen," said Daniel, reading their irritation at being grilled, "but we might know you from our past."

"I don't know how, since you folks are from Kentucky and we are from Snake Indian lands north of here," Jacob replied coldly, feeling a little out of sorts.

Then Martin remembered something and slowly said, "According to our stepparents, our fathers came from somewhere east of a river called the Mississippi in '29. They went to St. Louis and joined up with a fur brigade and went west, trapping beaver and other furbearers. To our understanding, they were young men at the time, hardly older than sixteen. They was killed in '36 by the Gros Ventre Jacob spoke of."

Daniel went almost white and appeared to be having a hard time breathing. Martin Jones rose from his seat on a log, and tears began streaming down his cheeks in torrents, an emotion rarely exhibited by an Indian.

Zeke spoke softly and in measured words to Jacob. "I think you are my long-lost grandson!"

Jacob looked at Zeke in stunned silence.

"And I think you are my grandson as well," said Martin Jones, looking at Martin in disbelief and awe.

For a moment there was stunned silence around their campfire, and the nearby campfires, overhearing the conversation, fell silent as well.

"How do you figure, Zeke?" asked Jacob in disbelief.

"My stepson, Jacob, was the son of my Uncle Lemuel and Aunt Sarah. His parents were killed by marauding Indians on their farm in Kentucky. My wife, Margaret, and I raised Jacob. When he grew up, he teamed up with his Delaware Indian boyhood friend, Martin, and they came west at the age of sixteen to join the mountain men in 1829. They too went to St. Louis, joined the fur brigades, and after that we lost track of them. What you two remember hearing about your dads coming up the Mississippi River in 1829 and going into the fur trade when they were sixteen years old, and the fact that they were named Jacob and Martin, more than likely makes you my grandson, Jacob. And Martin is Martin Jones's grandson!"

Margaret, Zeke's wife, stepped into the firelight and, looking hard at Jacob, said, "I can see the family resemblance now. Zeke, look at his nose and eyes! He is the son of our long-lost son, Jacob!"

She ran into Zeke's arms as tears rolled down her cheeks, staining the front of her dress just as they had many years before on the farm, the day Jacob and Martin had decided to leave home and venture west into the fur trade.

Neither Jacob or Martin knew what to say or do.

"If that be the case, then Martin and I are your long-lost kin," Jacob said slowly, still hardly believing what he was saying or hearing.

For a long time no one moved. Other members of the wagon train who had drifted over to Daniel's campfire stood frozen as the family histories unraveled in front of everyone.

Margaret left Zeke's arms and ran crying to the still confused Jacob. Jacob found himself holding her tightly, as if she had belonged there all along.

Martin Jones walked over to Martin and said, "The Great Spirit has smiled on me and my family this day. I had hoped before I passed over to the Cloud People, that I would see my son once again. But I have his son, and I will love you like my son, who is now with the Cloud People."

Not really knowing why, Martin walked into his grandfather's arms and felt at home with himself for the first time in his short life.

There was much laughing, crying, back-slapping and handshaking all around as the wagon train welcomed Martin and Jacob into their family in a way reserved for kin, however long lost. Soon Jacob and Martin's reserve had melted away as their newfound family members told them stories about their dads that matched what they had been told by their stepparents before they had been killed by the Lakota. Many present found themselves in tears, and then someone called out for a celebration.

Abruptly leaving the crowd gathered around Daniel's campfire, Jacob strode over to one of his and Martin's wagons. He returned carrying a small keg of whiskey, and a party such as had never before been seen on the California Trail whirled away into the wee hours.

The wagon train made only ten miles the next day, as the travelers rose later and moved more slowly than usual...

Chapter Nineteen

A DEER HUNT BRINGS SURPRISE VISITORS

THE NEXT AFTERNOON, as the wagon train settled in for the evening, Otis Barnes and Marvin Clary left the circle of wagons with their rifles. They had spotted a small herd of mule deer quietly feeding a quarter mile away in a creek bottom. Slowly sneaking up on the feeding animals, Otis and Marvin each picked out a large buck. The men settled into their rifles, and on a prearranged quiet count, they both fired. The roar from their two rifles echoed throughout the small valley, and the deer herd quickly sprinted for the safety offered by the surrounding sage-brush. Walking closer to the creek bottom, the men were pleased at what they saw. Marvin's large six-point buck kicked his last as the result of a fine head shot, and the deer shot by Otis, a five-point, had already stopped moving. The two men decided that Marvin would return to the wagon train and get several pack horses on which to load and carry the two large deer back to the waiting camp. Otis would gut the animals and wait for Marvin's return.

As he started to gut the second animal, Otis heard horses' hoofs as Marvin returned with some horses to carry the deer...or so he thought. Looking up, Otis was surprised to see not Marvin but about fifteen mounted Indians coming at him hell bent for leather! Quickly realizing that the rifle he had just grabbed had not been reloaded, he took off running all out for the protection offered by the wagon train several hundred yards away.

"Indians, Indians!" he yelled as he ran as fast as he could. However, his escape was not to be. The mounted Indians quickly surrounded the running man and forced him to a stop with a surround of their horses.

Hearing Otis's warning yells, Jacob and Martin mounted their horses and went at a gallop to rescue him. Seeing that it would do no good to race toward the Indians in such a threatening manner, since Otis had already been captured, the two men reined to a slowed canter with arms raised in the sign language of friendship.

Back at the wagon train, Jerry and Dave Hall

were making the frightened travelers form a defense against any attack. Kim and Amanda ran to the edge of the circled wagons, and their hearts froze when they saw Jacob and Martin riding into sure death if the Indians so decided! Then they were hustled back out of sight by their fathers as the men prepared to defend themselves against what they considered the heathen terrors of the plains.

In the meantime, the Indians forcefully took Otis's rifle. It was obvious in their eyes that the white man was soon going to die for trespassing and hunting on their lands. This prime hunting area had lately been overrun by the white-topped wagons and the white men and women who rode within them. They had killed or spooked off most of the game, muddied the watering holes, and grazed off all the grass with their ever-hungry livestock. If this flood of white men didn't stop soon, all the tribes in the region would starve to death or be driven from their lands, many of the Indians believed.

Many-Horses-Walking sat on his horse quietly looking down at the white man they had just captured. This man was concerned but appeared not to be afraid like all the others they had caught and killed in similar circumstances. *Yes, he was a brave one, thought Many-Horses-Walking.* Then he turned his attention to the two riders from the wagon train coming his way with their hands raised in the sign of friendship. He thought he would listen to what they had to say and then kill all three of them in front of the members of the wagon train. Then he would take their horses and firearms as tribute for their foolish hunting or crossing on Lakota lands.

Walks-in-the-Sun, son of Chief Many-Horses-Walking, patiently sat beside his father as they awaited the arrival of the two brave but heavily outnumbered men approaching their group of mounted warriors. Then, standing higher in his stirrups so he could see better, Walks-in-the-Sun strained his eyes in disbelief! Suddenly spurring his horse out from the group of warriors, he rode madly toward the two white men, howling like a banshee! Riding his horse directly into the side of Martin's, the young Indian jumped off, tackling Martin from his saddle and spilling both men off their horses and onto the ground with a resounding crump and a cloud of dust.

"Martin! Jacob!" the young Indian man yelled as he wrestled with Martin.

Removing his hand from the butt of his pistol, Jacob leaped off his horse and jumped onto the pile of Martin and Walks-in- the-Sun. All three rolled around on the ground like a bunch of goofy kids. This move by the howling Indian attacking Jacob and Martin and the three of them apparently locked in mortal combat caused near panic in the wagon train. Kim and Amanda turned away, not knowing what was going on but assuming the worst, and began crying.

Rising to their feet, the three men were hugging and talking in Lakota and sign all at the same time. The men in the wagon train and the mounted warriors waited in confusion as things began sorting themselves out. Chief Many-Horses-Walking rode over to the trio and quickly recognized Jacob and Martin. Quietly stepping off his horse, he strode over to Jacob and grabbed his shoulders in a sign of friendship. Then he did the same with Martin, who was happy to see his old friend. Confusion still reigned in the wagon train, but Dave and Jerry kept the travelers in check and at the ready as they waited for the outcome of the conference going on in the middle of the prairie between their wagon masters and the Indians.

Soon the worried travelers standing behind their barricade of wagons saw Otis Barnes striding across the field toward the wagon train carrying his rifle. Behind him came Jacob, Martin, and Walks-in-the Sun, followed by Chief Many-Horses-Walking and his warriors. The parade of men also included two warriors dragging the dead bucks toward the wagons behind their horses.

Arriving back at the circle of wagons, Jacob and Martin introduced their friends, Lakota Chief Many-Horses-Walking and his son Walks-in-the-Sun, to the still worried travelers. Soon everybody's hackles lay back down after the scare, and even more so when Jacob asked the women to prepare a big dinner using the fresh deer meat for everyone. Jacob also asked that a big pot of sweetened dried fruit be boiled, along with many pots of coffee. Then Jacob and Martin took the chief to their wagons and handed him several sacks of blue and red beads, several Green River skinning knives, some whetstones, a keg of powder, a sack of flints, a sack of coffee beans, and a sack of brown-sugar cones. The smile on the chief's face told everyone he was now more than happy. The chief in turn distributed some of his gifts to his men, which created even more smiles all around. Then Jacob broke out a keg of cigars and passed them around to everyone, and soon a happy haze of cigar smoke filled the circle of wagons. That was followed by many good smells from the cooking fires, and shortly thereafter the wagon-train travelers and the Lakota were happily enjoying a feast as friends.

That evening the Lakota guests and their horses slept within the circle of wagons beside the cooking fires. The next morning another feast of biscuits, honey, cooked mush with fruit, fried venison, and pots of scalding coffee was held in honor of the Lakota. When finished, the men bade farewell to their Indian friends, but not before giving them some more tobacco from Jacob and Martin's stores. Just as Jim Bridger had predicted: "Bring along plenty of supplies. You will never know when you will need them, especially for Indian trade."

But a somber note was sounded by some news passed on to Jacob and Martin at the same time. Their friend Cain, they were told, had wandered away from the tribe after his wife had died in childbirth. He was so distraught that he had left in the dead of night during a violent spring storm, and his Indian friends had never seen him again. Jacob and Martin were upset by the news because they felt that they had just lost a brother.

That was followed by more bad news. The Lakota under Chief Red Cloud were on the warpath, killing any white people going up the Fort Hall Road. They had had enough of the invasion and were doing what they felt was right in trying to keep the settlers from flooding through, destroying their game and lands. Jacob assured his friends that the people in his wagon train were leaving the Indians' lands forever and that he hoped they would have safe passage. Chief Many-Horses-Walking told him they would have safe passage, but they should leave before things got much worse. Jacob and Martin thanked their old friends and, after saying good-bye, watched them ride off. They saw Chief Many-Horses-Walking and his son stop on the top of a small rise, wave farewell, and disappear over the horizon. The brothers realized that another chapter in their lives had just been closed.

Chapter Twenty

FORT HALL, AND DR. LARSON SAVES THE DAY

THE FOLLOWING AFTERNOON the wagon train topped a rise, and there in the distance lay Fort Hall. At first excitement reigned at the prospect of visiting civilization once again, but that feeling soon disappeared. The closer the wagon train got, the smaller the fort looked until everyone realized the fort was nothing more than a small trading post. It was located on a barren plain next to a bend in the Snake River and was surrounded by several dozen tepees from members of the Shoshone and Bannock tribes.

Circling the wagons on a small grassy plain that had not been grazed to the dirt by previous wagon trains and leaving Dave Hall in charge, Jacob and Martin rode over to the fort. They were invited in by several of the fort's employees and met with the factor in charge of the trading post. To their disappointment, they discovered that supplies at the fort were very low and contained nothing that their wagon train needed.

As they walked out through the walls of the trading post, Jacob told Martin, "Good ol' Jim Bridger. If he hadn't insisted on us topping off with supplies and adding extra, we might be in trouble. All I saw in the way of supplies were mounds of buffalo hides, fresh buffalo meat, piles of moldy jerky, and slabs of half-rancid bacon left by those who came before us to lighten their loads."

"I agree," said Martin. "Those poor devils have nothing we want and are a lot worse off than we ever thought of being. Not to mention, they are surrounded by hostile Indians, and I doubt many supplies they need will be getting through now that Chief Red Cloud is on the warpath."

As they passed by some tepees, Jacob noticed a lot of sick children lying around on blankets, softly moaning and crying. Martin grabbed Jacob's arm in alarm and said, "We need to leave this area. They have white man's sickness that makes them vomit the black liquid. We need to leave this area of death fast!"

Jacob remembered a time in the Wind River Mountains when a small band of Shoshone had been wiped out by the white man's sickness called cholera. With that in mind, he spurred his horse, and the brothers rode quickly back to their wagon train.

"Hook 'em back up!" yelled Jacob, circling his arm in the air to emphasize the urgency of his command.

"There is sickness back at the fort, and we need to leave the area fast," shouted Martin.

Both men bailed off their horses and began helping the others gather their livestock and hook them up to the wagons. In about thirty minutes the wagons were once again strung out along the trail, heading southwest along the Snake River.

Later that evening they came to a dividing of the Oregon and California Trails. Remembering Bridger's instructions, Jacob pointed the wagons toward the trail heading almost due south. After traveling about a mile, they found good grass for their stock and a small creek of fresh water. They circled the wagons near the creek and let the stock out to feed and graze below the camp. Some of the party began the laborious job of trying to find firewood on the wood-scarce plains. Not finding any wood, they finally gave up. Needing fuel for their fires, they began bringing in armloads of dried buffalo dung, which was now also getting very scarce, and sagebrush sticks. Soon several fires were blazing merrily away, and from the comer of his eye Jacob saw Dr. Larson coming his way with a worried look on his face.

"Jacob," Howard began, "I think we might have a problem. We need to have everyone boil their water before using it for drinking or cooking with it."

"Why is that, Doc?" asked Martin.

"What you described at the fort back there sounded like cholera to me. If that be the case, we need to make sure all our water is boiled so we don't come down with the illness. Plus, I took the time to walk a short distance upstream from our camp and discovered that another wagon train had camped there earlier. They may have fouled our drinking water, so now I think it best to boil all water used for drinking or cooking. That should help prevent infection if anyone on that earlier wagon train had or was coming down with the disease."

"Are you sure, Doc?" asked Martin, carefully examining the doctor's worried face.

"No, I am not dead sure. But from everything I have read over the years about the disease, it seems it is more readily found in filthy living conditions and around fouled water," Howard answered with a seriousness neither Jacob or Martin had seen in him previously.

"Well, I don't want that kind of trouble in our wagon train," Jacob said firmly. "Martin, you tell those folks to the south of the circle of wagons, and I will tell those to the north about boiling all their water. Be sure and tell them that those are orders from the doctor!"

The two men made fast work of their mission, and just in time. Several folks were already at the edge of the stream starting to pull up buckets of water so they could refill their water barrels! That evening around a communal campfire, Howard gave everyone a lesson in trying to keep clean and making sure they boiled their water before drinking, eating, or washing dishes. There was some grumbling about needing a cold drink sometimes, but Dr. Larson held firm, as did Jacob and Martin. Death was the only alternative if anyone chose to be careless, to their way of thinking.

The next morning Jacob and Martin took a ride around their camping area. There was plenty of good grass and water as long as everyone boiled it. They decided to stay the day so the women could do some baking and wash their clothes for the next week. For the rest of the day the men greased axles, repaired harnesses, checked oxen shoes, hauled in what wood they could find, boiled water, and gathered a small mountain of buffalo chips for their campfires. The women washed their families' clothing, draping it over the wheels, sagebrush, and wagon covers to dry. Then they began baking the next week's breads, and soon the circle of wagons was full of good smells. Jacob and Martin went into a nearby sagebrush draw and brought back two fat doe deer over their saddles for fresh camp meat to be shared by all. They had hoped for a buffalo, but ever since they had left Fort Hall and headed into the sagebrush country those animals had all but disappeared. In their place roamed the mule deer, elk, and pronghorn antelope.

That evening the people in the camp celebrated their day's labors. Jacob and Martin spent their time catching up with and getting to know their newfound kin, learning family stories and more about the history of their fathers and the two clans.

Daylight the next morning found the wagon train continuing southwesterly by way of the Raft River. When evening came, the tired travelers were treated to one of Mother Nature's surprises. A jagged rock formation, looking somewhat like a city made from rocks, appeared along the trail. Since grass was good about one-quarter mile off the trail, Jacob and Martin called a halt to their travels once they reached the good grazing. Circling the wagons, the men unhooked their oxen and let them mingle, feed, and water with the horse and mule herd. Two heavily armed men, Rich Grosz and Mark Webb, took the women and children back to the City of Rocks so they could see the phenomenon close up. On the way back they gathered up what wood and sagebrush limbs they could carry for fueling the evening's cooking fires. Soon the dancing fires cast many shadows on the sides of the wagons, making the evening near the City of Rocks even more surreal.

What made that evening even more magical were the stories told to Jacob and Martin about their fathers when they were young men working on their farms. These tales featured their hard work ethic and their ability to shoot the heads off running turkeys. Jacob and Martin smiled at the turkey story because they too were crack shots in their own right. The evening also made for many longing moments for the boys as they realized how much they had missed in growing up without their real dads.

The following evening the wagons stopped at Goose Creek, aptly named for the large numbers of Canada geese along its banks and in the flooded meadows. While their animals happily grazed in belly-deep grasses, several of the men went goose hunting, killing enough of the large birds for the entire camp to enjoy. Aside from the hordes of mosquitoes, which left many red welts on exposed skin, the travelers had a pleasant evening until about midnight. Then the skies, which had been foreboding for some time and were now jagged with yellow flashes of lightning, opened up, and everyone found their sleeping problematic. It was hard to keep the wagons dry in such a downpour, not to mention the almost continual loud cracks of thunder. The rain fell by the bucket, and soon the two men guarding the animal herd within the circle of wagons deserted their posts for drier places under the wagon tops. In the cool of the next morning, much to everyone's relief, the camp was almost free of mosquitoes. The coolness also reminded Jacob and Martin that they needed to keep moving for fear of winter's heavy snows closing the high mountain passes over the Sierra Nevada mountain range before they got there.

The following afternoon Jacob slowly moved the wagons into the Thousand Springs Valley. Stopping on a hill overlooking the valley, he heard the sound of a horse moving up on his flank. Turning, he saw Martin arriving, looking intently into the valley ahead.

"What's up?" asked Jacob, sensing that his brother was on to something.

"Elk," quietly advised Martin, not taking his eyes off the brushy area into which the elk had vanished. "Over there by that big patch of willows near the cut in the bank of the stream," he whispered. Unable to see the elk and not wanting to scare them any further, Jacob held up his hand, signaling the trailing wagons to stop.

"Lead off, brother," he murmured.

Twenty minutes later the two brothers lay on a stream bank overlooking a small herd of quietly feeding and resting cow and calf elk.

"You take that big cow on the right, and I will take that lead cow looking in our direction to the left," said Martin as he moved the Hawken at his side into a shooting position.

Boom—boom went the heavy rifles, and the small herd of elk fled in panic into the dense willows along the stream, leaving behind two fat cow elk kicking their last. After gutting the animals, Martin mounted his horse and rode back to the wagons for help and a couple of horses to help bring back the meat. Leading one pack animal loaded down with fresh meat, Jacob stopped to talk to Dave and Jerry, sitting in their wagons at the head of the train.

"Have the wagons move to those yonder hilltops overlooking the edge of the valley. That way we will be out of the mosquitoes a bit, and they can circle the wagons there. Plus that gives us a good look over the valley below in case any Indians appear. Then have several of the men, at least six, mind you, bring the livestock down into the valley to water and feed. Make sure they are heavily armed because Martin and I are unfamiliar with the area's tribes and don't want any trouble having our critters stampeded off," he carefully instructed.

Jacob led the pack animal to the bluffs where

the wagons were to circle and unloaded the elk. Heading back down to the stream, he and Martin loaded the rest of the elk and then headed back to the hilltop to unload so the entire camp could partake of fresh venison for their supper.

"That ought to fill a few cooking pots for several days," said Martin with a good feeling, especially because he had seen the elk before his sharp-eyed brother.

"Good eye, Martin. I always did know you would be good for something," Jacob said with a laugh, spurring his horse out of the way before Martin could get even.

The brothers rode back down to a quiet, secluded pool on the creek and took a welcome bath, scrubbing off with sand to rid themselves of their many days of caked-on dirt, sweat, grime, and the smell of horse sweat and musty odor of freshly killed elk.

However, secluded as they were, they had been seen!

Riding back to camp, they passed the men bringing the livestock down to water and graze. There was a lot of good-natured ribbing as the two groups passed. Arriving at the pile of elk meat, Martin cut out one of the tender back straps and took it over to the Martin Jones camp.

Kim met him with a smile, saying, "Is that for me?"

"Well, you and the rest of the clan," said Martin

with a nervous blush. Damn, he thought, I can't do anything around her without turning red!

The next morning the wagon train hit the California Trail early. To the northwest rumbled thunder from ominous black clouds still many miles away. Jacob knew the freshening wind told him they were going to get wet before the day was done. Looking over at Martin, he knew his brother's senses were also reading the weather and telling him the same thing.

They moved the wagon train into the Bishop Creek area near a grassy flat beside the creek, and not a moment too soon as the storm broke in all its fury, with howling winds, pelting rains quickly turning to hail, and lightning strikes just moments apart all around. Quickly moving to form a defensive circle, the men ran their livestock into the circle of wagons to avoid any loss from a storm-induced stampede. The travelers huddled in their wagons for what comfort they offered. Between the hard work of getting through the rugged canyon they had just traversed, the violent summer storm, no chance for a fire for an evening meal, and the hungry livestock milling nervously within the circle of wagons all night long, no one got much sleep.

The next morning the wet and tired travelers built several cooking fires from the dry wood scraps picked up the day before along the trail,

234 | TERRY GROSZ

which had been tossed into canvas tarps carried under each wagon box, and started breakfast. As the campfires crackled to life, many of the women and young children stretched their damp bedding and clothing over the wagon wheels and nearby sagebrush to dry. Several of the men herded the livestock out from the protective circle of the wagons and into a nearby pasture area to let the hungry animals feed so they would be ready for the day's heavy hauling.

"We best stay the day and let everything dry out and the animals feed heavy after that hard trip through the canyon. My guess is that they are pretty well spent and hoof-sore," said Jacob.

Martin nodded in agreement, as did Dave and Jerry.

"It would be no good to beat the animals who worked so hard yesterday and have not had a chance to graze until this morning," said Martin, looking at the threatening rain clouds still ominously poised overhead and flowing in from the northwest.

"I agree," said Jacob. "By laying off for the day, that lets everyone dry their bedding and cook ahead for the next few days. Also, we can cook up the rest of that elk meat and prevent it from spoiling. Let's canvass all the wagons and see if anyone has stock who are really footsore after traveling that damn rocky canyon. If we find any, we can tie them off in the creek's mud to cool them off. That will reduce their soreness, draw out the inflammation, and make them less foot sore down the trail."

"Hey, we are missing three horses!" yelled Mark Webb from his post guarding the horse and mule herd.

Jacob and Martin raced out to where the herd was grazing and counted the remaining horses. Sure enough, three good riding sorrels were missing! Without a word, Jacob took a scout one way outside the circled wagons, and Martin went the other direction, looking for telltale tracks that would tell them what had happened to the missing horses.

"Jacob, over here!" yelled Martin.

Griping his Hawken, Jacob walked calmly over to where Martin stood, not wanting to raise any more concern among the travelers than they already had. There they were—the muddy indentations of the tracks of three horses leaving the circle of wagons and heading out into the countryside. Without a word and with the curious shuffle-like walk he used when tracking something, Jacob took off cold-tracking the hoof prints. Close behind him was his brother, with his Hawken at the ready just in case they were surprised by the horse thieves. Hard as he tried, Jacob soon lost the horses' muddy traces less than one mile from camp because of the heavy washing rains from the evening before. But his mind was now whirling. The horses had been walking, judging from the distance between the hoof prints. They were not running as they would if they had been spooked and stampeded by the storm. Looking up at his brother, he saw that Martin had already figured out why the horses were gone as well. Back at the wagons, Jacob called an assembly of the party.

"Folks, we lost three good horses last night during the storm. Like the other night when the storm got so intense, those guarding the herd left for the dry of the wagons. That was when we apparently had visitors. Martin and I tracked the missing stock as far as we could but eventually lost them because of the heavy rains destroying even the hoofprint indentations. However, my brother and I do not think they stampeded off because of the storm. Jerry and Dave, having been here before, think they were taken by resident Paiute Indians while we slept!"

He could see the effect of his words had on the assembly. The women and young children were terrified at hearing they had had wild Indians among them, and no one had even noticed their presence.

"Back at Fort Bridger we were told that the Paiutes could not be trusted and that they were horse thieves of the highest caliber once we got to this part of the trail. So we will now double our guards wherever the animals go and will post double guards in camp every night. Martin and I will draw the first night's watch tonight and Dave and Jerry the second night down the trail. I feel they will be back for more stock since they made such a clean escape, and we need to stop them before all of us are walking," he continued with a smile, trying to lighten the moment. If the grim looks of his fellow travelers meant anything, his effort hadn't succeeded.

That night, after the fires had died down and the light had faded, Jacob quietly moved to one side of the livestock resting within the circle of wagons, and Martin moved to the other. For hours everything was quiet, and then Martin noticed one of the bell mules looking intently in his direction. Straining his eyes for a long time, he saw nothing until—there it was! It was just the slightest movement by one of the wagon wheels next to the animals. Quietly notching the arrow in his bow, Martin waited. Two more forms silently slipped into the circle of wagons behind the first one, heading for several quietly standing but now alert horses.

Zip—thunk went an arrow from Martin's bow into the standing dark figure not six feet from where he knelt partially hidden behind a wagon box. A scream erupted from the man as he pitched forward, gurgling his life's essence into the soil.

Boom went Martin's pistol into another fleeing form at a distance of less than four feet, illuminating the face of a heavily painted Indian in the muzzle flash. Another scream erupted from that man as the heavy pistol ball blew away his lower jaw. *Ka-poof* went Martin's second pistol as it misfired at the third fleeing figure. Boom went the heavy roar of a Hawken as Jacob, having also seen the creeping forms, crept around the outside of the circle of wagons in order to draw closer and back up his brother. Another fleeing figure struck the damp ground after being hit by Jacob's rifle ball, never to creep into a wagon camp or steal livestock again.

By now the wagon train was in an uproar! Men were shouting and women were screaming as the herd of livestock, scared by the shooting and smell of blood, anxiously milled about within the circle of wagons, creating even more chaos.

"Hold your fire! Everything is under control! " yelled Martin, not wanting to get shot by mistake by the aroused travelers.

Jacob, on the other hand, stayed glued flat to the ground until the uproar settled down and someone lit one of the campfires. Then the two men moved to the outside of the wagons to see if any Indians remained. Seeing no one, they ambled back to camp as if nothing out of the ordinary had occurred. Lying there under Rich Grosz's wagon was an Indian with an arrow thrust deeply into the base of his throat. His eyes, wide open in eternal surprise, said it all. The man Jacob had shot had not moved because the lead ball from his Hawken had blown through his chest and severed his spine. Meanwhile, the man shot in the jaw by Martin was lying on the ground, gurgling and trying to crawl backward as if that would help with the intense pain. Without a word, Martin bent over and cut the man's throat to put him out of his misery. Looking up, he saw Kim looking down on the savagery from the back of her wagon. For once Martin did not blush over his actions.

"It's all over," Jacob said firmly, trying to reestablish a feeling of normalcy. "Let's get our cooking fires lit, take on some grub, and, come first light, graze our stock for an hour or so before we move on."

Martin moved to his brother's side and quietly said, "Best we move on before the rest of the tribe comes looking for the ones we just killed."

Jacob nodded in agreement but said nothing, for the look in his eyes said it all.

As the camp swung to life and the intense moment passed, Jacob and Martin dragged the dead Indians into the willows along the creek—but not before cutting off their fingers once they were out of the rest of the travelers' sight. Those were tossed to the four winds for the critters to enjoy and to cause the dead Indians eternal grief as they tried to enter the Happy Hunting Ground, being less than perfect in form.

Walking back to camp, they headed for Daniel's cooking fire and poured themselves some just-warmed over coffee as if nothing out of the ordinary had happened. Margaret paused in preparing breakfast to give the two men a big hug of thanks.

There really is something to this family thing, Martin thought as he happily settled down by the fire with a grin while the blood of the Indian whose throat he had just cut was not yet dry between his fingers.

Chapter Twenty-One

THE HUMBOLDT RIVER AND TROUBLE

AFTER SEVERAL MORE long days of hard, dusty travel with scant good water that didn't taste of alkali, the wagon train finally arrived at the Humboldt River just west of present-day Elko, Nevada. For the next week the group traveled almost due west along the river, enjoying the abundance of water and fair grazing. Just off the river bottom were miles and miles of sagebrush, rabbit brush, rocks, deep dust pockets, more rocks, fleet jackrabbits, and little else. The large game animals had mostly disappeared except in small numbers along the river. The hunters took every opportunity when the game showed themselves to freshen up the wagon train's fresh meat supplies.

One night Jacob signaled the wagons to circle

in a large meadow. Martin, riding up from the tail end of the train, looked upon the deep green of the meadow with relief.

"Brother, we best hole up here for a day. The animals are finding it harder and harder to pull these wagons living off the rank grasses we have found to date," he said.

"I agree," said Jacob. "This here meadow has the best eats for our critters I've seen in the last ten days. I think we need to rest for a day and let the stock recover and let the folks repair their tack, grease the axle hubs, wash, and bake. According to the Halls, the route ahead has some pretty sparse pickings, so we better make the best of what this area has to offer."

"Damn, I've seen some pretty poor land these last few days, and what still lies ahead, if it's like what we just passed, isn't worth owning," said Martin.

Jacob nodded in agreement as he looked ahead as far as he could see and saw nothing but more sagebrush, rocks, dust devils, and shimmering heat waves.

Dusk found some of the weary travelers tending cooking fires while others returned from the river's edge, where they had washed their clothing and taken baths. Standing discreetly around the women at the river's edge stood six heavily armed men, watching the surrounding terrain for any sign of danger. When the women finished, the men washed in shifts, always leaving an armed guard alertly on the shore. They had seen enough fresh Indian sign throughout the day to make them wary. Later that evening Jacob and Martin held a council of war with the two old but still hardy mountain men. All four realized they were near a band of Indians on the move. They also realized that the sharp-eyed Indians had probably already seen the plumes of dust raised by the wagon train that was closely following them across the high desert.

"Tonight I want all our livestock except for the slow-moving oxen double-hobbled in case someone from that band gets a hankering for some good horseflesh," Jacob said, sternly.

"Jerry, why don't you and I take the first watch tonight and let my brother and Dave take the second one?" Martin suggested through a cold mouthful of yesterday's biscuits.

"Sounds good to me, and if I might make a suggestion, I say we load our rifles with buck and ball this evening. My shooting eyes ain't what they used to be, and that surefire mixture of lead can give man or beast a powerful gut ache," Jerry answered with a knowing grin.

"Might not be a bad idea," said Dave, "because if and when they come, there might be a passel of them red devils on top of us all at once, and it is a damn sight easier to get their attention if the air is filled with lead heading their way."

Jacob thought over the suggestions and then said, "Them is all good ideas, and I was thinking more or less along the same lines. I want all of us to carry two pistols along with our rifles for the next several days until we can lose this band of Indians. I also want all of you to personally contact every male member of the wagon train who can shoot and make sure they're sleeping with their shooting irons close at hand and ready to go in case something happens."

For the next several days all was quiet along the trail and within the circle of wagons at night. They continued to see large numbers of moccasin tracks and unshod-pony hoofprints in the alkali dust, but nothing out of the ordinary occurred. Finally the tracks of the traveling Indians broke south around a small, shallow water pan toward a distant range of mountains and disappeared from the wagon trail along the Humboldt River.

Moving along the northwest side of the waters of the Humboldt Sink, Jacob turned in his saddle and looked back. Each wagon was traveling out of line from behind the one directly before it to avoid the choking haze of alkali dust raised by the feet of the oxen and wheels of each preceding wagon. Far to the rear, beside the last wagon, was the dusty gray figure of his brother, alertly watching over their charges.

My, how love blinds one's vision, Jacob thought with a grin.

Kim and some of her family members were in the last wagon that day, and Martin faithfully stuck close to the wagon so he could visit with her. Each day the wagons moved up one place in the train and the lead wagon went to the rear so that the miserable traveling conditions of riding "drag" at the end of the line were shared equally.

Turning back in his saddle, Jacob continued smiling through gritty teeth as he looked for a spot to rest for the night that had some good grazing. Good grazing was scanty in that part of the desert, but he finally settled on an area beside a small, shallow pond where the animals could water and feed. Firewood was scarce, and the party would have to scatter among the nearby rocky hills to gather sagebrush limbs and roots for their evening's fires once again.

I'll have to break out some of my remaining sacks of wheat and oats to add to the oxen's feed this evening, Jacob thought. Otherwise they will soon lose too much muscle mass to be able to pull the wagons unless we find better grass.

Riding ahead, Jacob signaled with his raised arm to circle the wagons in the spot where he sat on his horse. Soon the wagons were circled as the men hustled to unyoke the oxen and let them feed among the sparse grasses as long as possible. The horse and mule herd was already grazing, and the oxen hurried to join in before all the good grass was gone. The women and children tumbled from the wagons to pick flowers, scrounge sagebrush firewood, and soak their bare feet in the warm waters and mud of the Humboldt Sink. The men were still heavily armed and set up a guard around the livestock or quietly stood near the women and their activities. Soon fire pits were dug, and any wood gathered during the day's travel along the trail was retrieved from the tarps swinging under the wagons. In short order fires blazed and coffee merrily bubbled away in blackened coffee pots hung on rods over the fire pits.

Groups of children scurried over the hills, picking up bits and scraps of wood as several groups of watchful men stood guard over those activities as well. As darkness fell, the men brought the livestock in from the meadows, and Jacob, Jerry, and Dave managed to grain all the oxen while keeping the other animals from helping themselves to the oxen's fare. The great smells of baking biscuits and many pots of cooking stews soon prevailed in the cooling desert air. Jacob, Dave, Martin, and Jerry settled around the campfire of Jacob and Martin's kin, and soon the fatigue of the day began to melt away, especially when Margaret served up large, golden-brown

Dutch-oven biscuits smothered in a heavy, gravy-laden venison stew. That was followed with a cup of scalding black-as-night coffee, and life was good.

After dinner the men gathered for their evening's assignments, and shortly thereafter Howard Larson's imported English pipe tobacco could be smelled around the inner circle of wagons. That was soon followed by the scent of strong-smelling cigars from Jacob and Martin's stores being smoked by the rest of the men who enjoyed tobacco.

The cool of the evening from the evaporating water pans in the Humboldt Sink quickly enveloped the wagon train. Cooking fires slowly died down into the orange eyes of coals staring skyward, and except for the nervous shuffling of the tired livestock, the camp quieted down for the evening.

Thump went the dull sound of a tomahawk into Jacob's cousin Bill's skull, killing him before he hit the ground in a lifeless, crumpled pile. This was sixteen-year-old Bill's first and last watch over the livestock.

At the front of the nearest wagon two Paiute braves reached for the back of the man mountain named Chris Grosz, who was watching the other side of the herd. The first brave, a large man himself, grabbed Chris's shoulder in order to pull him to earth and swiftly cut his throat with his knife. The Indian was surprised to grab something that felt as solid as a large rock. The rock whirled in an instant with the quickness of a cat, grabbed the brave, and broke his neck with a savage twist. The remaining brave's tomahawk thumped into the shoulder of the large man. Then it was taken from his hands, wrenched from the wound, and smashed into his forehead, spoiling his white-striped face with the rich color of his own fresh blood.

"Indians," Chris yelled as he grabbed his rifle, whirled, and broke his rifle stock over a third Indian rising from his position of concealment. In that instant, Chris had broken the Indian's back. Immediately after that, the man gurgled his last as Chris's knife cut his throat.

Moments before Bill had been killed, Martin and Jacob had been awakened by an increase in the shuffling sounds from the horse and mule herd. Realizing something was afoot, both men had slipped out from their sleeping furs and quietly awakened Dave and Jerry. Then they disappeared into the darkness on each side of the ring of wagons. Jacob drew first blood from an Indian reaching for the sleeping Amanda just as Chris yelled his warning. Grabbing the brave from behind, Jacob severed his spine with a brutal knife thrust in the back. Unseen by Jacob, however, another brave was quickly closing in behind him. Boom went a rifle from the back of Rich Grosz's wagon. Rich had neatly shot the assailant in the head from a distance of about three feet! By now, hell had no fury like the fast-awakening wagon-train members, leaping from their beds to the sound of many yelling Indians within the circle of wagons!

"Indians among the stock!" yelled Mark Webb as he cut one down with a shot from his pistol as the brave attempted to lead a horse from the inner circle.

Another Indian attempted to crawl up into Chris's wagon, only to have Chris's wife, Lisa, shoot him clear off the seat of the wagon with her shotgun. The close-in blast hurled him backward into the brush, dead before he hit the ground. Then everything dissolved into a dusty swirl of fighting, grappling men and milling livestock. For several moments all that could be heard was the heavy thump of rifles and pistols going off, the lighter thwack of tomahawks, and the zip sounds of arrows passing at too-close-for-comfort range.

Daniel managed to shoot an Indian who had a neck lock on his son, Jeremiah. That Indian dropped in his tracks, and not a moment too soon, as Jeremiah was immediately locked in mortal combat with another brave who made a fatal mistake in grabbing the stout farmer. Martin Jones and his three boys were all locked in a swirl of tomahawk-swinging Indians, which was soon broken up by the addition of Dave and Jerry. Only one Indian limped away from that part of the fight; he was found the next day, hiding in a thick stand of rabbit brush and slowly bleeding out. The hungry magpies and local desert ants had discovered what was left of his life and had already feasted.

Then it was all over, and aside from the many questions hurled back and forth as the travelers checked on each other, things began settling down. Soon sparks from old fire pits were rekindled with fresh wood, and the travelers surveyed the bloody scene.

Martin had been hit by a low-flying arrow that had passed clean through his cheeks, chipping a tooth in the process. At his feet lay two dead Indians, one killed by a pistol ball and the other by a knife in the throat. Jacob was unwounded except for a loud ringing in his left ear caused by Rich Grosz shooting over his shoulder and killing an Indian who was racing up to Jacob with an upraised tomahawk. That was a small problem, to Jacob's way of thinking. Bill had been killed at the beginning of the fight. Chris Grosz had suffered a deep tomahawk wound to his left shoulder that had slashed clear to the bone. At his feet lay three raiders who would raid no more. Jerry and Dave had each killed an Indian after they had left the fight at the Joneses'. They had caught two raiders racing for the outer circle of the wagons, each trailing a horse. The accurate shooting by the two old mountain men had been dead on the mark regardless of their constant carping that they couldn't shoot straight. Mark Webb had caught an arrow in his right thigh and a cut to his left hand when he had exchanged knife thrusts with an assailant. Despite his wound, Mark had hit his target. Martin's grandfather had been shot clean through his side, probably by a friendly shooter in the wagon train, but not before he had killed two raiders with his tomahawk and knife. Otis Barnes had killed one Indian as he had raced by with a horse on a lead rope and broken another's jaw with a right cross as that man had tried to help a fellow Indian escape. That Indian was soon dispatched by one of Martin's cousins, who took his scalp in the process. Marvin Clary never had to leave his wagon. Two Indians tried to come in the front and another in the back. All three died from close-in shots by a rifle, a pistol, and a scattergun wielded by the straight-shooting Clary.

A guard was posted, and as daylight began to break, the wagon train fell into cleanup mode. Dr. Larson was tending to the company's wounds as if such battles were an everyday affair. Jacob and Dave dragged the bodies of the Indians to a nearby gully to leave them for the scavengers, and everyone else tended to the business of getting ready to quickly move on from the bloody battleground.

Bill was sadly buried in a deep grave in the center of the trail yet to be traveled. The grave diggers laid stones in the last two feet of cover over him so that animals would not be able to dig up his body. A final layer of dirt covered the stones, and they finished by building a bonfire over his grave. When the fire had cooled, everyone said their good-byes and sorrowfully drove their wagons over the gravesite to disguise what lay underneath. A practice that was common with westward travelers so the gravesite would not be discovered and disturbed.

None of the livestock had been lost to the Indians, but one of the oxen had been killed by a stray arrow. Before the travelers left the scene, they took what meat they could use and then dusted the remains of that oxen with cyanide powder that they had brought along to poison wolves once they reached California. Then the sad and sore company turned their eyes toward the horizon to the west and never looked back — except in their hearts and minds over the years that followed.

Chapter Twenty-Two

TRUCKEE RIVER, NEVADA TERRITORY

JACOB AND MARTIN kept the train moving southwest on the California Trail, mindful of the rugged Sierra passes and their propensity to fill up with early winter snows. According to Jim Bridger, once they left the Humboldt Sink area, they would be looking at many miles of sparse grass and even scarcer good water. He had told them to maintain a west-by-southwest bearing, and after several days of hard travel, they would reach what he called the Truckee River—a river named by earlier pioneers after a friendly Paiute Indian chief. As they prepared to leave the Humboldt Sink, Jacob had everyone fill up every water container they had. The whole company spent the next day cutting any and all grasses they could find for the animals to eat the next day out from the sink. Since they had a full moon, Jacob suggested to Martin that they start in the evening and move through the cool of the night, following the existing trail. That way the livestock would be less apt to wear out in the drying desert heat.

Martin thought over his brother's suggestion and said, "By gum, you might be right. If we can do that, it would cut down on the water consumption, and with that, coupled with our cut hay and the last of our oats and grain, our animals should make it."

Jacob called a meeting of the men and laid out what challenges awaited them over the next several days on the trail. "Men, we are looking at forty to fifty miles of hard going with the prospect of little water and even less grass. We can beat the heat by traveling at night and resting during the high daytime temperatures. We must ration our use of water, saving it for the animals, because if they don't make it, neither will we. According to Jim Bridger who has traveled this way several times before, and the Hall brothers, there is a large river at the end of our trail through this inhospitable part of our travels. It is supposed to have good grass and lots of cool water without the alkali taste we have been used to because it is fed by the snows in the high Sierra Nevada Mountains. So plan on our normal evening meal, and then we will set out on this difficult part of the trail. Are there any questions that come to mind before we leave?"

None of the men raised any issues because they were all familiar with the trials to date on the trail and had come to expect more of the same in order to reach California.

"Good," said Jacob. "Let's fall to on any remaining chores and be prepared to leave tonight once the cool has set in."

The men broke ranks and headed for their wagons to make ready for their first experience of nighttime traveling. Groups of women and children quickly gathered and, accompanied by a few heavily armed men, spread out over the surrounding area in order to gather what wood they could. That was now especially important since they would not be able to find any fuel while traveling in the dark and resting during the day.

Looking back over the wagons, Jacob turned his horse down the trail toward where the Truckee River was supposed to be, with Jerry's wagon following. Soon the train was strung out with Martin riding alongside the wagons, making sure they kept up and stayed together. He kept a tight rein on their formation because he didn't want them to straggle too far apart and thus be more vulnerable to another Indian attack. He had no way of knowing that the hostile Indian band had feasted on the remains of the poisoned ox that they had left behind, and many of them would never again attack a wagon train...

For the next four nights the tired oxen plodded along the trail, resting and eating as they could during the heat of the day.

The wagon train's travelers struggled in the dark over the broken trail. They tried to rest during the day's heat and kept looking to the southwest with hopeful eyes for the promised Truckee River and their salvation.

Toward the end of the fifth day, the horses and mules became even more alert than usual and started eagerly moving ahead of the wagons as if they knew something no one else did. Jacob's horse also perked up and kept his head raised, even though he was tired and thirsty, as he continually looked to the southwest. Trotting ahead of the wagon train, Jacob soon saw a cut in the rugged desert terrain with a river lying in the bottom. Racing back to the wagon train, he alerted those driving the oxen to hold their reins tightly.

"Hold them tight and don't let them get their heads, or they will break for the water and wreck the wagons!" he yelled.

The horse and mule herd, controlled more loosely than the oxen, eventually broke for the river and disappeared in a cloud of dust. The drivers held the oxen, and when the train approached a flat along the river, they were unhitched and let loose to drink their fill along with the rest of the livestock. A number of the people jumped into the cooling waters of the river with shouts of joy. The more reserved just took off their shoes and soaked their feet in the cool waters in relief at having arrived safely. After an hour of celebration along the river, Jacob and Martin made everyone hitch up their oxen teams and circle the wagons in a defensive position along the river. Then the oxen were once again released to feed under a heavy armed guard.

That evening there was much celebrating. The women had a chance to do their washing and cooking as the men made repairs to their tack and wagons. There was plenty of cottonwood timber along the river, and soon campfires burned hot and brightly. The air was laced with the great smells of baking bread, biscuits, and steaming pots of bacon and beans, intermingled with the smell of several boiling coffee pots.

"Well, you did it, brother," said a smiling but still dusty Martin.

"Last time I looked, we both had our hands in the pot," said Jacob as he smiled back at his brother.

Margaret came over to the two boys, gave

them each a hug, and told them to get washed up because supper was ready. Dave, Jerry, Martin, and Jacob walked to the river and cleaned themselves as well as they could, enjoying the cooling waters for the first time with great relish.

"Tomorrow I suggest we stay here and rest up our stock and let them feed to their hearts' content. Me, I plan on riding up the river to a settlement that is supposed to be within a day's ride of here," Jacob said, referring to a community that became the town of Reno in 1862. "According to Jim Bridger, this settlement is a supply center for the silver mines in the Virginia City area. If that be the case, I will scout to see what they have in the way of supplies, and when our wagons arrive several days hence, we can head straight into the emporiums and resupply so as not to waste any travel time. I am still fearful of those rugged passes over the Sierra Nevada Mountains and don't want to leave my bones there because of being slowed in our travels. In the meantime, I want the three of you to watch over the camp. Make sure everyone's wagons are repaired and cared for. Also, have the men check the shoes on their livestock. If some are badly worn or need replacing, get it done. The mountains ahead will give us our toughest challenge, so I want everyone to be ready to go. We are racing the arrival of winter, and I don't want to get caught in the mountains or on this side of them come winter."

The three men nodded in agreement, realizing that the real challenge was yet to come and they had best be prepared or they would leave their bones in view of the lands of California.

The next morning, long before daylight, Jacob saddled his horse, packed some jerky, and headed along the Truckee River toward the settlement and the adventures it would bring.

Arriving at midday, Jacob looked upon a sprawling boom town of brightly painted mansions and crude log-and-mud huts along with false-fronted commercial buildings trying to look more imposing than they really were. These were interspersed with tent villages all jammed together, indicative of the rapid growth and temporary nature of the community. Melded into that view were the sound of barking dogs, the crack of teamsters' whips, the firing of guns into the air by drunken miners, the din of blacksmiths' shops hammering iron, and a million other assorted noises that were foreign to his ears after the many quiet weeks on the trail.

Stepping over garbage, the contents of chamber pots strewn in the dusty streets, and animal droppings were crowds of people. Everyone seemed in a hurry to get somewhere. Jacob finally reined his horse up in front of a large sign reading, "ROSE AND ERNIE EATON'S EMPORIUM—dry goods, ammunition, whis-

key, medicinals, patent medicines and notions."
Tying his horse to the hitching rail, he entered
the store. There before his eyes lay all the goods
anyone could want! Boxes, bags, kettles, jars,
barrels, and sacks were strewn about in an organized confusion, containing what had to be
all the world's treasures, he thought. Walking
across the uneven wooden floors created from
using green, uncured lumber when building in a
hurry, Jacob became aware of the smells of stale
cigar smoke, the cheap perfume worn by some
busily shopping ladies of the night, and the odor
of many unwashed bodies.

With a tired smile, he thought that the whole
movement of humanity among the store's goods
reminded him of a bunch of maggots on a three-
day-old buffalo carcass in the prairie sun.

"May I help you?" came a pleasant voice
from a middle-aged woman with a mischievous
twinkle in her eyes. She wore a bright red apron,
and at her waist hung a skinning knife. From the
looks of it and her hands, it had been used very
recently.

"Yes, ma'am," replied Jacob. "I will be bringing a small wagon train into town shortly. They
are camped a few miles out and are getting ready
for a trip across the Sierras. As near as I can figure, we will need some supplies such as flour,
salt, pepper, stick candy for the kids, cornmeal,

bacon, sewing needles, feed grains, horse and oxen shoes, and such."

"Well, sonny, you came to the right spot. This is the largest place of commerce this side of the Missouri River, and we have more goods coming in every week by wagons from back East. So what we don't have today, we may have tomorrow," she replied happily. "My name is Rose Eaton," she added as she extended her hand in friendship. "My husband, Ernie, and I own the place and we pride ourselves on providing most everything needed with a smile and the lowest prices to boot in this here settlement."

Jacob shook her hand and said, "Pleased to meet you, ma'am. My name is Jacob. Is there someplace nearby where a man can circle his wagons and still have walking access to your place of business?"

"You are in luck, stranger," she replied. "Ernie!" she yelled.

Soon a man lean as a ridgepole stepped out from behind a stack of boxes he was inventorying and walked over to Rose wearing a smile that was more than genuine.

"What do you need, honey?" he asked as he patted her bottom with a grin.

"Don't you get fresh with me, Ernie Eaton," she replied, but with a look of approval. "Take this man out back and see if his wagons will fit in our back pasture behind the store," she ordered.

"Yes, dear," he said as he turned and headed for the back of the store—but not before playfully patting Rose on the backside once more. This time he had to duck a broom hastily swung by the object of his affection.

Not wanting to get a swat from the broom as well, Jacob quickly ducked and followed Ernie out the back door. Directly behind the store was a thirty-acre grassy lot that would more than satisfy the needs of his wagon train and provide the necessary feed for his livestock for a short time as well.

"What be the charge to use your lot for a few days, friend?" asked Jacob.

"Nothing," replied Ernie, "if you buy your supplies in our store."

"That be fair," replied Jacob. "I plan on having my group here sometime in the next couple of days. Once here, we can begin shopping in earnest."

"Where you be headed?" asked Ernie as the two men walked back to the store.

"Somewhere in California where we can farm, raise cattle, and start a family without the thought of Indians lurking around the next corner wanting to lift our hair," he replied.

"Well, that sure be the place. Most Indians there are what Californians call Digger Indians, and they is fairly peaceable. The soil is good, from what I hear, and the weather fairer than most places," Ernie answered.

"Sounds just like where we want to set down our roots," Jacob said with a grin.

Back in the store, Jacob purchased several items, and Rose wrapped them up in plain brown paper, tying them off with butcher's twine.

Stepping back outside onto the wooden walks, Jacob noticed a place of business just across the street. The white sign with red lettering on its false front read, "LARRY DAVIS GUN SHOP— Gun Repair, Ammunition, Edged Weapons, Purveyor of Fine European Firearms, Powder, Primers, Beaver Traps and Such."

My brother and I need to visit that place, Jacob thought. There are many new types of firearms that don't require reloading every time one has to shoot that we could use. That may be the way to go in the future, especially in this new land where we have to deal with white varmints instead of red ones.

Getting back on his horse after tying the wrapped items behind the saddle in his bedroll, Jacob spurred the animal back toward the wagon train. It had taken him less time than he had expected to size up the settlement and locate a place to resupply their depleted stores and a place to circle his wagons. This place sure has more to offer than Fort Hall, he thought with a smile as he rode east into the oncoming dusk.

Back at camp, Jacob was guided in by the light from several still burning cooking fires. Stepping off his horse outside the wagons, he was immediately challenged by the camp guard.

Recognizing the voice of the challenger, Jacob replied, "It's just me, Jerry."

Walking into the circle of wagons, he was met by Martin and Dave as well. All three had a ton of questions about the town until they were interrupted by Margaret saying, "You men leave him be. He probably hasn't had a dam thing to eat all day and is tired. You will just have to wait until I get him fed before you ask him all those dam-fool questions." With that, Margaret took Jacob by the arm and marched him over to her cooking fire. She sat him down on a log and gave him a cup of scalding coffee. She was right—he had been so eager to get to town that he had forgotten to eat. Then he had been so eager to get back to camp with his news that he had again forgotten to eat anything. Now he realized just how hungry he was and smiled not only at her actions but at all the motherly attention he was getting as well.

"Margaret," Jacob whispered.

"What?" she said as she returned to the cooking fire with a full plate of biscuits and freshly cooked venison from a deer one of the men had shot earlier that day along the river.

Jacob handed her one of the wrapped pack-ages he had brought from town with a smile on his face.

"What is this?" she said as she took the package after laying down his plate of food on a nearby wagon tail gate.

"Well, open it and see," Jacob said with a grin.

When she opened the package, several long tails of brightly colored cloth tumbled from the package; they were attached to a light pink sun-bonnet in the newest style, decorated all over with yellow, red, orange ,and blue flowers.

"Oh, it's beautiful!" Margaret gasped. "May I try it on?"

"Well, I would say so, once you give me my supper to eat," he joked.

Margaret hurriedly gave Jacob his plate and then, like an excited little girl, took the bonnet and put it on over her tousled hair.

"Oh, Jacob," she said gleefully, "I will be the prettiest lady in the train."

Happy his present was so well received, Jacob signaled Martin, who was standing nearby, to come over to him as he hungrily wolfed down a biscuit.

"What's up, Jacob?" Martin asked.

Reaching behind his log, Jacob picked up an-other package and handed it to his brother.

"What's in the package, Goose?" Martin asked.

"Oh, just a little something pretty. That is, if you had a little gal in mind to give it to," Jacob replied with an impish twinkle in his eyes.

Martin, without a moment's hesitation, took the package and headed straight over to Martin Jones's wagons to see Kim.

God didn't raise a turnip in that lad, Jacob thought with a grin.

Next he signaled Jerry and Dave with a "come here" jerk of his head.

"Here, you two. Don't ever say I am always forgetting you," he said as he handed each man a large package containing several pounds of fresh, rich-smelling chewing tobacco.

"Hot damn!" said Jerry as he recognized the luxurious smell coming from the package.

Dave didn't dally a bit. Ripping open the package, he took out a huge wad of the fresh chewing tobacco and stuffed it into his mouth until he looked like a big chipmunk with a cheekful of seeds heading for his burrow.

"Thumph, boff," said Dave.

"He is saying, 'Thanks, boss,'" said Jerry, also stuffing his mouth with the fresh chewing tobacco as he headed back to his guard post. Once his mouth was full, he turned and gave Jacob a thumbs-up sign of thanks.

Kim and Martin walked into the light of the cooking fire. Kim was wearing a bright red apron with ruffles like Rose Eaton had been wearing earlier in the day.

Smiling from ear to ear, Kim said, "Thank you, Jacob. That was very sweet of you for getting me this. It is very beautiful, and my favorite color too."

"You need to thank Martin," he replied. "It was him that suggested I bring you back a play pretty." He lied, but it was just as well because Kim once again looked dotingly at Martin as they walked away from the circle of wagons and down towards the river.

Finishing his supper, Jacob put the dishes into the pan of wash water; then, taking his last package, he walked over to Rich Grosz's wagon. The inside of the wagon was dimly lit by a candle. As he drew closer, Jacob could hear Rich reading to his wife and kids from the Bible.

"Anybody home?" Jacob asked in a subdued voice.

"Sure are," responded Rich. "Come on over."

Walking around to the back of the wagon, Jacob said, "Good evening, all."

"How was town?" asked Rich.

"Crowded, noisy, smelly, people and barking dogs everywhere, and wonderful all at the same time," Jacob replied as he looked over at Amanda with a smile.

She returned his smile in such a manner that Jacob almost forgot why he was there.

"Rich, I found a small thing in the store I was in for Miss Amanda. I wondered if it would be all right with you and your wife if I gave it to her?" asked Jacob.

The look Rich gave back would have leveled a grizzly in a charge if his wife, Carrie, hadn't broken the spell with "Well, why, yes. It was so nice of you, Jacob, to remember her when you were in town."

Still not daring to look directly at Rich, Jacob handed Amanda the last package. She shyly opened it to find a beautiful dark blue heavy wool shawl for the upcoming fall and winter in the nearby Sierra Nevada Mountains.

"Why, Jacob, it is beautiful!" she said as she tried it on.

The shawl hung over her shoulders beautifully, and Katelyn, her younger sister, and Carrie had to finger its fine quality.

"Well, I have to make my rounds and meet with Martin, Jerry, and Dave to see how things went while I was gone. Excuse me, folks." Jacob strode off into the cool night, glad to be away from Rich's intense, disarming stare.

Daylight the next morning found the wagons rocking along the banks of the Truckee River as they headed for town and what laid beyond. Because of the close confines of the riverbanks and the nearby rocky hills, the travelers had lunch without circling the wagons as the livestock grazed and happy laughter rang throughout the Truckee River campsite.

Pushing the wagons hard, the company arrived in town at dusk. Jacob headed over to Rose and Ernie's Emporium and requested guidance on how they wanted the wagons placed in their back pasture. Soon the wagons were circled in the large pasture, and the livestock had been turned out to graze quietly. Campfires were built with the cottonwood limbs picked up along the river trail en route to the settlement, and soon numerous good cooking smells prevailed. After supper was over and the chores were done, everyone turned to getting out their best duds for the morrow's trip into civilization. Some folks even quietly washed up in their wagons in preparation for the big event. However, Jacob and Martin had much on their minds as they sat by a campfire wondering between themselves about the rugged trip over the Sierras that lay ahead. Neither looked forward to that part of the trip as they remembered Jim Bridger's words of caution about the early winter snows and rugged trails they were soon to travel.

They didn't realize that Jim Bridger's reputation had preceded them and that there would be good news for the wagon train when it came to crossing the Sierras...

Chapter Twenty-Three

TRUCKEE RIVER, NEVADA TERRITORY

EARLY THE NEXT MORNING, the wagon train's travelers streamed out of their protective circle and went their separate ways as they explored the settlement and what it had to offer. However, Jacob and Martin went directly across the street and into Larry Davis's gun shop. Entering, they smelled the familiar odors of gun oil, cleaning solvents, wood smoke from a badly leaking stove at the rear of the store, and the strong smell of cigar smoke coming from a tall, rugged-looking individual working behind the counter. The man, who appeared to be a gunsmith based on the work he was performing on the lock of a rifle, was being watched intently by a dark-skinned, medium sized grizzled man who appeared to be the rifle's owner. The rifle was a well-used and somewhat abused Hawken, similar to the ones Jacob and Martin carried.

"Damn, Jim, I think you have done it this time. You just have to shoot straighter in the future at the griz instead of trying to club him to death with what used to be a fine rifle. The lock is really messed up this time, and I don't have the parts to fix it. In fact, I don't even have the right kind or temper of iron to build you another hammer and flat spring," stated the gunsmith as he shook his head over the poor condition of the well-used rifle.

"Wagh!" replied the man with the broken rifle. "That there smoke pole is the only thing that will kill that damn griz with one shot if'n he is hit right!"

The two boys took a closer look at the man with the broken rifle. He was a dark man, but not as dark as Cain. Maybe he was a cross-breed, Jacob thought. He had long, unkempt hair that flowed past his shoulders and wore buckskins that were somewhat the worse for wear. He was shod with beaded moccasins with beautiful Crow Indian beadwork and carried a long gutting knife in his much-decorated belt, along with a large-bored, single-shot pistol. Jacob and Martin thought he had the look of a well-used mountain man.

"Be with you two boys in a moment once I get rid of this here ring-tailed twister," Davis said with a grin of admiration for the man standing before him.

"No hurry," said Jacob. "We will have a lot of questions for you once you're finished with your customer because it looks like we'll need a lesson or two on some of these here newfangled firearms in your display cases anyhows."

"I won't keep you from good business, Larry. Just hand me 'Old Meat in the Pot,' and I will be on my way," replied the mountain man.

"How the hell you goin' to defend yourself or kill some eats if your rifle doesn't work for a damn, you old poop?" the gunsmith shot back.

"Don't rightly figure. Maybe sell off some land or some livestock, but sure hate to part with my Hawken. It has seen a lot of trails and saved my hide many times," the other man replied, running his fingers lovingly along the scarred barrel and stock.

"Maybe we can help," said Jacob right out of the blue, surprising even his brother.

The two men looked over at Jacob and Martin.

"We both shoot Hawkens, and if I am not mistaken, we have a keg of Hawken parts back at our wagon just in case we broke our rifles. Got them from Fort Bridger afore we came west," Jacob explained.

"Fort Bridger!" yelled the mountain man. "You boys seen or knowed Jim?"

"Yes," said Martin. "He is an old family friend and our friend as well."

"Well, I be damned and turned inside out like a beaver hide. How is the old crapper? Is he still aboveground and well? When did you seed him last?" The questions flew from the mountain man as fast as a rainbow trout striking a grasshopper flopping on the surface of a cottonwood-fluff-covered beaver pond.

"Whoa there, old-timer," said Jacob. "Them's more questions than we have had to answer in a passel of days."

"Jim Beckwourth here," said the mountain man as he held out his worn hand for the boys to shake. "Any friend of Jim's is a friend of mine. Who might the two of you be?" he asked, looking both boys in the eyes intently as if trying to remember their identities from his long-ago travels on the beaver trail or at one of the Rendezvous.

"We be Jacob and Martin from the Wind Rivers," said Jacob.

"Holy cow!" said Jim as he slowly sat down on a keg of broken gun parts. "Be your namesakes from your dads? Jacob, a white man from Kaintuck, and his partner, Martin, a Delaware Indian from the same ground, and both as mean and as big as a he-griz in rut?"

Both boys felt a shiver go down their spines, as if someone had just dumped a cup of snowmelt water down the backs of their buckskins.

"That be us," Martin answered slowly while Jacob just looked at the man in disbelief.

"Hell, I met the two of them first time in '33 at the Horse Creek Rendezvous. And it goes without sayin' we tipped many a tin cup of old top-knot remover celebrating our friendship. Even helped the two of them out of a scrape or two with the Indians. In fact, the two of them went to the Wind Rivers to trap with my good friends Tom and Albert Potts. Them Potts brothers was killed by Blackfeet, but your dads cleaned out the whole damn nest of killers in revenge, if'n I have my facts right. Then we met once again in '34 at Ham's Fork on the Green for a rip-snortin' good time at that rendezvous. They had two of the prettiest damn Snake Indian wives at that rendezvous, if'n I remember the facts right. Must have been your mas. Saw them two boys again in '35 at Horse Creek on the Green, and they had you two along, but just as little guys. Then your dads teamed up with Leo and Jeremiah, two boys they had bought out of a life of slavery from the Utes years before. By then them two boys were full-fledged mountain men and free trappers. The whole kit and kaboodle went back into the Wind Rivers, and your dads and moms was kilt in the spring of '36 by the damn Blackfoot or Gros Ventre, if'n my memory don't fail me. It also seems them two boys, Leo and Jeremiah, tracked down and avenged your folks by killin' the whole nest of hostiles who had murdered your folks."

Neither boy dared to move or breathe for fear of breaking the spell of history flowing from Beckwourth's lips. He was covering history that dovetailed with what Leo and Jeremiah had told them as youngsters. It was as if a small window had been opened and the boys were wonderfully allowed to look back into their past.

Jim, noticing the shock registering on the boys' faces for the first time, stopped and said, "You boys all right?"

"We're fine, Jim. Just a little startled at meeting someone who knew our families before they were killed and who could give us a fresh look into our pasts like you have just done," Martin replied quietly, as if not wanting to break the spell.

"I am sorry if'n I have opened up the hurt on you two boys over what I just said. Many folks who know me say I have a big trap, and most of that which comes out one can't hang their hats on. But as God is my witness, what I spoke of here today is to the best of my memory," Jim said with a serious look. "Say, how be them two adopted boys of your folks, Leo and Jeremiah? Now, them was two ring-tailed twisters. Some of the best shots and trackers I ever did seed. They was as gentle as baby rabbits and just as mean as full-growed griz if'n you cornered them or hurt their kin. Now, them two were real men of the mountains. How they be and where do they be?" asked Jim as he finally ran out of questions.

"They both be dead, and their wives as well," said Jacob slowly. "They was killed by a raiding party of Lakota out by Fort Bridger way, but not before they killed a passel of them Indians. Then Martin and I cold-tracked those still living after we got back from our first buffalo hunt and killed all of those Indians from that raiding party still left alive."

"Well, I be damned! I am sorry to hear that. This country sure can be rough on a body even if he is on the lookout for the trouble that comes with the wonder of it. But from the sounds of it, you two boys sure be of their stock," Beckwourth said as he carefully looked Jacob and Martin over closely.

There was a long moment of silence, and then Jacob said, "Jim, what you said here today opens up more memories for us and gives us additional details on the lives of our folks afore the Indians killed them. So don't be ashamed for what you said."

"Damn, boys, them was some good folks and always treated me as an equal even though I come from half-slave and half-Indian stock myself. If'n there is anything I can do for the two of you, you just let old Jim know," the older man said with a big grin.

"Well, for now, I think there is something we can do for you. I am sure we have the kind of parts fer that Hawken you need and would be glad to part with them for old times' sake," Martin said with an answering grin. "Especially for a friend of our parents."

"That would be one hell of a help. Man can't get around in this country without his smoke pole because of all them varmints, man and critter alike. I sure would be obliged fer the help," Beckwourth responded.

"Mr. Davis, will you be open later on in the morning or tomorrow?" asked Jacob.

"Sure am planning on it," the gunsmith replied, "unless the good Lord takes a likin' to me in the dark of the night and comes alookin' fer me."

"Good," said Jacob, "because me and my brother will probably have some business with you in the area of some of those newfangled pistols that shoot more than once before having to reload them. There also appears to be several of them new Sharps rifles in the corner we might be interested in as well."

"That be fine with me, but just be aware you have mentioned several of the most expensive firearms in my whole shop," Davis replied with a serious business look on his face.

"If they do the job, that is fine with us regardless of the price," Martin answered.

The two boys and Jim left the gun shop and headed back to the wagon train. Jacob and Martin were surprised at what awaited them there. As they rounded the corner of their wagons, Jim stopped dead in his tracks, then sprinted over to their campfire and picked up Jerry Hall from behind. With that, he flung him down to the ground in a heap of dust and dried horse manure left behind by previous campers.

"Jerry!" yelled Beckwourth, "you old scudder and leaky bottom of a whiskey barrel, how the hell you be?"

Jerry scrambled to his feet, preparing to do battle before he quickly recognized the face of his old friend. Soon both were talking and laughing as fast as they could. The noise level only heightened when Dave rounded the wagon with an armload of wood for cooking. When he saw his old friend with his brother, the sticks flew into the air, and soon all three men were talking and slapping each other on the backs like the long-lost mountain-man friends they were.

Jacob and Martin looked on in amusement. After things had calmed down a bit, Martin went to one of their wagons and brought out a small keg of the hell-for-stout uncut Kentucky whiskey they had purchased from Jim Bridger. It didn't take long for all who imbibed to get a little loose in the wheels, so to speak. However, cooler heads prevailed, and soon Jacob was digging around in their barrel of spare rifle parts. Spotting what he needed, he retrieved a complete lock-and-hammer system for a Hawken, with a spare set thrown in for good luck in case Jim had to whang another griz on the head with the business end of his rifle.

"Chris," yelled Martin, "how about a hand over here?"

The man-mountain blacksmith and gunsmith ambled over and, after hearing about Jim's problem, took his rifle and examined it. Soon he had the new lock installed and working properly. Then Chris was into the whiskey cups with the rest of the men, and a grand time was had by all.

"Jim, why don't you stay the night with us and partake of some great home cookin'?" asked Jacob.

"Don't mind if'n I do. That is, if'n it won't be a burden on you good folks," replied Jim.

"Not in the least way. That is the least we can do for a man who is a friend of the family," replied Martin, smiling.

"Then by gum, you will have an eager eater as your guest this evening," said a happy Jim Beckwourth, still a little deep in his whiskey cups.

At dinner, Jacob introduced Jim to Daniel and Martin Jones. Soon the whole clan was quietly listening to the story Jim had to tell about his time with Jacob and Martin before they were killed in '36. There were tears in a lot of eyes after Jim finished. But there were also proud looks in Daniel's and Martin Jones's eyes as Jim spun more and more tales about their two dead sons. It was like a whole new, wonderful world had been opened for the two old men.

After supper and storytelling time, things began to quiet down in the wagon train. Then Beckwourth asked of the little group still sitting around the campfire, "Where you boys headin'?"

"Well, we don't rightly know at this point. Just somewhere in California where we can farm and ranch in peace without looking over our shoulders all the time for hostiles," responded Jacob. The cigar smoke rolled lazily over the heads of the men as the question and answer hung in the cool night air for a moment.

"I know a place where there is room for everyone in this train and where cattle are growing fat as I speak. The place I speak of is one in which folks can grow corn, beets, spuds, onions, grain, apples, and the like. There is plenty of water, the four seasons are not too harsh, and there are only the friendly and poor local Indians running around. They might steal a cow, pig or chicken once in a while but nary a thing more," Beckwourth said.

"Where might this piece of milk-and-honey land lie?" asked Jacob with more than passing interest.

"Over the lowest pass in the Sierras. One I discovered myself, and a few days' easy ride west from here," Beckwourth replied, aware of the change in tenor and tone of Jacob's voice.

"Are you saying we can avoid the rugged passes in the Sierras, go over a lower one, and a few days later be in such a place in California?" inquired Jacob. He wasn't the only one interested in the answer if the intent looks on the others' faces said anything.

"Sure do, and it is only a few days' easy travel to this pass and then home to more land than anyone would want," Jim quietly replied.

"Jim, this ain't one of your windy tales you spoke of earlier, is it?" asked Jacob.

"No, I would never do that to the sons of my dear departed friends. What I speak of is a high mountain valley a few days' ride from here with more than enough room for everyone to farm and raise cattle and their families in peace. An area full of pronghorn antelope, rolling fat mule deer, great-tasting elk, good grasses, plenty of water, and soil that will grow most things, and a griz or two thrown in for the spice they offer" Beckwourth answered seriously.

"How do you know of such things?" asked Jacob, now very serious as he stepped into his role as wagon master.

"Because that is where I have my ranch," said Jim with quiet emphasis.

"How much land are we talking about that might be available?" asked Jacob.

"At least twenty thousand acres of farm and grazing land and another area like in size of forested land, if n anyone is interested," Jim replied with a twinkle of anticipation in his eyes.

"How did you come to find this place?" Jacob asked again.

"Because the place I speak of was deeded to me by the king of Spain and authorized by the Spanish governor Vallejo before the Californians won their independence. He did so for my service to the Spanish crown as an explorer," Jim answered proudly.

"But that is your land," said Jacob.

"That is right, but those are the lands I would be willin' to sell to you good folks if n that is what you want. I am growing too old to farm and ranch such an expanse of land. So I would be willing to sell off a large amount of it to get out from under so much work. Then I might like to retire on a smaller ranch that I also own near Grizzly Creek at the west end of the valley I call Sierra," Jim explained. "Plus, I would be surrounded by newfound friends and a ready-made market for the lumber produced from my mill for new houses, barns, fences and such."

"Sounds good to me, but I would have to present your offer to the people of the wagon train and see what they think," Jacob said, feeling very excited but still very much under control.

Looking over at his brother, Jacob could tell Martin was excited at the prospect of such a piece of property as well. Especially one so close at hand that did not include a difficult trip over the dangerous Sierra Nevada Mountains during the fast-approaching winter.

The next morning there was a colder-than-usual chill in the air and a timely dusting of snow in the Sierra Mountains lying to the south and west. How prophetic, thought Jacob as he called the men from the wagon train together so they could hear Jim's offer.

Jim covered the same ground he had spoken about the evening before with Jacob, Martin, and the Hall brothers. The only extra things he threw into the conversation were the price of the land at fifty cents per acre, which could be paid off as the crops came in, and over several years' time. And he mentioned that he had a small sawmill along Grizzly Creek that could produce lumber for the building of homes and barns. Then, as if just remembering, he said there were two additional mountain valleys lying just to the north of his lands, Clover Valley and Squaw Valley, that would be available for the raising of cattle or dairy herds as well.

Many questions flew from the gathered men, but most seemed to be very interested in Jim's offer in light of the land's closeness, the fair price, and the easy mountain pass through which they would have to travel. The one nagging question most had was where the nearest markets would be for their crops and beef cattle.

"This settlement we are in right now is still growing by leaps and bounds. Then there is Virginia City and several smaller towns called Truckee, Sierraville, American Valley (Quincy today), and Mormon Junction (Portola today). "All of them would be nearby markets for your crops and cattle."

He also pointed out that their first couple of years would be spent breaking the ground and raising seed crops, so most production would be self-consumed. After that time, there would surely be better and closer markets for their crops and beef. Beef especially would be in demand in the small towns springing up in the surrounding areas where gold and silver were being mined because the miners had shot and eliminated so much of the wildlife in the surrounding areas. Jacob and Martin could tell that Jim's offer excited the men. They as a group, were happy at the prospect of ending the trip and getting on with their lives.

The next day, after the camp had slept on the offer and mindful of the approaching winter, the closeness of the proposed destination, and trail-weariness, they took a vote. To a family, everyone decided to join with Jim Beckwourth and head west to his lands of promise. Then the work and preparation in the wagon train truly began in earnest for the final leg of their trip.

Chapter Twenty-Four

CALIFORNIA BOUND!

JACOB AND MARTIN led a delegation of travelers from their wagon train into Rose and Ernie's Emporium the next day at daylight. As everyone gawked at all the available wonders, Jacob and Martin waited for Rose to finish with a customer.

"Good morning, Rose," Jacob said to the lady with the red apron when she came over to them.

"Good morning, Jacob. What can I do you in for?" she answered with a smile.

"These good folks are part of our wagon train and have need for enough supplies to last until we can return in the spring and resupply. They will need the usual staples as well as stock tack, buffalo robes if you have any, and notions for the ladies and kids," said Jacob.

"That be fine with us, Jacob. And how do you to propose to pay for this world of goods your folks will more than likely need?" asked Rose in a business-like tone.

"My brother and I will pay you in gold," Jacob said quietly.

"Then let us get down to the brass tacks and gather up what these good folks need. That plus we will have some fair ideas of our own based on past needs of wagon-train travelers going to California.

"Ernie," she yelled, "get your carcass out here. We have a passel of good folks here who need a pile of what we have to offer and have just a short time to get it thrown together."

"I am on the way, dear," Ernie replied as he entered the store. "Where do you folks want to start?" he asked, and the shopping began.

As Jacob and Martin left, they noticed store prices at $4 per barrel for flour, sugar at $1.50 per pint, coffee at $1 per pint, bacon at $.01 per pound, and so on. Waving Jerry and Dave over, Jacob told them to get what would be needed to last them throughout the winter into spring. Then, as an afterthought, Jacob said, "Make sure that list includes at least ten buffalo robes if they are available, and thirty pounds of chew." Those last words put grins on the faces of both the grizzled old mountain men.

Jacob and Martin headed back to Davis's gun shop across the street. They found Larry behind the counter working on a broken pistol. Walking over to the gunsmith, the boys greeted him and asked if he had the time to show them some of the latest firearms. Getting up from his workbench, he pushed his glasses back onto the top of his head and without a word headed for the back of his shop. Once there, he reached into a closet, pulled out two heavy-barreled Sharps rifles, and handed them to the boys for examination.

"That is the latest in rifles, boys. Them are Sharps rifles, weigh about nine and a half pounds each, and will shoot a 500-grain bullet a thousand yards, according to some," Davis informed them.

Both boys hefted the rifles, and it was an instant love affair. As they shouldered the rifles, they got huge grins on their bearded faces. Both men were not only very strong but larger than most men of the day, and for them, hefting such rifles was child's play. Their weight and arm strengths were a perfect match for the heavy rifles. They laid the firearms on the counter as Jacob said, "We will take these and two more of the same caliber if you have them."

Davis rustled around in the closet among other firearms, brought forth two more of the heavy-barreled rifles, and laid them on the counter as well. "This is all I have, boys. The first two are

.50-caliber, and the last two are .45-caliber. But all of them are sound as a blacksmith's hammer."

"We will take all four of them, Mr. Davis, but you will have to teach us how to load and shoot them since we are used to our Hawkens and these appear quite different," said Martin.

"That won't be a problem. I have a shooting range out back, and I can show you boys how they operate, but you are quite right. They are totally different from your old Hawkens, which are still good shooters, but you will find these far better, more accurate and faster to reload," Davis responded.

"Now," said Jacob, "how about giving us a look at them pistols over in that display case?"

"I can see you two appreciate good firearms. Them is my latest acquisitions just in from back East. Them is Colt Walker pistols. They are .44-caliber, six-shot cap and ball, and weigh in at four and a half pounds each. Heavy enough to bang someone over the head once you run out of shots if need be."

Hefting the heavy handguns, Martin got a huge grin and said, "Now, that is a pistol with more than just a little sand, to my way of thinking."

The look on Jacob's face said the same thing as he also lifted the new firearm.

"Mr. Davis, my brother and I will take two of these if you have 'em," said Jacob.

"Damn, boys, you are about to clean me out of my new stock of smoke wagons!" Davis replied, happy at what the sales would bring him before it was all over.

"With the addition of these, we will need bullet molds for every caliber and several extra in case we lose or break them. Then we will need a large stock of powder for each weapon, extra cleaning rods, caps, extra cylinders, and anything else you deem we will need," said Martin.

"One thing you will need is a pile of linen cartridges for the Sharps and some bullet pullers in case of a misfire," said Larry as he began calculating what would be needed with the purchases.

Minutes later the three men went out behind the gun shop, and the boys began learning to shoot their newest acquisitions. After about thirty minutes of shooting and reloading, they were more than satisfied and proficient with their new weapons. They shot straight, reloaded easily, and aside from the normal amount of fouling due to the standard use of black powder, they were superior to anything they now carried.

Back inside the gun shop, Davis continued to gather up accessories for the weapons.

Martin and Jacob each took a Sharps and one of the Colt Walker pistols, and after telling Larry they would be back to settle up with him, they went down the street to a leather shop. There they ordered scabbards to be built for the rifles and belts and holsters for the big Walker pistols. Then the two men walked back to their wagon and, digging under a bunch of empty feed sacks and furs, took out a large tube-like poke of the gold nuggets they had mined so long ago in Clear Creek Canyon.

Walking back to Davis's, the two men quietly waited for Larry to cipher what the costs would be.

"Well, boys, hang on to your hats. This here pile of smoke poles and all the things that go with it comes to $320.00. Now, I know that is high, and if you want to pay for the lot on time your credit would be good with me," said Larry.

Without a word, Martin took the poke full of gold nuggets and began spilling them onto Larry's counter. "Stop us when you figure we have our bill paid," said Martin.

Larry just looked on in amazement at the golden hoard spilling over his counter and finally said, "Whoa, boys. That appears to be more than enough! Let me put a scale to 'em before you go any further."

Taking the front of his dirty apron, Larry formed a pocket and scooped the gold off the counter into it. Then he headed for his gold-weighing scale in the back room. Jacob and Martin followed, and after a time Larry handed back a handful of nuggets that exceeded the bill owed by the two men.

As they put those nuggets back into the leather poke, Davis said, "I don't know where you boys got that poke full of gold and don't want to know. But I would suggest you keep your hoard and the location of your diggin's out of sight and out of mind, if'n you get my drift."

Both boys nodded at Larry's words of wisdom, and then Jacob said, "Mr. Davis, are you saying all that firepower you just sold us isn't any good in a fight?" with a smile on his face for the joke he intended.

"You boys may be big and damn good shooters, but a shot from the dark of an alley here in this town is a great equalizer," Davis said with grim emphasis.

Jacob, feeling chastised, grew stem and said, "You are right, Mr. Davis. After we settle up with the Eatons we will be on our way with Jim Beckwourth, and hell will follow anyone who decides to tail our wagon train for the gold it may still carry."

The rest of the day was spent moving their firearms back to their wagons, picking up their new leather gear for the weapons, and loading up the mound of supplies from Rose and Ernie's Emporium. Then it came time to settle up with the Eatons.

Jacob and Martin walked into the emporium and headed for the back room as Ernie gestured for them to follow. In the back room, out of sight and mind of the public, Ernie was finishing up his tally of goods procured by members of the wagon train.

"As near as I can figure, you boys owe us $1,897.60. If you would like a breakdown, I can have that for you in about an hour," he said.

"That won't be necessary, Mr. Eaton. You and your wife appear to be fair people, and we don't suspect you are out to cheat us since we will be lifelong customers if we settle where old Jim wants us to," replied Jacob. "Pay the man, Martin," he instructed his brother. Martin began spilling gold nuggets onto the counter from the elk-leather poke.

Ernie's eyes grew big as saucers at the hoard of large gold nuggets spilling over his counter and running over onto his sawdust-covered wooden floor.

"By the God eternal, where did you boys get such a hoard?" he asked.

"We mined them near Fort Vasquez when we lived there," said Jacob as he studied the questioner closely, looking for any evil intent in the question.

"Holy cow!" exclaimed Ernie as he began gathering up the nuggets in amazement. "I will need to get my scale in order to get a proper figure on what you boys have dumped here. It looks like too much, but I will need my scale."

He began quietly weighing out the nuggets at $16 per ounce.

"There she is, boys. We are even, and you still have some left over," Ernie stated.

"Now," said Jacob, "we will be leaving in the morning with Jim Beckwourth for his ranch. I would be obliged if you and the missus didn't take that pile of gold to the bank until we are long gone so someone doesn't get the idea from whence it came and come looking for it."

"Count on it, boys. Nary a word from our lips will be heard," said Ernie seriously. "Besides, Rose and I have a big iron safe downstairs where we put our valuables. That is where your gold will go and be used over time as our needs dictate. 1 wouldn't want to lose such good customers," he continued with a genuine smile of friendship.

The men shook on the deal and left the store for their wagon train circled out back. In short order they informed everyone that they would be leaving the next morning at daylight. Then the men were all gathered around and told the bill had been paid with gold nuggets. Jacob and Martin explained that if word of the gold got out, they would probably have a handful of ruffians hot on their trail. Because of that, each man would remain heavily armed and alert to anything out of order until they made it to Jim's Sierra Valley. Stern faces told them that the word was well received and the orders would be carried out to the letter. Then, to a man, everyone thanked Jacob and Martin for their generosity in supplying the train through the coming winter months. It was at that moment that the brothers finally understood what Jim Bridger had told them about the brotherhood and family of a wagon train and why it was so important that they be alert to their people and travels. It now also became very obvious why their dads had valued Jim's friendship so highly...

≈⊙≈

AS JACOB SAT on his horse beside Jim Beckwourth, waiting for the wagon train to get under way, he saw his brother walking toward him. Beckoning for Jacob to lean over, Martin whispered, "We still have over six hundred pounds of gold nuggets and all the golden ingots our parents saved for us. I think that will be more than enough to build our future ranches and have some left over for me to see that big pond everyone calls the Pacific Ocean."

Jacob smiled as he watched Martin walk back into the predawn darkness around the wagon train, mount his horse, and take his position alongside Kim's family's wagon.

"Jim, we are ready to go. Lead the way," said Jacob.

"Wagons, ho!" shouted Jim and started to move out of the settlement heading north.

Soon the wagons were spread out in a long

line and moving easily behind Jacob and Jim. Leaving town, they climbed up some rolling hills and onto a huge sagebrush flat as they continued northerly. The travel was not difficult, as they followed another well-used wagon trail, and soon it was midday. Then the wagon train was filled with voices warning that a stagecoach was coming by. Within a moment and in a cloud of dust, a three- span pulling a grand Concorde Stage sped by, leaving a cloud of dust amid the jangling of harness chains from the teams of beautifully matched horses.

అఱ

AFTER TWO FAIRLY EASY days of travel, Jim abruptly swung the wagons off the well-beaten trail heading them onto another one, less well traveled, heading into some higher, rolling sagebrush hills to the west. As expected, the oxen had to work hard for the earlier part of that day getting up over the hills. Then all of a sudden they crossed through a low pass and into a huge mountain valley lying to the west.

"Stagecoach, ho," came numerous shouts from the wagon train as another stage, this time a Mud Wagon, a type built for rougher trails, came alongside the wagons as the driver walked the horses up the east side of Beckwourth Pass. Once on top, the driver's whip cracked and the three-span of horses leaned into their collars as the Mud Wagon picked up speed. It only went a few miles along the trail before them and then turned south into a large stage station built from rock to change the horses and rest the dusty and weary travelers.

The wagon train crept along on the trail heading west until late afternoon. Then Jim Beckwourth moved the train out into a large meadow to the south where a stone walled, artesian well was spewing clear, cold water high into the air for all to see. Circling the stoned-in well site, the wagons made ready for the evening.

"Jim, what a great place to stop," said Jacob.

"I know," Jim replied, beaming. "We now are at the edge of my ranch, and soon we will view a small, wooded mountain range where we will stop and see if your people are interested in settling down in the area just passed or if they wish to move on into the Sacramento Valley to a town called Marysville. That is at the end of the Beckwourth Trail, one that I blazed many years ago as a fur trapper."

A pleasant evening was had by all, but they could tell that winter's nip was in the air. Around the campfire after supper the five mountain men talked far into the night. Jacob had decided that he would continue with those in the wagon train who wanted to move into the Sacramento Valley, farther west. Martin, Dave, and Jerry would remain behind to help those who wanted to take Jim up on his offer and make a new life in Sierra Valley. Jacob would return after helping the other group reach its destination and make his new life on Jim's ranch as well. From what he had seen, the area was perfect for farming and raising cattle.

Jacob thought he would like to make his new home here with his brother, and he hoped Rich Grosz and Martin Jones would do the same, for obvious reasons...

During the next day of travel in Sierra Valley, the men often walked alongside the wagons, gathering handfuls of soil and slowly letting it flow through their fingers as they evaluated its quality. Others rode short distances from the wagon train, looking over the abundant water supplies and grazing prospects for future cattle operations. They were amazed at the quantity of pronghorn antelope, elk, mule deer, sage grouse, black-tailed jackrabbits, and golden eagles that they saw as they moved along the dusty trail.

On the second day of easy traveling through the valley, the wagon train came to a range of pine-forested hills at the west end of Sierra Valley. Since it was well into the afternoon, travel was called to a halt by a small creek coming from the mountains to the north named Grizzly Creek. On the northeast side of Grizzly Creek and the north side of the Middle Fork of the Feather River, most of the wagons circled for their last time together.

Wood was hurriedly gathered from the forest floor, and soon many cooking fires were ablaze. They filled the cool evening air with the smell of pine smoke and hearty meals cooking.

"We will rest tomorrow and let the stock graze and the women wash and cook," said Jacob as he helped load a pack horse for Jim to take to his home cabin several miles from where the wagons now stood.

"Thank you for the supplies, Jacob, and I will see you tomorrow morning. Maybe your folks can talk about staying or moving on this evening," said Beckwourth.

"We will have the coffee pot on, partner," said Martin as he slapped Jim's pack horse on the rump to get him started. Jim rode off into the rapidly settling dusk toward his nearby cabin and his Crow Indian wife.

Around ten the next morning the men gathered near a central campfire, sitting on several logs. Their wives and children stood close behind so they could hear the discussion on whether to settle in Sierra Valley or move farther west into the Sacramento Valley.

You could cut the tension in the air with a knife, thought Jacob as he surveyed the scene.

Serious looks were on all the men's faces as

Jerry, Dave, Jim, Martin, and Jacob took center stage.

"You all know why we're here this morning," began Jacob. "We have had a chance to look over the valley as we crossed it to see if it would suit us for our future homes. There appears to be much here to satisfy anyone who wants to farm or ranch cattle. There is good grass, the soil appears to be tillable and fertile, there's game galore, there's timber for the taking to build our homes and barns, and water doesn't appear to be an issue. Jim has made what I consider to be a fair offer, and he has a small working sawmill on Grizzly Creek that can turn out any amount of lumber we might need if we stay here. The only thing I can see that remains is to make a decision to go or stay. And if you stay, what part of Jim's ranch you wish to buy. For those who wish to move on and see what is on the other side, Jim and I will lead you to a town in the Sacramento Valley called Marysville. There you will no longer have to travel in a wagon train but move among your own because that is as civilized as it gets. So that is about it.

"Now what I would like to do is go around to each of you men in the group and see just what you want to do. For those who want to move on, we will leave tomorrow because winter is coming and we need to get you across the remaining mountains to lower elevations. For those who wish to stay, we have to get cracking and get our winter homes built and prepare for what Old Man Winter will throw our way. I would like to start with Daniel and his clan."

Without hesitation, Daniel said, "I have talked to all my clan. We wish to stay in this valley and begin anew. It appears to hold everything we would ever want and then some."

Looking over at Martin Jones, Jacob said, "What say you, Martin?"

Martin, like his grandson, was a man of few words. "We all wish to stay as long as the payment timetable for the lands is reasonable," he said.

"Doc, what are your wishes?" asked Jacob.

"Well, I am not a farmer or cattleman and must make my living taking care of sick people. This group is healthy as a bunch of horses unless we run into a band of Indians, it seems. My wife and I would like to move on to the town called American Valley, which, according to Jim, is just a few more days' travel on the Beckwourth Trail to the west," Howard said, referring to the present-day town of Quincy. "That way I would have enough patients to make a living and eventually raise my family."

"Okay, Otis, where do your interests lie?" asked Jacob.

"I think I would like to explore Clover Valley and Squaw Valley to the north and see what they be like. If they are half as good as this ground, me and my family would like to settle there. Thataway, we won't be crowding these good folks wishing to settle here," he replied.

"Marvin," Jacob asked, "what are your druthers?"

"Jacob, I am inclined to look at the other two valleys to the north with my cousin Otis. If they be good lands, me and my family will settle there as well."

"Chris," asked Jacob, "how about you?"

"'Pears to me this valley and the nearby town of Mormon Junction could use a good blacksmith and gunsmith. Me and my family will settle here somewhere along Grizzly Creek if those lands be available," Chris replied with his usual big grin.

"Rich, what about you and your family?" asked Jacob, scarcely daring to hear his response.

"I plan on settling along Grizzly Creek as well. Someone needs to keep an eye on my younger brother," Rich said with a smile directed toward Chris.

Jacob's heart sang with those words. Now maybe he would have a chance to court Miss Amanda properly if he could somehow win over her stem father.

"Mark, what are your druthers when it comes to settling here or moving on?" asked Jacob.

"We plan on settling here in this valley. The soil looks good to me, and the grass will help me raise some cattle. Plus, the hunting looks good here in the valley and thereabouts, so here is where we will make our new home."

"Well, that leaves you, Jerry, and your brother, Dave," said Jacob turning to face the two old mountain men.

The brothers looked at each other, and then Jerry rose and said, "As long as you and Martin will put up with two old men waiting to die, we would like to stay with you two and live out our lives wherever you decide to light down."

"That settles it, then. Otis and Marvin, you two need to ride to Squaw and Clover Valleys as soon as possible and see what you think. I will escort Howard and his family to American Valley so they can settle in at their home. As for the rest, you need to pick out your new home sites and settle up with Jim. Then everyone will fall to cutting down some of this fine pine and fir timber so we can all pitch in and build our winter homes before the snow flies," said Jacob, still mindful of his responsibilities as wagon master.

Turning to Martin, he said, "And you, my brother, can wipe that goofy smile off your face. You will be doubly tasked in helping Martin Jones and his clan get settled in and ready for winter."

Martin continued to smile knowingly.

The following morning, Howard Larson and

his wife said their good-byes to the people of the wagon train, and Jim and Jacob took them to American Valley. Once there, Howard rounded up some carpenters and began building his family's new home on some recently acquired property on the American Valley Ranch home site. The next day, Otis Barnes and Marvin Clary saddled up two horses and a pack animal. With a wave of their hands, they headed over the mountains toward where Jim had directed them to Squaw and Clover Valleys.

When Jacob and Jim returned from getting the Larson's settled in American Valley, they learned that Otis and Marvin would settle in Squaw Valley and begin their lives anew. However, for the coming winter, they chose to live close to everyone else and planned to wait until spring to build their homes and livestock barns in Squaw Valley.

For the next three weeks, Sierra Valley hummed with the sounds of its new inhabitants. The sounds of double bucksaws and axes rang throughout the hills adjacent to Grizzly Creek. Whips cracked as the settlers urged their mules and oxen to lean into their traces as they pulled cut and limbed logs down to a central log deck. Women and children cut mounds of hay from the meadows to be used in the caulking of the cabins and for winter livestock feed. Jim's sawmill, operated by Maidu Indians, with its water-powered circular saw whined sixteen hours a day, cutting green Ponderosa pine and Douglas fir lumber for roofs, doors, and windowsills. Soon the men gathered at each homesite and began cutting and notching logs to length for the cabins and barns. With as many willing hands as they had, they discovered they could build a large family cabin and modest barn in two and a half to three days! Soon everyone had a new, freshly caulked cabin in which to live through the oncoming winter. Then they moved the wagons and livestock into the new barns and corrals and all the dry goods and staples into the cabins from the covered wagons for safekeeping from the weather and animals.

Then the woods rang once again with the sound of axes and double bucksaws as the men began cutting and hauling dead, dry timber so each family would have a winter's supply of fire-wood. Once finished with that chore, into the hay meadows went the men with their wagons to cut more hay for winter storage in the lofts of their new barns. There they discovered rich mountain hay belly-deep to their draft animals. Last but not least, hunting parties led by Mark and Rich went into the valley and forests, and soon many deer, elk, and pronghorn were harvested and carried back to their settlement for processing into jerky and other smoked and brined meats. Jacob and Martin, with their new Sharps rifles in tow, hunted the length of Grizzly Creek and into Clover Valley for any black and grizzly bears not yet in hibernation. Seventeen fat bears fell to the men's new rifles, and the guns were deemed superior even to Larry Davis's fitting description.

Jerry and Dave Hall hauled the bears back to the home sites in wagons, and the women rendered the fat out into some fine cooking oil while the hams were smoked for winter and the hides dried and tanned for trade at nearby Mormon Junction. They finished all their hurried activities on a Saturday, and a celebration was planned for the next day. After a church service led by Daniel giving thanks, the cooking, feasting, and celebration of the travelers' good fortune on their new lives began.

After everyone had eaten more than they should, Otis and Marvin broke out the fiddle and banjo, and the festivities got lively as everyone danced far into the night. Martin and Jacob were even able to dance with Kim and Amanda, although only two dances each. It seemed that many of the other younger single men wanted to dance with the two pretty girls, so Jacob and Martin had to wait their turns. Finally the fires burned low, and everyone, exhausted from many days of hard labor, retired to their cabins. The next day, they awoke to a foot of freshly fallen snow and temperatures in the upper teens.

Walking out to feed his horses, Jacob was pleased. They had beaten the dreaded winter snows in the Sierras by one day!

Chapter Twenty-Five

THE SACRAMENTO VALLEY, THE PACIFIC OCEAN, AND SAN FRANCISCO

WINTER PASSED QUICKLY that first year in the valley, with everyone using their time to make new clothes, shoe livestock, repair weapons, prepare equipment for the spring plowing, hunt game, trap, and break the ice on Grizzly Creek each morning so everyone could have fresh water.

Finally enough grass pushed through the cold spring soil in 1858 that anyone traveling would have good horse feed along the way. With its arrival signaling the end of winter, Jacob sat down with Martin, Jerry, and Dave one morning after a breakfast of biscuits, honey, and bacon.

"I think we need to make ready and push on down to Sutter's Fort in the Sacramento Valley, as Jim suggested last year. While there, we need to purchase some bulls, cows, and hog brood stock for our ranches. That way we can support our farming with the addition of livestock and have lard on the hoof instead of hoping the bear population holds out in the fall so we can render their fat," said Jacob. "We also need to talk to our neighbors and see what they might need from civilization since what Mormon Junction has to offer is really very little and very high priced due to all the mining activity in the area. Unless you guys think differently, we could also make a trip to the ocean so Martin can realize a dream he has had all his life. Then we can travel back to Sutter's Fort, pick up our stock, and, according to Jim, go on to the hog farm near the town of Marysville to purchase some brood sows and a few boars. By then things will be blooming all over the place, and we can trail our critters back over the mountains to our valley." Jacob looked at his companions for their thoughts as he sipped his second cup of scalding coffee.

"Fer certain, Jacob? We going to see the ocean?" asked Martin, very excited.

"Well, what the damn hell did you think when we started moving West? That we was coming way out here to go to a church social?" Jacob replied with a grin.

Martin smiled, but immediately followed it with a frown. "How long we going to be gone?" he asked.

"Reckon it will take us about two months of hard riding, looking, and dickering about prices for our cattle and hogs. Then we have to purchase wagons and our next year's supplies plus hire some extra hands to help move our stock back here to our valley. Suppose it will then take about another two to three weeks to wind ourselves back to here over the Sierra Mountains on the Beckwourth Trail," Jacob answered.

Before Martin could chime in again with his thoughts, Jerry spoke up. "Jacob, if'n you two don't mind or need us, we would like to stay here in the valley and get ready for your return. The both of us are so stove up after the long ride out here and our creeping age that we would only slow you down if n we went with you. Besides, that will give us a chance to build more corrals, fix up our barns proper-like, and work on our cabins."

Jacob thought for a moment and then said, "That will be all right. It will be a long ride to all the places we want to go anyway. We can hire some cowhands to help bring the herds of cattle back. Then we will hire some Mexicans to drive our new high-walled wagons full of pigs once they are purchased at Sutter's Hock Farm."

The relief was as evident on Jerry's and Dave's faces as was the concern still on Martin's. Still mindful of the dance before the winter's snow and the hard time he'd had in getting to dance with Kim, he said, "Will we have a few days before we go, Jacob?"

"I would like to leave in a day or two, if possible. That should give the two of us time to visit the ladies and let them know we will be back shortly. And ask them to hold good thoughts for us and our travels," Jacob replied, mindful of his feelings for Amanda as well.

The next two days flew by like the wind. Every chance Jacob and Martin had outside the preparation for the trip, they were at the sides of Kim and Amanda, promising a quick return. Even Rich Grosz and Martin Jones seemed to realize the situation and gave the two mountain men the opportunity to visit their daughters as much as possible.

The evening before Jacob and Martin left, the four mountain men dug up some of the pokes of gold nuggets that had been cached in the floor of their cabin. Once they had a supply for their trip, the wooden box still held at least five hundred pounds of nuggets and all of the golden ingots their parents had left them. It is a fortune to anyone s way of thinking, thought Jacob as they shoveled dirt back over the box containing the golden metal that made men mad.

The next morning, Jacob and Martin had breakfast with their two ladies. The women were trying hard not to show any concern, but the tears in their eyes betrayed their feelings. It was obvious that during the long trip from Fort Bridger to Sierra Valley, the men had won the hearts of the girls as well as those of their parents.

Mounting up, both men shook the hands of Rich, Martin Jones, Dave, and Jerry and then hurriedly turned their horses and pack animals away as they headed for the town of American Valley some thirty miles away. But not before hugging two very concerned young ladies.

Pulling into American Valley later that evening, the two men stabled their riding horses and pack mules in the local livery. Then, shouldering their rifles and pokes full of gold nuggets, they headed over to Doc Larson's house. They spent the evening getting reacquainted and enjoying a wonderful meal provided by his wife Mary Ann.

Before daylight the next morning, the two men mounted up and headed down the Beckwourth Trail toward their first stop at Bucks Ranch. There they holed up for the night, sleeping in a bunkhouse with the snoring and smelly hired hands. Again rising before daylight, they headed down the mountains toward what was called the French Hotel, some twenty miles farther west. There they had a bath and an evening meal of bear steaks, biscuits with homemade blackberry jam, and a hot apple pie fresh out of the wood

314 | TERRY GROSZ

stove. Following their routine, they were again gone before daylight en route to Peavine Ranch, some nineteen miles away. There dinner consisted of a piece of meat later discovered to be porcupine, one stale biscuit, and a cup of black coffee that could have floated a mule's shoe! After a restless night's sleep in the barn, the men were awakened by the tinkling of many small silver bells. Hurriedly getting dressed and peering out from the barn, they saw a mule train of about forty-five animals stopping in front of the ranch. Four mule skinners were hurriedly unloading numerous packs from the mules and spreading some of their wares out on the ground for the now arriving local groups of fellow ranchers, miners, and woodsmen. The first shopper in line was the wife of the ranch's owner, and soon great smells began emanating from the open kitchen door. These aromas foretold better food soon to come than the previous night's fare. Soon Jacob and Martin were treated to fresh trout, fried eggs, pan-fried spuds, biscuits, and coffee that tasted like real coffee, all courtesy of the mule pack string and its supplies fresh from the large mining town of Oroville.

Leaving the Peavine Ranch behind, the two men continued moving down the ridge trail until they arrived at what was known as the Mountain House some nine miles away. Observing ap-

proaching storm clouds and fearing a wet afternoon on the trail, they stopped and had a lunch
that was one of the best meals they had eaten in
over two years! Much to their surprise, five miles
down the trail, they were so sick from eating apparently tainted food that it soon had them bail-
ing off their saddles and running at both ends!

Stopping after making only fourteen miles
and weak from their bouts with food poisoning,
the brothers holed up at the Berry Creek House,
going to bed early in the adjoining bunkhouse.
Come daylight, they awoke famished because
they hadn't had anything to eat that had stayed
down since their lunch the day before. At the
breakfast table they discovered flapjacks by
the small mountain, homemade jams of several
kinds, fried ham steaks, small mounds of spuds
fried in bear grease, biscuits, and coffee that was
out of this world. They fell to and soon could
hardly move. However, they did find room for a
wonderful freshly baked blackberry pie, consuming the whole thing between them at one sitting!

Finding themselves at the Mill House some
eight miles from the Berry Creek House around
noon and discovering that it was the last eating
house before Oroville, the men loaded up on
what that establishment had to offer. Realizing
they were possibly headed for a night on the trail,
Jacob and Martin purchased some cold fried ven-

ison and biscuits to take along. Then they headed toward Bidwell's Bar, a wild gold mining camp on the Feather River. Arriving late at night, they boarded their animals and then, not trusting the local hell-raising, drunken mining inhabitants, slept in the barn with their stock.

They were awakened the following morning by the cracking of whips and jingling of many horses in their traces. Rolling out from their buffalo robes, Jacob and Martin were surprised to see a Concorde Stage rolling to a stop in front of their livery. It was being pulled by a three-span of good-looking but heavily sweating horses and was loaded to the gills with people, including a number who rode on top of the coach with the luggage. Soon the area was alive with stagehands unhooking the team and leading another team of fresh horses into their traces for the eight-mile run to the next stage stop. The change was accomplished in a very short period of time by a practiced stage-stop crew.

"Load up!" shouted the shotgun as the passengers began stumbling from the stage-stop kitchen with cups of spilling coffee and buttermilk biscuits in hand. Soon the stage was nothing but a cloud of dust, jingling trace chains, and a memory swaying up the road toward Hearts' Mill for the official breakfast stop, still some eight miles away.

Saddling their horses and repacking their mules, Jacob and Martin led them to the tie-up in front of a clapboard shack doubling as an eatery. Walking inside, they were met with the smells of overboiled coffee, burned biscuits, and meat frying in a pan without enough grease. Martin and Jacob just looked at each other, turned around, and left. Fishing out some jerky, they rode away from Bidwell's Bar on the trail toward Oroville. A short way down the road, they were confronted with a suspension bridge crossing the Feather River. Never having ridden across such a swinging contraption, they dismounted and walked their nervous horses and mules across before remounting.

Later that evening the men pulled into the booming mining town of Oroville. Even at that hour, the scene was a madhouse. There were gas lights flickering everywhere, sounds of off-tune, clanking pianos emanating from each saloon, streets crowded with noisy or drunken miners, and the occasional smell of Chinese cooking, which was foreign to their senses. Mingled with that was the smell of human offal and animal manure thickly deposited in the streets and the sounds of barking dogs, squealing pigs running loose in the alleys being kicked by an angry miner, wagons moving to and fro, and loud, happy sounds coming from all places selling liquor.

Grinning at such exuberance, the two men pulled into Jason's Livery, which happened to be across from Ma French's Boarding House and Eatery. Giving the liveryman a dollar to curry down and grain their animals, the men took their saddlebags and leather pokes of gold nuggets and carefully walked around all the manure left by the mule and oxen trains going to the mines, across the street and up the steps to the boardinghouse.

"That'll be fifty cents for each of you for one bed," said a bored, half-asleep clerk after Jacob inquired about lodging.

Not having any coin, Jacob laid down a small gold nugget, which the clerk's greasy hand instantly plucked off the counter so he could eye it for authenticity.

Satisfied, the clerk said, "That'll be room 101 at the head of the stairs and to the left."

"Where can a man get some good eats at this time of the night?" said Jacob.

Pointing to an open door to the left, the clerk said, "Through that door is some of the best grub in Oroville."

Thanking the man, the brothers entered an eating area and took a seat at a table. They soon were visited by a Chinese waiter who told them the only thing available from the kitchen this late at night was bacon, eggs, warmed-over spuds, and coffee.

"That be fine with us," said Jacob. "Oh, and by the way, can we have a bottle of whiskey?"

The waiter nodded and soon returned with a bottle, glasses, and their silverware.

As they drank whiskey from dirty water glasses, Jacob said, "Brother, we must find a place to cash in some of our gold for money. I don't like the idea of giving away our nuggets for the attention it brings. Plus, I am not sure what they are worth and if we are being taken advantage of."

Martin nodded as he took a long pull of whiskey from his water glass and then refilled it from the bottle.

"Right now, brother, all I am interested in is some grub and a couple of quiet hours in bed to get rid of this flattened-out saddle feeling from my last part over the fence," Martin replied with a grin.

"I know how you feel. Right now I feel like I am married to the backbone of my horse," Jacob replied, grinning as well.

Early the next morning the two brothers visited the Pacific Bank and Trust on Third Street. Spilling out about five pounds of nuggets from one of their elk-skin pokes, they waited and watched as the bank clerk weighed out their gold on a fancy set of scales.

"That will be $1,280.50 at $16.00 an ounce," the

clerk announced. "I won't be able to give you all that back in U.S. coin, but I do have some gold slugs minted by respectable assay houses in San Francisco and Sacramento. They are just as good as any U.S. coin in the hands of a merchant."

"That be fine with us," said Jacob as he closed off the end of his poke in order not to spill out any more gold nuggets for everyone with eyes and a nosy streak to see. Leaving the bank, the men retrieved their livestock and, after getting directions from the liveryman, they headed down the trail as directed toward the towns of Marysville and then Sacramento.

In their travels to Sacramento, they had the opportunity to see wildlife everywhere in abundance. They saw grizzly bear, tule elk, thousands of ducks and geese on every spot of water, and mule deer everywhere in between. They were also passed by many stagecoaches and mule trains, empty and packed, as they headed for the gold fields or returned for more goods to deliver to the miners. They were amazed at the frantic activity of the miners in the Oroville area and on the Feather River. Entire sections of the river had been blocked off with a temporary dam and a flume, which took the waters below the obstruction. The miners were like ants in the bottom of the emptied riverbed, hauling out the large rocks and stacking them in huge piles along the banks so they could get to the bedrock and mine the leavings. They also saw many streams being mined where the water ran dark brown with the flow of muddy effluent from the busy mining activities. They just shook their heads at the land's destruction by men acting crazy in the head to get at the yellow metal.

Days later found the men in Sacramento, parts of which proved to be just as wild as Oroville. They spent several days in Sacramento, resting their livestock and themselves. During that stay, they visited John Sutter at Sutter's Fort. He was a tough old man from a country called Switzerland, and he drove a hard bargain, but soon the brothers had arranged to purchase two thousand head of cattle, ten bulls of breeding age, forty brood sows, and five boars from his hock farm. They also purchased ten milk cows and two dairy bulls along with eight heavy-load-carrying wagons and teams with a promise of teamsters and cowboys to assist them in their travels back to Sierra Valley. When the bargaining was finished, the brothers were surprised to still be in possession of one set of saddlebags containing gold nuggets and over a thousand dollars in gold coins.

They also discovered that a series of steam packets plied the nearby Sacramento River and could take them straight to San Francisco and the Pacific Ocean. Agreeing to return in two weeks, the brothers left their newly purchased livestock in John Sutter's care, booked passage on a boat plying the Sacramento River for San Francisco, boarded their horses and mules, and boarded a steam packet for the Bay area the following morning.

Having paid for first-class passage on the steam packet Micky O 'Brien, the brothers were surprised at their accommodations: a spacious cabin with hot and cold running water, three meals a day with real linen napkins, and river scenery to rival much of what they were used to in the mountains. There were pairs of waterfowl everywhere on the river, bald eagles in many of the huge cottonwoods along the river, fishermen pulling giant white sturgeon and the smaller green sturgeon from the river, and numerous herds of tule elk watering along deserted shorelines in the mornings and evenings.

This sure is a far cry from watching out for the Lakota on a daily basis so they didn't lift one's hair, Jacob thought with a relaxed smile.

Several days later, the Micky O 'Brien pulled into a set of docks in San Francisco by what the boys soon learned was called the Embarcadero. As the boat anchored alongside many other steam packets and dozens of sailing ships, the brothers stared in awe at the spectacle. The docks were a frenzy of activity. There were carts with sweating men pushing loads of goods to individual docks to be unloaded and just as many men pushing their carts dockside with goods offloaded from the sea of ships at anchor or tied alongside the wharfs. The stevedores shouting, cries from whirling gulls overhead, the smell of salt water, and the smell of rotting fish associated with such an active waterway, assaulted the men's senses. For several hours all they did was wander around and stare at a scene they had never even dreamed about. Then it was off to Market Street in a horse-drawn carriage and then up to Geary Boulevard and west to the Pacific Ocean.

Upon arriving at the shoreline, Martin got out of the carriage, took off his moccasins, and walked briskly into the surf. For a long time he just stood there. Then he turned and said, "Jacob, you don't know how long I have waited to do this. Ever since the mountain men at the rendezvous talked about this big, salty pond, I have wanted to see it. Now I am here, and it is everything I hoped it would be and then some!"

Jacob smiled at his brother's child-like antics, then took off his moccasins and joined him. It was a personal moment between two brothers and the realization of a dream. The cold water finally numbed their feet, and the men walked out of the water, cleaned the sand from their feet, put on their moccasins, and got back into the waiting carriage.

"Carriage man," said Jacob, "take us to a part of San Francisco where my brother and I can celebrate our arrival, have a drink or two, and get something good to eat."

The carriage man got a twisted grin on his face and clucked his horse into action. Shortly thereafter, he stopped the carriage in a rough-and-tumble section of San Francisco known as the Barbary Coast. Raucous-sounding bars lined the streets, and sailors were everywhere, walking arm in arm with obvious fallen doves. In between was every kind of street vendor. Gun and knife fights erupted at least once per block, and the gutters were lined with men who had fallen from blows in a fight or from imbibing too much John Barleycorn.

Grinning at the opportunity for entertainment, Martin paid the carriage man, and the brothers looked around for a place to start. A large, brightly painted bar named Maggie's of Ireland caught their eye.

"What say you, brother? Shall we go forth and see what San Francisco has to offer?" asked Martin with a grin of anticipation.

Jacob nodded, pleased with his brother's playful attitude. After all, Martin had always backed his hand, and now it was time for Jacob to let down his guard and allow Martin the chance to see a part of the world he had always longed for.

Without a backward glance, the two brothers entered a rather rough- and-tumble bar in which, from the sounds inside, everyone was having a glorious time. Stepping over a drunken sailor lying on the floor, the two men settled down at an unoccupied table. Soon they were visited by several rather rough-looking young ladies, obviously looking for more than a free drink. Remembering their pledges to Amanda and Kim, the brothers demurred and asked for some of the establishment's best whiskey. Within moments, a barkeep approached with a bottle of whiskey and two glasses. The two brothers laid their rifles across the table, toasted their safe trip across the Western reaches with the wagon train, and then ordered dinner off a menu scrawled in chalk on a wooden board. Soon a corned-beef-and-cabbage dinner arrived, and the two men fell to as they watched the happenings around them in amusement. They witnessed ladies plying their trade among the young sailors, lumbermen trading punches with seafaring men, fishermen trading some of their freshly caught wares for those of the ladies, and everything else in between. After dinner the brothers ordered a plum pudding for dessert and another whiskey. After that drink, they decided to leave and try another establishment. Wobbling out and singing an old mountain-man ditty, they staggered into a bar across the

326 | TERRY GROSZ

street advertising freak shows. Sitting down in front of a stage, they ordered several more drinks and watched in disbelief as a man swallowed a sword and then took it back out without dying or bleeding all over the place! Then a burly sailor approached and asked if they were looking for a stint at some good sea duty.

Jacob answered, "Not really; we are nothing but cattle ranchers out for a good time, and we're not interested in going to sea."

That was the last thing either man remembered as they were struck from behind by two other unseen sailors! The next thing Jacob knew, he was being bound and gagged as he lay in the slop in the bottom of a dinghy heading out into the harbor toward a square-masted rigger. Squirming around and squinting through the pain in his skull, Jacob could see his brother and another man lying with him in the bottom of the boat. Looking up, he observed two men rowing the boat while a third manned the tiller. Remembering the bar scene, Jacob realized that the man steering the boat had been the one in front of their table, distracting the brothers with his seafaring question before they had been hit from behind. Then a boot came crashing down on his head from one of the men rowing the boat, and the lights went out once again.

Chapter Twenty-Six

SHANGHAIED AND SEA DUTY

THE NEXT THING the brothers knew was the pitching and rolling of a ship under way. They heard numerous orders being shouted above the hold where they were lying. They also became aware of the stench of rotting things, their dry throats, and the crushing ache at the backs of their heads where they had been struck by belaying pins. That was quickly superseded by the nausea that comes from being a landlubber experiencing his first bout of seasickness. Soon the men were violently retching. As Jacob vomited for the fourth time, he was glad their captors had removed their gags and damn unhappy he had feasted earlier on the rich, greasy corned beef and cabbage dinner.

Martin rolled over after retching for his fifth

or sixth time, and there was fire in his eyes! "I will kill the first man I get my hands on for doing this," he uttered through clenched teeth and a beard splattered with pieces of vomit.

"Careful, my brother," said Jacob. "Let us see what the odds are and what circumstances we now face before jumping into something we can't handle."

Martin understood the wisdom of Jacob's words, but he had never been bested on the field of battle and sure as hell was not going to start now! A murderous hatred was boiling up within him—as was more puke as he retched deeply once again.

"We will wait until we see the odds," Jacob said, also through clenched teeth. "If they are not good, we must bide our time and do as we are told. Then when the opportunity arises, we will strike and kill everyone responsible for this."

The soft pitching and yawing of the vessel continued to worked its magic on the two men. The vomiting began again in earnest until both men figured they had expelled everything they held, including some necessary body parts. Then Jacob remembered their rifles, cash, and saddlebag of gold nuggets. A quick scan of the dank hold in which they lay revealed nothing but a cat-sized black rat staring back at them from several feet away.

"Git, you son of a bitch," yelled Jacob, and the rat, sensing this would not be an easy dinner, scurried out of sight into the blackness of the hold.

By now the other man who had been brought to the ship with the brothers began groaning and bleeding even more heavily from his head wound. Soon he quieted and moved no more. Then the light of a lantern penetrated the dank hold, and two barefoot seamen approached the jumble of men who had been shanghaied earlier that afternoon.

"All right, you lubbers, rise to your feet so the captain can see you," yelled a scrawny man with a heavy beard. The command was followed by a swift kick to all three men by the man holding the lantern. Martin rolled over and exploded to his feet so fast the two antagonists did not have time to move out of his way. One swift kick to the groin felled the man with the mouth, and the one with the lantern dropped it and attempted to escape back up the ladder. Martin threw a shoulder block into the man, crushing him against the stairway and causing him to scream in intense pain. Jacob, surprised by his brother's actions, rolled over to the fallen sailor, who was softly groaning. Squirming around, he attempted to get the man's knife with his tied hands so he could cut his bonds. Then he heard the thundering of feet from the deck above, and down the stairway into the hold came more men. Soon the two brothers were beaten senseless by four other sailors with belaying pins.

About an hour went by before the brothers awoke again.

"Jacob, are you all right?" asked Martin, his voice sounding very worried in the dark of the hold.

Rolling over and aware of the intense pain coming from his neck, head, and shoulders, Jacob said, "Well, I have felt better. How about you?"

"I am all right except for a ringing in my head that won't go away," Martin answered.

"Next time I tell you to lay low until we can strike, you had better damn well listen to me. I can't remember when I have taken such a beating and couldn't fight back," Jacob mumbled through a badly split and still bleeding upper lip.

"Sorry, brother. That won't happen again—at least not until you feel ready to act," said a contrite and very sore Martin.

A short while later, the soft padding of bare feet could be heard once again coming down the stairs. Rolling over, both men waited to see what fate awaited them this time.

"Gangway," yelled a booming, commanding voice as the men on the stairway split to let a monster of a man through. "I am the chief boatswain's mate on this here ship called the *Sea Witch*, and you mates now work for me. Grab 'em up and let's take the three of them topside to the captain for a look-see."

The hands roughly grabbed the three men and dragged them up the stairway and out into the light of day on deck. Then the three men were hurled down on the decking at the feet of a man who was obviously the captain.

For a long time the captain just looked down on the three men. Then he said, "This one here is dead. Toss his miserable carcass overboard, and the sharks can have an early dinner." Two sailors rushed forward, quickly picked up the man with the crushed skull, and tossed his body overboard. Then the captain looked down on Jacob and Martin.

"Which one started giving you men all the trouble?" he asked. "That one!" said the scrawny one with the heavy beard as he pointed to Martin.

The look in Martin's eyes foretold that they were looking at a mouthy dead man if he ever got the chance. The mouthy one, seeing the deadly look in Martin's eyes, drifted back into the group of sailors standing around the captain for the protection their numbers offered.

"Lash him to the main," said the captain.

The sailors split Martin's buckskin shirt open down the back and lashed him to the main mast.

Then, taking a whip that had been coiled in his belt, the captain methodically lashed it across Martin's broad back in a practiced way until Martin finally fainted from the pain.

"Cut him down and toss a bucket of seawater on the wounds," said the captain as he slowly re-rolled his whip and placed it back under his belt.

When the seawater hit Martin's back, even though he was out cold, he moaned softly in pain as the salt stung the ripped and bleeding flesh.

"Chief boatswain's mate," bellowed the captain, "I want these two horses of men kept healthy. They will be of advantage to us once under way and harvesting the fur seals and sea otter. If nothing else, they will be good fodder for rowing the killing boats."

By the captain's feet, Jacob spied his saddle-bags holding the gold nuggets. Stepping forward and looking the captain straight in the eye, he said, "Captain, what about my saddlebags at your feet? What is in there belongs to me and my brother."

"You forfeited any rights you had when you came aboard my ship," the captain yelled. "Lash his arrogant ass to the main as well," he screamed as his eyes almost popped out of his head in crazed fury.

Within moments Jacob was feeling the sting of the whip. He vowed not to pass out so he could remember every bit of pain he would inflict on the captain when he had the chance to kill him for this and for what he had done to his brother. On the fifteenth lash, however, Jacob found himself slumping into a quiet and darkened world without pain.

Coming to, Jacob could feel the pain in his back from the lashing plus that of several rats tearing at his torn, bloody flesh!

Staggering to his feet, he shook off the rats, which continued feeding on his back as he rose. As they fell off, he smashed one flat with the heel of his moccasin. Instantly the other two rats were on the dead one, dragging it off into the darkness of the hold to be eaten. Then Jacob heard his brother softly moaning off to his left.

Reaching out to the sound in the darkened hold and feeling his brother's shoulder, he asked, "Martin, can you hear me?"

"Yes, and by God I sure do hurt. I really pity those you and I finally get our hands on when it comes time to kill them," Martin answered in a voice weakened by the beating.

"I agree on all counts, but for now we need to lay low and not make a stir until we heal up and feel we can win. Then and only then will we make our move," Jacob uttered through gritted teeth.

The dark, wet hold became silent as the men

quietly endured the pain in their backs and fended off the hungry rats coming at them in droves, energized by the smell of fresh blood.

"Avast, ye lubbers," came a voice from the top of the stairs as the hatch was thrown open once again and muted light and fresh salt air streamed in. "Move your miserable carcasses from down there and up onto the deck. We have work to do, and you might as well get started in your new life."

Painfully staggering up the stairs, the brothers emerged into the dim light of a deck shrouded with a wet, heavy fog.

"I am Able Seaman John Paul. The captain has assigned you two lubbers to me, and between the three of us, we have our ship's duties to perform. Now, for your own good, I suggest we try and get along. Currently we are at least sixty miles from the shore and heading north to the sealing grounds off the coast of Canada. If either of you wants to escape and cares to swim that far, now is the time to have at it."

There was a long pause as John Paul looked closely at the faces of the brothers for their reactions to his words. Not seeing any emotion other than cold stares, he continued, "Now, there is some able seamen's clothing behind you. It is warmer and will wear better than those buckskin duds you are wearing. I suggest you get rid of your old clothing and put on the new."

Jacob and Martin sorted through the pile of discarded clothing until they found some that more or less fitted their massive frames. However, it took both of them several minutes to put on their shirts because of the pain from their badly damaged backs.

"By cracky, the two of you just might make seamen yet," exclaimed John Paul as he looked them over approvingly. "Now, we must hollystone the aft decking by the rendering pots. That is where we skin our catch and render out their fat. That portion of the deck gets covered with fats and oils during the butchering and skinning process. So we must holly stone the deck or it gets too slick to walk on." John Paul pointed a bony finger toward the plunging bow of the ship and said, "Aft is thataway."

Walking forward, the three men were soon scrubbing the decks with buckets of seawater and pumice stones. Throughout the process, Jacob and Martin continued dry-heaving with continuing bouts of seasickness. By now nothing came up because it had been two days since they had eaten.

Soon the ship broke free of the damp, misting fog, and the brothers had their first chance to look around. They saw nothing but empty sea for miles and a large fog bank to the east covering the land. Looking at each other, their eyes said it all.

We will wait for now, thought Jacob. We need to see how many other men are on board and how many of them are like us, looking to escape. And figure out how to run this ship without sinking it on some rocks.

"I know what ye are thinking, lad, and I would warn ye away from such thoughts," said John Paul, squinting at Jacob. "I am in the same boat, having been shanghaied four years ago. Since then I have had the chance to look around and see if I could escape. The captain and those loyal to him are hard cases, and they run a tight ship. But if ye do figger out a way, count me in, for I would like to see my family on the mainland once again afore I become meat for the crabs."

Jacob and Martin did not let their feelings show any more during that conversation, not knowing if they could trust John Paul. However, they kept the possibility of having him as a comrade in arms in the back of their minds in case it came to choosing sides in a mutiny.

For the next several weeks John Paul and the brothers quietly worked together as instructed by the captain. During that time, John Paul taught the brothers about shipboard life. They learned knot tying, how to set and release the sails, how to weather their less frequent bouts with seasickness, and how to stomach the lousy food served by the ship's cook. They also learned to avoid the captain and blows from the chief boatswain's mate. And they began to learn the sealing and sea otter fur trade and oil business.

Since they did not have the complete confidence of the captain, they had to watch the harvesting process from the ship's rail. The process included lowering four or five whaleboats, each carrying two rowers and a tillerman who also acted as a shooter. The boats would approach resting seals and sea lions on the rocky coasts and shoot into the massed animals, killing as many as they could before they slipped off the rocks and into the deep. Then they would fire at those trying to swim away, trying to kill them with head shots so they would not sink immediately.

The process for taking sea otters was different. The killing boats would quietly move into a resting pod of sea otters in the kelp beds and begin head-shooting the hapless, trusting animals. Those that did not sink were retrieved and loaded into the longboats. Once the boats were loaded with fresh carcasses, they returned to the mother ship and offloaded their catch. Then, as with the seals and sea lions, a crew onboard began skinning their catches and stretching the valuable furs on metal hoops. The skin sides were fleshed out, salted down, and placed forward in a special fur hold. The bodies were then placed in the huge shipboard rendering pots and the fat rendered.

When the oil had floated to the surface of the pot, it was ladled off, poured into wooden kegs, and bunged shut. Those casks of valuable oil were also placed forward in the ship in a separate hold to be sold later for use in lamps, lubricants, and additive to various patent medicines. Then the carcasses were thrown overboard to the waiting sharks except for some select pieces, which were mostly served to the crew in a strong-tasting, oily stew accompanied by wormy hardtack.

One day Jacob got a plan and, after discussing it with his brother, approached the captain and said, "Captain, I have a plan on how to increase your harvest of sea otters and seals if you are interested."

The captain looked long and hard at the man he considered a troublemaker and then said, "It had better be good, or it's back to the mast and the sting of the whip."

Figuring he would just add the man's acid tone to the list of grievances he was holding in his breast, Jacob continued, "My brother and I are better shots than all of your men put together. We spent years in the West as mountain men and were known throughout the region as the keenest shooters among all the trappers. My brother and I, since we are part of the crew and because all of us get a cut of that which is taken, wish to improve not only our lot but that of the ship's company. We figure we can do that by doubling the kill with less use of powder and ball if you are inclined to consider my suggestion."

Looking down on Jacob from the bridge, the captain considered his words. He still did not trust either of the two men even though they had somewhat assimilated into his crew after being shanghaied. However, that level of adjustment was not normal, to his way of thinking. It was best he kept his guard up against these two bearded giants, no matter how well they seemed to adapt to life onboard. But he was also a greedy man, and what Jacob had said was in fact true. His best shooters missed more than they hit even on their better days.

"And if you can't? What then?" the captain asked with interest.

"Then you can take me and my brother's share of the take and keep it for yourself," Jacob replied with a grin, realizing he had the captain's rapt attention even though the man tried hard not to show it.

"All right, tomorrow you will go out with my chief boatswain's mate. He will be armed as well, and if you try anything he will shoot you and dump your miserable carcass overboard!" the captain said with a vicious look.

Jacob returned to his skinning and fleshing detail. On the way, he caught Martin's eye and winked. Their escape plan was being set into motion.

Chapter Twenty-Seven

THE HUNT FOR THE SEA OTTER AND FREEDOM

THE FOLLOWING MORNING, when the longboats were lowered, Jacob sat in the front of one of them. Sitting immediately behind him was the grim-faced chief boatswain's mate with two Remington .44-caliber pistols tucked into his belt. Two other men at the oars pulled hard, and soon their boat was in a giant kelp bed full of the unsuspecting, gentle sea otters.

"It is time, mountain man. Let me see what you can do. Just remember, if you so much as squirm the wrong way, I will shoot you in the back of the head and dump your carcass overboard!" snarled the chief boatswain's mate.

Lying in the bow were four rifles. Taking one up, Jacob hefted it and checked its sights. Sighting on a large sea otter some thirty yards away, he cleanly killed the animal with a head shot. Without looking back, he handed the empty rifle into the hands of a rower behind him who was acting as loader, grabbed the next rifle, and cleanly killed another otter. Handing that rifle back, he continued the routine until all the rifles were empty or being reloaded. This process was repeated eighteen times until the chief boatswain's mate said, "Let's load up what we have already killed. I think we may have a load of otters that might swamp the boat if we try to load any more on board."

All the floating dead otters were loaded into the boat, and with only about three inches of freeboard, they carefully rowed back to the mother ship. Jacob could tell the captain was pleased as he looked down into the boat. They were fully loaded with sea-otter carcasses and had come back before any other killing boats could even think of returning.

"Eighteen shots and eighteen sea otters," the chief boatswain's mate yelled up to the captain. Jacob could tell by the look on the captain's face that he was awestruck over their success and Jacob's shooting ability.

"Offload the catch, and let's see what he can do once again," shouted down the captain.

The hot-and-heavy killing action continued all day long. Even the chief boatswain's mate lowered his guard and helped load the rifles so more otters could be killed faster by the sharp-shooting mountain man. By day's end Jacob had killed 113 sea otters and 2 harbor seals that had wandered into his killing zone. The other three boats hunting in the same area brought in only 87 animals altogether!

The next morning when the boats were lowered, Jacob sat in the bow of one and Martin in another. Throughout that day and the others that followed, the crack shooting of Jacob and Martin kept the skinning and fleshing crews more than busy. With the end of each day of shooting success, Jacob and Martin noticed the crew becoming more friendly to them, as did the ship's cook. They were finding many choice morsels of food in their tin plates now that they had become the ship's top shooters. The cook realized that every day the brothers went out meant that his pockets, like those of his shipmates, would be lined with more proceeds than ever before.

Soon the *Sea Witch* was loaded to the gunwales with valuable hides and kegs of marine mammal oil. In fact, the ship ran out of wooden kegs in which to store the oil, and the extra carcasses had to be tossed overboard without being rendered. The hold used to store furs was full, and extra furs were being stored in the captain's mess, his bedroom, and in every other place where they could be kept dry. Finally their supply of salt ran out, and the captain had to turn the ship south toward the nearest port where he could offload his catch. It was two months earlier than he had ever left the killing grounds!

Another benefit to the two brothers was that those in the crew loyal to the captain were slowly lowering their guards more and more as they accepted the two ex-mountain men as genuine sealers and shipboard mates.

"Port, ho!" yelled the lookout as the *Sea Witch* turned landward toward where San Francisco lay.

The crew lined the rails as the ship moved closer to the docks, anticipating the debauchery that would follow their landing. Jacob and Martin had quietly agreed that if they were let free on the docks, they would kill any of their captors who were close at hand and then lose themselves in the waterfront crowd before the law could swap one form of captivity for another. But alas, it was not to be...Hearing the click of rifles being cocked, the brothers turned to find the chief boatswain's mate, his first mate, and another seaman pointing rifles at them.

"What the hell!" exclaimed Jacob.

"The captain does not feel you two are entirely trustworthy, and until we leave port you will be confined to the lower decks. That is, until we resupply and leave for the sealing grounds south of San Francisco," the chief boatswain's mate coldly replied with a leering grin.

The brothers were escorted below decks and chained so they could not escape.

Jacob quietly put his finger to his lips for Martin to see as they were being chained to a ship's timber. Martin caught the sign and held still, honoring his pledge to wait before he exploded at the crew members loyal to the captain.

When their captors had left and were out of earshot, Jacob said, "Well, this is something I had not planned on. In the future, we must secrete away a file and hammer in this area so if they do this again and the time is right, we can free ourselves and escape."

"When they free us, my brother, I will go to the ship's carpenter's stores and steal a file, cold chisel, and hammer. Count on it being here the next time this happens," Martin said through clenched teeth, a sign he was ready to kill someone once again.

For the next three days, as the *Sea Witch* took on supplies and offloaded casks of oil and piles of furs, the brothers remained chained to the beam below decks. They were fed and watered but never allowed on deck. On the fourth day, the *Sea Witch* sailed south on the evening tide. When land was several miles off the port beam,

John Paul came below decks and freed Jacob and Martin from their shackles. With everyone falling to on the deck and setting the sails, no one noticed Martin's brief absence. When he reappeared, he glanced over at Jacob and gave him the high sign that they now had a file, chisel, and hammer hidden near the place where they had been confined.

It will be a cold day in hell before we will be at the mercy of the captain and his cohorts again, thought Jacob.

For two days the *Sea Witch* slowly sailed south along the shore of California, finally dropping anchor in a quiet bay some forty miles south of Monterey. Sea otters abounded in the area along the coastline in the kelp beds, and soon the killing commenced.

It quickly became apparent that Jacob and Martin with their keen shooting eyes could provide far more sea otters than the crew on the ship could process. To rectify that situation, the captain reduced the kill boats from four to two, leaving Jacob and Martin as the main shooters in each boat. The crews from the two boats removed from the killing detail were then assigned to skinning and fleshing duties in order to keep up with the loads of otters and the occasional harbor seal or California sea lion provided by the brothers.

For the next several months, other than when the brothers were detained in the safety of the mother ship because of winter storms, the killing continued unabated. Christmas that year was celebrated with an extra cup of strong rum and nothing more. When the spring of 1859 arrived, the killing continued until the sea otters were decimated in their area. When that happened, the *Sea Witch* would pull anchor, move a few miles farther south, and drop anchor for the killing process to begin once again. Other sea-otter hunters were in the area, but the captain managed to keep those ships at bay with the liberal use of a swivel gun mounted on the flying bridge. After several shots through the offending ships' sails and rigging, they got the message and moved to less dangerous hunting areas far from the *Sea Witch* and her crazy captain.

When the ship ran low on the firewood used to heat the rendering kettles and had holds almost filled with oil casks and sea-otter skins, the captain decided to head north to Monterey to take on more firewood and sell his oil and salted hides. He also planned to give his trusted crew members a day of shore leave to take out the kinks and take advantage of the "shady lady" trade.

"Monterey," rang out a shout from the crow's nest. The lookout followed with the command, "Ten degrees to starboard." Reefing in his mainsail, the captain moved into the port of Monterey running on his jib and boom an hour later. Slowly running with the tide, he adroitly maneuvered his ship alongside a long dock jutting out into the bay. Seamen jumped from the deck onto the dock and secured the *Sea Witch* tightly with hawsers both fore and aft. The first mate ran out the ship's gangway, and the captain, leaving the chief boatswain's mate in charge, headed for the port authority building at the end of the pier.

In the meantime, John Paul and an armed able seaman escorted Jacob and Martin below decks, where they were once again shackled to avoid any attempt at escaping.

When the two seamen left, Martin turned to his brother and said, "Do you want to try and escape now?"

Jacob thought for a moment and said, "No. They have an armed gang on the dock plus several more loyalists close at hand. If we tried to escape now, we would be shot down like the dogs they are."

Martin, not to be denied, said, "Jacob, I have the hammer, chisel, and file hidden within reach. We could overpower the crew, take their rifles, and shoot those on the deck."

"And then what? The captain would have the law on us in an instant, and they would believe him over a couple of scruffy - looking seamen, especially if we killed some of his crew. No, we will wait for a better opportunity, and for some reason, I have a strong feeling that is soon to come."

Chapter Twenty-Eight

A BLACK MAN COMES AGAIN,
AND TROUBLE FOLLOWS

JACOB AND MARTIN were awakened from a fitful sleep by the arrival of drunken sailors returning from the shore party. Much yelling and singing was accompanied by someone lifting the deck hatch over where Jacob and Martin were shackled. Three bodies were roughly rolled down the steps to their level, and the hatch was once more quickly latched shut.

Three more men shanghaied, Jacob thought disgustedly.

The men groaned softly and soon lay still in deep sleep from having been drugged before being taken. Unable to do anything or even see in the dark hold, Jacob and Martin just sat there. Soon they could hear running feet and extra activity taking place on the ship's deck. Then they could feel the ship slowly moving, followed by the command to unfurl the mainsail. Within moments, the sails filled with a spirited wind, and the usual creaking and groaning of the ship under full sail could be heard. That motion soon rocked the two brothers back into a fitful sleep until they were awakened several hours later when the hatch was loudly opened and the bare feet came running down the stairs.

"A vast, you sons of a whore, it's time to hit the deck and earn your keep," shouted the chief boatswain's mate.

Three armed seamen loyal to the captain stood on the stairway to the hold, hollering and prodding the three recent additions to the crew. It took some work to get the drugged men to rise, but eventually that was accomplished, and they staggered up the stairs onto a rain-covered deck.

While waiting their turn to be freed and let out, the two brothers sat looking on in shock at the three men leaving the hold in the light of day. One of the three was a huge black man! It was none other than Cain, their long-lost brother from the plains!

Jacob and Martin just looked at each other in profound disbelief, so surprised that neither could utter a word. The last they had heard of Cain was the Indians' tale of his walking away in the middle of the night during a blinding spring snow storm after he had lost his wife in child-birth. Now, bigger than life, there he was back from the dead!

Jacob got hold of his senses and whispered to Martin, "Don't let on we know him. If we do, the captain will keep us isolated from one another out of mistrust. Let's try to give Cain a high sign telling him to remain quiet. Otherwise we may not get the chance to team up and get off this rat-infested bucket."

Martin nodded as he understood the signifi-cance of Jacob's words. It was apparent to them that Cain had been drugged and shanghaied. If they could team up with Cain and possibly the other men dumped in the hold with him, along with John Paul, then maybe they could take over the ship and escape. For the first time in months, they thought they saw a possibility of escape so that they could return to their life as ranchers and finally marry the loves of their lives, who they hoped were still waiting for them in Sierra Valley.

Their rapid thinking was interrupted when John Paul came down the stairs and released them so they could return to their duties on deck.

"We best hurry and get up on the deck. The captain is in a killing bad mood, and we don't want to make him any madder," whispered John Paul.

Scrambling up on deck, the brothers could quickly see why the captain was so mad. One of his eyes was closed, and the other was bloodied and almost closed. His lip was split, and he had a huge cut over his left eye that still trickled blood down the side of his face. Then they saw the first mate, who was another evil son of a bitch. His jaw hung limply, looking as if it had been broken in a vicious fight, and the entire side of his face was purple, black, and blue. His left arm also hung limply as if it had been broken, and one of his eyes was a reddish-purple, swollen orb. It quickly became obvious that the captain and the first mate had tangled with something neither of them had ever faced before and probably never wanted to face again.

"Lash that black bastard to the main!" bellowed the captain.

It took four men to lift and secure the semiconscious Cain to the main mast, but they finally got it done. For the next five minutes the captain took out his fury on the back of the black man with his whip. Finishing and out of breath, he had his chief boatswain's mate continue the beating with his one good arm. Soon Cain's back was a mass of torn and bleeding flesh, with the white bone of his ribs and backbone showing.

"That is enough!" shouted the captain. "I want that bastard to live so I can grind him into the decking as an ordinary seaman."

Cain had long since passed out, and when they cut him down, he collapsed onto the deck in a bloody heap.

"John Paul," yelled the captain, "you, Jacob, and Martin take this piece of crap below decks and shackle him with leg shackles. He is one mean son of a bitch, and I don't want him roaming the ship unless he is shackled."

"Aye, sir," said John Paul. He turned to Jacob and Martin and said, "Give me a hand with this bastard so we can do as the captain says."

Jacob and Martin, not wanting to face the captain's wrath at that time, jumped right in to grab Cain. Leaving a bloody smear along the deck, they dragged him to the hold. As the ship's carpenter manacled Cain's legs, Jacob and Martin looked at each other with a knowing grin. Both could tell it would be a real battle among the three of them, once Cain healed and they found an opportunity to right their wrongs, especially as to who would get to kill the captain.

"Jacob, go up and get me a bucket of seawater. We need to fix the back of this man or he will be crippled all his life. Martin, go see the carpenter's assistant and tell him we need some thread and a sail needle so we can sew him up before infection sets in," ordered John Paul.

As the *Sea Witch* sailed south before a brisk winter wind, Martin, Jacob, and John Paul bathed

Cain's back and sewed the loose chunks of flesh into the holes in his massive back where the captain's whip had tom them free.

It took Cain three days to come out of the delirium caused by his brutal whipping. But when he did, he found himself looking into the grinning faces of Martin and Jacob. When he recognized the two brothers, his eyes looked as if they would pop out of their sockets. Then he reached out with his massive hand as if to convince himself and touched both men. Tears came to his eyes, and then he passed back into his world of pain — but not before Jacob had whispered to him that he was not to mention that he knew them, and when he was feeling better they would let him in on why they were on the same ship.

Anchoring sixty miles south of Monterey, the captain sent Jacob and Martin overboard to kill sea otters. Before going, Jacob and Martin conferred with John Paul, whom both men felt they could now trust, and told him to take good care of the black man. Not knowing what was going on but now being a good friend to the brothers, John Paul agreed.

For the next month, between bouts of winter storms, the brothers killed sea otters as if nothing were out of the ordinary. In their spare time in the evenings, they could be found huddled with Cain below decks as John Paul kept watch. As

Cain healed, the brothers had the opportunity to fill him in on their lives after they had separated. They also used the time to explain how they had come to be working on the vessel. Cain in turn brought the brothers up-to-date on what had happened to him after he had disappeared from his band of Lakota. In a daze of grief, he had wandered the mountains trapping and killing animals to live. Finally running out of supplies and recovering a bit from his personal losses, he had ventured to Fort Bridger. While there in conversation with Jim Bridger, Cain discovered that the brothers had taken a wagon train to California. Remembering that Martin had always wanted to see the Pacific Ocean, he too came west looking for his friends. After crossing the Sierra Nevada Mountains on horseback, he landed in Monterey and found work in the fur houses processing sea-otter pelts. One evening while drinking at a bar called the Sandpiper, he had run across the captain of the *Sea Witch*. The captain had offered to buy him a few drinks and had spiked Cain's drink. Cain was such a big man that the potion only half knocked him out, and when the first mate and the captain tried to shanghai him, he naturally resisted to the point that he was really working the two of them over when the rest of the crew jumped in by cracking him in the head with a belaying pin. That was the last thing he remembered.

Upon hearing the story, Jacob had to quietly laugh. Cain was still the horse of a man he had always been, and with him at their side, the brothers began to seriously plot their escape.

One evening, as the men relaxed, Jacob asked Cain how his back was. Cain moved his huge, muscular arms over his head, and Jacob saw him wince in pain.

"You still have a way to go before you are your old self, my brother," said Jacob.

"Give me another month and I think I will be all right," said Cain.

"Either way, my brother, you must be at full strength. We mean to take this ship over at the earliest opportunity and kill about half the crew who either support the captain or were in on our being shanghaied. As near as I can figure, we will have John Paul at our side, and that is good because he is a good shipwright. I am also hoping that when the time is right, we can count on those two men who were shanghaied along with you. That might just give us enough men to take the ship, kill those needing killing, and sail her back to San Francisco and our freedom," Jacob said grimly. "It would be better if we had a few more men for the crew, like another shipwright and a good helmsman, but when the time comes those few of us willing to fight will just have to make do."

"Jacob," said Martin, "one of those guys that came with Cain is named Ran Slaten. He has been on ships that sailed to Alaska, and I think he might join us. I will feel him out some evening when we are up on the deck having a smoke, and if I am wrong, I will break his neck to keep him quiet and toss him overboard to keep our secret."

John Paul couldn't keep to himself after hearing bits and snips of the mutiny being hatched. "Jacob, I just can't sit here and be the lookout. I need to say something," said John Paul. "That other fellow who came onboard with Cain is named Bill Black. He used to be a ship's master till he ran aground in the fog off the coast of Alaska. His helmsman at the time had been drinking and got off his bearings. When the ship went aground, he drowned trying to get into a lifeboat. According to Bill, he fell from the deck into the longboat, bounced out into the icy water, and was never seen again. As a result, there was no one to testify on Bill's behalf that he wasn't manning the ship at the time, and he lost his ship's papers. He bounced from pillar to post until he, like the two of you, was shanghaied. I am here to tell you, we had better hurry if either of you wants to kill the captain because Bill is already planning to do so even if he is killed in the process. He is that good of a man."

"I will meet this fellow where we can talk,

and if what you say is true, we will include him. However, if he is not what he represents himself to be, I think a trip to Davy Jones's locker will be his fate as well," Jacob said quietly.

"There is another good man in the crew, Jacob," continued John Paul. "His name is Leo Suazo, a Mexican, and one hell of a man with a knife and pistol. He is my friend and can keep his mouth shut. He also has a hankering to kill the first mate for all he has done to him and would welcome the chance to join our merry band if it meant his escape."

"Then it is set," said Martin. "I will get together with my man, and you do the same with yours, Jacob. If we are successful, there will be six of us to take over the ship and do what needs doing. I will also get together with this Mexican fellow, and if he is what John Paul says, then we will have a seventh man in the fold. If not, he will float clear to Mexico with the gulls picking at his flesh before anyone knows he is gone."

With their plans set into motion, the men went about their business as usual. Cain, now sufficiently healed, was given skinning and fleshing duties but was always in manacles and watched closely by the first mate. That way the captain felt that if Cain tried to get at him, he would have time to draw his pistol and kill him since he could only shuffle slowly while his ankles were chained together.

When the end of spring came, the escape plan was bearing fruit. Martin had talked to Ran Slaten and found a more-than-willing ally. Jacob had discovered that Bill Black was a true and determined partner in the mutiny and, as John Paul had said, an ex-ship's master who was more than qualified to navigate the *Sea Witch* back to San Francisco. Martin had met with Leo Suazo and found that him to be a rather stout fellow also ready to join the plot. Suazo told Martin outright that he alone would be the one to kill the first mate because of all the old scores he had to settle with the man. Now all the seven men needed was the right opportunity, and then hell would come riding in on a black horse even though they were at sea...

For the next thirty days, the ship's company was stirred into action. The captain wanted to clean out the sea otters from the southern reaches of California, offload in Monterey, resupply, and head for the waters off Alaska to hunt fur seals and kill more sea otters. Jacob and Martin saw to it that sea otters flowed rapidly into the ship so they could get on with their plans. Finally the ship was more than full of curing otter hides and casks of the valuable marine-mammal oils.

With a freshening wind, the *Sea Witch* turned north to begin her trip to Monterey. However, it was not to be a fast trip. The next day, the ship was buffeted by intense northerly winds and late-spring storms and was soon blown five hundred miles off course. Finally the weather relented, and with strong southerly winds, the *Sea Witch* arrived in the port of Monterey a month and a half later than planned.

Upon their arrival, they found that all the dock space was taken up by other seagoing vessels, so the *Sea Witch* had to anchor slightly off the end of the pier, and the crew had to ferry all their oil casks and sea-otter pelts to the docks by longboat. Several weeks of backbreaking work transpired, and at the end of each day, Jacob, Martin, and Cain were chained below decks to prevent them from slipping over the side and swimming to shore.

One evening, the captain, having been paid for his cargo, returned rip-roaring drunk to the *Sea Witch*. With him he carried a heavy wooden strongbox. The chief boatswain's mate and the first mate joined him, and it soon became apparent that none of them were feeling any pain as the drinking continued. However, the first mate wisely didn't join the captain and trusted members of his crew until Jacob, Martin, and Cain had been chained to the ship's timbers in the hold.

Realizing the time for escape was right, Martin retrieved the hidden tools and began quietly filing through the chains that held his brother and him to the ship's massive framing. Laying a heavy rag over the action dulled the filing sounds as Randy, John, Leo, and Bill Black made their way into the hold. All carried knives stolen from the galley and quietly waited for the brothers to free themselves. Once that was done, they filed the chains off Cain's ankles.

Jacob placed his index finger against his lips to indicate silence, and the seven men quietly climbed out of the hold and squatted on the deck until their eyes adjusted to the dim evening light. Using hand signals to show that he was carrying out the next step in the plan, Bill crept over to the hatch leading down to the crew's quarters. Quietly lowering the hatch cover over the snoring men sleeping below, he latched it with a locking iron pin so no one could come up. Then he padded soundlessly, back to the group of men waiting in the shadows below the bridge. From there, John Paul made his way to the ship's lookout, and soon a soft thud told everyone that his belaying pin had found its mark. Rejoining his mates, John Paul signaled the fate of the lookout with a finger run across his throat. Then Ran Slaten silently padded across the deck and crawled up the stairs to the bridge, and soon they heard the dead body of the helmsman hitting the water. Slaten lashed the wheel of the ship and returned to his shipmates on the main deck. With that, the seven men made their way to the door of the captain's cabin and paused. Inside, they could hear a wild party going on over the prices the oil and sea otter pelts had brought. It was apparent that the rum was now flowing freely among the trusted members of the captain's crew.

Throwing the door open suddenly, Cain burst into the cabin, heading for the captain's dinner table, which was bathed in the soft glow of several candles and surrounded by eight men drinking heavily and laughing loudly. The laughter stopped immediately as the seven men from outside surged in. Without a moment's hesitation, Leo Suazo sprinted across the floor and into the surprised arms of the first mate. There was a soft groan as Leo thrust his knife deeply into the first mate's heart, followed by a loud crash as Leo's momentum carried both men away from the captain's dinner table and onto the floor. Boom went one of the captain's Remington .44-caliber black-powder pistols, hitting Cain dead center in his upper chest. Cain slumped to the deck, and before the captain could get off another shot, Martin was on him in all his anger. Jacob and Bill Black hit the beefy chief boatswain's mate at the same time, and all three men sailed across the floor and into the wall in a human ball of fury. John Paul broke out an able seaman's teeth with the swing of his belaying pin, and when the man grabbed his mouth in agony, that same club found the back of his head, spilling his brains all over the floor. Ran Slaten jumped over the captain's overturned table and sailed into a group of surprised able seamen, slashing wildly at numerous faces with his knife as he went. Rising from his pile, Jacob in a frenzy lifted the chief boatswain's mate clear off the floor and smashed him in the face with a crushing right fist. The man, although he had been hit with a fist holding the power of an angry mule's kick and then slammed to the floor, scrambled back to his feet in an instant like a crazed animal. He let out a loud roar of anger and tackled Jacob in his midsection. Both men slammed to the floor, and then the chief boatswain's mate moved no more as Bill Black, in one fell swoop, grabbed his long hair, jerked his head violently back, and slit his throat. Lying underneath the dying man, Jacob was drenched with his blood. *Boom—boom* went more shots from pistols fired by the clump of sailors huddled in terror in the corner of the captain's cabin, held there by the knife-slashing Ran Slaten. One shot went into Ran's leg as he finished off one able seaman on the floor with a knife thrust to his throat, and the other sailed harmlessly into the main beam running the length of the cabin. In an instant, a revived Cain, Jacob, and Leo hurled into the three remaining sailors, killing all with knife thrusts to their vitals. Rising slowly with only a knife slash across his ribs, Martin viewed his work with satisfaction. The captain lay lifeless on the floor with a twisted grin on his face and a broken neck to match. Then all was quiet except for the heavy breathing of the survivors. That was followed by yelling and banging under the deck hatch from the rest of the crew. A crew who and had been roused by the violent sounds of shooting and fighting only to find themselves trapped below decks.

"Everyone okay?" said Jacob as he placed a lighted candle on the now upright table.

"I'm fine," Martin answered quietly, happy to see that his brother was also all right.

"I hurt like hell," replied Cain, "but the bastard only shot me in the muscular part of my chest. I don't think the bullet went any further than my breastbone, thank God." He slowly got up from the floor and eased himself into a chair.

"I hurt like hell also," said Ran Slaten, "but the bullet that hit my leg didn't break any bones. It just ran down the full length of the bone and out the heel, so I think I am all right."

"I am fine as frog hair," Bill Black said happily, "especially since I got to kill that son of a bitch who made my life so miserable."

Leo said something in Spanish, and Jacob said teasingly, "Leo, you are in America. As long as you are in this country, you have to speak American."

"I am fine, chief," said Leo, but that was followed by more Spanish, obviously a friendly insult hurled Jacob's way.

"John Paul, how you doing?" asked Jacob.

"Like Leo said, boss, I couldn't be finer since I now am a free man to do as I please."

An hour later, when things had settled down and the seven men had armed themselves from the ship's gun locker, they opened the hatch leading to the crew's quarters. Out stormed the thirteen remaining crewmen, only to be faced by seven determined and heavily armed men, one of whom was pointing the swivel cannon at the crew from the bridge above.

Without looking over his shoulder at Leo, who stood ready at the swivel cannon, Jacob said, "Leo, if they get out of hand, shoot down the lot of them!"

Those words and the determined faces of the men awaiting them on the main deck quelled the feelings of the remaining crew except for a few grumbles.

"Men, we seven stand before you as shanghaied members of the crew. All of us were removed from our lives, but now we have taken them back by the same force that took us. The captain and his loyal crew are all dead and no longer a threat to any of us. With that in mind, are there any of you who would care to throw in your lot with us?"

It was a long moment after those words were spoken before anyone answered, and then an able seaman known as Ross, a known troublemaker, said, "None of us want this rotten fish you have given us. A ship's mutiny is a hanging offense in this country. So you can take your offer and stick it."

"Is that how the rest of you feel?" asked Jacob.

No one moved or spoke, so Jacob said, "That be fine with us, men. All of you will return below decks, and if anyone tries to escape or cause trouble, he will be killed just as dead as your captain and his body tossed overboard for the sharks."

With more grumbling, the men shuffled below decks to their quarters, and the mutineers pinned the hatch cover shut once again to prevent escape from below.

Gathering the seven men around him, Jacob said, "Bill, you take the helm. The rest of us will quietly slip farther out to sea under reduced sail so as not to cause any suspicion. Once out to sea, we will increase sail and set a course north toward San Francisco. However, before we get there, we will release the rest of the crew in longboats along the coast in some deserted area between Monterey and Frisco. By the time they get back to civilization and raise the alarm, we will be in Frisco, off this bloody ship, and long gone. Any questions?" Not hearing any, Jacob went on, "Then let's get cracking and get the hell out of here before anyone on shore is any the wiser!"

Slowly the *Sea Witch* moved offshore and into the ever-present fog bank off the coast of California. Bill set the ship's course north toward San Francisco under reduced sail as Jacob had the assistant ship's carpenter come forth from the hold. Once the man was on deck, Jacob ordered him to tend to Cain's and Ran's wounds. In a matter of moments, he had dug the flattened bullet out of Cain's chest. He offered the information that Cain had a cracked sternum, which although painful would probably heal. Then the assistant ship's carpenter cleaned out Ran's bullet hole, poured the wound channel full of whiskey from the captain's stores, and bound it tightly with a piece of clean gun cotton. He was escorted back below decks, and the hatch to the crew hold was again locked and guarded by an armed man.

Once safely away from the harbor and miles out to sea, Martin and Jacob hurled the bodies of the captain, the chief boatswain's mate, the first mate, and their henchmen into the sea. Since sharks usually followed in the wake of the ship, the men were assured that any evidence of the killings would soon be lost to Davy Jones's locker.

The following day, Jacob had Bill put into a quiet, uninhabited bay along the California coast south of San Francisco. As the untrustworthy crew members got into two longboats, Jacob came forth from the captain's cabin. Carrying a wooden chest, obviously heavy with gold coin, he paused at the rail.

"Men," he shouted, "we found the take from our several voyages in the captain's cabin from the sale of sea-otter pelts and oil. I have counted out each man's share according to rank and service. Each of you will find that share in individual canvas sacks with your name pinned to the bags. I have also split up the share from the dead men and included that in your bags. Bill Black tells me that according to our charts, there is a small harbor town ten miles to the northwest along the coast. I suggest you head that way, and you will be there sometime tomorrow or the next day. Good luck, men, and Godspeed."

He handed the heavy chest down to one of the boats' coxswains. Then the men pushed off, happily talking among themselves about their good fortune in finally getting paid their rightful shares.

Quietly pulling in among the dozens of abandoned sailing ships in San Francisco Bay whose crews had deserted so they could work the gold fields, the *Sea Witch* dropped anchor several days later. Waiting until dark, the seven men left the ship in a longboat pulling for the docks of San Francisco. They quietly landed at the end of a series of docks, and Leo disembarked as planned, disappearing into the dark of the night. An hour later, he arrived back at the docks driving a heavy wagon with a span of horses that he had rented from a liveryman in the city. The men climbed into the straw-filled wagon box after loading over $90,000 in gold coin from their labors as sea-otter hunters and one set of saddlebags still full of gold nuggets that had been taken from the brothers when they had been shanghaied almost a year before.

Chapter Twenty-Nine

HOMEWARD BOUND

IT HAD BEEN OVER a year since Jacob and Martin had left Sierra Valley. As they made their ways back toward Sutter's Fort to reclaim their already-paid-for cattle, hogs, and high walled wagons, Jacob turned in his saddle and had to smile. Behind him rode Bill Black, Ran Slaten, Leo Suazo, John Paul, Cain, and Martin. Aside from his brother and Cain, Jacob had expected the other men to return to their seafaring lives. But to his happy surprise, all of them had decided they wanted to remain with Jacob and Martin and see if they wanted to settle down as ranchers and farmers in Sierra Valley.

The California sun and the soft blue sky greeted him as he turned back in his saddle and headed northeast toward Sacramento and Sutter's Fort,

373

and he silently gave heartfelt thanks for their survival during the past year.

"Veil, I be a son of a monkey's uncle!" came the heavily Swiss-accented voice of John Sutter as he entered the room in which the brothers waited at his fort. "Vere haff you two been? I already giff you up for lost ven you didn't return in two veeks like you said."

"It is a long story, Mr. Sutter, but suffice to say we both were shanghaied and put to work on a vessel hunting sea otters and seals along the coast of California. But that escapade is now ancient history as far as we are concerned. We are here to pick up our cattle, hogs, and wagons so we can return home," said Jacob.

"Veil, you two look none the vorse for vear, so let's get down to business," answered Sutter with a big grin and a friendly wave of his massive, paw-like hand.

One week later the seven men were pushing a herd of cattle and dairy cows toward Sutter's Hock Farm. During the week they had waited for Sutter to round up their cattle, the men had shopped in nearby Sacramento for the staples they thought the valley residents would be able to use in the season ahead as well as purchasing the newest in rifles and pistols because theirs had been lost. They filled four of their remaining eight wagons with those goods and staples.

The saddlebags full of gold nuggets that they had retrieved from the captain's cabin just about paid for everything. And they still had $90,000 in silver and gold coins and California Territorial gold slugs taken from the ship after the deadly battle for their freedom. Additionally, Sutter lent the men six Mexican cowboys from his vast holdings to help in the cattle drive.

Arriving two days later at Sutter's Hock Farm near Marysville, the men lined their remaining four high-walled wagons deeply with straw. Then they loaded their hogs and bags of feed into them for transport to the ranches in Sierra Valley. Sutter had warned Jacob and Martin that to trail the hogs along with the cattle would invite trouble. He felt the area they were going into was still full of grizzly bears, mountain lions, and gray wolves. Under such conditions, he felt that trailing the slow-moving hogs would invite heavy predation and losses. But Jacob and Martin decided to go ahead after hiring four more Mexican laborers from the hock farm to drive the wagons and tend to the pigs and a fifth to drive the chuck wagon and act as the group's cook. The following morning, the men began their long trek back up over the Beckwourth Trail leading back towards their ranches in Sierra Valley.

Trailing the herd across the Sacramento Valley was easy, and the group of men made good time.

Their first trouble occurred just east of Oroville as they headed for Bidwell's Bar and mining camp. Stopping one evening high up on a ridge overlooking the Feather River, the men were preparing for their evening meal when several shots rang out near where the herd was grazing. Racing to the scene, Jacob and Martin discovered several Mexican herders standing guard over two sad-looking California Maidu Indians. It seemed that the Indian camp was down along the Feather River, and the lowing of the cattle had brought the Maidu men to investigate. Coming across a feeding steer, they had shot it with their bow and arrows and prepared to carry it back in pieces to their band. However, before they could accomplish their mission, they had been discovered by the Mexican cowboys, who were now prepared to kill them. With the arrival of Jacob and Martin, the cowboys backed off, and the brothers looked down on the obviously very poor examples of hungry Maidu humanity.

"Does anyone speak their lingo?" asked Martin.

"I do, señor," responded one of the Mexican cowboys.

"Ask him why they killed my steer," said Martin.

The Mexican spoke to one of the Indians in the Maidu language, and they responded.

Turning, the Mexican cowboy said, "They say they are very hungry, patron."

After looking at Jacob, Martin turned and told the Mexican, "Tell the Indians they can have this one animal to eat, but no more. Let them know in the clearest language that if they try to kill any more animals, they will be shot on sight and left for the birds to eat."

The Mexican cowboy relayed Martin's stem words, and both Indians nodded and said something in return to Martin.

"They say, 'Thank you,' patron," said the cowboy pleased with his bosses' decision.

Martin and Jacob smiled and then ordered the rest of the men back to camp so they could have a hot meal after a long day on the trail. No more cattle disappeared during the rest of the trip as the herders continued crossing the lands of the Maidu.

Aside from meeting the stages and mule trains on the narrow trail, the next rite of passage became the swinging bridge over the Feather River. When confronted by the strange contraption, the cattle would not cross no matter how hard the men tried to push them. Finally Jacob got the idea of dragging across the leader of the herd. With several rope loops across his head and horns, he was dragged bellowing in fear across the swinging bridge. That settled it as the herd, seeing their leader on the other side of the river, almost stampeded across the bridge, causing it to groan and swing wildly. Soon everyone was across the Feather River and began the long trek up out of the canyon and onto the ridge trail from Bidwell's Bar to Bucks Ranch.

For the next four days, they trailed the herd back over the Beckwourth Trail to the small mining town of American Valley. Here they rested the herd for two days so the animals could feed on the valley's lush grasses on the Thompson Ranch several miles east of the town.

Realizing they were less than a week's travel from Sierra Valley, Amanda, and Kim, the boys went into town where they purchased new clothing, got haircuts and shaves, and took long, hot baths. When they returned to camp, they took a lot of razzing for getting "all gussied up." Jacob and Martin took the razzing in good spirits, and their improved appearance wasn't all they had up their new sleeves. They had purchased not only many fine ladies' clothes but perfumes and two diamond rings as well! Grouchy fathers or not, the men had it in mind to propose to the two ladies, eventually marry, and settle down in Sierra Valley as wealthy cattle ranchers. They would also be made even richer by the wealth of Spanish gold bars and pokes full of nuggets still buried in their cabin's floor awaiting them.

The following morning the men and the herd left Thompson's Ranch, and a week later they left the small town of Mormon Junction. A short time later, they arrived on a small ridge overlooking Grizzly Creek at the entrance of Sierra Valley. The brothers could hardly wait as their tired herd and slow-moving wagons seemed to just creak along. Finally they arrived at the brothers' two cabins, barns, and sets of corrals, only to find them burned to the ground! Quickly riding to their original home site, they discovered two stark wooden crosses at the head of fresh mounds of earth.

Leaping off their horses, Jacob and Martin hurriedly walked over to their cabin's ash heaps and, after a brief look of disbelief, moved over to the two crosses. One was carved with the word "Jerry" and the other with "Dave."

As the herd arrived and began to mill around and the wagons full of squealing pigs braked to a stop, the two brothers could hardly believe their eyes. Both looked wildly around as if the culprit would still be nearby, then quietly accepted the scene of death and destruction spread out before them.

"Men, we will camp back along Grizzly Creek this evening and just let the cattle roam nearby. In the meantime, let's build a corral that will hold the pigs and let them out from their wagons so they can move around a bit," said a very grim-faced Jacob.

His grimness turned even darker when his brother returned from the cabin where their gold nuggets and bars had been buried.

"Jacob, someone discovered our gold cache, dug it up, and spirited it all away!" said Martin with his typical someone-is-going-to-die-for-this look.

"Are you sure?" asked Jacob, feeling his killing edge coming on as well.

"Sure as I am standing here. There is a hole on the northeast side of the cabin that is at least four feet deep with nary a nugget or gold bar left," Martin grimly responded. "Not to mention someone killed our two friends the Hall brothers in the process of robbing us."

As all this ugliness came to light, their crew of herders and friends from the sea gathered around, listening and looking on quietly.

"Cain, will you take charge of the crew and things here? My brother and I have to ride over to Jim Beckwourth's cabin in order to get to the bottom of this," Jacob said with a distinct killing tenor in his voice.

Cain, sensing the seriousness of the moment, nodded in agreement as Jacob and Martin swung back into their saddles and galloped off in the direction of Jim Beckwourth's cabin.

"Hello, the cabin!" yelled Jacob as he and Martin rode up. In a second, the door flew open, and out strode Jim Beckwourth with a look of wonder on his face and rifle in hand.

"Where the hell have you two ring-tailed cats been? Do you realize it has been more than a year since you two showed your ugly mugs in this here valley?" he asked, obviously astonished yet happy to see his two given up for lost friends.

"What the holy hell happened, Jim?" asked Jacob in a tone not to be misunderstood as he swung down from his horse.

"I take it you two boys have been over to your place and found it burned to the ground. Well, as near as anyone can tell, Dave and Jerry let four travelers stay for the night in Martin's cabin since he wasn't using it. The next thing we knowed was the cabins were burning, and Dave and Jerry were dead."

"Who did it, Jim?" asked Martin in a hard voice.

"Don't rightly know for sure, but talk in Mormon Junction was that four mean-as-a-skunk miners from a camp called Rich Bar over on the Feather River were tossed out of a saloon in town after killing another miner in a suspicious fight during a card game. The last anyone saw of them they was headed this way just before Jerry and Dave were killed. Two days after they was reported in the area, I went over to your cabins to borrow a sack of flour. That was when I discovered the burned cabins, barns, and corrals, all your stock missing, and the bodies, or what were left of them, inside the cabins' remains. I took right off after giving Dave and Jerry a proper burial and tracked them four varmints and a slew of packhorses they stole from you as far as the outskirts of the Truckee River settlement afore I lost their trail. However, I went into town and met with Larry Davis, the gunsmith, and he said there were four miners who have since bought the Majestic Saloon adjoining Stockley's Gaming Casino, the Bucket of Blood Saloon, and Molly's Sporting House. Hell's fire, boys, they now own a block of the town's finest gaming and sporting houses purchased with a hoard of gold they got from somewhere!"

Martin turned to Jacob and said, "Yes, and it sounds like they did so with our stash of gold that we left buried in our cabin."

"How the hell did they find it?" returned Jacob with a questioning look.

"I might have an idea," said Jim. "From the looks of one of the Hall brothers, his hands and feet were wired together when I found them."

"That be the only way," said a grim-faced Jacob. "They had to torture it out of those fellows because they knew where the gold was buried, but they were loyal to us to a fault."

"Jacob, if that be the case, we have some killing to attend to," Martin uttered quietly.

"I would be obliged if'n you boys would let me attend that event as well. If'n for nothing else, to keep the wolves from your backs during the hurrah and to avenge the loss of my two old mountain-man friends," Jim said with a killing glint in his eyes as well.

"Can't let you do it, Jim," replied Jacob. "You of all people deserve to live out your string in peace in light of what you done for the West and all of us here in the valley."

Realizing the truth of Jacob's words and his creeping age, Jim said, "If'n you need help, I think you can count on Davis to give you a hand once you get there in town."

"That would be good," said Martin, "because by now them four varmints have hired others like them to protect and watch over their backsides."

The ride back to their cabins was a quiet affair. When they arrived, it became apparent that word had gone around the valley that the boys were back because Rich Grosz, Mark Webb, Daniel and his clan, and Martin Jones and his clan had appeared. There was much happiness in evidence as the people were only too pleased to see the return of the long-lost brothers. But there was also much sadness over the loss of the Hall brothers.

After much explanation about what had happened to the brothers and about their yearlong absence, Jacob quieted the crowd, and the talk turned serious.

"Folks, we have a lot to do and not much time to do it, so we had better get started. Firstly, we have four wagons heavily loaded with winter supplies. With the help of our hired Mexican hands, I suggest we get those goods distributed to all of you so they are not stolen by outsiders or ruined by the weather. Secondly, we have the issue of our livestock and pigs. Again with the help of our Mexican hands, I suggest we distribute them equally among the families at hand for safekeeping until my brother and I return from a task awaiting us along the Truckee River settlement. If we return, my brother and I will settle up with all of you for caring for our stock. If we don't return, then you will have starter cattle and hog herds, and we will be even.

"Now, we have another issue. It appears the men who killed the Hall brothers are in the Truckee River settlement. That being said, my brother and I propose to go there and prove that is the case—and given the chance, we will kill every one of them! Again, if we are successful, we will be back. If not, then you can split up our things and divide our ranch and its lands equally among yourselves because it is all paid for."

"Jacob," said Cain, "what about us who were your shipmates and came with you to settle here as farmers or cattlemen?"

"You can stay and share in our supplies and herds as well. You will need to get together with Jim and purchase some land from him from our cache of coins we brought with us because that opportunity hasn't changed. You don't need to get in harm's way and risk your lives with us for a score we need to personally settle," replied Jacob.

"The hell you say!" said Cain. "We were brothers once and still are as far as I am concerned. Count me in on the killin' trip. After all, I got shanghaied looking for the two of you in the first place, and now I'll be damned if I let either of you out of my sight again to get into trouble without me."

With that, Cain rode his horse over to where Jacob, Martin, and Jim were mounted and took his place beside his brother mountain men.

"Well, if that don't take the cake!" said Bill Black. "Here we have the chance to get into a real hell-raising and aren't even invited. I would say that borders on some of the worst manners I have ever seen. What say the rest of you bilge rats? Are we in, or are we out?"

En masse and without hesitation, Ran Slaten, Leo Suazo, Bill Black, and John Paul rode their horses over to where Jacob and company stood and reined in behind them.

"Well, if all of you wish to become damn fools,

I guess I won't object," said Jacob with the first smile he'd shown since his arrival home. "If that be the case, we best get cracking and get ready because I plan on leaving for the Truckee settlement at first light."

The rest of the day was spent in getting ready and paying off the Mexican cowboys so they could go home once they had moved the cattle, hogs, and food supplies to the various ranches. During that process, Rich Grosz, Chris Grosz, and Mark Webb approached Jacob with fire in their eyes.

"Jacob, you can count us in on this fracas as well. Jerry and Dave were our friends too, and we feel we owe them something," said Chris.

Jacob looked for a moment at the three hell-for-stout men standing solidly in front of him, then said, "No, I think not. I didn't drag you three all this way just to have you killed in a brawl in town. Besides, all of you have families, and we don't. If any of us get killed, it don't matter. But if you do, then your families are at a loss."

The three men tried to object, but Jacob stood firm. Seeing that Jacob's mind was made up and that his words made sense, the three men fell to the work at hand helping in the dividing of the winter food supplies and animal herds.

Martin Jones approached Martin and had a similar quiet conversation in which he offered to go with Martin, as did his sons. Martin, like Jacob, thanked his grandfather for the offer. But he told the older man that he and his sons needed to continue their new life in a land where being an Indian did not matter but being a man of his word did. After more quiet conversation, Martin's face clouded over, over what his grandfather had just told him. Then Martin Jones and his boys fell to with the others trying to carry out Jacob's wishes regarding the placement of the supplies and livestock.

Walking over to Jacob, Martin said, "Kim is married. She waited for me, and after no word on our whereabouts for over a year, she married a dairy farmer from the east side of the valley. Martin tells me she is happily married, and I best not let her know I am back because according to him, she loved me dearly, and that might cause problems in her marriage."

Jacob could see the heartbreak in his brother's eyes. He put his arm over Martin's shoulders and walked him away from the other men and their activity.

"I just learned from Rich that Amanda is also married. Like Kim, she waited, then, fearing I was dead, married a man in Mormon Junction who runs the town's largest emporium. She too is happy and in fact is with child. I do not plan on visiting her or upsetting her life either. From what I can see, the two of us are brothers once more with little opportunity to settle down and have a family in this valley," Jacob said sadly.

"Well," said Martin, "we were gone a long time, and I don't blame them. But for once things sure seemed to be going our way, and now we must once again start over and face our mortality."

"I can't think of a better person with which to do that than with you, my brother," Jacob said quietly.

The brothers hugged and then, without another word about what might have been, returned to the preparations at hand. Once they finished, they had some unfinished business to attend to, and that included a whole lot of bloodletting to their way of thinking...and not their blood

Chapter Thirty

THE FOURTH OF JULY

DUSK THE NEXT DAY found seven heavily armed men entering the firearms shop of Larry Davis. Recognizing the brothers and sensing that something serious was up, Larry walked by the group without saying a word, put a closed sign in his window, and drew down the shades.

"It is good to see you two boys once again," he said with a big grin and hearty back-slap.

Introductions were made all around, and then Jacob said, "We have come to claim what is rightfully ours and kill four thieving, killing sons of bitches and anyone associated with them for what they did to two of our friends in Sierra Valley."

"I take it you mean those and their small army of confederates who walked into town some time back with leather sacks of gold nuggets and Spanish ingots and now own half of Main Street," Larry responded seriously.

"That sounds like them," said Martin, deadly serious over the violent business to come.

"Well, after talking with Jim from over your way, I figured you might eventually show up with blood in your eyes and have taken it upon myself to do some groundwork. Sheriff John Dale is my friend and also realized there was something stinking in the henhouse with the arrival of those four and their instant wealth. Especially in light of no news of a new gold strike for many months in the territory. However, those chaps have surrounded themselves with an army of local outlaws, and the sheriff is unable to do anything about it because he doesn't have very many good men," said Larry. "But I will tell you what we need to do. I need to go get John and see if he will meet with the seven of you. That way we can get his support, and when we drop the anvil on these killers, we will have the legal sun at our backs in a manner of speaking."

"Larry, when can you get the sheriff to sneak over and meet with us?" asked Jacob.

"How about tonight? You can bed down in the back of my store, and I will get Rose from Rose and Ernie's Emporium to bring us some chow when no one is looking. In the meantime, you had better get out of sight in case anyone looks past my shades. It seems Royce Hubert, the leader of the gang of four, has spies everywhere. And by the way, count me and my artillery in on this shindig whenever it comes down the pike."

Jacob had to smile at Larry's offer, and from the tone of his voice, the request was not to be questioned but counted on as gospel.

As they stood around Larry's wood stove in the back room, waiting for the coffee to boil and the sheriff to arrive, there was a loud bang as the front door opened and then slammed shut. Each man went for his shooting iron, only to be met by Rose carrying in a huge crock of bean soup, an armload of fresh homemade bread, and several crocks of butter.

"Larry said you boys might be hungry after your long ride, so I loaded the tray up pretty good. I will leave it here and go back for another, so eat hearty."

She was gone just as quickly as she had appeared. Hungry and not wasting any time, the men dove into the food with gusto. The dishes were clean as a hound's tooth when Rose entered with another tray carrying more of her hearty soup, homemade bread, and a fresh-cut apple pie still crackling hot from the oven in her wood stove.

Taking the empty tray, she asked, "How you

fellas fixed for ammunition?" Before anyone could respond, she said, "I see most of you are wearing Remingtons. I will have Ernie stash some .44 cartridges in the next load that comes over." Then she was once again gone just as fast as she had appeared.

The back door opened, and in walked Larry and a smallish man with arms as muscular as a blacksmith's.

"Evening, gents," spoke the new man, who was wearing a badge.

Stepping forward, Jacob introduced himself, as did the rest of the men crowded around the coffee pot on the stove.

"Larry tells me you men are here to lay claim to that which was taken from you. If that is the case, how do you know that these four men are the culprits? I need to know because I don't want you shooting up my town without good reason. But if you have something on that nest of snakes headed up by Royce, let me know, and I will be happy to lead the way."

"Well, I can add something that may be of assistance," said Davis. "Beckwourth told me he tracked those devils here shortly after they had killed the Halls. He only went after them when he discovered from the good folks in Mormon Junction that these four skunks had been kicked out of that town because they had killed another miner in a suspicious gunfight. Once here, he heard about this Royce fellow throwing gold nuggets about like he had just made a big strike. In fact, while at his saloon in an attempt to gather information, Beckwourth overheard one of Royce's group talking about purchasing the whole block and, 'using their Spanish ingots of gold to do so.'"

"Sheriff, we had 126 ingots of Spanish gold along with six elk-skin tubes of nuggets stolen from our cabin when the Hall brothers were killed," added a stony-looking Martin.

"Royce showed me one of those Spanish gold ingots some time back when I was there in his saloon on another mater," the sheriff said thoughtfully. "Say, before I forget it, did you boys lose any Hawkens? I ask because there were six of those hellish good rifles stacked in the corner behind the bar in Royce's Bucket of Blood Saloon for sale one day when I was there. To be frank with you, they are a sight scarce out in this neck of the woods. That is why I took an interest in seeing six of them all in one place other than at Larry's here."

"Sheriff, we had four Hawkens in our cabin, and the Halls had two more. In fact, those four we had came from our folks who are now dead, and to be sure, both Martin and I would kill anyone taking such pieces of family history for that alone," Jacob said.

"Jacob, you are not known in these parts. How about the two of us going over to the Bucket of Blood Saloon and having a drink? Maybe with a little luck I can get Royce or one of his three henchmen to show us one of those Spanish ingots if I tell him you are interested in such history. What do you think?" said the sheriff as if turning over the plan in his head.

"When do we go?" asked Jacob.

"I can't think of any time better than right now," said the sheriff with a twinkle in his eyes.

Walking into the Bucket of Blood Saloon, the sheriff and Jacob had to muscle up to the bar in order to get served. The next day was the 4th of July, and many locals were already starting to celebrate Independence Day. Waiting for the barkeep to make his appearance and serve them, Jacob chanced to look over the bar into a nearby corner. Standing neatly there in the corner were the six Hawkens the sheriff had spoken about. As he looked them over carefully from a distance so as not to arouse suspicion, Jacob realized that one of the rifles was the one that used to belong to his father. The sheriff felt Jacob go taut as a buggy whip, as if he had just seen a grizzly bear.

Placing his hand on Jacob's forearm, the sheriff whispered, "Hold it there, big fellow. I don't want any killing afore we are ready and it's time."

Jacob's eyes never left the rifle standing in the

comer behind the bar, but he regained his composure as the barkeep approached the two men. The sheriff had told him that this man was one of Royce's original gang of four.

"What will it be, gents?" the barkeep asked.

"Whiskey for me and my friend," said the sheriff, fearing Jacob was too enraged to speak civilly.

"Coming up," said the barkeep as he lifted a bottle from beneath the counter and poured the sheriff and Jacob two fingers of the stout, twice-cut, fiery frontier staple.

"I don't need to see any more," Jacob said coldly through clenched teeth. "That rifle third from the left is mine, and the last one along the wall on the left is Martin's. The one with the tacks in the stock with an Indian design is Dave Hall's, and I would bet that upon closer examination, I could tell you that the rest are ours as well. We can leave anytime you are ready."

"Don't you want to see them Spanish gold bars?" the sheriff asked quietly.

"No need," said Jacob. "I have seen enough to know these fellas are the ones that need killing for what they did to the Hall brothers! Why else would they have the Hawkens?"

"Well, if you are sure on the rifles, that is enough for me," said the sheriff.

"I suggest we drink our whiskey and leave

before I start the 4th of July early," said a grim-faced Jacob as he tossed down his warm glass of whiskey.

Back at the Davis Gun Shop, Jacob slowly wiped the sweat from the liner of his hat with his handkerchief before he spoke.

"Didn't get to see the Spanish gold bars but didn't have no need. Them Hawkens standing in the comer for sale are yours and mine, Martin," Jacob finally said. "Plus, there is one there with tacks driven into the stock like the Crow used to do to their rifles. Dave had done that to his rifle, and the design is the exact same one he had."

"What do you want us to do?" asked Martin.

"Well, afore we decide that, boys, there is a thing or two you need to know," said the sheriff in an equally grim tone. "Tonight I noticed that Royce had two guns posted on the second floor of the saloon so they could watch over what was going on below them. Then there was a hired gun running each of the two faro tables that I am very familiar with. The barkeep is one of Royce's right-hand men and is one mean son of a bitch who will kill at the drop of a hat. In fact, he keeps a 12-gauge 'street howitzer' behind the bar just in case any trouble rears its ugly head. Lastly, the two dealers at the card tables are Royce's other friends. One is called Buckeye Dan, and the other calls himself California Joe."

"Is that all they have?" asked Jacob.

"Yep, except for Royce, and he can be found in his office counting his money or drunk most of the time. However, don't let that fool you. He too is one killing son of a bitch, fast with the iron, and will back-shoot you in a heartbeat," said the sheriff.

"Do you have a good vigilance committee here in town?" asked Jacob.

That question caught everyone off guard, prompting Martin to ask, "What you got in mind that we can't handle by ourselves, brother?"

"I am thinking on killing Royce and the bar-keep right off the get-go. Then, if possible, we can take the rest alive. That way we can let all of them dance at the end of a hangman's rope for all to see and remember," Jacob said quietly. "I have had enough of killing, and if we do it that way, maybe seeing all those necks stretching in ropes will have a settling effect on those who think they can rob or kill at will. 'Sides, that would back the hand of the sheriff and let him accomplish what he needs to do in the future in keeping law and order in this here town."

The sheriff nodded in agreement, and then Jacob started to discuss his plan: "I will kill the barkeep and keep him from using his scattergun and maybe killing us or an innocent bar patron. Martin, I want you to confront Royce and see if he will confess. I want you to take the sheriff along just in case he does. If not, kill him in a fair fight, and I don't care how you do it. Cain, I want you and Bill Black each at a faro table. The minute this 4th of July celebration gets rolling, I want the two of you to draw down on them cohorts guarding the tables and hold them as prisoners for the hanging. If they object, kill them. Leo and John Paul, I want the two of you in a card game at each table. When the time is right, draw down on them two skunks guarding those tables, and if they want a fight, shoot them in the head. Larry, do you know them two skunks who be guarding the scene from the second floor?"

"Sure do," Larry replied. "They bought their pistols here at the shop, and I think I can get in close enough to get the drop on them when the time is right."

"All right, but for sure, I want you in their midst when the shooting begins to control their every move," said Jacob. "Ran, I want you at the front door. Anyone associated with this gang who tries to come to their aid or leave afore we finish with them, blow them down where they are so they are out of our hair. I would suggest you start with a scattergun and go from there with your hog-leg as it becomes necessary."

Without a word, Ran nodded, and Jacob, remembering his actions in the fight in the captain's cabin, knew he would be there when the devil had his due.

"Well, Sheriff, have we left anything out?" asked Jacob. "Nary a thing, son," the sheriff replied with a grimness in light of the killing to come, "other than this. All of you raise your right hands so I can swear you in as my deputies."

Within moments, that act was done.

"Good, then it is done," Jacob said coldly. "Tomorrow will be a 4th of July that will long be remembered in this town if we have our way."

"Oh, there is one thing. We need to stagger in at different times after ten in the morning. That way they won't be any the wiser like they would if a slug of us entered all at once," the sheriff suggested wisely.

Ten o'clock the next morning found the men leaving Larry's Gun Shop in ones and twos. First to depart was Jacob, followed by Martin and the sheriff. Last to leave was Ran Slaten. On his hip, he wore a Colt Dragoon, .44-caliber, good in any gunfight or used as a club, and he also cradled a 12-gauge double-barreled shotgun carrying double-00 buckshot.

Jacob entered the saloon, strode over to the bar, and ordered a beer. Because it was the 4th of July, the bar had filled early, and by now the entire saloon was awash in half-drunk, celebrating humanity.

Nursing his beer so the others could get into position, Jacob found it hard to take his eyes off the Hawkens in the comer. The more he looked, the madder he got. However, he was not so mad that he didn't notice Larry finally enter, order a bottle of whiskey, and then walk up to the two men overlooking the floor below carrying three empty glasses. Once he was in place, Jacob gave the high sign as Martin and the sheriff left the crowd and, carrying a bottle of expensive whiskey themselves, went up the stairs, knocked on the door, and went into Royce's office as if to celebrate the holiday.

"Barkeep, I need a bottle of your finest, and don't spare the cost!" yelled Jacob to get the bartender's attention.

Realizing he had a chance to gouge a customer even more than usual with an expensive bottle of whiskey, the barkeep reached into a cabinet under the mirror behind the bar and took out a fine-looking bottle of imported whiskey. Walking down the line of men drinking at the bar, he placed the bottle in front of Jacob and said with a leering grin, "That will be five dollars, partner."

Without missing a beat, Jacob said loudly enough that he could heard over the crowded drinking establishment, "Don't call me your partner, you killing, thieving son of a bitch!"

"What did you say?" the barkeep asked with

an instant snarl on his lips as if he needed the words repeated.

"You heard me, you back-shooting son of a bitch. You and your kind tortured my two friends in Sierra Valley and then killed them after finding the gold buried in our cabin. Then you burned our cabins to the ground to hide your tracks," Jacob said so that others along the bar nearby could hear his fighting words and have time to clear out of harm's way.

The bartender went white in the face, mouthed something that could not be heard, and went for his hidden shotgun under the bar.

Jacob waited until the bartender's shotgun emerged from under the bar, then shot him just under the chin with his .44 Remington.

Boom went the pistol at point-blank range. In fact, the range was so short that the pistol's blast burned the barkeep's face a dark black as he staggered backward. He crashed into the whiskey bottles on the far side of the bar and then dropped to the sawdust-covered floor in a bloody, twitching heap.

At the sound of the shot, the two men on the second floor went for their shooting irons only to have Larry Davis make his move. Swinging into action, he drew his heavy Colt Dragoon pistol and swung it hard at his closest opponent, smashing in his skull. That man dropped as if shot, and when his partner turned to see what had happened, he discovered he was facing down the menacing muzzle of a grim-faced Larry's pistol.

"Hand your iron over!" yelled Larry.

For a moment the man froze. Then, with a snarl forming on his face, he said, "You little piece of shit!" With those words, he suddenly flew over the bannister to the floor below with a .44-caliber hole blown above his right eye and powder burns all over his face from Larry's close-in pistol shot.

With Jacob's shot, the saloon went instantly silent. With Larry's shot and the outlaw crashing headfirst to the floor below, chaos erupted! So many running men scrambling for cover hit the swinging doors of the saloon at the same time that the doors and their framing exploded outward. That crash and the sounds of feet running to other exits was made all the more frantic with the explosion of another shot behind the door in Royce's office. The two outlaws around the poker tables and the two at the faro tables all went instantaneously for their shooting irons, only to be stopped cold in their tracks by four pistols leveled at their heads by men who had been innocently gambling just moments before. Those four were quickly stripped of their weapons and lined up along a back wall of the saloon by Jacob and Martin's loyal henchmen.

Jacob lunged over the bar with a single bound,

took the 12-gauge hammer gun from the barkeep's cooling hands, and ran for the stairs leading up to Royce's office. Taking the stairs three
at a time, he slammed through the closed door to
find his brother and the sheriff dressing a super-
ficial head wound on Royce.

"Sorry, brother. When he went for his gun
I tried a head shot and just grazed him," said
Martin.

"That is all right," said the sheriff. "This is the
one bastard who really needs to swing, and now
it looks like he will get his chance."

"The lads downstairs have the situation well
in hand, Sheriff. We have the four at the gambling tables and one of the guards from up on
this floor that may still be alive. The barkeep is
dead, however. He went for the shotgun, and
just as it cleared the bar, I ended his time here on
earth. Plus one of the guards on this floor tried
Larry on for size and found he didn't fit, if you
get my drift," said Jacob, still coming down from
the killing frenzy.

About then the head of the town's vigilantes
burst through the door, followed by four more
heavily armed and grim-faced men.

"All of you carrying iron, throw them down,
or by damn we will send all of you into eternity!"
yelled the leader of the vigilantes.

"Hold her, Bob!" yelled the sheriff from upstairs. "Those men are with me and just helped clean up Royce and his nest of snakes."

With that, things quickly came under control, and the six remaining outlaws were tied up and herded into a log hut with a heavy iron door that served as the town's jail. Posted in front of the jail and behind it to prevent escape were a dozen members of the local vigilantes. Soon a crowd began to form, consisting of miners and men from every other walk of life who had been cheated, roughed up, or survived being shot by the Bucket of Blood Saloon gang.

Gathering up the Hawkens, Cain laid them on the bar for safekeeping, and then, leaving Ran Slaten to guard them, went upstairs to make sure Jacob and Martin were all right. He found Jacob, Martin, and the sheriff opening Royce's safe with the combination he had given them before being led out to the jail. Inside, the men discovered over $120,000 in coin, gold nuggets, and dust. Also at the back of the safe, stacked in a neat pile, were 126 Spanish gold ingots. The Spanish gold true to form, had carried its curse to its recent owners, including those about to die as a result of the saloon gunfight.

"Well, gentlemen, I don't know if that will cover all your losses, but it is a start," said the sheriff with a grin of satisfaction.

"Sheriff, we figured before we left for Sutter's

Fort that we still had at least five hundred pounds of gold nuggets from our labors in Clear Creek. That comes to about $128,000 at today's price of gold at $16 per ounce. I would say we are a little short of even," said Jacob.

"Well, son, you have this entire block of saloons and sporting houses that once belonged to Royce. Since he still owes you, I would say they be yours to do with as you see fit…They will sell fast in light of the fact the old owner no longer has any use for these properties," replied the sheriff with a grin.

&

STOPPING ON TOP of Beckwourth Pass and looking back, Jacob and his men rested their horses and pack mules. On the pack mules was about $150,000 in coin, gold nuggets, and dust. That did not account for the 126 Spanish gold ingots also in the packs! Royce's properties had quickly sold to other local saloon operators, and the boys figured they were even except for the loss of their friends, the Hall brothers.

Unexpectedly, Royce and his cohorts had been dragged from their holding cell before a federal marshal could arrive from Virginia City and had been hanged by a lynch mob in the cottonwoods behind the Larry Davis Gun Shop on the 4th of July. They remained in that position for several weeks until someone cut them down and spirited away the badly rotting bodies in the middle of the night.

Jacob, Martin, and their companions had not attended the ultimate 4th of July celebration and neck-tie party that followed. As Jacob had said, he was tired of killing.

As for the curse of the Spanish gold, the ingots were back in the hands of their previous owners, with an evil purpose yet to be served...

Chapter Thirty-One

SIERRA VALLEY AND POINTS WEST

DROPPING DOWN INTO SIERRA VALLEY, the men made good time to their home site at Grizzly Creek. When they arrived, they discovered that someone had cleaned off the ruins of the old cabins and had rebuilt one cabin. On the other site, another cabin was in the process of being built. The corrals were up, and a large hay barn had been built where the other one had stood. The two men were sitting on their horses looking on in disbelief when they heard a familiar voice from behind them.

"Hello, you two. I was hoping you would make it through the Truckee River battle and eventually come home," said their old friend Jim Beckwourth as he rode up on a mule.

"Hello, Jim," Jacob and Martin said in unison.

"What the dickens is all this?" said Martin, pointing toward the new structures.

"Well, all of us in the valley figured you two were too tough to get kilt in the fight, so we got together and built everything back up so you would have a place to stay. Also, I hope you noticed that we built them big enough to house all of you chaps," said Jim as he made the rounds shaking the hands of all the other men. "We also reburied Dave and Jerry proper-like over there on that hill where they can overlook all our ranches."

Getting down from their horses, the men stretched their tired frames as Jacob and Martin thanked Jim for what he had done for the Halls. Then they inspected their new cabins, barn, and home site.

"The people you brought across in the wagon train figured it was the least they could do for you two since you saw to it they had supplies and herds of livestock, and you staked them on the trail from Fort Bridger," said Jim with a twinkle in his eyes.

"Well, I'll be horsewhipped," said Jacob, still amazed at the results lying before him in all their fresh-peeled pine and Douglas-fir log splendor.

"If we are to sleep with a roof overhead tonight, we had better get a roof on this second cabin," said Cain with a big grin as he took off his shirt so he could get down to brass tacks.

Looking over at the half-bare man, Jacob could still see the whip scars across his broad back inflicted by the captain of the *Sea Witch*.

Never again will anyone do that to anyone in my new family, he thought grimly as he pulled off his own shirt in preparation for the labors ahead. In so doing, his scars from the whip were also evident to all.

Jim left to tell the folks around the valley that the boys were back, and the men left behind finished the second cabin in a long afternoon. They put all their pack animals and horses into the new corrals as the men moved into their new homes lock, stock, and barrel.

Martin killed a nice California mule-deer buck for dinner, and soon the smell of beans cooking over the open fire and corn- bread in the Dutch ovens graced the cooling night air. Bill and Leo came back from Grizzly Creek, each holding a dozen fat trout strung through their gills on a willow stick.

"Breakfast," said Leo with a grin as he held up his catch.

"Hell, man, you have just enough for me. What about all the rest of the guys?" said Cain with a big grin.

"Thought you might grumble about our catch," said Leo as he dug a twenty-six-inch cutthroat trout out of a tote sack and held it high in the air for all to see. "This one is for you, my always hungry big friend," he said with a grin.

Cain, realizing he had been bested, reached over, picked Leo up, and held him and his big trout high over his head, saying, "I think I will have both of these little trout for my breakfast," to the laughter of all the men.

"Chow is ready," said Martin as he took the lid off the Dutch oven to reveal golden-brown cornbread. Soon all was quiet as the men fell to dinner with appetites brought on by the clean mountain air and hard work. Afterward the men squatted on their haunches or sat on a log pulled up to the cooking fire and quietly smoked their pipes. They let the quiet of the evening surround them and their deepest thoughts.

"Why such deep thoughts, Bill?" asked Jacob.

"Well, I have been thinking. I miss the gentle rocking of a ship, the sound of wheeling gulls, and the smell of the salt air. I thought I had enough of that life, but traveling all this way and the fight in the saloon has gotten me to thinking. Maybe someday I will go back to my home on the sea," Bill said with a faraway look on his face.

"I have been thinking the same thing," said John Paul. "It is hard to get the sea out of my blood and away from my thoughts. Besides, it is hard to walk on ground that does not move like the pitching timbers of a good ship under full sail."

"Not me," said Leo. "It's solid ground for me and my kind. You can take that sea duty and give it to the bears."

"I agree," said Ran Slaten. "I plan on making my home in that little town of American Valley we passed through some days past. That whole area is really pretty and seems like a place where I would like to settle down."

Cain, Martin, and Jacob sat quietly, lost in their thoughts and considering the remarks of their friends. They too had found that they missed the thrill of sailing and the sea—a place that was like the old frontier, not crowded with people and still loaded with adventure.

Early the next morning the men rose from their sleeping furs to the sounds of braying mules, men talking, children laughing, and dogs barking. Stepping out from his cabin door, Jacob was confronted by all his friends from the valley, including Kim and Amanda along with their new husbands. Tumbling out behind Jacob came the rest of the men, surprised at the numbers and noise from the many people in front of their cabins.

"We came to finish the second cabin," said Chris Grosz, "but it appears someone has already done so." Then everyone closed in around the men fresh from the Truckee River fight, and hundreds of questions flew back and forth as the tale of the fight was told and retold.

After half an hour of getting reacquainted, Rich Grosz said, "Well, since the work is done, what say we have a big feed? I will bring one of my steers over this evening, and we can kill it and prepare it for an old-fashioned open-pit cookout."

That suggestion met with lots of support, and instantly the women in the party wanted to go home so they could cook their favorite dishes for the morrow's feast. Soon the crowd was gone as fast as it had materialized.

Jacob and crew, realizing they had a ton of work to do, got cracking. First they dug a big fire pit and lined it with stones from Grizzly Creek. Then they dragged dry cottonwood logs to the pit and set them afire so they would have plenty of coals in which to cook a whole beef the next day. As the pit gained heat, a fresh trout breakfast was quickly served, and then the work continued for the festivities to come.

Jacob and Cain began cutting up numerous small logs so they could make chairs for the crowd soon to come. The rest of the men hauled more cottonwood for the fire pit and built pine-log tables for the community feast. Soon things began to look shipshape as the men brought buckets of water to dampen the dust around the cooking area, tables, and fire pit. About then Rich Grosz returned with a large beef, which was soon butchered and spitted over the fire. Leo Suazo, a cook beyond compare, prepared a wet sauce to be slopped over the slowly cooking meat as Bill Black and Ran Slaten went to Mormon Junction and returned around midnight with a pack mule loaded with bottles of beer and a case of whiskey for the celebrants. That evening the men sat around the slowly cooking beef, drinking beer and talking about old times, most of which were sea related.

The following morning, as the ranchers began arriving from around the valley, the women began preparing the tables for the welcome-back feast for the brothers and the rest of the men in the Truckee River battle. As the morning heat increased, cold beers were retrieved from the cool waters of Grizzly Creek, and soon most of the men had forgotten about their many war wounds...

Jacob and Martin had an opportunity to wish Kim and Amanda well in their new lives and to give them the gifts they had purchased in San Francisco. They gave them everything but the diamond rings they had purchased to aid in their proposals of marriage. Since that was now not to be, they later tossed the rings quietly into a deep, trout-filled pool in the cold waters of Grizzly Creek without a backward glance.

Then the feast began, and what a time was had

by all, especially when Otis and Marvin got out their fiddle and banjo and many feet began to fly. The music wafted far into the night and off into the evening's cooling breezes. People finally drifted off to their wagons to sleep off the good food and to dream about the day's festivities. The next morning the celebration began all over again until the beef and beer were gone. Then the parties left to go back to their ranches so they could take care of their livestock and crops.

The quiet after the celebration was appreciated by Jacob and Martin and their companions, all of whom were used to long spells of solitude broken only by Mother Nature's beauty. Lighting up their pipes and filling their mouths with good chew, the men sat back and rested from the rigors of too much partying. Bill Black was the first to break the welcome silence.

"Jacob, if it be all right with you, I would like to return to San Francisco so I can sign on with a good ship and return to sea duty."

"Bill, if'n that is your druthers, how about a companion along the way? Maybe we can sign on to the same ship," said John Paul.

Jacob looked hard at Martin and Cain, and they stared back at him. In a moment of inner recognition, all three realized that the West was changing, and not to a way of their liking as mountain men of old.

Jacob spoke slowly, saying, "Our land is changing, as are the times and our lives. After all this time of wanting to settle down, I am not so sure now that is what I really wanted. Maybe the sea is the place for me as well. At least there we are not bumping elbows, having to fight our way out of saloons, and having to watch almost everyone so they don't clean us out. In fact, we just have to worry about the freshening wind and rogue waves. What say you, my brothers?" he asked, turning to Cain and Martin.

Cain spoke first, saying, "You have been more than a brother to me ever since we met over that moose carcass so long ago. I will happily go to sea with you, my brother."

"I guess that about settles it," said Martin. "I have really come to love that big pond they call the Pacific Ocean ever since I took off my moccasins the first time and waded in it by San Francisco. I go with you, my brothers, until the end of our adventure, wherever it carries us."

"Not me," said Ran Slaten. "As I said earlier, I plan on settling down in American Valley, raising a family, and going into the cattle and dairy business. Just looking around, it seems there is lots of demand for milk, butter, cream, and meat in all the surrounding towns and mining camps."

Leo spoke last, saying, "I will miss all you big lugs, but I would like to stay here in Sierra

Valley, raise a family, and go into the dairy business. Like Ran, I can see a market for dairy goods in Virginia City and every point in between. So here I mean to stay. No more stinking holds of ships, rats as big as cats, and me seasick all the time. I like it here just fine."

"Then it is settled," said Jacob. "Martin and I will give you our ranch and lands, which are already paid for, Leo. Then we will split the take from the fight, except for the Spanish gold. Martin and I inherited that and intend to keep it for down the line when we might need it. But we will split our gold nuggets and coin with all of you equally. With that, you will be able to start out and have a good life no matter what you decide to do." There was a murmur of approval over the fairness of his words, and Jacob continued, "Let's get cracking, for we have a lot to do before tomorrow at daylight. There is no use sitting around here when we can once again feel the roll of a ship under our feet!"

Sitting on his horse, Jacob looked down at Leo and said, "Leo, let the good people in the valley know the cattle and supplies we brought back from the Sacramento Valley are for them to share equally with no strings attached. Please let our good friend Jim Beckwourth know that all of us felt it better to leave this way because we are tired of the killing that seems to follow us everywhere and all the sad good-byes. Also, let Jim know we really appreciated all he did for us over the years. Please let all the families, especially those from Martin's and my clans, know we love them but felt it best to move on into wherever this new adventure and time takes us, just like our dads did."

With that, the friends shook hands all around, and then their horses and pack strings faded into the early-morning dark of the forest as they headed west toward San Francisco.

With them went the curse of the Spanish gold…

Chapter Thirty-Two

THE RAVEN AND THE LAST GOLDEN BAR

JACOB AND COMPANY entered the office of the San Francisco Port Authority and stood quietly to one side as the port manager finished his business with another customer.

Finishing, the portly port manager said, "What can I do for you lads?"

"We are looking for a good ship, preferably a whaler, and if one is not available, a square-masted rigger at least one hundred feet in length that could be converted to a whaler," said Bill. Then, looking over at Martin and Jacob for confirmation, Bill continued, "Oh, one with an iron bottom would be even better because we are going to use it in the northern waters around Alaska and its ice fields."

The port manager got out his eyeglasses,

pulled a heavy, leather-covered book from under the counter, laid it on top, and opened it. For about five minutes he ran a greasy finger down the entries in the ledger before he stopped at one.

"Here is one that fits the bill. It's an old whaler but was built by a master shipwright in Massachusetts eight years ago. It is three-masted, one hundred and sixteen feet in length, has a twenty-six-foot beam, is iron-hulled, draws ten feet, and has a fifteen-horse, coal-fired steam engine with a single screw for emergencies. What do you think, lads?" he asked as he looked up from his ledger.

"Sounds like just what we want in a ship for the uses we have in mind," said Bill.

Jacob nodded, deferring to Bill's expertise in ships, and then said, "When can we see her?"

"I can have a lad and a longboat here within the hour if you gents would care to wait," said the port manager with a smile.

"Sounds good to us," said Jacob. "Is there a saloon nearby where we can have a drink and get something good to eat without being shanghaied while we wait?"

"Yes, sir. Go back down this dock and turn east at the first street. You will see a saloon called the Sea Serpent Inn. They not only serve drinks but a good meal as well if you are interested," said the manager. "By the way, boys," he continued, "without knowing it, you may have struck it rich in a manner of speaking. Ever since this gold rush started, ships have pulled into the bay with their cargos and then the crews desert for the diggings. As a result, our bay is full of ghost ships rotting at their anchors. This one we are talking about, the *Raven*, arrived less than a month ago and since the crew and her captain deserted has just been sitting there waiting for a crew to take her to sea. Her owners, a New York firm, have lowered the price more than $20,000 just last week. So if you are really serious about taking her to sea, you might just be able to get her for a real bargain."

"Bill," said Jacob, "if this be our ship, how many more men would we need to crew her?"

"Counting all of us and knowing what you want her for, I would say at least sixteen more mates would do it," Bill replied.

"Where the devil we going to get sixteen more men," asked Jacob, "in light of everyone running off to the gold diggin's?"

"Pardon me, gents," said the port manager. "I couldn't help but overhear your conversation, and I may have an answer. Not everyone ran off to the diggin's. There are a few old salts not interested in going to the gold fields over at the Longshoremen's Office, two blocks down from your saloon and eatery. You could check in there and see if there are enough good men lying around looking for a pitching deck under their feet with which to crew your ship."

"That we will do, old-timer, but first a good shot of whiskey to ward off the damp air and something to eat to hold our ribs apart, and then we will go and check. Oh, by the way, when your man arrives with the longboat, just send him down to where we are at the saloon," said Jacob.

"Got you, mate. Will do," said the port manager, and Jacob and his friends left his office for the saloon.

"Ain't you gonna ask him the selling price?" asked John Paul.

"No reason," said Jacob. "We will know when we see her if she is the ship we want or not. Besides, we are carrying enough gold coin and Spanish ingots to purchase any ship in the bay, I would wager, and still have enough left over to not only crew her but supply her as well."

Walking up the dock to the street, the men turned as instructed and soon found themselves sitting around a large table in the Sea Serpent Inn. They were careful to sit in such a manner that none of them could get hit from behind and shanghaied. Then they ordered drinks, which were followed by a generous helping of steak, spuds, eggs, and homemade bread. During their meal, they were interrupted by a lanky seaman sent to fetch them so he could take them out to the *Raven*, as promised by the port manager.

"Sit down, lad," said Jacob, warmed by his second two fingers of whiskey. "Have you had anything to eat this morning?"

"No, sir," replied the lanky man.

Jacob pulled out an extra chair for the man to sit. Soon he was also eating breakfast, and from the way he was wolfing down his food, it seemed it had been some time since he had seen his last meal.

"What's your name, lad?" asked Martin.

"Jacob Dean, sir," he replied between mouthfuls.

"That be a good omen, boss," said Bill with a grin.

"I am also called Jacob," said Jacob with a grin as he formally introduced the new Jacob all around to the men.

"Is it true, sir, that you may want to take the *Raven* to sea once again?" asked Dean.

"If she be a good and sound vessel," said Jacob, "then she will go to sea once again so we can hunt sea otter, if we can find a crew."

"If you be looking for seamen, I would like to throw my hat in the ring," Dean said with a grin.

"What did you do at sea before you were land-locked?" asked Bill.

"I was a shipwright, and a damn good one," he replied.

Then there was a flurry of questions as John Paul tested the man's knowledge of a ship and its workings. As this question- and-answer period went on, the rest of the men looked on and listened with keen interest.

"Jacob, I am satisfied this man is what he says he is. 1 would suggest we hire him as our second shipwright," said John Paul with a twinkle in his eyes.

"Lad, you just joined our crew, and if we can get a good ship, you will have a new home," said Jacob as he stuck out his hand to seal the deal.

"Jacob, I have two younger brothers who were able seamen for six years, the same as me, and were landlocked as well here in San Francisco when our ship sailed in and the rest of the crew deserted. They tried their hands at gold panning and found the work hard, the meals few and far between, and the payoff poor. They have returned to San Francisco and live with me in a one- room flat. Would you and your mates be interested in talking to them about joining the crew as well?"

Jacob looked at Bill and grinned. If Dean's two brothers were anything like the lad sitting before them, they would soon have two more good men on the crew.

"Finish your breakfast and then go get them and see if they are interested in going to the waters off Alaska on a blubber, oil, and sea-otter-hide run. If so, bring them back so Bill and I can take a gander at them," said Jacob with a grin.

Dean wolfed down the last of his breakfast and bolted out the door as if this opportunity would vanish into thin air if he waited too long. Forty minutes later he returned trailing two other young men who appeared to be in their middle twenties. Dean introduced his brothers to the men sitting around the table, and for the next fifteen minutes or so Bill talked to the two newcomers about their experience, likes, and dislikes. Then Bill nodded to Jacob and Martin, letting them know these two new additions would make good seamen. Jacob welcomed the two new men with a handshake, as did the rest of the men sitting around the now crowded table.

As Dean rowed the men out to where the *Raven* rested at anchor, Jacob and Bill looked on keenly as they approached the vessel. Bill had the man slowly row the longboat around the ship as his practiced eye checked out her hull and super-structure.

"Jacob, from here she looks like a damn fine ship. But let's get aboard and check her out from stem to stem before we settle in our minds what we want to do," said Bill with excitement building in his voice.

For the next four hours, all the men carefully checked out the ship as she quietly rested at anchor as if not wanting to spoil the moment for her potential new buyers.

Jacob gathered all the men on the deck and, sitting around on whatever they could find, they discussed the condition of the *Raven*.

"Dean," said Bill, "what did you see that needed fixin'?"

Without missing a beat, the young man said, "She will need some extra sail for the hold. Her bilge is fine. Her main masts are made from the finest oak. She will need an assortment of new ropes for the hold and rigging. She will need some new steering chains that are heavier than normal if we are going into Alaska waters, and she will need a complete resupply of water casks, food, and wood for the deck boilers and coal for the steam engine. Other than that, this is one fine-looking ship."

"Bill, what are your thoughts?" asked Jacob.

"My thoughts mirror those of our newest shipwright. This is one of the finest ships I have been on in a long time. And Dean's assessment on the steering chains is right on. Alaska waters and storms will try even the best of steering chains, and we need the best since we will be close in to the coastline most of the time, seal, walrus, and sea-otter hunting."

"What say the rest of you?" asked Jacob.

For the next hour the men supplied their

thoughts and suggestions, and when it was all done, Jacob looked over at Martin. Martin quietly gave a nod indicating that he was comfortable with his brother's decision to purchase the ship.

Walking back into the port manager's office, Jacob said, "We like what we see on the *Raven*. Who do we go and see to purchase the ship and settle up?"

"That would be the Carriage State Bank on Market Street," the man answered with a grin.

"How do I get there from here?" asked Jacob.

"I will call you a carriage. How would that be?" asked the port manager.

"That would be fine," said Jacob, "because that bank is where my brother and I have our money, as it just so happens."

As the port manager sent a runner for a carriage, Jacob turned to Martin and Bill, saying, "The two of you go to that Longshoremen's Office up near where we ate and see what you can gather up as a crew. I don't want any troublemakers, just good seamen who are willing to work for a share of the take. Also, Martin, I plan on using the Spanish ingots to parley into our ownership of the *Raven*. Any problems with that?"

"I don't have any problems with that, Jacob. We have been carrying those ingots ever since our stepparents were killed, and I think it is now time to use them to help us achieve our goals. I know Mom and Dad would have approved, so go for it. And in a manner of speaking, it seems as if we have almost been cursed for as long as we have carried those ingots around. Especially in light of all we have had to do in order to keep them. But maybe that is just the Indian superstition in me, huh?" Martin replied with a grin.

∽∾

SITTING IN FRONT of a banker, Jacob waited for him to finish the paperwork on purchasing the *Raven*. "There you go, sir. Everything is signed and sealed. You have purchased the *Raven* for the princely sum of $38,000. How do you propose to pay such an amount?" the man asked.

"My brother and I have in your bank a cache of gold coins, gold nuggets, and 126 Spanish gold ingots. I would like to cash all that in for coin and pay for the ship today," said Jacob.

For the next hour, the bank manager and a clerk weighed out all the gold and arrived at a figure based on $16 dollars per ounce, which was satisfactory to Jacob. Then the bank manager wrote a draft on his bank for $38,000 to the owners of the *Raven* back in New York and converted the rest of the gold into U.S. gold coins and $50 and $100 gold territorial slugs from local banks and assay houses in the San Francisco area. After paying for the ship, Jacob and Martin were left with a balance of $157,800!

Jacob returned to the Sea Serpent Inn, where he met his brother, the rest of the crew, and fifteen more men of motley looks and seafaring attire. Buying all the men a drink, Jacob motioned Martin, Cain, and Bill into an unoccupied corner of the saloon and said, "What is the deal on all these men?"

"Jacob," said Martin, "these all appear to be pretty sound seafaring men. Bill had at them with many questions while I just watched. He ended up with the best of the lot at the Longshoremen's Hall, and unless I miss my guess, they seem pretty solid of timber and mind."

"I count fifteen new men. I figured we only needed an additional thirteen after we took a look at the ship," said Jacob with a questioning look.

"You are right, brother, but we found fifteen good ones and just figured if someone ever got sick or hurt, we would still have enough men to do the job. Besides, as you know, there is always plenty of work onboard, especially when the rendering work starts. With that, I figure we can keep all of them more than busy," replied Martin.

"Good thinking, you three," Jacob quickly replied. "Well, here it is. Our new home for as long as we desire." He unrolled the bill of sale for their new ship, the *Raven*, for the others to see.

The three men each held the official document

and then grinned at each other like a bunch of school kids who had just put a live frog in the teacher's desk.

"Dang, Jacob," said Martin, "when I said I wanted to see that great pond to the west, who would've figured that was where we would end up."

Jacob just smiled at his brother's words, as did Bill and Cain. Then the four men returned to the noisy gathering of seamen.

"Men!" said Jacob in a loud voice. "We have just had the good fortune to purchase a sound ship named the *Raven*. She is a three-masted whaler with an iron bottom and a reserve steam engine for emergencies and is of sound timber, having been built on the East Coast by master shipbuilders. She has a large, comfortable crew quarters with a fire box below decks to provide heat. She also carries a large galley where half of us can eat at a time, good storage both fore and aft, a roomy officers' quarters, and a double wheel up on the bridge by the captain's quarters. She can pile on plenty of sail, and her masts and spars are of the finest oak. She is only eight years old and was abandoned by her crew when they arrived in San Francisco some days back.

"I need all of you to gather up your sea bags and be on Dock Number 3 by seven in the morning tomorrow. We will board her and make her shipshape while my brother, Cain, Bill, and I start making arrangements for the ship's stores. All of us will fall to when they arrive and store everything below, both forward and aft so they are out of the weather and in balance with the ride of the ship. We will also be replacing our steering chains because we are going to the waters off Alaska to hunt walrus, fur seals, and sea otters. Now, let's us eat and drink because it will be some time before we put in to shore for more of the same," said Jacob.

There was a rousing cheer, and then the festivities began in earnest as the whiskey and rum flowed and the food ordered, and soon served, overflowed the tables.

At seven the next morning, Jacob, Cain, and Martin stood on the end of Dock 3 and looked over their charges. It was plain that many had more than enjoyed the previous night's festivities, but every one of them stood steady on the end of the dock in anticipation of sea duty once again. As two longboats took the men and their gear to the *Raven*, Jacob and his handpicked companions moved into San Francisco on a spree to supply a ship for the waters off Alaska. Two weeks later, the ship had been supplied to the gills. Many cords of oak wood for the crew's quarters and the deck's rendering boilers had been stowed aboard as well as small mountains of coal for their steam engine. In addition, the hold had been stuffed with new wooden barrels to hold the oils rendered from the walrus as well as those filled with drinking and cooking water. Bill and Dean oversaw the replacement of the steering chains and added a larger rudder to make it even safer and more maneuverable when moving among the rocks off the Alaska shoreline.

On the day of departure, as the tide turned and the wind freshened, the anchor was lifted from San Francisco Bay, and the *Raven*, as if happy in its own right, moved gracefully out to sea. Turning north, Bill steered the *Raven* towards southeastern Alaska and the fabled sea-otter hunting grounds. By the time they arrived, the men and ship had been shaken down and were operating as an efficient team.

That first evening on the hunting grounds, Jacob, Martin, Cain, Bill, and John Paul, who was now the first mate, gathered in the captain's cabin for a special dinner. One of the men who had been hired in San Francisco had previously served as a ship's cook. As it turned out, he was a good one, possessing many fine culinary skills. That evening for their dinner, the men feasted on Pacific black brant, sea geese killed from the deck as they had flown by, beans, cornbread, and an apple pie made from dried apples.

"Here is to a meal fit for a king and a good voyage ahead," said Jacob, holding up a cup filled with whiskey. All the men did likewise, and soon they fell to the dinner, eating as if it had been a long time since their last meal. As Martin reached for the decanter holding more whiskey, he noticed that it was sitting on top of a single Spanish golden ingot.

"Jacob, what is this?" he asked as he hefted the brick of gold.

"Oh, I couldn't sell off all of the Spanish gold. We had too much family history in them, plus we lugged them around for so many years, I kind of got attached to them. So I kept one back for good luck and to remind us of our roots," Jacob said quietly.

For a moment, the melancholy of the moment reached all around the table, with each man aware of his own history and that of the golden ingots. Then Martin hefted his glass and said, "To us, our parents, mountain men, the vanishing West, and our time." That broke the spell, and the men fell once again to their dinner, followed by the still steaming apple pie from the galley.

The next morning, three longboats were lowered into the inland waterways just north of the Russian community of Sitka. In one longboat as a shooter sat Cain, and in the other two sat Martin and Jacob. Soon the bodies of the hapless otters were being hoisted aboard the *Raven* for pelt-

434 | TERRY GROSZ

ing and rendering. For the next two weeks, the *Raven*'s crew shot hundreds of otter and a few seals as they moved farther and farther north along the coastline of southeastern Alaska. Then, as summer beckoned, Jacob, Martin, and Cain decided it was time to fill their holds with valuable walrus oil. They asked Bill to set a course for Saint Lawrence Island in the Bering Sea.

Sailing up through a break in the Aleutian Islands through Unimak Pass, the *Raven* proceeded to the northwest side of Saint Lawrence Island into the broken sea ice. There the gunners in the longboats shot hundreds of the trusting walruses off their icebergs, and soon the rendering fires burned day and night as the light walrus oil was funneled into waiting wooden casks. Once filled, they were bunged shut and stored below decks in ever-increasing numbers.

On one occasion, Bill said to Jacob, "Boss, the ship is riding lower and does not react like she did to the tiller when we were empty. It is pretty plain we are taking on a good load of hides and oil, which will please the crew over their shares when we sell our cargo."

"Well, since we are here, we will kill and render as many animals as we can, but when you feel the sea ice is closing in and we need to scoot south, it will be your call," said Jacob.

Soon more and more storms rolled in from the

Bering Sea as the summer waned, making the shooting and hauling of the heavy bodied walruses back to the ship by longboat problematic.

One evening, as the tired and wind burned men ate supper, Bill said, "I think it is time we take what we have and run south. Storms in these latitudes can be rough, and I noticed the smoke from several other whalers on the horizon yesterday. All were heading south. I think we best follow. Besides, weather permitting, we can still take some otter along the coast of southeastern Alaska and Canada before we head back to Frisco."

"What do you think?" said Jacob to Cain and Martin.

"Bill is our ship's master and has been here before. I say we take his advice and head south," said Martin.

"Yeah, I don't cotton to freezing to death up here nohows," said Cain with his typical grin.

"Then it is done," said Jacob. "Just give us one more day hunting walruses, and with that we will have filled all our casks." The following day, a quicker step could be seen among the crew as they moved around the ship. The thought of going home and spending some of their share monies seemed to lighten their feet as they moved around the deck. As promised, when the last of the hunters' longboats were loaded back on deck in their housings, Bill turned the ship south and loaded on the sail. Throwing over the last of the rendered meats from the walruses, the men squared away the deck and holly-stoned all of the oily spots so they wouldn't slip while working if hit with a storm.

Just off the coast north of Sitka, the *Raven* hove to as a winter storm lashed its decks with freezing seawater. The crew had to turn to with belaying pins and hammers to knock off the heavy load of ice forming on the decks and superstructure to prevent dangerous ice buildup and the possibility of a rollover.

Over the howling winds and salt spray, Bill yelled at Jacob, "I think we need to move farther south and get out of this ice. We are heavy with cargo anyway, and this extra ice freezing on the decks and rigging doesn't do us any good in the steering department!" The howling winds made it necessary for Bill to repeat his words before Jacob understood.

With a wave of the hand pointing south, Bill set a new course.

South of Alaska in the Hecate Straits off the coast of Canada by the town of Prince Rupert, Bill and his second helmsman fought the wheel of the *Raven* for control. Because of the weight of her cargo, the strong, still howling onshore winds, and the iced decks and rigging, the *Raven* was responding to the rudder like a barge to Bill's way of thinking. On deck, the exhausted crew continued slipping and sliding as they tried to bust the heavy ice forming on everything. Finally Martin went up on the bridge to relieve the second mate manning the helm so as to help Bill at the wheel. Jacob was on the pitching deck busting ice with the men with a frenzy born of his innate survival instincts.

"Rogue wave, rogue wave!" shouted Bill over the howling winter winds.

Bill and Martin spun the wheel hard to starboard to meet this new threat. Slowly, ever so slowly, the *Raven* turned into the swiftly onrushing wave and, because of Bill's skill at the helm, safely drove through the towering wall of water.

"Another one!" Bill shouted into the roaring winds and hellish flying partially frozen salt spray as he rung up full power from their hardworking steam engine, hoping the extra thrust and the wind in the sails would carry them over this wave as well. The *Raven*, like the good ship it was, swung into the onrushing wave, knifing through it as if it had been there before.

❧

FOR TWO MORE DAYS, the winter storm howled as it spun crazily out from the Bering Sea. Finally the winds subsided, as did the raging surf, and the sun finally shone weakly through the roiled heavens. Little Raven, son to Chief Orca of the Tlingit Indians, the *Raven* Band, rolled out from his sleeping furs and, careful not to waken anyone else sleeping in the long house, dressed and headed for the beach. As he always had, he would walk the shoreline in front of his tribe's village to look for anything of value washed up on the sand by the recent violent storms.

Standing on the bank overlooking the shoreline, he was amazed at what he saw! Wooden casks were floating in the water and cast up on the shore. Bundles of sea-otter skins floated everywhere, and were stacked up along the surf line. Wooden wreckage floated and bobbed everywhere, signaling it represented flotsam from a large ship.

Running down to the shore, Little Raven began pulling in the valuable bundles of sea-otter skins and anything else he could find above the surf line. Then he spotted a partially sunken longboat bobbing in the surf at the water's edge. Running over to the longboat, he swung its stern shoreward and dragged it up out of the still foaming surf. Peering inside the longboat, he saw nothing. Then he noticed the name on the longboat and smiled. The partially shattered transom board on the stern had a name painted on it in dark letters, and it appeared to be the same as his name—*RAVEN*...

A LOOK AT JOSIAH PIKE BY TERRY GROSZ

JOSIAH PIKE, CAPTURED BY THE SIOUX! A novel, but also an in depth look into the western wilds and the life of the tribes.

Terry Grosz has an extensive background in the wilds of the West, as a California Fish and Wildlife warden and later a U. S. Fish and Wildlife agent, serving from California to North Dakota.

His contact and interaction with the tribes of the West, gives him in-depth knowledge of Indian life, and he passes that along in Josiah Pike. The book is a novel, but written in a style that not only entertains but educates. It's dense with tribal life, yet vibrant and compelling as Pike is captured then taken to the bosom of the Sioux.

Available from Wolfpack Publishing and Terry Grosz.

About the Author

WHETHER AS A PROFESSIONAL in the field of wildlife law enforcement or as a prolific writer, Terry Grosz has distinguished himself with a kind of passion, dedication, integrity and professionalism that often exemplify Humboldt State alumni. The beginning of his 32-year career in wildlife law enforcement came in 1966 with the California Department of Fish and Game in Eureka. After several years and a transfer to Colusa, he was hired by the U.S. Fish and Wildlife Service (FWS), moving into increasing responsibility for conservation and wildlife law enforcement in successively larger geographic regions, from jurisdiction over the central half of Northern California to finally Assistant Regional Director for Law Enforcement where he supervised FWS's wildlife law programs covering 750,000 square miles.

When Grosz became the FWS Senior Special Agent, he wrote regulations, policy and procedures, responded to congressional inquiries, provided advice, guidance and expertise. But it wasn't just a desk job. He also traveled throughout Asia assisting foreign governments in curtailing the smuggling of wildlife and establishing cooperative international law enforcements programs. In all the various positions held by Terry, he supervised agents who protected wildlife from being smuggled or imported illegally into the US, protected eagles from being poisoned or trapped, and more.

In 1998, Grosz retired from the FWS and began a second career as a prolific writer, and has since authored and published seven books, with several more on the way. Clearly, he's got a lot of material to work with. Many of his stories have hilarious moments and hair-raising adventures, some others are sad and tragic, they are all about the men and women who work as wildlife conservation officers trying to preserve our natural heritage for future generations.

Find more great titles by Terry Grosz and Wolfpack Publishing at wolfpackpublishing.com/terry-grosz/

www.ingramcontent.com/pod-product-compliance
Lightning Source LLC
Chambersburg PA
CBHW030849030726
47495CB00005B/1451